D1524211

The Book of Riley: Part 1
My Name is Riley

Mark Tufo

Cover Art:
Cover Art by Shaed Studios, shaedstudios.com

Dedications: To my wife, who somehow is miraculously able to put up with me. I never figured myself as high maintenance, who knew? Thank you for all your hard work on being able to get this book out on time. I love you and I hit the lottery the day you said yes.

As always to the men and women of the armed services, thank you for all you do!

To my readers, who make all this possible, without your continued support I would be that weird guy washing windshields at that really long traffic light that you just want to turn green QUICKLY. I feel like I should say more than Thank You, but please know that I mean it from the bottom of my heart!

Foreword: Hello all! Many of you know that Riley started off as a short story as part of an anthology. I was limited to 5 thousand words, which, for those of you that know anything about me realize this is a near impossibility. You only need to look at the Zombie Fallout series that spans seven and a half novels (at the moment) to realize this! So five thousand quickly became ten thousand which I posted online. Then ten became twenty five and I realized I had a novella on my hands. What you hold here is all four Riley novellas together for the first time ever! And then as an added bonus I have included the first part of a new book I am working on entitled Pulse. It is my sincerest hope that you enjoy the stories contained within.

Table of Contents - Riley Part 1
Prologue
Chapter One
Chapter Two
Chapter Three
Chapter Four
Chapter Five
Chapter Six

Table of Contents - Riley Part 2
Chapter One
Chapter Two
Chapter Three
Chapter Four
Chapter Five
Chapter Six
Chapter Seven
Epilogue

Table of Contents - Riley Part 3
Prologue
Chapter One
Chapter Two
Chapter Three
Chapter Four
Chapter Five
Chapter Six
Chapter Seven
Chapter Eight

Table of Contents - Riley Part 4
Chapter 1 - Riley
Chapter 2 - Jess
Chapter 3 - Riley
Chapter 4 - Ned
Chapter 5 - Icely
Chapter 6 - Riley
Chapter 7 - Riley
Chapter 8 - Jess and the Gang
Chapter 9 - Riley
Chapter 10 - Icely
Chapter 11 - Jess and the Gang
Chapter 12 - Icely
Chapter 13 - Riley
Chapter 14 - Icely
Chapter 15 - Jess
Chapter 16 - Jess plus four
Chapter 17 - Alex

PULSE
This is how the end began

PROLOGUE

Hello Dear Reader you hold in your hands part one of four of The Book of Riley. This first installment of the novella serialization is entitled My Name is Riley. Here is the how this book came about, a couple of years ago when I was *brand* new to the independent author arena, a fellow author by the name of Armand Rosamilia contacted me and asked if I wanted the chance to have a short story published in his upcoming anthology. I was extremely excited at the prospect and then he sort of put the fear of God into me when he mentioned some of the other authors that would be included, Joe McKinney, Ian Woodhead, Scott Nicholson and Armand himself, those are some pretty huge names in my genre. I wanted something unique, that is the reason I went with a zombie apocalypse through the eyes of an American Bulldog, if you know me at all you are sitting back and scratching your head, 'Why didn't he use an English Bulldog like Henry?' Oh I thought long and hard about it, but being around English Bullies for as long as I have been I know that a great many of them, my Henry included would sleep through the vast majority of action sequences and I wanted the story to be as believable as possible given the circumstances.

So there I was, Armand had imposed a harsh word limit, by my standards, of 5000 words, before I knew it I had hit that number and was ready to keep going. I had a satisfactory ending at that point but not a conclusive one. And who am I kidding, I was enjoying the characters and their interplay immensely, within a few months during off time I rounded out the first installment to around 26 or 27 thousand words. My goal is to do another three installments roughly all the same length. Again if you know me this will probably end up being 15 or 16 installments, but first things first, I really hope you enjoy this story!

CHAPTER ONE

My name is Riley and this is my story. The fact I am a ninety pound female and a mere three summer seasons old should in no way dissuade you from how tough I am. I can run faster than any person I know, and I have a bite that might not be enough to snap a cow's leg but is certainly enough to cause a human - even a dead one - some serious problems. I am what the two-legged animals call an American Bulldog, although I have the heart of my wolf ancestors. Unlike what some misinformed scientists have claimed, I *am* self-aware. I love my pack of humans. There's the Alpha male named Charles, the Alpha female Heather, the oldest female cub Jessie (my favorite), the younger male cub Daniel (who needs a lesson in manners, if he pulls my ears one more time I will relieve myself on his pillow) and the infant cub who is my second favorite, Zachary (he always has so many unique smells going on). I tolerate the little pain in the ass Yorkshire Terrier known as Ben-Ben, that thing yips when the wind blows. Haven't a had decent night's rest since they brought him back from the animal dumping facility, or to you humans, the pound. And last *and* definitely least is the cat; one of these days I'm going to catch that little fleabag and... well let's just say it won't be pretty. I don't know what kind of spell she has over the humans because they absolutely adore the purring pestilence known as Patches.

The night the world changed I had hopped the dog gate to get away from Ben-Ben. I was sleeping on Heather's couch in the living room. Ben-Ben wouldn't shut up.

"Definitely something out there, Riley," he kept saying over and over. I couldn't bury my head deep enough in the cushions to drown him out. "Don't you hear it Riley?" he asked, getting louder and louder.

"I can't hear anything over you!" I shouted at him. Damn, I had to be quiet. If I barked any louder one or both of the Alphas would wake up and come downstairs. I could get back over the gate before either got here but oh, the bother of it all. The couch was so comfortable. Ben-Ben was in the other room and if that little bitch cat snuck down here at any time like she does, I might have gotten a shot at curtailing her worthless life.

"Rileeeeyy, you should get in here!" Ben-Ben whined.

"Shut up Ben-Ben!" came from the pack leader's bedroom.

Dammit, Ben-Ben, I thought. *Now I'm going to have to come back into the dog room.* I hated his whimpering, not much of a Wolf's heart beat in his thin chest. I got off the couch, not even caring I had knocked off two of the pillows, and yes I can count. So let's get all these misconceptions out of the way before I go any further. I can and *do* watch television but I can't stand most of the stuff they have on unless it involves cats falling off of things. I can count, I admit not much higher than seven though. I do understand the passage of time. I know what the humans are saying to me when they use their strange language, I just choose which parts I want to listen to, especially if the word 'cookie' is thrown in there somewhere. I absolutely *loathe* begging but I am not above it. Never once have I thought my meat flavored kibble bits tasted better than a cheeseburger or French fries, or French toast or even plain toast with some jelly or butter, I'll even eat just the butter if I can get a hold of it. They've learned since the last time I jumped up on the counter to always make sure it is put away back in the cold box. But the Daniel cub usually forgets and I can get a few good licks in on the stick before someone realizes his mistake.

I hopped back over the gate nearly landing on Ben-Ben's head; he was crouched up next to it. "I smell fear urine," I nipped at him. I hated that smell; he had done it for the first week after they had brought him here. I had told him I would eat him if he kept doing that and if he didn't quit all of his barking. One year later and I still haven't persuaded him to be quiet, though the urination has stopped.

"Riley, there are people in the backyard," Ben-Ben said as he tried to retreat farther into the shadows of the room.

I perked up now. Nobody came into my yard unless the humans said it was okay and even then the visitors still had to get my approval. I strode quickly (because running was undignified if the situation didn't necessitate it) to the backdoor and moved the curtain so I could see outside. What met my eyes was an abomination. Warm urine ran down my leg.

"Oh, this is bad, bad, bad!" Ben-Ben whimpered.

I was inclined to agree with him. There were many more than seven human things in the backyard. I really wished now I had paid more attention when the Daniel cub was doing his math homework but I'd never been able to steal more than seven cookies before I was found out and never saw a reason to go past that number. What was in the backyard was human once but no more. They smelled dead, not long, but dead all the same. Yes, I know the concept of death too, I mourn like almost every other animal on the planet, except for cats. When I was brought to my new pack I had the honor of knowing and loving the dog that was here before me. King George was an English Bulldog who took very little guff from anybody, especially a wet nosed puppy. He taught me all about the people who lived here, who was the easiest to beg food from, who gave the best walks and tummy rubs, who dropped the most food, and who was absolutely the best to snuggle with. Zachary had not yet been born, though Heather was heavy with him. When my best friend died, I did not sleep or eat right for almost a complete cycle of the moon. King George will always be the noblest dog I have ever known.

"Ben-Ben, bark louder!" I shouted, doing my best to match him in volume. I never could figure out how such a little dog packed such a loud punch. The only thing I had going for me was that I barked so infrequently that when I did it generally signified something important, and the two-leggers would usually come quickly. This time was no different; the Alpha Charles was muttering something as he switched on the kitchen light. He started swearing after his toes slammed into the dog gate.

When he finally moved the gate out of the way his cursing grew even louder and more colorful as one of his sock covered feet splashed in Ben-Ben's fear urine. "Oh, for the love of all that is mighty and good, Ben-Ben, what the hell are you barking at?" Ben-Ben was damn near invisible as he hid behind the kitchen table. The human noticed me standing at the door, back ramrod straight and I hated to admit it but my hind legs were quivering. "What's a matter, girl?" he cooed. "Something out there?" I could hear the fear in his voice as his words lost most of their volume. He cursed softly as his one still dry foot found its way into my fear urine. "What the hell is going on, girl? This isn't like you," he said as he stroked my back. I was thankful for the contact but still scared out of my wits.

Ben-Ben was still whining. "Rileeeeey, are they any closer?"

"Shut up!" both me and Alpha Charles said.

"What the fuck?" Alpha said as he peered through the glass on the doors. "Damn punks." I could sense he wanted to open the door and yell at them, but even humans with their horrible sense of instinct can still tell when something is so stupendously wrong. That and I know he could count way past seven and one against way past seven was not great odds, unless the enemy were cats and then all bets were off.

"You with me on this?" Alpha asked me. This was one of those times I wanted to pretend I didn't know the meaning of his communication. Cookie or not, I would stand with the pack leader. I looked up at with him with my best pleading eyes, imploring him to not open that door. I barked once in warning negation but I think he took that as a sign of my acquiescence. He opened the door slowly. The smell coming from the yard was worse than Zachary's diapers, which actually isn't a fair comparison because I find his offal to be somewhat sweet even if the rest of the members of my pack felt otherwise. Alpha was having a difficult time breathing in the stink I was experiencing many more times than seven.

He was hunched over preparing to evacuate the salami sandwich he had shared with me earlier. My stomach was roiling too but that meat had been entirely too tasty to let it hit the ground; I could have done without the mustard but the cheese was an added bonus. The *things* in the yard all started to come toward the porch steps. Alpha looked almost as bad as *them*, and still he hadn't thrown up or looked up. I bit him a little harder on the leg than I had meant to.

"Fug, Riley!" he yelled, choking back vomit. "What are you doing?"

I turned away from him and moved to the bottom step, which was exactly two steps away. I know two is less than seven but not by how many. Didn't matter, though; the approaching *thing* was a lot closer to us than we needed to be to it. Alpha had followed my line of sight. He reached over and roughly grabbed my collar and pulled me back in the house. I don't know why he felt the need to do that; I wasn't going to attack that thing. No sooner had he closed and locked the door when he tossed his dinner and after dinner snack all over the floor. Even Ben-Ben, the dog equivalent of a waste bucket, wouldn't come out from his hiding spot to eat the floor buffet and I'd seen that little pecker eat his own turds. I always laughed (yes, dogs have a sense of humor—haven't you noticed how we *always* walk right in front of you and stop abruptly? We find that to be just about the funniest thing ever when you do everything in your power to not run into us) when Daniel would let Ben-Ben lick all over his face. I would have stopped it but that cub always takes my toys—fair is fair.

"Heather!" Alpha screamed as he stood up, swaths of brown-tinged spittle hanging from his face. Before she could respond, the closest *thing* slammed into the door. Alpha and myself both took an involuntary step backward. I stood there transfixed by the image on the other side of the glass. Alpha slipped once as he hit Ben-Ben's piss and then he was down the hallway yelling for his wife to 'get the kids up and get the guns'. I hated the noise the fire sticks made but I saw the wisdom in them at the moment.

"Riley, is it safe to come out?" Ben-Ben asked.

The *thing* I was to learn was a zombie stared at me with one good eye. The other was streaked in blood; someone had scratched runnels from the top of the zombie's forehead through its eye and halfway down his cheek. It did not seem to care that it would never see from that side again. That one good eye, though, would not stop following me as I backed out of the room. I couldn't really stand the little dog, but no one deserves to go out that way. "Let's go, Ben-Ben," I said with more force than I felt.

He never looked at the backdoor as he scurried past me and into the living room, a fresh stream of piss following him. "Why don't you just leave a trail of bread crumbs?" I barked at Ben-Ben. (Yes, I like faery tales, Alpha female always reads them to her youngest cub; I find them completely entertaining to go to sleep with, especially the one about the big bad wolf!)

The glass backdoor breaking got me moving. I almost ran straight into Ben-Ben who was shaking so uncontrollably his bowels had loosed. I was thinking if not for the zombies, Alpha female would send him back to dog prison. I hurdled over the much smaller dog and waited at the landing to the top floor. I could hear the kids asking what was going on. She Alpha was trying to use her talking device. "Charles, there's no answer at the police station!" she shrieked.

"No time!" He was yelling from the room where he kept the fire sticks, I could hear him loading the lead bees. He needed to hurry; my incessant barking should get him moving.

The zombie had broken through the door and was walking down the hallway. Ben-Ben was still shitting; it was like he had been holding his stool for four days. Liquidy brown refuse pooled on the floor behind him, yet the stink of it could not mask the creature walking toward him.

"Ben-Ben!" I barked.

He spared a look over his shoulder. "I can't stop, Rileeeeey!" he cried.

"Do it while you run, Ben-Ben!" I growled and barked with my most ferocious, menacing face, trying to ward off the zombie with my potential attack. It didn't even notice me; it was fixated on the Yorkie. Finally, the dog's mud flap closed and he sprinted past me and up the stairs, leaving poop laced paw prints halfway up; the She Alpha was not going to be happy. The thing, which had been a normal two-legger once, slipped and fell in Ben-Ben's excrement. *Whoa! So he is good for something!* I thought. The zombie flopped around in the hallway, getting Ben-Ben's waste over most of his body. Shit intermingled with the blood running from his face, chunks of it lodged in his multiple wounds that looked like they had been inflicted by the leaden bees. Brown dripped from various places as the zombie regained his balance and stood. I had once seen He Alpha stop everything he was doing when he had accidentally mowed over one of my refuse piles with the grass cutter and some had gotten on his pants. You would have thought he was on fire the way he peeled his clothes off and went into the water pourer. This monster before me took no notice of the crap or my growling as I bounded up the stairs.

Boy cub Daniel was still half asleep as he came to the head of the stairs. He looked like he wanted to go down, so I jumped up the remaining three stairs and knocked him over. His crying only added to the cacophony.

"Dad!" the cub screamed. "Riley is trying to eat me!"

He Alpha came out of the room where he kept his fire sticks. He took one look at me and then down the stairs. "Riley just saved your life," he Alpha said grimly as he placed the stick to his shoulder. "Stop or I will shoot!" he told the thing ascending the stairs.

She Alpha screamed as she came to the head of the stairs next to her husband. She cub Jessie was behind them both. The cub Daniel was able to peek past my body to see what everyone was staring at. His eyes seemed to grow large with fear, his bladder let loose much like mine and Ben-Ben's had only moments earlier.

"*Dad*, it's a zombie! Shoot it in the head!" the boy cub screamed.

I got off the boy's chest. This is when I learned the name for the beasts, but I still didn't know what it meant. It was halfway up to us before the Alpha shot; the noise from the blast was incredibly loud, but the ensuing quiet was among some of the most peaceful I would ever have left. At least until Zachary awoke crying from the shock of the noise, add Ben-Ben's mewling and the damn cat's yowling and it was beginning to get very loud.

"My God!" Heather said. "What the hell is going on? You killed that man!" she said to her mate in an accusatory tone.

He was visibly shaking. The thing on the stairs began to stir. "Shoot it again!" Heather screamed.

"The head, Dad, the head!" Daniel yelled to match his mother's entreaties.

The bee did its work as the zombie's head ruptured all over the wall behind it. Rotten gray matter rolled down, but some stuck in red bloody clumps. (Yes, I can see color.)

Jessie was vomiting behind her mother; it smelled like gummy worms and spaghetti.

"Is it safe now, Dad?" The boy cub asked its sire.

You didn't need to have dog ears to hear the commotion going on at the back of the house. More were coming.

"Heather, get the kids and lock yourselves in the bathroom. Me and Riley will stay here."

I was not thrilled I got included in his plan, but I would never abandon one of my pack. That pussy Patches had no such qualm as I saw her dash into the back bedroom where the big human waste room was.

Ben-Ben came out from under the bed, his tail tucked deep under his legs and crap dripping from the tan fur of his tail. "I'll stay too, Rileeey," he whined bravely.

His stock went up in my eyes.

"Oh, Christ, there's another one!" Alpha said.

My fur bristled; Ben-Ben crouched down but did not slink away. One would have been more preferable than the amount that ended up coming up those stairs.

I could hear the cubs and She Alpha cry out after each shot from the fire stick, the problems would arise when the booming stopped. The stairs were choked with the carnage of destroyed human bodies. Blood, intestine and brains mixed in with the remnants of our fallen neighbors. The smell was stifling; I was thankful for the acrid smell of the leaden bees.

Sometime later Alpha looked over to me with resignation in his eyes. "Out of bullets, girl," he told me. I watched as he turned the fire stick around to use more like a regular stick. The quivering pile of bodies at the foot of the stairs was disturbing. Most were not moving but some were. Add to that the zombie creatures desperately trying to get around or over the putrid pile of their brethren. They hunted like a pack but did not have a pack mentality; they cared not for their fallen. It was a younger she two-legger that made it through first. This seemed to have a debilitating effect on my pack leader. I didn't see the problem—male, female, big, or little an enemy is an enemy.

I put my front paws down onto the first step, saliva dripping from my maw as a growl rumbled deep in my chest. Alpha was backing up as the zombie girl was advancing.

"It's Daniel's friend, Denise," Alpha choked out between sobs.

She didn't smell like Denise, I thought as I launched off the step. My jaws encircled her entire face, I bit hard and deep, I could feel the delicate bones start to crumble. I shook violently from side to side. The skin of her face shredded in my jaws. As she fell backward I could feel the tear of flesh from membrane. Red muscle and tendons stared back at me as she righted herself and started back up the stairs, I had ripped her face clean off. The taste in my mouth was foul, way worse than Jessie's attempt at meatloaf. Who uses tofu to make meatloaf? Nobody ate it, well scratch that, Ben-Ben did, although he was sick the next day. I told him not to touch it, but he wouldn't listen.

Alpha male was retching; Ben-Ben was at the top of the stairs yelling. "More are coming, Rileeeey!"

I turned and got back to the top of the stairs. Alpha stood up and moved in front of Ben-Ben and me. He was struggling to hold down his gorge as the girl thing came up the stairs, her blood red smile leading the way.

"God, forgive me for what I do," Alpha said as he mightily swung the club down on top of the thing's head. With the bones in her face broken and most of the skin torn away it was no surprise when both of her eyeballs popped out with an audible sucking sound. I do not think Alpha was aware of what was going to happen, he dropped his stick and fell to his knees. The thing twitched a few times and then laid still. I still could not get the taste of it out of my mouth as I licked the carpet. I pushed my snout into Alpha's face, more of the beasts were coming up the stairs and he was still not moving. He pushed me away; salty water flowed from his eyes, misery rolled off him in waves.

"Ben-Ben, we need to stop these things!" I barked.

Ben-Ben took one look at our fallen pack leader and stood paw to paw with me. Three of the things were fast approaching us. I leaped again, and I'll give him credit, so did that damn little Yorkie. We fought savagely. Thick black blood flowed from our enemies; I thought we might be able to hold them off. They seemed much more interested in Alpha than in either one of us; they did not defend against our bites. All that mattered to them was to press on. I ripped calves open; I tore throats out and watched naked Adam's apples bob up and down. I attacked and crushed genitalia of both genders. I ripped more than one belly open to have many feet of intestine spill loose and still they advanced. Ben-Ben was lost at some point in the fray; I could no longer hear his battle yipping. Even as I fought on I found myself mourning his passing, for all his bad traits he had stayed true at the end.

"A wolf's heart after all!" I howled. I had been pushed back up to the top step. Alpha was gone. I could smell his scent heading to the back of the bedroom where the human waste room was. I did not feel betrayal; Alpha's actions are not for me to question, a little help would have been nice, though. I had nothing left; I had burned through all of my energy, zombies streamed past me on their way to the rear of the sleeping chambers. I bit at a few as they went by but my jaws hurt so bad I could not apply enough pressure to dissuade them from their course of action. More than seven were in the bedroom, but not many more than that. I could hear my pack screaming as the zombies started to hammer on the door. I was so hot; I could not close my mouth for fear if I interrupted my panting I would overheat.

I took a quick glance down the stairs to see if anything alive or dead was still coming, the pile of strewn body parts twitched a bit but it did not appear that anything was going to dislodge itself from that mountain of human remains. The zombies were pushing up against the door. The wood was not very strong—I should know, I used to chew it as a puppy. It was very thin and if I remember right it did not taste good, either. The door was splintering under the assault, I barked at their backs but none of them turned.

"Riley, run!" I heard Jessie shout.

Where would I go? This was my pack.

"No, Charles!" I heard She Alpha yell.

"They're going to break in soon, at least some of us will be safe," I heard him answer.

Jessie was full on crying. I pulled my ears back and started tearing at the dead two-leggers. Meat sloughed off some of the ones that had been dead longer. I had dropped my third one when the door to the water pourer room finally gave out. Alpha fought hard for a minute or more but when a zombie bit two of his fingers off he again dropped to his knees, blood pouring through the stumps where a moment before his fingers had been. Another zombie bit down hard on the top of his exposed scalp. I did not think two-leggers had enough force to bite through bone. I thought wrong as I saw the exposed brain of Alpha glistening wetly in the harsh light. Alpha's arms and legs began to twitch violently as the zombie bit even deeper into the pink goo. She Alpha Heather was shrieking violently as another zombie got to her neck, it tore out a fair portion of her throat. The screaming stopped suddenly but not the violence of the will to exist. She fought valiantly for her survival as her life-blood leaked onto the floor. Another zombie had torn through her shirt and like a suckling infant went right for her teats, unlike a baby though, it tore the breast clean off. The pain of existence became too much. She Alpha fell.

No matter how hard I tried and how much damage I inflicted on my pack's killers I could not get through the doorway. Daniel was trying to get out of a window Ben-Ben would have just barely fit through. The top half of his body was outside, the other half was still in, his legs were thrusting violently but with nothing to seek purchase on he was wedged tight. I had always tried to get him away from the game playing picture box and throw the ball with me and now I regretted not trying harder. His screams as a zombie tore open his thigh had thus far been unrivaled. The zombie clenched onto a strip of flesh and pulled, a piece of Daniel about the size of a good steak sheered free, and blood pooled on the bathroom floor. The legs that a moment before were going a mile a minute fell still. I had failed; all of my pack was dead. I was about to do as much damage as possible before I fell but then I realized Jessie and the baby cub Zachary were not visible, neither did I smell their remains. They had to have come in here with the Alphas.

"Mom?" I heard from outside. "Dad? Help!"

The Jessie cub was outside! I ran down the stairs and over the pile of death and out the backdoor. Jessie was holding her baby brother; tears flowing freely down her face. I was almost to them when I was attacked.

CHAPTER TWO

Something landed on top of me, a razor sharp claw narrowly missing my eye. I rolled over onto my side and the pain in the ass cat Patches fell off my back.

"Sorry," she said. "I thought you were attacking the children."

"You talk?" I barked at her.

"Of course I do, I just never had anything to say to the likes of *you*," she stated matter-of-factly.

I had been wrong on two counts tonight, Ben-Ben's bravery and Patches' willingness to protect the pack. What else would I learn I was wrong about before the night was out? Hopefully, I would figure it out before it was too late, the four of us were now the pack and even animals know there is safety in numbers. If I could find enough living beings to make our pack more than seven, then all the better.

Jessie was crying uncontrollably and barely acknowledged my presence. She was looking up. I followed her line of sight. Daniel's dead body hung limply from the window, blood dripping from his mouth and landing not three feet from where we stood.

Patches walked over to the growing puddle of viscous liquid. "He has the disease," she stated.

"The dead disease?" I asked her. "You can smell it?"

"Can't you?" she asked disdainfully.

I walked over to the blood and sniffed around. I didn't know what the conniving cat was talking about. I could only smell the fat-soaked iron rich blood smell the humans produce.

"I thought as much," she said as she licked a paw.

"How'd you like me to rip that paw off?" I growled at her.

Jessie finally seemed to take notice as she heard my threat to the cat. "Riley? Oh, God, Riley!" she cried as she got down on one knee and wrapped her free hand around my neck.

I licked her face, the bitter tears washing away the vileness of my opponents.

"Riley, they're all dead!" she cried again. Zachary shifted some in her other arm but did not awaken.

"And we'll join them if we stay here," Patches added.

I would have liked to help the cat along on her journey to the afterlife, but not just yet.

"Oh, I know what you're thinking, you big dumb dog. It'll have to wait."

"Wow, you really *aren't* as dumb as you look," I told her.

Jessie had put the baby down and looked like she wanted to lie down next to it. I nipped her arm.

"Riley, stop," Jessie said without much force. "I'm so cold and they're all dead," she cried.

Now I know human females, unlike any other animal on the planet, have a tendency to get overly upset for the least reason. Daniel had once told her her pants made her look fat and she had cried and had thrown things around for two days. I thought it was funny that he wasn't even looking her way when he said it. And maybe if she had shared a little more of her food with me, he wouldn't have had to say it. I'm just saying. But this was not one of those times. Our pack leaders and pack mates had been killed and it was cold out. Even I was feeling the effects and Jessie did not have her cold protective clothing on.

I nipped her arm again. We would not be safe here long or at all.

"Get them moving, Riley. They're coming," Patches said

as she came back around the corner of the house. I hadn't even noticed she was gone.

Jessie pushed me away as I went in for another more vigorous warning.

I knew the zombies were coming and stealth right now was the best option, but Jessie was angering me, I had never seen her just give up. I barked loudly once in her ear. The sound should have conveyed to her the danger we were in and that we had to get moving to survive. I don't know why she didn't understand it. I had spent the first year of my life learning their language; I don't know why the two-leggers didn't feel the need to do the same.

"She wishes to die, Patches," I said disparagingly.

"Grab the infant," Patches said, coming up beside me. "We should go into the house with the big wheeled machines."

"She's part of our pack," I said to Patches mournfully.

"Are you including me in that?" Patches asked, looking up at me.

I looked down. The cat was within biting distance. I had been waiting for this moment almost my entire life and that all seemed like wasted time now. "I guess I am," I said, bowing my head and grabbing the infant's swaddling. "How will we get in?" I mumbled, the words difficult to get out around the bundle in my mouth.

"Watch," Patches said as we started to walk over to the machine house.

"Riley, Patches, where are you going with Zachary?" Jessie asked, raising her head from the ground.

"Don't turn around!" Patches hissed at me. "Keep walking, maybe even a little faster."

"She's one of us, Cat!" I said as loud as I could whilst not waking the baby.

"Does that squished-in face of yours affect your brain?" Patches asked with an evil grin.

"I will eat you!" I told her. "And I don't even like mangy

food!"

"You'll wake the infant and the noise will bring the dead ones."

"Riley, you come here now!" Jessie yelled.

"Is she getting closer?" I asked Patches. The need to pay heed to who was now the pack leader was like a physical pull.

"See, I know what I'm doing."

"Oh, she's following us!" I yipped excitedly.

"There's hope for you yet," Patches said derisively.

"I will still eat you, but later."

"Fine, fine. Hold onto that thought if you can, but you had better move faster or it won't matter."

"Dead ones?" I asked as my lips pulled back. "I can't smell them through this one's waste, smells a lot like broccoli and those delicious sweets in the foil packs." I took another sniff to be certain. "Strawberry, I believe."

Patches got to the door first and begin to caterwaul loudly. "Hurry, human!" seemed to be the loose translation. She usually only reserved this for the most dire of situations, like when her yarn was tangled or it was din-din time or pretty much anytime the little princess felt like she needed something quickly. I'd let it slide this time.

Jessie caught up to me just as I got to the door. She opened the door without any further prompting from Patches. Her will to live beginning to return, she would need to tap into her survival instincts if she wanted to make it through this night and the next. She grabbed Zachary from my jaws, I was thankful to let the bundle go. My mouth still hurt from earlier.

No sooner had the small door shut when Patches turned to me. "This shouldn't be a problem for you, but you need to relieve yourself."

"What? Indoors? I will not do such a thing," I said indignantly.

"I remember when you were a puppy, you used to do it

all the time."

"I did not know any better," I said ashamedly.

"You must, Dog, the scent will throw the dead ones away from here and from them." She motioned with her head.

"They are scent-driven? How do you know this? The humans can't smell anything with that little nose."

"Be that as it may," Patches started, "but those things out there are not human and I've watched them sniff the wind to find a scent."

"I do not know if I believe you, but even if I did and I thought I would not get into trouble by relieving myself here, I cannot. Pack leader took me out earlier and I took care of business then. Why don't you do it?" I asked her. She looked at me like I had asked her to mate with a chipmunk.

"Me?" she fairly spat. "I go in the same bathroom as the pack leaders!" she huffed.

"Please!" I answered. "You go in a dirt box and then try to cover it up, thinking no one else will know. Let me tell you, your pee burns my nose."

"It does no such thing!" she said peevishly.

"Patches, Riley, be quiet," Jessie whispered, looking through the window. "They're coming."

"Now or never, oh dainty one," I told Patches. I nudged Jessie to get away from the outside viewer, or window, that was what the two-leggers called it. I wasn't sure if the cat was completely right about the scent thing or not, but standing in front of the glass was still not a good idea. Jessie slowly backed up to the big-wheeled machine.

She seemed to get an idea as she opened the door to what the humans called a Hummer. All I knew was I loved to be inside of it. The wind as it blew past my face was exhilarating, so many scents so quickly it was impossible to define them all, but yet I tried. *Happy times*, I smiled as I thought to myself. I watched as Jessie strapped the cub into his special seat, he had fallen back asleep after the fire stick battle and had stayed that way. Lucky for him, the dog gods were looking out for all of us.

"Shit, keys," Jessie said softly.

"The janglers!" I barked softly. Pack leader would always shake them in front of me when it was my turn to go for a ride.

The acidic smell of cat piss hit me just as Patches rounded the front of the large riding machine, her tail swishing triumphantly high in the air.

"You did that on purpose," I told her.

"Of course I did," she answered, not trying to hide anything.

"It's awful, it's burning my throat."

Patches made sure her tail rubbed up against my nose as she passed by. I sneezed loudly.

"Riley, be quiet!" Jessie said sternly. Patches openly laughed. "I need to think. Dad told me once he had hidden keys for this thing. But he never let me drive it so I didn't bother to try to remember."

"What's she talking about, Riley?" Patches asked.

"The janglers, Cat. Don't you know anything?" But how would she? As far as I knew Patches never got to go for rides and now I felt something I'd never felt for the cat: guilt. "It's the things that make the machine come to life," I told her. "Kind of like giving you catnip."

Patches got a faraway look in her eyes, remembering the mind-altering spice.

"Cats," I said contemptuously, walking away. I was pretty sure I knew where Alpha kept an extra jangler. He was always leaving the big bunch of them inside the car, why he didn't just open the door and get them I'll never know. We were at the dog park once and had to wait for a very long time while another human came and had to open the door for my pack leader. Alpha was pretty mad about it. I was pretty happy, I got to run around the park with the other dogs for a lot longer than I usually got to. After that, though, he had put a single jangler on the outside of the wheeled machine.

"Where'd he put it?" I thought out loud, but softly. I walked around the machine. Pack leader's scent was strong where the door opened and by where the liquid went that smelled worse than Patches' pee, but those weren't the right spots. I came around to the back of the wheeler and got another strong scent of him by the door handle and again by the piece about level with my nose. I whined softly until Jessie came over to see what the matter was. I pawed the location where the lone jangler was hidden. Jessie just stared at me.

"They're coming," Patches said as her tail jigged and jagged back and forth rapidly. I always wanted to bite that thing and this was no exception.

I banged my paw on the bumper this time harder, but Jessie was looking toward the front of the machine house. We all heard it; I definitely smelled it and so did the cat as she walked back around the way she had come. I batted Jessie's leg with my paw; she reached a hand down to brush me away. *Alright, so much for subtle,* I thought grimly. As her hand came down again I clamped a hold. She cried out in surprise. It wasn't even close to being enough pressure to break skin, but I wasn't letting go. I dragged her hand over to the bumper; her eyes glistened with fear.

"What, Riley! That really hurts," she yelled as loudly as she could without getting past a whisper.

I made sure her hand touched the bumper before I let go. She immediately pulled her hand up and rubbed it. I noticed where my large teeth had put indents into her hand. Maybe I had bit down a little harder than intended. I was scared too. Jessie kept rubbing her hand, but her eyes were at least on me, so I put my paw back up on the back of the machine.

"The bumper, Riley? What about... oh shit, *that's* where he put the key!" she said happily. "How did you know, good girl?" she said as she patted my head.

"Because I'm smart!" I yipped quietly.

"Yeah, regular genius," Patches' voice came faintly from the other side of the garage.

"When this is over, Cat, I will catch you. We have a score to settle."

"Please," Patches said, now magically sitting by the front wheel licking her paw. "You couldn't catch your own tail."

"You know that's not fair, Cat, I don't have much of a tail," I growled.

"Like I said," she finished as she licked the rest of her paw.

"I'm not really sure what that means but it doesn't sound good," I told her.

"Hah, got it!" Jessie said triumphantly. "Come on, Riley girl, let's go for a ride!" she said excitedly.

I looked over to Patches; she looked like she had swallowed a lemon. "What's the matter? Got your own tongue?" I laughed.

"Yeah, never heard that one," she answered nervously.

"Come on, Jessie is driving the wheeled ride. As much as it pains me to say this, you need to get in," I told her.

"I'm not getting in the car," she hissed. "Every time I do, some strange guy tells me how cute I am right before he stings me with a metal stick."

"That thing is called a what? And the animal doctor? You're afraid of the animal doctor? But they always give treats," I tried to assure her.

"You're just too dog-id to realize, Riley. That's where they brought George when he was sick and he never came back. I wish he were here now," she cried.

"George? Why? I mean I wish he were here too."

"Are you really that stupid?" she asked with that look of contempt only a cat can pull off with an air of indifference.

I took a step toward her. "I can only suffer your attitude for so long, Cat, no matter the dangers lurking outside."

"Fine," she fairly purred, the edge of her muzzle pulling

up in a supercilious smile. "George and I were the best of friends."

"You lie!" I barked in her face. I noticed with satisfaction she flinched when my spittle sprayed her face.

"Riley! Shut up, they're going to hear us," Jessie cried in alarm.

"Oh, it's true," Patches replied, rubbing her paw on her face to wipe away the majority of the offending liquid. "I knew George for eight seasons before the humans made the mistake of bringing you home."

Eight? I don't know how many eight is. I didn't know what else to do, I was in shock so I did the best thing I could think of, I growled at her.

"We were almost as close as litter mates."

I think my jaw dropped.

"I can't be expected to remember that far back. Has to be ten winter seasons ago and I was very young. I can't say for sure which one of us was here first, but I remember the heat of him as we slept curled together."

Ten! Dammit, another number I did not know, but it sounded like it must be more than seven. "He told me how he hated cats, Cat!" I said triumphantly.

"That may be the case," she answered back coolly. "But did he ever mention me specifically?"

"Well… well, not specifically, but it was implied!" I told her, believing I had for certain won this skirmish. "I watched him chase you," I added, believing this to be the knock out paw to the side of the head.

"It was merely for the amusement of the two-leggers."

"What?" I asked incredulously.

"The humans thought it funny, plus they would give him a cookie if he stopped. Part of which he always shared with me."

"The secret stash? He shared his secret stash with you? He wouldn't even let me *sniff* anywhere near it."

"Well, that should tell you something," Patches said

arrogantly.

I growled deeply.

"Are they getting closer, Riley?" Jessie asked. "Get in the car." She leaned over and opened the passenger door.

"Cat, if you don't get in this machine I will have to eat you now and since I still have the taste of the dead ones in my mouth I would not be able to enjoy it as much. So get in the car," I rumbled menacingly.

Patches looked toward my drool-dripping maw, to the garage door where something banged up against it, and to the open door where Jessie was encouraging her to enter with hand motions and gently cooing. She took the less threatening alternative and jumped onto the seat and then into Jessie's lap.

"Shut the door, shut the door," Patches meowed to Jessie.

"Be quiet, Patches," Jessie murmured.

"You're about as trustworthy as a French poodle," I growled to the cat as I raced around the Hummer and hopped up onto the seat next to Jessie's.

"Take it back," Patches hissed, showing her claws.

"I'd rather mate with a snake," I told her, which was pretty low as far as dog swears went.

"You will regret this," she told me, her green eyes narrowing with animosity.

"Already do," I said as Jessie stretched her arm across me to shut my door.

"I will urinate where—"

"Shut up!" I snapped. I paused for a second. Everything was quiet. "Did you hear that?" I asked her.

"How could I? I don't have those big Dumbo ears."

I didn't know what 'Dumbo' meant but it came from the cat so it couldn't be good. "There it is again."

Patches tilted her head.

"Oh, no!' we said in unison.

"It's Ben-Ben," I finished.

"This night couldn't get any worse," Patches sighed.

It could get worse for you, I thought. Ben-Ben had climbed my respect ladder tonight but he was still a pain in my rear quarters.

"Rileeeeyy," came Ben-Ben's yipping. "Where are you, Rileeeeeyyy?"

"Dog couldn't find his own scat if he stepped in it," Patches offered.

"That's pretty funny, Cat," I told Patches. She dipped her head in acknowledgement. "But he stood his ground with me when all, including yourself, took flight."

Patches looked at me defiantly. "Who do you think showed the two-leggers the window to get out?"

"You? The humans could not think of it on their own?" I begged to differ.

"You were not in there, Riley. The panic pheromones flooding off them were horrible. They were hiding in the water collector; I jumped up onto the ledge and beat my paw against the glass. It was then your Alpha and my Care-Giver thought to open it and look around to see if the dead ones were out there. I jumped down first to make sure the coast was clear and meowed back up to him that everything was okay. He lowered Jessie down first, then dropped Zachary into her arms. The fat one that always pulled my tail did not fit."

"You did all that?" I asked. *How could I have been so wrong about Ben-Ben and now Patches?* I wondered. "I still do not know if I will ever like you, Cat, but I thank you for saving these two cubs."

"And I thank you for giving me the time to do it," she replied.

"This is going to take some time to get used to," I told her.

"Agreed," she said. "But can't we leave Ben-Ben behind while we figure it all out?"

"Damn, Ben-Ben. I had almost forgotten about him."

"Reason twenty-two why cats are better than dogs."

"I hate numbers, Cat."

"I know," she purred smugly.

I barked once at Jessie who had turned to check on Zachary. "Shhh, girl, what's the matter?" she asked softly.

Certainly she could hear Ben-Ben now even with those useless little round things the two-leggers called ears. How do they have every other species on the planet afraid of them? They are slow, they cannot smell or hear well. Their teeth are small and not very intimidating, and they don't see particularly well in the dark. As dogs we were smart enough to realize why we should ally ourselves with them but we could not figure out their secret of domination.

Jessie took in a great gulp of air. "Is that Ben-Ben? If Ben-Ben survived, did the rest of my family?" she asked me. "Oh, Riley," she cried and grabbed both sides of my head, weeping.

Nobody else from her pack survived, I had seen the damage done. Jessie leaned away from me to open her door. I jumped over her as her door came completely open. I landed awkwardly on the ground but hurt nothing. I turned to Jessie and barked once, telling her to *stay*. She looked at me with a funny expression and then shut her door. Maybe there was hope for her yet.

"Hey, Brainiac," the cat yelled. "How you going to get out of the garage?"

I did not know 'brainiac' or 'garage', but I pieced together the getting out part and considering the speaker, figured it was some sort of insult.

"I'm not as dumb as you look, Cat," I told her.

"We'll see," she said aloofly, looking out the window.

I gripped the metal door handle tightly with my jaws, which were still sore from earlier, and twisted. At first my teeth just slid uncomfortably along the cold fixture. I could hear the cat chuckling but I tried to ignore it. I twisted the other way, my teeth were still slipping but this time the handle was turning. I bit down harder, my jaw muscles ached. The door was loose! I backed up and the door swung inwards. "Hah!" I barked in triumph a little too loudly.

"Who else you going to let know?" Patches asked with a sneer.

I ignored her as I listened for Ben-Ben's telltale yipping. He was on the far side of the house away from the 'garage'. I could smell the dead ones and they were close, even the cat's piss could do little to disguise it.

"Rileeeey, they're chasing me!" Ben-Ben yipped fearfully.

He was running the other way, away from Jessie, Zach, the other, and me. I ran to the corner of the house to see which way he was going. Ben-Ben was looking over his shoulder as maybe twenty-two dead ones were chasing him. I couldn't exactly tell because twenty-two is a very large number. *If the cat knows the number then so do I*, I thought.

"Ben-Ben!" I barked as loud as I could. He stopped dead in his tracks. "Stupid dog! Keep running or they will eat you. Run around the two-legger's house next to us as fast as you can and then come to the wheeler house," I barked, my throat raw from the effort.

"Rileeeyyy!" Ben-Ben squealed in happiness as he abruptly turned and started running directly toward me, his tongue lolling, eyes wide with fear, gore and gristle probably from twenty of the two-leggers dripping from him.

"Oh, Cat crap," I moaned. The zombies were trying to get a hold of Ben-Ben as he dodged in and out of outstretched hands, but what was worse were the ones he got past were now starting to follow.

"Ben-Ben, I'm going back to the wheeler house, when you get there jump in to the wheeler!" I turned to start to run.

"Can't, Riley," he panted. I felt bad; the little guy was starting to tucker out. "Too high," he got out hastily.

"Just get there and be quick."

"I love you, Rileeeey," he yipped excitedly.

"Fine, just keep running." But I smiled all the same.

Jessie was out of the car; at least that's what I think the cat called it.

"Oh, Riley, you're back," Jessie said happily. "I was so worried. We need to go, girl."

Figured that part out on my own, I wanted to tell her. She reached over and pressed a button, a large sound overhead caused the big 'car' door to open. "Come on, girl," Jessie said as she ran over to the car and patted the seat for me to get in. She got upset when I didn't immediately follow her command. "Please, Riley, we need to go." I could tell she was close to tears. Just then I watched as her head swiveled up to the sound of Ben-Ben's yammering. "Ben-Ben?" she fairly cried. "He looks like a zombie."

I turned to see the approaching Yorkie. I could see her point. He had more life fluid on the outside of him than he probably contained on the inside.

"They're close, Rileeey," Ben-Ben needlessly told me.

He darted past me and up to the first step of the car, where Jessie was looking down at him in disbelief. Humans are so funny with their fear of what they consider gross stuff, but yet they defecate in the same place they live, so who's gross now? I ran over to the car, grabbed Ben-Ben by the scruff of his fur and launched him inside. He did a quick shake all over the seat Alpha used. *Someone was going to get dirty*, I thought as I hopped in. "Backseat, mutt," I barked at him. He didn't so much as register a complaint he was so happy to be 'safe'. I had to admit I was happy to see him too.

"Disgusting!" Jessie said looking at her seat. She was hesitant to get in until I started barking past her and at the figures in the doorway. Gross seat was WAY better than Dead Ones. Apparently, Jessie thought the same thing as she hastily hopped in and shut her door.

The first of the Dead Ones hit the side of the car before Jessie got the jangler turned. Her shriek was so loud it hurt my ears. Ben-Ben was yipping at the window like he wanted to exact some revenge, and who knows, maybe he did.

Patches looked indifferent but her fur was bristling. I could tell she was ready to leave. "Make the girl do something, Riley," Patches said with annoyance. "She looks like those metal things humans are always making of each other."

"Statues," Ben-Ben said, turning to look at her. "They build them to honor their great pack leaders."

I was feeling confused and a little worried; I always marked those when we went to the park. But I should've been alright, the air rats are always scatting on them and they never get in trouble. Maybe that's why the two-leggers put them up. I don't know, I've seen them do way weirder things.

"Riley!" Patches shouted.

"Sorry, Cat. *Move!*" I barked at Jessie.

She looked over at me like she couldn't believe I had just done that, but it seemed to have the right effect. The wheeler turned on and we started moving; she hit two of the Dead Ones as she left the garage. I could smell a welling of saliva frothing in Jessie's mouth and she looked very pale. If she threw up maybe Ben-Ben would be able to eat now. I smiled. I was just happy to be moving away from them. I would miss the Alphas and maybe the Daniel cub a bit, definitely my warm bed, and my toys. I had Jessie, Zachary, to a lesser degree, Ben-Ben, and I would have to suffer through Patches.

When we got out onto the large hard-packed pathway, there were cars everywhere without people in them. There were also many things on fire. Jessie was moving very slowly as she looked at all the things now wrong in our world.

"Riley, where will we go?" Jessie asked as she turned to me.

I told her to go to the park, why would Dead Ones want to go there? But she didn't respond. Her mood changed from despondent to hopeful as she pulled out her talking box from her pocket. She slowed even more as she pressed on it with her fingers. Any slower and the Dead Ones would start to pass us by. I was looking out the windows and noticed nervously we were starting to become the center of attention. Now don't get me wrong, I'm all about being the center of attention but only when it is going to benefit me, like if I get my belly rubbed or get a piece of cheese or maybe even a hotdog, then it's all good. But the Dead Ones were looking at us like we were the cheese and the hot dogs. I wanted to leave. I whined loudly, Jessie looked up and realizing they were getting closer, made the car go faster.

"Come on, come on, come on!" Jessie said into her talking box. "Where are you, Justin?"

"Did she say Justin?" Patches asked me.

"Yeah wasn't that the boy cub who always came over before the Great Move?" I replied questioningly.

"His pheromones dripped off him every time he was around Jessie," Patches laughed. "Hers did too."

"He always gave me snacks and rubbed my head," I told Patches. "I think it was so I would go away, though, and he could put his face to hers—another strange two-legger custom."

"At least they don't sniff each other's butts," Patches said in challenge.

"I love sniffing butts," Ben-Ben said dreamily.

"I bet you do, Dog," Patches said with disdain.

I left it at that. I had a feeling the cat was pretty smart and if I couldn't chase her or eat her, I didn't want to get in an argument with her I might not win.

"Just a busy signal, dammit!" Jessie yelled angrily. "How far is California to Colorado?"

I started to think back to the Great Move. It took two cycles of the burning disc to get to our new home. I remember the smell the most; the salt in the air stung my nose at first. Must have sneezed every day for the first two new moons. But how 'far' I don't think even the haughty

Patches knew the answer.

"Well then, that's it, we'll go to Colorado, there's nothing left for me here," Jessie said with a sob. "How hard can it be? I just need to drive east."

I didn't know what 'east' meant but I was all for finding the Justin boy. He cared for Jessie and me and I for one would welcome more into the pack. So started our journey to find a place free from the Dead Ones.

CHAPTER THREE

I was exhausted; Jessie had been driving for a long enough time I felt I had missed my early morning meal. Her head kept bobbing up and down like she wanted to sleep, but when her head went down the car started to go off the hard-packed path. More than once I had to bark to get her attention, she would look over to me with red blazed teary eyes and then swerve the car to stay on the path when she realized why I was barking in the first place.

"I need some sleep, girl," Jessie said to me. "And I'm hungry."

I barked in agreement to both things she said.

The bright disc was just becoming visible; I was looking at a sea of what looked like kitty litter, as if on cue the cat spoke up.

"Can you make the human stop, Riley? I have to relieve myself," Patches said.

I looked around. There was only one other wheeler and it was just barely within my field of vision. I barked again at Jessie, her head had not even been drooping but it was close.

"What, girl?" she asked.

I pawed the door.

"You need out?" She yawned.

"Well, the cat does, but now that you mention it, I could do with a little stop, myself," I told her. "And maybe a meat treat." But I didn't smell any on her.

The car came to a lurching halt as Jessie stepped on the stopping pedal a little too hard; there was a loud thump as Ben-Ben rolled off the seat and onto the floor, followed immediately by a 'yip' of surprise.

"Please, don't send me back! I'll be good!" he barked loudly before he completely woke up.

"You alright?" I asked him, looking around the seat to where he was splayed upside down on the floor.

"Sorry," he replied with his tail tucked between his legs.

"Nobody is ever going to send you away, Ben-Ben, not after what you did last night," I told him.

He struggled to gain his footing and get back on the seat. "Thank you, Riley," he responded with his head hanging low. His tail had come somewhat out from under him but not completely.

It was tough to tell with him if the abuse from the two-leggers at his first home had been caused from his behavior, or his behavior had been a result of the two-leggers' abuse. He had more than proven his worth to me last night and I would forgive him many things I had previously found bothersome.

I was still looking at him when the car stopped completely. Jessie had gotten out and was stretching, Patches was out immediately after her and heading for some small bushes on the side of the road.

"Don't go far!" I barked.

"Do you mind if I relieve myself in private? I'm not a dog. I have dignity. Always scatting and peeing in front of the humans as if you're proud of it," Patches mewled.

"Why wouldn't we be, Riley?" Ben-Ben asked me.

"Don't listen to her, she's just a cat."

"I can still hear you," Patches grunted from the side of the pathway.

"Let's go out, Ben-Ben, I think we're going to rest here," I told him. I took a quick sniff of Zachary. He was still asleep but I didn't think he would be for long, he smelled like he was sitting in his own offal and he didn't usually care at first but eventually he would get angry about it.

I put my paws far out in front of me and arched to stretch

my back, I was thirsty and hungry and needed to relieve myself. I would have done so right on the pathway, but the damned cat now had me thinking about it. One more strike against her.

"Ben-Ben, keep an eye out for the sick ones, I have to do something," I told him.

He looked longingly at me, hoping I wouldn't be gone long, I would imagine, but he didn't say anything.

Patches was just coming out of the brush as I was about to enter.

"Where you going?" she asked.

"Nothing! Looking for something!" I barked hastily.

She laughed her cat laugh at me. "Looks like there might be hope for you, after all," she said as she walked away leaving me to my business.

"We need food and water," Jessie was saying aloud, not really directed to me but more to all of us.

I finished what I needed to do and came back to the wheeler and looked in.

Zachary began to leak water from his face, I knew this for the precursor that it was, he was about to bellow loudly; for someone so small the sound belied his stature.

"Oh, Zak, you must be starving," Jessie said with concern as she took the human cub out of the car. "Oooh, and you need a diaper change." Jessie's face wrinkled up from the smell.

Zachary was beginning to hitch with his breathing as his cries became even more voluminous.

"Mom always kept emergency stuff in the back," Jess said as she found something next to her seat that made the back of the car open.

I smelled food; I went to the back of the car.

"Yes, diapers," Jessie said happily as she pulled a big bright bag out of the car. She spent the next few moments changing the cub's clothing and then began to rummage through the big pack. She was pulling out all sorts of delicious looking treats by this time; Ben-Ben and the cat were bearing witness.

"Water, formula, breakfast bars, pretzels, and whatever this is," Jessie said, holding up a small tinfoil pack of the treats I knew Daniel loved. He called them Pop-Farts or something like that. It was a funny name, but I'd tasted more than a few during my life and they were delicious.

Jessie put what she called 'formula' into a container for the baby cub and gave it to Zak; she put him back in the car where he drank greedily. Jessie ripped open one of the bags she called breakfast bars and was devouring it almost as greedily as her pack mate. She looked up from her food to see us all staring back. She broke the remainder into three equal parts and handed the first one to Ben-Ben.

"Gentle!" she shouted when he accidentally nipped her fingers.

"Sorry," he mumbled. He swallowed his before Patches had even finished sniffing her portion.

"Take it," Jessie urged the cat.

"There's no meat in this," Patches said indignantly as she kept sniffing the food. "Or fish." She swished her tail. "I will not eat this," she said turning her tail on the proffered food.

I was not happy that the piece Patches had sniffed all over and refused was the piece Jessie now offered me, but my belly would suffer the slight. I gently took the piece and chewed as slowly as I could, it would do little to stop the pang in my belly but it tasted so good.

Ben-Ben was already back sniffing at the last piece remaining. "Mine, mine, mine!" he kept yipping excitedly.

Jessie popped it into her own mouth. Something deeply instinctual was beginning to reawaken in my head that had long been asleep. The two-legger was no longer going to be able to keep my belly full; if I wanted food I was going to have to get it myself. But this wasn't going to be as easy as prying open a door in the human's food room. The animals that had sometimes entered our outside area—like squirrels and rabbits—that I had chased for the fun of it would now be things I would chase to eat. I caught them or I would starve.

I was going to need help and right now I was looking at a small dog that was running in circles for a long eaten human hand-out, and to a cat. She at least had some skill; I'd seen her on more than one occasion drop a bird or a mouse on the front stairs of the house of the humans.

"Cat," I said. She completely ignored me as their species tends to do. "Cat!" I said a little louder.

She glared up at me. "It's Patches, you mongrel, and if you can't bother to say it right then I shan't bother to listen."

"Fine, Ca—Patches."

"That's better. Was that so hard?" she asked me.

"Strangely, it was," I told her.

"What do you want?"

"I want food." I answered. The cat began to eye me suspiciously. "Not you, I imagine you'd be stringy without much flavor."

She hissed at me. "What do you want from me, then?"

"We need to hunt."

"We?" she asked. "I don't need any help."

"We need to get food for the baby cub and your Jessie."

Patches kept looking at me and then the corners of her mouth pulled up slightly. "And?" she asked, waiting patiently for my answer.

"And what?" I asked, defending myself.

"Say it dog or I will not help you."

"You will not provide food for the two-leggers? After all they have done for you?"

"What they have done for me?" she yelled loudly. "I have given them my attention in exchange for their food and shelter—was that not a fair trade?" she asked and she meant it. "I do not 'owe' them anything."

"You cannot be serious!" I said heatedly. Had I been too hasty in giving the cat any sort of fondness or credit? "We are a pack, we help each other. We do things together so we can survive together."

"You have it wrong, Dog. Pack mentality is something you and the humans share, Cats do not work like that. I will take their food because it suits me, but I am quite capable of surviving on my own."

"Until now I never knew the depths of your selfishness. Had I known I would have snapped your neck when I had a chance."

Patches bristled. "You have never had a chance." She hissed, arching her back for size and to be able to launch an offensive strike if it came to that.

Ben-Ben picked this inopportune time to come around the car to see what was happening.

"Whoa, Riley why does she look like she's going to stick her claws into you? Those things hurt," Ben-Ben said, bowing his head and rubbing his snout with his paw where Patches had ripped open Ben-Ben's muzzle a year ago when the incessant little Yorkie wouldn't leave her alone.

"Stay out of this," Patches said, "or I'll do it again."

"Ben-Ben, can you hunt?" I asked, never taking my gaze from Patches.

"You mean catch stuff and eat it, Riley?" Ben-Ben asked.

"Yes, Ben-Ben, Catch stuff and eat it."

"Why would I want to do that?" Ben-Ben asked.

"Fine, Cat!" I spat out. "I need help in catching food for the two-leggers and me and Ben-Ben."

"I knew you would eventually come around and realize my superiority. Why didn't you just save us all this trouble and just say so?" she asked, standing back up normally.

"What just happened?" Ben-Ben asked confusedly.

"Progress," Patches answered, but I sure didn't see it that way. If anything, dog advancement had just taken a huge hit. I had just admitted to a cat I needed its help, I was glad none of my forefathers were there to witness it. I growled my discontent.

Jessie was feeding the baby and she appeared to be almost asleep as Patches, Ben-Ben, and I figured out how we were going to get some food. The more we talked about it the less Ben-Ben seemed interested.

"Why don't we just find stuff the two-leggers open up and give us?" he said. "Especially the wet meat when they use the loud whirring thing," Ben-Ben finished, his tail wagging involuntarily as he thought about it.

"It's a can opener," Patched told him.

"What's a can opener?" Ben-Ben asked, his reverie snapped.

"The wet meat comes in a can and the humans use a can-opener to get at it." Patches elaborated.

"Yeah, yeah, wet meat—why don't we just go out there and find some of those?" Ben-Ben asked, looking off into the large sand area.

"Meat cans don't come from the desert," Patches said.

I was glad she clarified that because I wasn't exactly sure and I didn't want to say anything in front of her to make me look not smart.

"Are you sure?" Ben-Ben asked. "Because that would be great, just round up a bunch of those things and we could eat all day!" Ben-Ben said excitedly.

"Has he always been this stupid?" Patches asked me.

"Pretty much," I answered; Ben-Ben was paying no attention to either of us as his muzzle was leaking drool.

***

Within a few minutes, Patches and I came up with a plan of attack, Ben-Ben was relegated to guard dog; I hope he snapped out of his wet meat dream soon enough to do a good job.

"Ben-Ben!" I barked. "You need to keep an eye out for anything coming and then give a warning yell."

"I heard you," Ben-Ben whimpered. "No need to yell."

Patches and I headed into the small brush.

"Could you try to make a little less noise, you're not much better than a human," Patches hissed at me.

She was probably right, but coming out of her mouth somehow made it worse. I watched my footing as best I could, but until we got out from under the bushes it was going to be difficult. She was small enough that she could stay under the branches. I didn't have that luxury as the sticks poked and prodded me relentlessly. When we finally emerged on the other side I was greatly relieved, but I did not like the barrier between the human cubs and me. If they needed my help it would take me longer than I wished to get back to them.

"I smell rabbits and something else," Patches said, pausing to try to locate the smell. "I think it is a lizard."

"The green slimy thing?" I stuck my tongue out, wiping away the imaginary taste of what I thought the thing tasted like. Daniel had got one a season ago, I remember looking at it, wondering why he would want the thing and when he had stopped feeding the thing it had died. I was not saddened at the loss. It was never part of the pack.

"They taste like chicken," Patches said.

"I like chicken," I told her, almost getting that faraway look in my eyes like Ben-Ben. "Are there chickens out here?" I asked, hoping.

"You've been hanging around Ben-Ben too much," she replied.

I'd known the cat long enough to realize this wasn't a compliment, but I hadn't figured out quite yet how big of an insult it was. "No on the chickens then?"

"No chickens," Patches said, shaking her head in a very human, disapproving way.

Patches showed me how to lay low and wait for animals to come our way, but the fire disc was hot and the ground was getting even hotter. I wasn't getting any fuller waiting for stuff to come our way and besides it just *felt* wrong. I was supposed to be *chasing* things not slinking around waiting for something to come our way. I was panting hard, I was getting hot, and in some real need of water.

"You sound like a train, could you maybe shut up a bit?" Patches asked contemptuously.

I didn't know what a train was but they must be loud. "I've had enough of this. I'm finding food," I said stood up.

"Wait! It was almost here," she said resignedly to my retreating hind quarters. When I had stood I startled a rather large lizard within a couple of strides. It looked about half as big as Ben-Ben.

"You're fast," I said to the lizard bounding away toward the roadway.

"Stupid, stupid dog," Patches said behind me, she had joined in the pursuit. "A hundred more heartbeats and it would have came to us."

"This is funner," I barked, I was staying even with the lizard, no matter how fast I tried to run I couldn't catch it and it was heading for the bushes where its size would be of huge benefit for it. "You're going to have to get it when it gets to the bushes," I said to Patches.

"It's the same size as me, I can't kill that thing," Patches said as she caught up.

No wonder I'd never caught her, the cat was fast!

"Ben-Ben!" I howled. "Food is coming!"

"Wet meat?" he barked back.

"Sure!" I replied. The lizard ran straight under the bushes, Patches was no more than half a dog stride away. I had to slow down and get lower to get through.

"It's out the other side!" Patches said excitedly.

"Wet meat!" Ben-Ben said happily, then he must have caught sight of the lizard. "Oh, broken garage bags what is that?" he shrieked.

"Catch it, Ben-Ben!" I yelled.

"Are you sure, Riley?" he whined.

"He has wet meat!" I said trying a different tactic.

Howls and shrieks of pain and rage assailed my ears. I

struggled to get through as quickly as possible. When I finally got through to the other side, Patches was sitting on the edge of the hard pathway, her head shaking back and forth. She may have been smiling but it's tough to tell with her kind, it could just as soon have been a sneer.

"What's going on? Did it get away?" I asked her.

"Look for yourself."

I looked. Ben-Ben had the huge lizard protruding from his mouth. "Rastes rike ricken," he mumbled past the obstruction.

"What's all this noise?" Jessie asked rounding the corner to see Ben-Ben with the lizard in his mouth, she jumped back a step. "Ooh, gross, Ben-Ben what do you have in your mouth?"

Ben-Ben placed the lizard down and began yipping. "Chicken, I definitely have chicken," he said repeatedly.

I went over and nudged the dead lizard toward Jessie's foot.

"What are you doing, Riley? That thing is gross, just get away from it."

I kept rolling it her way and barking.

"This a gift? You want me to eat it? Riley, I don't think I can," she said, still backing farther away every time I nudged it closer.

"She's not going to eat it and I'm starved," Patches said, coming up alongside me. She was just about to sink her fangs in when I yelled at her. "Don't you dare!" This is for her." I growled.

"Do we get to have any of the chicken?" Ben-Ben asked, looking down at the lizard.

"This is a victorious kill," Patches said. "I will not see it wasted," she said biting into its midsection, blood and intestines streamed out. Jessie retched, turned away, and quickly walked out of sight.

My tongue was dry from the effort and somehow the green slimy thing did smell like chicken and it seemed like a waste not to eat. "Dig in, Ben-Ben," I said as I ripped a leg off. The meat was meager but it was somehow more gratifying that I had helped to kill our food. It felt good and deep down it seemed like the way it was supposed to be.

Five minutes later, what was left wouldn't have sated the infant. Patches was busy cleaning her paws and her mouth, Ben-Ben was still looking at the carcass probably hoping it would fill back in.

"I really like chicken," he said. "When are we going to get another one?"

Jessie slept as the burning disc got higher and then finally started to come back down. Patches and Ben-Ben got under the two-wheeler and were resting; I thought maybe a little too closely but the hunt may have done us some good and brought us all a little closer. I walked slowly up and down next to the pathway, trying my best to stay off it. The heat burned through the pads on my feet. On occasion I would rest under a bush getting away from the worst of the bright beams and when I felt better I would do my patrol again.

It was perhaps after my tenth, maybe seventh time I had done this when I caught whiff of something that did not smell quite right. It was still far away and I could not catch sight, but whatever it was, it was raising the hairs on my back. I barked once in warning.

"I'm sleeping over here," Patches said, opening one eye to respond, her head resting comfortably on her leg.

"Something is coming," I told her.

"More chicken?" Ben-Ben asked excitedly, bonking his head on the bottom of the wheeler as he got up too fast.

"Not chicken," Patches said, coming out from under the car, careful to keep off the part of the pathway that was still bright.

"You can smell that?" I asked her.

"My nose might not be as good as yours, but I think even the humans should be able to smell what is coming soon,"

Patches said.

I quickly crossed the path, it was not quite as hot as it had been, but I didn't want to stay on it any longer than I had to. Jessie was lying on her seat asleep, one of her legs was hanging out the door and she was wet with salty water all over her body and I began to lick it.

"Riley, leave me alone," she said with her eyes still closed. "I'm so hot and tired." She brought her hand up to wipe the liquid off her forehead. I greedily looked at the pooled fluid in her hand as she wiped it on her fake skins.

I almost forgot why I had come up to her when I caught an even stronger scent of the zombie coming our way. I barked.

"Riley! Shut up, the baby is sleeping!" Jessie yelled louder than I barked.

I was saddened to think I had upset Jessie, but right now it didn't matter, she wasn't getting the point and I needed to get more aggressive with her. I started outright barking. "Warning!" I was yelling to her. She sat up slowly, her eyes barely open. She looked a lighter color than usual, like maybe she was getting sick. She didn't smell sick but that could happen later.

"Riley, what girl? What's the matter? I don't feel so good." She clutched her belly.

Patches came up beside me. "The girl needs water."

"How do you know? She's covered in water," I told Patches.

"She's overheating. I can feel it from here."

"Why doesn't she just lick the water off her body?" I asked.

"First because it's salt water and second the dead ones are coming," Patches said. There was a slight hint of anxiety in her response, but she wasn't fully alarmed yet. "You need to get her moving or we need to leave."

"You would leave her?" I asked.

"To save myself, I would," Patches answered, not

disgusted with herself in the least.

"Something's coming, Riley, and it doesn't smell like chicken," Ben-Ben said and sneezed, trying to get the smell out of his nose.

I barked more warnings at Jessie; I could not understand how she couldn't smell it yet. "How many are there, Cat?" I asked.

"More than you can count," she answered back.

I couldn't tell if she was being condescending or helpful—this was getting old really fast.

Zach cracked an eye open.

"Great, Riley, you woke the little twerp up. I've been trying to get him to sleep all day." Jessie said looking back.

I moved back from the opening as Jessie swung her legs out of the wheeler. She stood, shielding her eyes from the flaming disc. "What is that smell?"

"About time," I responded.

"Ohmigod, zombies!" Jessie screamed. Patches hopped up into the car. I might not like the cat but if I wanted to live, following her might be the best thing I could do.

"Riley, we fighting or running?" Ben-Ben asked, looking from where the cat was perched in the backseat to the bunches of zombies as far as the farthest stick throw Alpha had ever made.

I barked again to get Jessie moving, she seemed to have been frozen and was now sending out panic chemicals.

"What do I do? What do I do?" Jessie screamed, hopping back and forth from foot to foot, her hands out in front of her swinging wildly from side to side.

"Riley, get the girl moving," Patches said forcibly.

"What do you want me to do?" I asked. Now I was panicking.

Ben-Ben solved the problem for me as he nipped Jess on the calf. I felt bad when her kick made him yelp and sent him sprawling some distance away. "What the fuck, Ben-Ben!" she yelled.

Whatever trance she had been in was broken by the pain of the bite Ben-Ben had inflicted. "Come on, Riley, let's go!" she yelled to me, patting her seat like I needed any incentive to get up there. I hopped up quickly and got into alpha female's usual seat.

Ben-Ben was still away from the car, his body low to the ground and tail tucked under in an apologetic gesture.

"Come on, Ben-Ben, let's go," Jess said with more than a hint of anger in her voice. "You shouldn't have bit me, but I'm not leaving you here."

Jessie didn't realize Ben-Ben's bite had probably saved us all.

"Come on!" I yelled to him, "we need to go!"

"She's mad at me, Riley!" he whined.

"Someone's always mad at you, get in this car!" I yelled back.

Ben-Ben hopped in and was smiling wide, his tongue lolling to the side as he crossed Jessie's seat and sat next to me.

"Nice view," he said to me as Jessie got in the car and closed her door. Within a few breaths we were again moving, the dead ones were following but they were far behind now.

I looked over to Ben-Ben. "I don't think so," I told him.

His expression dropped as he clambered into the backseat.

"Get off of me, you oaf!" Patches complained.

"Sorry," Ben-Ben said.

In a little bit Ben-Ben finally got situated. I turned to look at him. "Good work, Ben-Ben," I told him before I turned to look back out the front; I could see the pride in his eyes as he sat up just a little bit taller.

"Did you hear that?" Ben-Ben asked Patches. "Riley said I did a good job!"

"I'm sitting right next to you—how could I have missed it?" Patches said disdainfully.

I don't think he even heard her reply his tail was

wagging so fast it was thumping against the back of the seat.

Jessie turned to see what the noise was. When she saw Ben-Ben's tail wagging she spoke. "I don't know what you're so happy about? You're a bad dog, you bit me!"

I barked loudly at the side of Jessie's face, I could not understand how she could see Ben-Ben's actions as anything less than the heroic deed they were. Jessie turned quickly to stare at me. "What, Riley?" she asked me with a confused look on her face, one of her eyebrows arched in a questioning manner. I just kept staring at her.

"He bit me, Riley."

I barked, "Yup."

"The zombies were coming and he bit me," she added.

I barked, "Yup," again.

"And then we got in the car to get away from them." The questioning look on her face began to diminish and then disappeared altogether. Water leaked from her eyes as a cry escaped from her mouth, the car came to a slow stop. She turned around and grabbed Ben-Ben, hugging him fiercely. "You saved us!" she said, her mouth buried in his fur.

His tail, which I didn't think could go any faster, was now slamming against the seat, Patches was having a difficult time getting away from it.

"I'm so sorry—can you ever forgive me?" she asked as she pulled away to look into his eyes.

Ben-Ben licked from her chin, up to the top of her nose.

"Oh, gross, Ben-Ben," she said pulling back. "Who knows where your tongue has been!" She was smiling. "Thank you," she said, hugging him tight once more before turning to get the wheeler back in motion.

"I did good, Cat!" Ben-Ben said proudly.

"You did good, Ben-Ben," Patches said begrudgingly.

"I did, didn't I?" He yipped excitedly.

The high-pitched noise was enough to fully awaken Zach; his full-throated cry dominated the inside of the wheeler.

"Oh, Ben-Ben," Jessie said, having to again pull the car over.

CHAPTER FOUR

The events of the day had me more tired than I could ever remember. I tried to stay awake for Jessie, but I was so tired, the heat from the great sand pit had me exhausted. I fell asleep almost immediately. For a while in my sleep images, I was very happy. I was again asleep on Alpha Female's large couch. I had never been more comfortable! Baby Zachary was bringing me some of his cereal, which never happened. He didn't move around too much on his own but I would always stay near to his feeding grounds because the dry round O's he used to eat would always end up in my domain—the floor.

But in my sleep images he was walking and tossing the O's all around and most were luckily ending up in my mouth! Then it got bad—zombies had broken through the backdoor *on my watch!* One of them had Ben-Ben in its mouth and he was screaming to me for help. I was going into the kitchen when I saw more of them coming in through the backdoor, the zombie holding Ben-Ben ripped the small dog in half with its teeth but still Ben-Ben cried to me for help— 'Rileeeeey!'. I started to run away as life fluid poured from my small pack mate, no matter how hard or fast I tried to move I couldn't get away from the flowing blood or the zombies. I started to get stuck in the murky liquid. I was crying out for one of the alphas, anybody to help me, one of the zombies grabbed my side; I waited for the searing pain of teeth ripping through my flesh.

"It's okay, girl. It's okay—good girl," Jess was saying to me as I awoke with a jolt. "You just had a bad dream, girl, it's alright," Jess said soothingly as she rubbed my side. "You were yelping in your sleep and your paws were going a mile a minute." She laughed a little bit, but it was a nervous laugh. I did not believe she felt any merriment, I could not smell anything to indicate she was happy. Nervousness smells a bit like rusty iron and she was flooded in the flakes of it.

"I need to stop, Riley, I'm so tired. Do you have any ideas?" she asked me.

I didn't know how long I had slept; the burning disc was gone, replaced by the cool pale version, the moon is what my ancestors called it. The heat of the day was gone and I was now getting cold, hunger was still gnawing through my stomach like an un-chewed squirrel. I looked out the window, the sand was being replaced by more and more brush but it still looked very empty of everything two-legger built.

"She needs to find a house, Riley," Patches said, standing on the center console, looking out at the same scene I was.

I looked in the back of the wheeler. I didn't know if it was the light from the wolf howler (moon) or baby Zachary was sick but he looked pale and his breathing didn't seem right. In contrast, Ben-Ben who was asleep was still wearing that happy grin he had when Jessie had praised him. I felt good for him that he was happy, that dog had not done much right since he'd been reared and more praise and less scorn was always a good thing.

"Our house?" I asked Patches.

"Another's," she answered.

"Are you sure, Patches? Two-leggers are not always very accepting of each other. They reek of distrust when they come across others they do not know."

"The girl needs help. Food and sleep for herself and the baby is sick."

"Do you see anything?" I asked Patches, somewhat

ashamed I again had to defer to her better abilities. I would swear the cat could see with absolutely no light. There had been times at home when I knew she was padding around me as she thought I slept on the couch. I could smell her clearly, I could not see her, though, and that always angered me. She would come down when the skies were covered or the pale disc was not present. I would growl, she would laugh. I miss those times.

"Hi, Patches," Jessie said wearily as she stroked the cat's back. Patches purred in content and rubbed her head up against Jessie's shoulder.

"There is something coming on your side," Patches said. How she saw it I didn't know, her eyes were closed and her head was facing in the wrong direction.

The wheeler kept moving for a while longer before I began to make something out. It was a two-legger home but not nearly as big or nice as the one we had left. Large old rusted wheelers were in the front along with all manner of two-legger stuff, most of which I'm sure Alpha female would have called trash.

I barked as we got closer, pulling Jessie's attention away from the cat.

"A house," she said wearily, with a small measure of hope. At least that was what I got from the scent of her but then it flooded with mistrust, fear, and apprehension. "Sure is a pigsty. Trash all over the place, but it looks lived in. Should we try it?" she asked.

It was tough to not be swayed by her feelings, what seemed like a good idea a moment before now seemed dangerous.

"Cat?" I asked.

"Plenty of places to hide," Patches told me as she looked at the garbage strewn across the yard.

"This isn't all about you, Cat."

She looked at me as if to say, 'When did that happen?'.

"I'm starving, Riley."

I looked sternly at her.

"And the baby needs help," she added hastily when she realized I didn't like her first response, or her second for that matter. The baby did need help and I had to admit I was hungry too.

Jessie was pulling the car off the hard pathway and onto a smaller dirt path. She sat for long seconds just staring at the house. She took a deep breath, shut the car off and got out. I watched as she looked into the rear of the car at Zach. She seemed to be hesitating on whether to leave him there or take him with her. She thought it through and decided to let sleeping babies lay, I jumped out before she had a chance to shut the door.

"Riley, stay in the car. I just want to see if there is anyone here and if we need to leave in a hurry I don't want to have to wait for you."

I moved farther away from the door. She got the point.

"Fine, but you stay close," she told me as she quietly shut the door to the wheeler. "I don't like this place, Riley."

I didn't either; it smelled like rot and human excrement. I saw something walk by the windows, just a darker shadow against the dark inside. Jessie did not see it, my hackles were raised and I pulled my lip up in a threatening manner.

"You see something, Riley?" Jessie asked. "Was it a zombie?"

"Worse," came a voice from the now open door in the front of the house.

Jess turned to run.

"Don't even think about it," The male voice said menacingly. "I'll shoot you where you stand. Wouldn't be the first, won't be the last—that's the benefit of being the first house after the desert or the last one before going in." He laughed.

"Mister, we're just looking for some help," Jessie

said, turning back around, her hands raised.

"That's the problem, everybody's always looking for some help. Did you see a sign that said 'Help here'?"

"Sir, my brother is sick."

"Get him the fuck outta here then. I don't want no zombies on my property!"

"It's not like that, not that kind of sick," she entreated.

"Do you see the word hospital anywhere?" he yelled.

"Please," she begged. "Just a little food and water, maybe some medicine."

"What do you have for me?" he said. "Or am I just 'apposed to give that to you out of the kindness of my heart?"

"I... I don't have anything," Jessie said hesitantly.

"Oh, I think you do. Turn around for me."

"Please."

"*Do it!*" he yelled. "Umm, nice," he said as Jessie did a small circle. "I'd trade for some of that."

"We'll just get going," Jessie said, nearly crying now.

"You're on my property now, you'll leave when I say you can. Come closer."

"Please," Jessie said as she slowly inched forward.

I moved with her.

"Tell the fucking mutt to stay put or I'll shoot him out of principle."

"Ri... Riley, stay," Jessie said.

I didn't know what was going on, the man said he would trade some food, but he said it with an edge to his voice and I could smell excitement and dominance on him. It was not a healthy combination. Jessie moved a foot closer, and so did I. I was going to make sure she was alright. I heard part of the fire stick move that normally came before the metal bees. Jessie stopped and so did I.

"I'm going to blow that damned dog's head clean off if he takes another step," the man said.

"He?" I snorted. "You threaten me and my pack mate

and call me a '*he*'?" I was barking as I charged, the metal bee whined past my ear, by the time the man was able to make the loud clicking noise again I had already latched onto his leg. His screams of pain increased as I bit down harder. I had a firm grip on the front of his leg; I could feel as my teeth punctured through his fake skins and into him.

I kept biting, the man's screams increasing in volume and pitch. I could feel the bone in his leg starting to yield.

"*No!*" Jessie screamed. The man had somehow held onto his fire stick and was bringing it to bear on me.

I could hear Jessie running toward me to help, I bit as hard as my jaw would allow and shook my head from side to side. The fire stick fell to my side as the man toppled over. He was bellowing for the bitch that had whelped him. I finally let him go when he stopped moving.

"Riley, are you alright?" Jessie asked as she came to a skidding stop next to me. "You broke his leg," she said with what I smelled was a fair amount of appreciation.

"What now? What now?" she asked nervously. "We should just go. There's probably more of them."

I sniffed long and hard inside the house, there had been others but not for a while. I walked in, we needed food.

"Riley, what are you doing?" Jessie asked from the front step of the door. The man was moaning loudly.

I turned my head, hoping she would follow; she bent down and picked up the fire stick. She pointed it at the man on the ground then cautiously came in after me. Jessie opened the fridge and then quickly slammed it shut when the stench of things long rotten came out. I could have spent a little while longer exploring the scents but I understood about Jessie, two-leggers where very peculiar in what they liked to smell.

There is nothing quite like understanding your pack mates by sniffing at their offal, but the two-leggers were always lighting the small flowery smelling fires or spraying cans of scents that were supposed to make the 'bad' smells go away but are far worse than anything me or even Ben-Ben had ever produced. Maybe not the cat though, that thing stunk.

Jessie was on the far side of the kitchen going through the wooden food holders. "Food," she said excitedly. She moved away from the shelves with food and started to pull different things out until she found what she was looking for.

"I hope this is strong enough," she said as opened the bag up and started to shove all sorts of two-legger canned food into it. My mouth started to water just thinking about what might be in those cans, not all cans mind you, some of them have horrible smelling things that make my nose burn, like what the humans call onions or peppers. I don't know why anyone would want to eat those things. I shook a little just thinking about the time the Daniel cub had given me a handful. He had laughed for a long time while I tried to rinse the taste out of my mouth, but I was a fast-learning puppy. He never did find the toy he had received the day before, I chewed it up and Alpha female had discovered it, she threw it into a bag much like Jessie was using now.

"Bad girl, Riley!" Alpha had said to me. "Maybe Danny will learn to pick his things up now. I've told him puppies chew things." She had gently reached out and stroked my muzzle. She had said mad words but her tone and actions said otherwise. I would miss my den mother mightily.

My head whipped around when I heard the man begin to groan, Jessie also looked. Her eyes got wide as the fear in her bloomed.

"We should leave, Riley," Jessie said, almost letting go of the bag with the food.

"My leg!" the man screamed. "I... I think it's broken," he wailed. "You fucking did this to me!" He pointed at Jess. She turned to see if there was another way out of the house, besides an 'outside looker' there wasn't.

Jess ran over and fumbled with something on the window and tried to push it open. "It's painted shut, Riley.

Shit. Shit."

"I'm gonna fucking kill you!" the man said, propping up on his hands and dragging himself toward the food room.

Jessie looked close to panicking; I started barking loudly, that got the man's attention. His eyes now took on that wide fear stare. "Don't... don't you come any closer," Jessie said, her voice wavering, but I wasn't sure if the man even heard her, his eyes were locked on mine. I threw in a deep growl just for good measure.

"Keep that mutt away from me," the man said, now backing away.

I advanced on him.

"Just watch him, Riley. Rip his throat out if he moves," Jess said as she started to shove more things into the bag.

"That's my stuff, you can't just take it," the man said. "You come into my house, your mutt breaks my leg and now you're stealing my food?"

"And pointing your gun at me and forcing me into your house, that's acceptable?" Jess asked.

"Hey, nothing's for free and I... I was just kidding. I would have let you go."

"Before or after you had done to me as you wished?"

"It... it was just a joke," he lied again. The words he spoke did not match what he meant, even I could tell that. "You've got to at least help me splint my leg. You're as good as murdering me if you don't."

Jessie was hesitating and I thought maybe even considering his request. There was no way I was going to let her get within arm's reach of the man, he was not a good two-legger.

"I can't," Jessie said as she swung the bag over her shoulder. She headed down the long room toward him then abruptly stopped and headed back to the food room. I heard the hard metal of the things the humans used to eat with clattering about on the floor and then Jessie said, 'aha' and came back down the long room. She skirted around the man's legs and pushed the door open. "Almost forgot a can opener. Come on, Riley, we need to get out of here," she said.

"When I get better I'm going to hunt you down and cut your throat, but not before I make that fucking mutt of yours watch me do all sorts of things to you that would make a demon blush." He laughed.

Jessie quickly shut the door, but we were back in the car with the doors closed before we stopped hearing his laughter.

"Wet meat!" Ben-Ben said triumphantly as he stuck his nose inside the bag Jess had placed in the back.

"Are you both okay?" Patches asked me as Jessie got the car started and headed back out onto the hard pathway.

"Do you really care?" I snapped back.

"In so much as I either needed Jessie to open the car door so I could get out or her ability to get food so I eat, so yes I cared."

"There was a bad two-legger in there. He wanted to hurt Jessie."

"You stupid dog, you say that as if he's the only one. It's been my experience that two-leggers are more like that man than those that were in our house."

"Maybe to you because you're a cat. But most two-leggers just want to scratch behind my ears or sometimes give me a treat. The large dog area…"

"The park," the smart-ass cat filled in.

"The large *dog* area," I emphasized. "There were always lots of humans and they were always so nice."

"Not the ones I've seen, Dog. Have you ever come across another two-legger without the alpha male or female?"

I thought about it for a long time and except for the cubs, I had never interacted with other two-leggers before. Sure I had barked at bunches, way over twenty-two but never sat there and played with any of them. "No," I said sheepishly as if that made me a bad dog.

"The humans pretend a lot of things when they are around other humans."

"Pretend?" I asked her.

"Lying," she explained.

"The two-leggers are lying when they said they liked me?" I asked, astonished. Why had I never picked up on this before?

"Oh, I'm sure one or two of the idiots liked you, I don't know why but there are some dog lovers, but most of them would throw a rock at you before they'd ever pet behind your ears."

"You speak the truth, Cat?" I asked, turning around to see if I could sense that all she spoke was real, but her eyes were difficult to see in the dark and it was nearly impossible to tell what the oversized rodent was thinking anyway.

"They are unlike any other animal, they are even worse than dogs. They will say one thing while they are doing something else.

"We must stay away from two-leggers!" I nearly shouted.

"It won't be easy, Jessie will seek them out. They find comfort among their own kind."

That I could understand.

"What about Justin? The boy she would press faces with? She seeks him out."

"Better than most, I suppose," she answered, thinking carefully. "We are going to have to protect her."

"We?" I asked. "Since when did you begin to care?"

"My ability to survive is greatly improved with all of you around. It may not be entirely to my liking, but it is what I have right now."

"You always know the right thing to say," I told her.

"My hands are shaking," Jessie said aloud. "That was so close, he was going to kill me. And you saved me, Riley," Jessie said as she stopped the car and petted my head gently.

"Thank you." She placed her hands on either side of my face and looked into my eyes. "You guys keep saving my life and I haven't even fed you yet."

***

"Humans are good, Cat," Ben-Ben said as he licked clean the can of what Jessie called stew. "You don't know anything." He finished, looking up, his snout covered in stew goo.

"This one is, I agree," she answered, shielding her stew can from Ben-Ben's eager nose. "Get out!" she said loudly, "You already ate!"

"Why are you taking so long? Do you need some help with it?" Ben-Ben asked as he began to push her out of the way.

"You move any closer to my food and I'm sticking my claws in you!"

Ben-Ben immediately backed up, his rear end pressed up against the car outside viewer. "Is this far enough away?" he asked with genuine terror.

"Outside would be preferable but that's far enough away for now," Patches said with a small note of humor.

She began to tease him as she would take a small bite of her food, slowly chew it and then meticulously clean off her whiskers. Ben-Ben was leaving a small pool of drool as he kept staring at her food can. I had also finished mine and the hurting part of the hunger was mostly gone, but I could have eaten another can. I wasn't going to let the cat know that, though.

Jessie had the baby outside and was walking around the car with him in her arms; she was talking animatedly as she got him to eat some food. He smelled and looked better. I still didn't feel good about him.

As if Patches knew what I was thinking, she spoke. "The baby is not well."

"I am not in the mood to listen to you anymore, Cat." I was angry because I thought she might be smarter, that she really didn't need any of us and that she was pointing out something I feared. It wasn't truly her fault, but all the same I was tired of it. Of her.

"Nevertheless, the baby, I fear, is going to die."

I jumped in the backseat, her can of food spilled onto the floor, I revealed my teeth, I was within a whiskers' length from her head. The cat was afraid and I was happy for it. "Do not trifle with me, Cat, there is nowhere for you to hide now."

I'll give the cat credit she stood her ground, the hair on her back was raised and I knew she had her claws ready for action, I could kill her, but she would draw blood.

"I see things, Riley, things humans and dogs do not," she said, trying her best to move slightly to get her dangerous claws up if she needed to.

"I can smell things you can't even dream exist," I spat out.

"Riley, I'm sure you can. This has nothing to do with your nose. The infant carries a cloud around itself like a fake skin."

"The white softness in the sky that hides the burning disc sometimes?" I asked.

"No, this is black. And not like rain clouds."

"Why can I not see this?"

"George believed me."

"He did?" I asked, my lips slipping back into their normal place.

"Do you remember when Alpha Male's sire came to stay with us?"

"I was still a puppy, but he was always so nice to me, he used to play with me for hours."

"He came to be with his pack before he died, I told George as much. It is something the humans called a custom; they care for each other before they pass over."

"Pass over to where?"

"We'll talk about that later. But I told George and he

didn't try to rip my face off because of it. He loved the Alpha's sire and made sure to spend as much time as he could with the old two-legger before he went for good."

"I kind of remember that, I just figured it was because the human was giving him extra snacks."

"I knew when George was getting close too."

"You did? Did you tell him?"

"No, but he realized what was going on when I started spending more time with him."

"I wish George was here."

"Can I eat the wet meat?" Ben-Ben asked, staring intently at the spilled food.

"No!" Patches and I said at the same time.

Ben-Ben whined and sat back down, his eyes skipping back and forth between me and Patches and the food.

"Does the cloud always mean a passing?" I asked the cat. Her lack of response told me what I needed to know. Ben-Ben, at some point while I was thinking about this, had got onto the floor of the car and was slowly crawling toward the stew.

This time I left him alone as I turned and hopped back into the front so I could think about what the cat had told me. Jessie was straight ahead, frowning at the baby who was refusing anymore food.

CHAPTER FIVE

The next morning I awoke not because the burning disc was shining in my eyes but rather the heat inside the wheeler. I was panting heavily and my mouth felt like I had the cat shoved in there. Jessie was still sleeping but she was again bathed in salty water. Ben-Ben's tongue was hanging out and he was looking directly at me.

"I'm sorry, Riley, I really had to go," Ben-Ben said apologetically.

"What is wrong with dogs?" Patches said, moving even closer to her door if that was even possible.

"Ben-Ben, really? You did *that* in the car?" I would have berated him further but the baby cub looked even more unwell, his skin color looked bad, his breathing was shallow and instead of leaking water like Jessie he was shivering with cold. I was about to bark and warn Jessie, but Ben-Ben's stink had at least the benefit of that.

"What is that? Zombies?" Jessie said, looking around wildly.

Ben-Ben had turned so his face was in the rear of the seat and his backside was pointed toward Jessie as she turned to see what was causing the smell. She immediately opened the door when she discovered the origin of the stench.

I hopped out after her, the smell of the Ben-Ben processed stew was bad but not as bad as the heat. Patches was immediately behind me and headed off for the brush, at least she knew where to go. Why did Ben-Ben have to give dogs such a bad name?

Jessie ran to the other side of the car and got the baby

out. "Zach?" she asked. "Baby, are you okay?" she asked, looking at him. The baby was not responding to her.

"*Get in!*" Patches screamed, bolting for the door. She deftly jumped in and into the back making room.

I wanted to find out what was going on, sometimes cats can be drama-infused mischievous vermin, but she didn't look like she was acting. I barked wildly, but Jessie was busy examining the baby cub.

"Rileeeeey, they're here!" Ben-Ben was yipping wildly from the backseat. He charged at them across his seat, smacked his head hard into the outside viewer, and he fell over onto Patches. I would have enjoyed the whole scene if not for the three zombies making their way through the brush.

Jessie was still ignorant to my pleas. She might not know the zombies were there, but they knew she was. I ran to get between her and them. My aggressive display did nothing to stop their advance, I didn't think it would after our last encounter, but it was difficult to not try what has worked for so many of my ancestors.

The smell was zombie, but there was something else too, there was a familial relation. The zombies that were coming were a pack. It appeared to be a sire and two male offspring. All were larger than my alpha had been.

My flight instinct was in high gear, but Jessie was slow to the realization of what was happening. I sprang onto the closest of the three. Jessie's screams of alarm nearly drowned out the snapping of my teeth as I bit deeply into the flesh of the zombie's putrid arm. He paid me almost no attention even as I tried to drag him down to the ground. My teeth were sunk deep and I had my hindquarters braced on the ground trying to halt his forward progress.

The skin and meat on his arm were sliding down as they came loose from his bones, I was left with what Ben-Ben would've called wet-meat hanging from my mouth. White bone shone in the light as I stripped his arm clean. Not once did he scream in pain or rage. I spat the bad meat out and grabbed onto the back of the man's leg, his calf muscle, this time it did have the desired effect as he fell face forward into the hard pathway.

I yelped as one of the other zombies stepped on my front paw and his leg caught the side of my face. I staggered back, my thoughts clouded and unsure of what was going on. The fire stick changed that; it knocked the fuzziness I was feeling right out of me. The zombie cub that had run into me was now falling back over; I quickly dodged out of the way as his body went crashing to the ground. Half of his face looked like a bloodier version of what we had eaten last night, but I don't think even Ben-Ben would touch this.

"I don't know how to reload this damned thing!" Jessie screamed as she was using the fire stick to physically keep the last standing zombie at bay. But she was losing ground and the sire was now getting up. I remembered Daniel's words. "The head, Dad, you have to shoot them in the head!"

I hadn't figured out how to make the metal bee shooter work yet, but I knew how to bite. I wrapped my jaws around the back of the sire's skull. My jaw popped as I applied more pressure, the zombie was still trying to stand, my front paws were off the ground before my teeth began to crack through the creatures head. I could feel his skull beginning to move under the pressure I was applying. I didn't know how long I could support my weight and try to kill it as we arose.

Black fluid leaked from around my mouth, I was salivating like Ben-Ben had been last night but this was in an attempt to wash away the taste of the horrible creature. I was completely off the ground, the zombie within arm's length of my Jessie, I bit down harder. I thought the creature's head bones broke, but it just as easily could have been my jaw. We fell to the ground, the thing dead like it should have been all along and me buried underneath it. I was exhausted, I couldn't move, my jaw hurt so bad I whimpered. I heard the fire stick roar one more time before my eyes started to close, the cat would later tell me it was from lack of oxygen, whatever that was.

***

This time when I awoke I was on a soft floor, Ben-Ben was not more than an inch or two from my face.

"You okay, Riley, huh?" he asked at least seven times.

"Ben-Ben, let her be," Jessie said as she walked across the room to come sit by me. She wrapped an arm around each of us and held tight. It was dog heaven.

I went to lick her arm but it hurt to move my jaw, I just lay there contentedly as she rubbed my back.

"Where are we, Ben-Ben? And where's the baby cub?"

"They have meat snacks here Riley, can we stay?" Ben-Ben asked excitedly.

"Where is *here*, Ben-Ben?"

"It's the place with the meat snacks," he answered sincerely and with some confusion why I hadn't figured that out. "Are you okay? The snack givers said you might have hurt your head."

"I'm fine if you were wondering," Patches said from the windowsill above me.

I craned my neck to see her; I was not at all pleased to have her peering down at me.

I was somewhat glad the cat was alright but I didn't see the need to tell her that. "Besides being able to get meat snacks, can you tell me where we are, Cat?"

"Do you want the whole story?" she asked.

"Sure, it doesn't look like we're in any rush at the moment, but first, how is the cub?"

"He yet lives, but it is tenuous," she said.

I didn't know what 'tenuous' meant but it didn't sound good.

"After you crushed the head of the zombie, Jessie was losing her battle with the other one. I jumped out of the car and onto his leg; I ran up his leg and clawed out his eyes. After he was blinded, Jessie was able to figure out how to make the rifle shoot and the zombie died."

I had some doubts about the cat jumping out to save Jessie, but maybe if she thought Jessie was going to die and she wouldn't have a ride or anybody to open the cans of food she might. Maybe; it still seemed a stretch.

"The girl started crying and was getting back into the car when I ran over to the zombie that had landed on you, I bit down on his shoulder and started to pull him off of you."

"Really? You did that for me?"

"Sure, we're pack mates, you and me."

It had been a stretch of truth *before* she started talking about pulling a large two-legger off of me.

"Well, I wasn't able to get him off you by myself, but Jessie did realize she had forgotten about you and then helped. Together we were able to roll him off of you. Then I helped her drag you over to the car and inside. She put you in the back and let me sit up front because now I was her favorite for having helped out and saving her."

"Oh, Patches," I said.

"It's okay Riley, she still loves you, it's just that now I am at the top because of my heroics. It was me who found this home too," she added triumphantly.

I didn't think the cat was lying, I really think this was how she viewed the world, what a funny little cat mind she had. Daniel had said that zombies like to eat brains; I don't think the cat was in any danger.

"Thank you, Patches," I said more for the entertainment value of her story than for actually helping me, but she purred her satisfaction.

"What am I going to do, Riley?" Jessie asked as she buried her face in my fur. "You saved me again, girl. When am I going to start being able to take care of myself? The lady here said Zach was a day away from dying, said he had a fever of a hundred and two. They are still not sure he'll be alright."

I did the only thing I could, I nuzzled my head in her lap, two-leggers felt better when they were scratching dogs behind their ears, Alpha Female had said as much when she read an article about dogs staying with older two-leggers.

Ben-Ben was also resting his head on Jessie's other leg, his eyes were rolling up and he was snoring softly, I was moments away from doing the same when a new two-legger came into the room.

"He's much better," the female two-legger told Jessie.

Jessie started to leak from her eyes again. "Thank you, Faye," Jessie said as she gently moved mine and Ben-Ben's heads so she could stand up, she encircled her arms around the woman, I equated it with sniffing another dog's genitalia, it was their form of greeting.

"He was dangerously dehydrated and he has a high temperature from a virus," Faye said. "And no, not *that* virus."

I did not feel anything threatening from the woman, but Patches' words had traveled deep. I whimpered as I stood up so I could be next to Jessie.

"What a good girl you are," Faye said. "I heard what you've done."

She was scratching behind my ears and out of a pouch in her fake skins she produced a snack bone. *Could this day get any better?* I thought as I crunched on the treat, my jaw still twinged but it was worth it.

Ben-Ben, upon hearing me chew, was immediately up and at my muzzle. "Whatcha got there, Riley? Smells like bacon. Is there any more? I would really like a bacon treat!"

"Oh, I heard about you too, boy!" Faye said, reaching down and scratching his back. She produced another treat from her magic pouch.

"Oh, boy!" Ben-Ben said dancing from paw to paw.

"Chicken, Riley!" he mumbled around chews.

I went over to sniff her pouch. There were still treats in it. I would treat this old two-legger nicely until she proved otherwise.

"I guess I have a new friend," she said to Jessie and laughed.

I was still enjoying the different scents of the treats when another two-legger came out of the room behind Faye. I immediately backed up, my hackles rose and I found myself growling even before I had a reason.

"It's okay, girl," Jessie said, coming up to wrap her arms around my neck. I was straining against her embrace, partly to attack and partly to runaway.

The two-legger that came through the door was enormous, he had to stoop so he did not hit his head on the opening. He had hair on his face that was longer than Ben-Ben's tail. He laughed when he saw my reaction his full belly shaking up and down.

"Santa?" Ben-Ben asked, running up to the giant. The huge man gently picked up Ben-Ben in his huge hands; the small dog could have gone for a walk in the man's grasp. "It is Santa!" Ben-Ben said, eagerly licking the man's face.

The man's laugh was so deep it made the floor tremble slightly.

"Well, you're a friendly one," the man said.

Ben-Ben may have made up his mind, but I sure hadn't. I turned to see where Patches was; my back-up was nowhere to be seen. *Typical*, I thought.

"Ben-Ben, who is Santa?" I asked.

"Only the kindest two-legger ever. He brings treats to dogs every year! I saw him more than once on the two-legger picture box."

"That is certainly not Santa," Patches said from on top of the couch over to my left.

"How come everyone knows who Santa is except me?" I asked.

Riley: The Complete Book Of

"How could you not?" Patches asked snidely. "The pack cubs go on and on about him about this time every year. But I know, if it doesn't revolve around food you really don't pay attention."

"Be careful cat," I said.

"Anyway, that's not Santa, I heard the old woman call him Winke. And he has a cloud around him too."

"Well, aren't you full of good news," I said.

"His isn't as dark and pressing as Zach's was. He probably still has a few moons left."

"Is he safe?" I asked, still unsure about the giant two-legger.

"That I cannot tell, but he is a human and they can only be trusted so far. I will eat the food he gives me and I will accept the petting, but I will always have a way to escape."

"I haven't made up my mind about you yet, Cat, but you are smart."

"Not that I care too much one way or the other, but your words are agreeable to me."

I cautiously walked over to the man; I was low to the ground, hoping he wouldn't notice me as I got closer to smell around his fake skins.

"You coming around?" the big man said as he leaned down. "Faye, give me one of your treats."

My tail started to wag on its own just at the mere mention of a treat.

"We lost our dog the day the zombies came," Faye said sadly as she handed a treat to her mate. I could tell by their comingled scents now that I was closer. If the kind woman thought enough of the man to mate with him then he had to be alright.

"I'm so sorry," Jessie said.

"Oh, no, I'm sorry, hon," Faye replied. "Here I am going on about my dog after all you lost."

"It's okay, Faye," Winke told his wife, kissing the top

of her head. "We haven't heard from our kids since. We have one in Connecticut and another up in San Francisco. It's the not knowing that's difficult." Faye was crying. "On a good note, your brother, I believe, is going to be fine. I had to put an intravenous in him to get him some much needed fluids and I gave him some antibiotics. He had a nasty case of strep, couple more days and he'll be right as rain."

"I cannot thank you enough," Jessie fairly sobbed. "When would it be safe for me to travel?"

Winke and Faye gave each other a silent look; I had seen Alpha male and female do this many times when they sent each other a message without talking.

"Jessie, I've been talking to Winke; why don't you just stay here?" Faye asked. "We have the room and plenty of food for all of you."

"Wet meat?"Ben-Ben asked, looking from face to face for a response.

Winke spoke up, "It's not safe out there, we know there's someone in Colorado you're trying to get to, but there's not much out there anymore."

"I can't tell you how grateful I am for all you've done, but he's the closest thing I have to family left," Jessie said.

"You have to be realistic—have you heard from him?" Winke asked. "You've only been here a short while, but we've grown fond of you and your brother and your traveling companions," Winke said as he rubbed my head vigorously.

Patches was watching intently but she wasn't weighing in one way or the other.

Jessie's head drooped a bit and then she picked it back up to speak. "See, you don't understand; his dad is kind of nuts, he's one of those survivalists. He would always be talking about how zombies were coming and we should be prepared. Come to think of it, I guess he was right."

"Our neighbors were world class survivalists, even

wrote articles for Hunter of Fortune type magazines," Winke said.

"Were?" Jessie asked.

"We had to shoot them when they tried to come in the kitchen window, they were both zombies," Winke explained.

"But Mr. Talbot was a Marine," Jess countered.

"My neighbor was Special Forces, his wife was a ground pounder in the Army, they were both in their thirties, peak physical condition, had enough food to last them twenty years and that doesn't even begin to bring into account the arsenal of weapons I found in their underground bunker."

"Mr. Talbot talked about getting an underground bunker but he lived in a townhouse. What am I going to do?"

"That's easy, stay here dear," Faye said putting her arm around Jessie.

"Can I think on it?"

"Sure, there's no time limit." Winke laughed. "At the very least you should stay a few days until we're sure the antibiotics we're giving Zach take hold."

"Maybe you could even stay through Christmas?" Faye asked hopefully.

"Christmas?" Jessie asked. "I guess it is December, I hadn't even really thought about it."

"I told you he was Santa!" Ben-Ben said excitedly, again lapping the man's face.

"He likes the idea," Winke said, putting the small dog down.

"Thank you," Jessie said.

"Sure, dear, come on, I'll show you your room. It's Bonnie's old room," Faye said wistfully.

"And what should we do with you all?" Winke asked us.

I trotted off after Jessie, as did Patches.

I guess that leaves you and me, Ben-Ben," Winke said.

"You and me Santa!" Ben-Ben said excitedly.

CHAPTER SIX

Zachary steadily improved over the next few days. We had been there close to what the humans call a week when Jessie again began to ask me if she thought we should stay here or move on. It was a daily occurrence; she changed her mind more times than I could count, probably even more than the cat could too.

"I want to see Justin, Riley. Do you think he's alive?" Jessie asked me.

I hoped he was, he seemed like a good human. Being honest with myself though, I liked Faye a lot and I think I loved Winke. I'd never met a two-legger so happy; if he had a tail it would wag constantly. Ben-Ben hadn't left his side since we got here, even got to sleep in their bed. Faye had complained that even their Dora hadn't been allowed to do that.

Winke would always laugh and say we were guests and we could do as we pleased.

"Winke, don't get too attached to that dog," Faye said as I padded into the kitchen. Jessie was still asleep and I needed to go outside.

"Why wouldn't I?" Winke had asked her as he held the small Yorkie up to his face. I think he could have fit all of Ben-Ben in his mouth without even trying.

"I don't think she's going to stay," Faye said.

Winke turned to her. "What makes you say that?"

"It's in her eyes, she misses that boy."

"Then all the more reason I should love this little guy even more," Winke said, gently pressing Ben-Ben to the side of his face.

"I just don't want to see you hurt," Faye said tenderly.

"Oh, Faye, I have so little time left myself, I might as well enjoy every minute of it."

"Don't you talk like that!"

"Come on, Faye, you have to be realistic. Even with the chemo the doctors were only talking about another six months to a year, tops. Hell, I'm thrilled the zombies came when they did or all this would be gone," Winke said, pulling on his impressively long face hair.

"I should have been so lucky," she said, getting on her toes for a lip press. And they called dogs' rituals weird. I scratched on the door.

"Well, hello, Riley," Winke said, "At least you know where to go the bathroom," he said as he looked playfully at Ben-Ben.

"What?" Faye asked. "Where?"

"I cleaned it up," Winke said cheerily.

"I've seen the way you clean—where was it?"

Winke looked out the door viewer first then opened the door for me. "Stay close, I'll be right back, Riley. I'm in a little trouble." He winked.

He walked off to show Faye where Ben-Ben had his accident. Dumb dog still hadn't figured it out. When I realized I was outside all alone in the early dark with zombies, I thought maybe he had figured it out after all. I was midway through my stream when I heard the clumsy sounding fall of feet as humans walked, but this was even clumsier. Zombies were close.

So far the dead two-leggers had shown no interest in eating dogs or, unfortunately, cats. But if I had the choice between a hamburger and dry dog food, I'd eat the ground up beef every time unless there was no more hamburger, then I'd eat whatever I could. How long would it be before there were no more two-leggers for the zombies to eat?

I wanted back in the house, but I didn't want to alert

the zombies to my presence. They didn't yet sound like they were on a hunt, but merely trying to pick up a scent. I waited by the door, occasionally lightly scratching at it, hoping to get someone's attention.

"Well, hello there, Riley!" Winke said much too loudly as he opened the door.

I ran straight into his tree-like legs when I heard the zombie footfalls become purposeful.

Winke bent down to rub his shins. "Let me know next time if I'm in your way." He smiled.

I barked vociferously in his face, "*Shut the door!*"

"Whoa, girl, it's alright," he said, mistakenly thinking I was barking *at* him. He slowly stood up and then noticed the real threat. "Shit," he said slamming the door shut just as a zombie banged into it.

The door rattled, it did not look very sturdy to me.

"What is all this racket?" Faye asked as she shuffled into the room.

Winke and I were looking at the backdoor. Light was beginning to filter in around the edges every time the zombie walked into it. All three of us were frozen right until the zombie broke the door viewer.

"Gonna need a gun, Faye," Winke said, never taking his eyes off the door; I guess he was hoping if he kept willing it shut it would stay.

Ben-Ben came back with Faye who had a very small fire stick.

"Why are they at Santa's house?" Ben-Ben asked.

Wood was splintering when Faye sent the metal bee flying. The zombie fell backward. Jessie was in the kitchen by the time the next one took its place.

"Give me the gun, Faye. Go out the front and get everyone over to Sean's house," Winke told his wife.

"I'm not leaving you here," she told him.

"Faye, this door isn't going to hold much longer, get them over there now. I'll be right behind you."

Faye was looking suspiciously at him.

"I'll be right behind you—*go!*" he shouted as he let fly another metal bee.

I couldn't see how many zombies there were, but when one fell another immediately took its place.

"Riley, come on," Jessie said a moment later. Zach was in her arms and Patches was at her feet.

"I'll watch out for the girl and the cub," Patches said.

"Go!" I barked at them much like Winke had earlier. Jessie turned to leave at Faye's urging. Ben-Ben came up beside me; it was good to have him.

"Nobody messes with Santa," he told me seriously.

"You two along for the ride?" Winke asked.

A car ride right now sounded like dog heaven, but when we didn't move I figured he meant something different. Humans were funny like that. Their words did not always equal their actions.

Winke fired a few more bees, then rushed over to one of the wooden food containers. He grabbed a box of bees and quickly placed some in the small stick. More wood had splintered while he wasn't shooting, zombies would be inside soon. I hoped Jessie and Zach were at the neighbor's and the cat had kept her word, might as well have asked a squirrel to give up some of its nuts.

The door swung in just as he started firing again, the lead zombie came to a halt mere whisker-lengths away from my muzzle. Winke kept firing until he ran out of bees. "That's it, guys. That should have given them enough time, we have to go."

Winke turned to leave. A zombie came running into the house at full speed. It was later I would remember that until this point all the zombies had been slow but right then I had to help save Santa.

The zombie ran into Winke's back and he probably would have fallen backward from the impact with Winke but Winke's foot got caught up in the food room's chair. He fell over, with the zombie on top of him. Ben-Ben was there before me; he bit deeply into the zombie's neck. The zombie was trying desperately to get through Winke's fake skins.

"Ben-Ben, watch the door, I'll get the zombie on Winke's—I mean Santa's back!"

Ben-Ben was reluctant to leave but when I grabbed the zombie's leg and had him half off he went to the door, there wasn't much he could do because of his height except trip the zombies up, but that was enough. Winke was scrambling to get up on his knees as I was pulling the zombie off. Winke screamed as he turned and laid a ham sized fist into the zombie's nose. Winke got completely up as I dragged the zombie a little bit away from him.

"Let's go," Winke and I said almost in unison.

Ben-Ben was limping but he didn't say anything as we ran for the front door. Winke held it open for us as we raced through. He slammed it shut as zombies poured into his living room. I saw Faye frantically waving and tapping a home viewer from across the yard. She looked scared, we were in agreement there. We were halfway to the house when we were seen by the hunters. Winke's log legs were serving him well, he ran pretty good for a two-legger, Ben-Ben was having difficulty keeping up, I grabbed him by the scruff of his neck and lifted him much like I would my young if I had had any.

"This is better than running!" Ben-Ben said, his tongue lolling and his tail wagging.

"Stay still," I mumbled.

"Come on, you damn fool," Faye said to Winke, urging him into the house.

Winke fell onto the floor and we were right behind him. Faye slammed the door shut as Jessie placed a large metal bar in place to secure the door. The door shook a little but it was in no threat of giving like Winke's.

"I got bit!" Winke said. He lifted the blue fake skins on his leg.

"Are you sure?" Faye asked, getting down to get a closer look at it.

"I think I'd damned well know if I got bit," Winke said.

Faye had a sharp intake of breath as she looked at the bite. She ran her finger over its outline. "Thank God it didn't break skin."

"You sure?" Winke asked.

"I think I'd damned well know if I saw blood," Faye said, throwing his words back at him. "You fool, you could have got yourself killed."

"It would have been worth it to be sure you made it. These two saved my life," Winke said, grabbing Ben-Ben and me. "These are some special dogs," he told Jessie.

"I know," she said, getting down to pet us.

"If it wasn't for me they would never have made it over here," Patches said indignantly. "I showed them how to walk quietly."

"Now what?" Faye asked as she looked through the viewer to her domicile.

"Well, I guess this is home now," Winke said as he got up and stood next to her. We could clearly hear things breaking and smashing across the way.

"Is this place any safer?" Jessie asked.

"This is a small fortress," Winke said. "This was our neighbor, the survivalists', home. We should have just moved in after... well, after they left."

"You know I couldn't," Faye said. "That's been our home for the last forty years. I couldn't stand the thought of leaving our kids' bedrooms, it would have been too final."

"I know, Hon, I know," Winke said, putting his arm around his wife. "We left most of their stuff here just usually came over and grabbed what we needed, kind of like a 7-11, I guess. I just always knew this day would come and it would be better to have everything here."

"Come on, Faye," Winke said leading his wife into

the new food room. Sit—me and Jessie will get some breakfast going."

"I'm staying with Santa, Riley," Ben-Ben said.

The sadness wafted off Faye. I stayed with her.

Patches hopped up onto the ledge of the home viewer. "More zombies are coming," she said.

My body shuddered; I hated the dead ones. Winke and Jessie came back a few moments later with their arms full of food boxes. "Faye, they have an indoor vented generator," Winke said excitedly.

Faye didn't respond.

"You know what that means, don't you?" he asked. She still didn't respond. "How does the idea of a hot shower sound?"

At least this time she looked up.

"Lights," he said. That one word seemed to have a big effect as a grin spread on her face.

"I'll be able to read at night?" she asked.

"Hell, you'll even be able to plug in your e-reader." He laughed.

"It's at our house Winke," she said resignedly. "And don't you even think about going and getting it."

"We'll see," he said as he pulled on his long face mane.

"Oh, a shower would be so nice."

"Go take one. I'll get some eats ready.

***

It was a few cycles of the burning disc before the zombies in Winke and Faye's house left or at least figured how to get out. Winke told me we would wait one more day before we went back to get Faye's stuff. Even then we would wait until she was asleep because if she knew he was going out she would kill him.

I didn't think she would, but Winke was scared of her and that was good enough reason for me to wait also.

The wolf disc was shining bright the night Winke

asked me if I wanted to go for a walk. I knew immediately what he was talking about. The house was quiet except for Faye's snoring, which in its own way was a comforting sound.

Winke talked to me as he looked through the viewer. "It's Christmas Eve and I want to get my wife something special. You ready, girl?"

I was. I had kind of hoped Ben-Ben was coming, the little dog had proved himself over and over in battle and not having him along by my side was slightly disturbing. But I understood it; the big man considered Ben-Ben like a child cub and would not put him in danger.

"I'm coming too," Patches said as she rushed out the door before Winke could stop her.

"Patches," Winke said softly. "Come back here, you'll get me in trouble with Jessie."

Patches was already heading for the other house. "Well, at least she's going the right way," Winke said as he looked both ways and stepped out. He had a very large fire stick with him and for that I was thankful.

"Oh, it stinks over here," Patches said as she rounded the corner to get to the back of Winke's house.

"Did you stream over there?" I asked.

"Funny, no it's the dead zombies," she said as Winke and I came up behind her.

"Well, they definitely don't bury their dead or eat them. I was wondering if they would or not. Too bad about that, we'd be able to get rid of them a lot quicker if they started to take bites out of each other," Winke said as he prodded it with his stick.

After a while of nothing happening he carefully stepped over it and into the house. The smell outside was nothing compared to what assailed us from the inside. Winke had to step back out, he took a smaller piece of fake skin from the pouch of the skins he was wearing and wrapped it around his face. I wondered if that would work for me. I waited by the door for him, partly because I didn't want to go in, either. Patches strolled in, seemingly unaffected.

"Wooo, if it wasn't Christmas Eve I wouldn't be doing this," Winke said.

"He shouldn't be doing this at all," Patches said to me.

I had to agree, if only because of the smell, not even including the danger. I heard something rustling on the far side of the house but I noticed most, if not all the outside viewers were broken and I could see the material covering them was moving back and forth and that easily could have been the source of the sound.

"Hard to believe this was my house for so many years, doesn't even look the same," Winke said with a choked voice.

Home was where my food bowl was, I thought. I wanted out of this place, it smelled worse than death. Death has an earthy naturalness to it, none of that was here. Broken clear viewer pieces crumbled under Winke's feet as he stepped farther in, I was careful to avoid the twinkling bits.

"Seems empty, girl," Winke said, I think to calm me, but more probably to soothe himself.

We walked farther in and then off to the right we went down the dark skinny room to the room Winke and Faye rested. I heard something move, but it sounded no louder than a mouse or maybe a rat. I had not seen the sharp-toothed ones eat any of the zombies yet but wherever there was a free meal they would follow shortly.

Patches came up behind me. "Nothing in the kitchen," she said.

"Did you hear the rat?" I asked her. Thinking she'd be curious and maybe go kill it. She shook her head. "You going to check it out?" I asked. She again shook her head. Whatever I was picking up on, so was she. I gently gripped the bottom of Winke's fake skins, halting his progress.

"You don't like this, either?" he asked me. "We'll be

out in a minute." Whatever a minute was I thought it was too long.

We finally came to the end of the skinny room and into the room of rest. It made the destruction in the house pale in comparison. A pack of rabid hippos couldn't have destroyed this room as thoroughly, I thought.

"I can't even see her nightstand—how am I going to find her ereader?" Winke asked.

Nightstand and ereader were both new words to me; I was not going to be of any help. Patches went to the far side of the room where there seemed a path to walk in. Winke seemed about to follow her when he spotted something on our side.

"I think that's her stand, I see reading glasses!" Winke said triumphantly.

I looked back down the dark long room something wasn't right but I couldn't sense it properly, the abundance of smell had me off balance. Then Winke screamed. Patches came hurdling over the turned over human resting pad. I thought heading for the door but she was heading for Winke. Winke was still cursing as he pulled his leg free from something I could not see from my vantage point. I could smell his blood and even in the soft light I could see it staining his fake skins.

"Zombie!" Patches yelled. She had her sharp claws out and was attacking. I rounded a broken large wooden piece humans put their fake skins in. Trapped underneath the debris was a zombie, its cloudy eyes were fixed on Winke, its mouth was crimson with the blood of Winke. Patches raked claws across its eye, it would never see out that side again, not that that would be a problem for long. Winke urged the cat away as he placed the fire stick up against the zombie's head and pulled the trigger. The smoke from the stick was still swirling in the air when I began to hear properly again. I was waiting for either more zombies or Faye to start screaming, nothing happened.

"You alright, Cat?" I asked.

"I am, but the human is dead," she responded.

"He's fine, there's not enough blood to be a problem. He'll put one of those sticky skins on it," I told her. Cats were always expecting the worst.

"You don't know anything, Dog," Patches said as she left the room.

Winke grabbed a chair and sat it upright; he then sat down so he could pull up his fake skins. "Well, it got me," he said, looking at the wound. He grabbed some fake skins out of the broken furniture to wipe the blood away; he then tied it around his leg.

"See, Cat!" I yelled. "You can barely see it."

"Shh, Riley. I don't want to wake the missus," Winke said.

"If she didn't hear the fire stick, she didn't hear me," I told him, quieter.

"Well, I'll be damned," he said as he leaned over. He grabbed something that looked much like the books Jessie used to read only thinner, then leaned over again and came up with a small leash the humans put into the wall that seemed to keep their devices from walking away.

"I found it, Riley. I guess that makes it sort of worthwhile. I wonder how much time I have left?"

I cocked my head to the side; I didn't know what he was talking about. Did he hear the cat?

He sat there a long time, sometimes his head between his hands, sometimes his hands were clasped together and he was mumbling with his face upturned but mostly he was silent. We stayed that way for a long time until the disc began to again brighten the darkness.

"So far, so good, girl," Winke said to me. "Let's go celebrate Christmas."

"Where have you been?" Faye asked as she met us at the door.

I scooted by Winke, to smell bacon after what was in

his other house was too much.

"I had to get you a gift!" Winke said enthusiastically. "Merry Christmas!" Winke handed her the thin book with the leash.

"My ereader! You shouldn't have, Winke," she squealed as she kissed his cheek. "Winke, you're hot." She touched his forehead. "You're burning up! Come on, go sit down."

"Now that you mention it, I don't feel so good," he told her.

"Is Santa making bacon?" Ben-Ben asked coming down the hallway.

Patches was at Jessie's room, meowing loudly.

"Cat, you're going to wake her," I said.

"I know, I'm trying to, we need to get out of here," she answered .

"Bacon, bacon, bacon," Ben-Ben kept repeating as he walked around in small circles in the food room.

"Patches, what?" Jessie asked as she opened her door. She first looked down at Patches who was now running back toward me and over to the room of living where Faye was helping Winke lay down.

"Is he alright?" Jessie asked as she also came down the hallway.

"He's burning up—could you please get me some water?" Faye asked.

Jessie ran to get him some water and then handed it to Faye. I saw her put her hand to her mouth and that's never a good human gesture.

"He's almost a zombie, Riley, make the girl get moving," Patches said.

"What?" I asked. I wasn't putting everything together.

"When a zombie bites a human, that human becomes a zombie. And that man is almost a zombie—we need to leave."

"I don't believe you," I told her.

"These humans feed me, they clean up after me, they provide me with a warm, safe place to rest—why would I want to leave?" Patches said.

I ran down the skinny room and into Jessie's rest room. I grabbed her fake paws, ran back down the hallway, and I placed them down loudly by her feet.

"I'm busy, Riley, I'll take you for a walk later," she told me.

I barked aggressively.

"Are you okay, Faye?" Jessie asked.

"I think so," Faye answered without looking up from her husband.

"I need to get dressed, apparently someone needs to go outside *real* bad." She rubbed my head.

I barked loudly at the doorway to baby Zach's room. No response. I barked louder.

"Stop, Riley, you're going to wake—dammit," Jess said as Zach began crying in earnest. "Now I'll have to take him, that's not a good girl."

I was fine with it. Not much time passed, but it was enough. I was beginning to get anxious and Ben-Ben wasn't helping.

"Riley, she's burning the bacon," Ben-Ben said. "I mean, I'll still eat it, but I like it when it's all wet and soggy like when the humans drop it on the floor. Santa needs to come over here and get the bacon."

As he tried to walk past, I barred his way.

"Riley, I just want bacon," Ben-Ben moaned.

I stalled him long enough; Jessie was coming back down the skinny room. "A walk first and then bacon."

"A walk? Why? Santa doesn't care where I go," Ben-Ben said.

"Have some pride, you're coming out and then we'll get some bacon," I told him. If he questioned me again I was going to nip him and I think he knew it.

"Promise?" he whined again.

"Sure, let's go," I told him. Patches was already at the door.

"You too?" Jessie asked.

"Faye, I'll be right back," Jessie said as she let us all out, including herself. She had no sooner shut the door and walked a few steps away when we heard a blood-curdling scream from Faye.

Jessie turned to run back, I got in her way like I had with Ben-Ben.

"Riley, stop!" Jessie said, trying to force me out of her path. I kept jumping back. Faye's screams got louder and finally stopped as Jessie fought her way through me and to the door. She opened it and stuck her head in, letting out a small gasp before quickly closing the door and then the heavy metal one in front. Something banged up against the now closed door.

"Santa?" Ben-Ben asked.

"Not anymore," Patches said.

"So no bacon then?" Ben-Ben asked.

I answered him by walking away.

Jessie was crying as we started out again to find Justin. It was the two-leggers' day of Christmas but none of us felt like celebrating.

The Book of Riley: Part 2
My Name is Riley

Mark Tufo

This book is a work of fiction. Names, Characters, places and events are a product of the author's imagination. Any resemblance to actual names, characters and places are entirely coincidental. The reproduction of this work in full or part is forbidden without written consent from the author.

Dedications:

To the missus, thank you for all that you do. (Especially when I injure myself in a variety of new and unusual ways)

To Katherine Coynor, your input and attention to detail is always appreciated.

To Paul Erickson, thank you. (I could go into a long and detailed explanation but he'd probably get embarrassed.)

To Max Heron, be well little one.

To the men and women of the armed forces, my unflagging gratitude for your sacrifices.

My Name is Riley - From the Book of Riley - Volume 2

Part 2 continues the saga of Riley and her pack, picking up exactly where part 1 ended.

CHAPTER ONE

We got back into Jess' car. Her hands were shaking as she placed the janglers into their resting spot. Water leaked from her eyes, splashing off the steering wheel. Ben-Ben was licking it up.

"It's salty like bacon. Do you want me to save you some?" Ben-Ben asked me.

"You thought him worth saving?" Patches asked me as she sighed from the back seat.

I turned my head to the side, which I think is near the same as when a human shrugs their shoulders. "He has his good parts," I told her.

"Let me know when they show, get the girl moving," Patches told me.

"You are a bossy little thing," I snarled at her.

"I'm a cat and I'm female, I fully expect others to do my bidding."

"Shouldn't we allow her to rest?" I asked Patches. "She just watched two of her own die."

"More will be coming. I cannot imagine you with that preposterously large nose not being able to smell them," Patches said.

Ben-Ben's water slurping was not allowing me to think clearly. "Sit down!" I barked at him.

"I just wanted some bacon," he whined. "I miss Santa, and the Alphas, even Alpha-cub," he whined softly.

I missed them, too, and I felt for Ben-Ben; but we needed to leave. Survival was all that mattered. Instincts that had been muted my entire life were now coming to the fore. I barked to get Jessie's attention and again when she didn't respond.

"Riley, what?" she asked with a pained expression.

I barked through the front viewer.

"I don't see anything," Jessie said, peering.

"She really needs to learn animal-speak, this is as bad as *Lassie*," Patches said.

"Who's Lassie?" Ben-Ben and I asked.

"If you two stopped playing tug-of-war with your tails you'd know," Patches said snidely.

I turned to the front when the four-wheeler awoke.

"Again you guys saved me," Jessie said, stroking the side of my face. Ben-Ben nudged me away so that his face was now in contact with Jess' front paw. "Oh, Ben-Ben," Jess said as more water flowed from her eyes.

"Think she could fill a bowl with that?" Ben-Ben asked me. "I'm very thirsty. I ate the casing the bacon came in."

"Dumb dog," Patches chimed in.

"What? Faye threw it in the giant dog bowl...I figured it was mine to eat!" Ben-Ben exclaimed.

"That's the trash," I said, shaking my head back and forth.

"Yum! It's all the same to me!" Ben-Ben said excitedly, his tail wagging furiously.

"I have got to start thinking on my own," Jess said to us. "I have Zachary to think of. It's just *us* now," she said as she snuggled up to my face. My whiskers tickled as she did so; I sneezed in her face. "Why thank you for that!" Jess said, pulling back a bit.

She put Zach in his special seat. I could tell from the smells that were leaking from him that he was in desperate need of elimination. I have yet to figure out why the two-leggers make their young keep the waste in their fake skins. Even the lowly cat doesn't walk around with offal in its coat. When I was a summer younger I thought it might just be my Alphas that did that, and then I went to the kid zoo—or they may have called it the park, I can't remember—but all the little ones there had fake skins on, and more than seven had waste tucked in with them. Two-leggers are a funny animal. And then I remember Ben-Ben when I think sometimes that we dogs are the superior being; he brings it all back. Patches might have it right, not that I'm going to let her know it. The only thing we have in common is that we're both females.

The wheeler was moving, and just in time, I saw zombies coming from around Winke's house.

"Something is wrong with Santa!" Ben-Ben howled.

I turned; my fur bristled as I saw him standing at the window. He looked to be eating a particularly large hunk of meat, it was not bacon, of that I was sure. Jess did not see, and I was thankful for that, she would have just leaked more eye water.

"I need to get to Justin," Jess said aloud. I could sense the desperation in her voice. "Until then, though, I'm going to start doing what it takes to keep us alive," she said with some determination; not much, but at least it was there.

"Finally, now I can take this burden off my back," Patches said as she puddled her tail around her body.

"As if," I snorted at her, she paid me no attention. "Typical cat, do nothing and take all the credit."

"I'm sleeping, dog, why don't you be a good second-class animal and shut up," she told me.

If I thought I could get into the back without hurting Zachary, I may have done so. I wouldn't hurt her, mostly. Maybe just fit her whole body in my mouth and give her a shake or two, let her know who was boss. I drifted off to sleep with that image in my mind; one of the better sleep thoughts I'd ever had.

"Nevada!" Was what I heard Jessie shout as she took me out of my sleep; good thing, too. I had been chasing a fat squirrel, and then when I got close, he stopped and turned towards me. His eyes lost the fear of the pursued; they turned as black as the night my pack died. And then he started to run *towards* me! A squirrel started to chase me! I would have been embarrassed if any of my dog friends had seen. Like sometimes during the autumn months when the two-leggers would parade me and Ben-Ben around in fake skins like theirs. Ben-Ben loved when they dressed him up. Last time he had looked like an orange toy ball, they kept calling him a pumpkin, but he sure didn't smell like one.

They put some frilly scratchy thing on me, said I was a ballerina, whatever that is. I tried my best to get away from the two-legger tether, but they offered a peanut butter cookie, and I'd do just about anything for a peanut butter cookie. Walked around the whole neighborhood with the Alphas, Zachary, and Daniel. They made sure to go to *every* house, kept saying something about 'tricks or treats' it was alright at some of the houses as the two-leggers that lived there would give me and Ben-Ben something. And then it got bad when that big Siberian Husky, Duke, saw me. He was howling in laughter. I made sure to mark his fence. He couldn't get past it to get to me. He was soooo angry!

"We're in Nevada!" Jessie shouted again.

"Cat, what is Nevada?" I asked. I hated to, but what choice did I have.

"We crossed an imaginary line in the dirt the humans created to mark their territory. We left what they call California and are now in Nevada," she answered.

I didn't have a clue what 'imaginary' meant, but I didn't want her to think I didn't. "So we've almost completed the big move?" I asked, trying to sound smarter than her.

"Dogs had to team up with humans or you would have never made it," she said, curling back up to go to sleep.

I looked around trying to figure out what made Nevada any different than California; I couldn't see anything besides dirt and rocks. Yup pretty much looked the same…except for the change in Jess. She seemed happy once we crossed that funny line. I would be happy with her; I just wished I knew how many more funny lines we would need to cross to see the pheromone boy.

"I think we'll go to Las Vegas," Jess said as we were driving along.

As long as they had food I would go willingly. We stopped once so that Zachary could get a new set of fake skins. I gladly got out and relieved myself behind the wheeler, I made Ben-Ben get up too and go outside. He would have been just as happy to go on the back seat. Patches hopped down and walked right under me, her tail smacking into my nose. I had visions of grabbing her by that offensive tail and sending her for a little 'fetch' ride.

Zachary was screaming; I went over to sniff him while Jess was busy digging the fake skins out. His bottom was the same color, Jess' skin had been this summer when she fell asleep outside. I don't know why it wouldn't be, he was sitting in his filth and he had no fur to protect himself. I smelled something else, too, the baby cub was sick. I could smell it in his breath. It wasn't bad yet, but it would be. I could only hope that this 'Las Vegas' would offer some help.

***

Zachary had been full-throated screaming since we left our relief station. The wheeler was traveling faster as maybe Jess realized something was wrong and was trying to get some help. If she was merely trying to outpace the noise, she wasn't doing such a good job.

"Shit!" Jess said, slamming her hands against the wheel. "We need gas."

I thought that was actually pretty good since we were just about to pass one of the smelly liquid dispensers. That was until I saw the dead ones walking around the pumps.

"Shit, shit, shit," Jess said. "We need gas or we're going to be walking." She looked over at the three dead ones who were now approaching, as she pulled in.

I alternated between looking at Jess and the dead

ones. Jess was alternating between looking at them and looking down at the number gauges on the wheeler. She reached behind the back seat and took out a metal stick, and then she got out of the car. She almost slammed my head in the heavy door as I tried to follow her.

"You watch out for Zach," she told me. I barked furiously at her.

"Cat, what is she doing?" I kept barking.

"This is bad," Ben-Ben said as he piddled.

"And that's going to help?" Patches said as she jumped into the front with me to get away from the stench and flow of Ben-Ben.

"I wish Santa was here," Ben-Ben said as he watched Jess.

"She's going to try and kill the zombies," Patches said.

"She's a fool!" I growled.

"Get me out of the wheeler, cat, NOW!" I was barking so loud I was actually making the baby cub stop his screaming as he looked in wonder at something that was actually complaining louder than he was.

Patches moved her paw to a button on the door. I heard something click on all four doors.

"Wrong button," Patches said, looking down at her paw. "I think I locked the doors."

The zombies were getting closer to Jess as she had come to my side of the car. She started to wildly swing the hooked metal stick. "They're going to kill her, cat. Get me out of this thing!" I was howling.

I heard a whirring sound as the window in the back on the driver's side began to go down. I had already jumped into the back seat and into Ben-Ben's urine when the other windows began to go down. The triumphant words of Patches were cut short as I dove through the opening.

"A thanks would be nice," I thought I heard her say as I came to a skidding halt when I landed.

I yelped a moment when I felt something in my paw tear. I turned my body and started to run around to the front. Jess had just hit the first zombie on the shoulder with her stick. It had no effect; his hands were reaching out and were about to close on her neck as I launched off the ground, my momentum taking us all to the ground.

I saw Jess' look of surprise and relief as I wrapped my muzzle around the creature's neck. Skin practically sloughed off in my mouth as I dug my paws into the ground pulling the monster off of her. She scrambled and got out from under us; she stood back up as I was shaking back and forth violently. I wasn't satisfied until I heard the bones in its neck begin to snap, and still the thing tried to bite at me.

"Back!" Jess screamed loudly.

I had just let go as she brought the metal stick down on the top of its skull. The splintering of its head was loud. Finally, it lay still. Jess was heaving from the exertion and the stress; I turned to face the remaining two.

"Oh God!" Jess bawled.

Unlike the Alphas' home, these zombies were much more interested in me than they had been. I knew what was happening. They were hungrier now, I might not be the favorite food choice for them, kind of like my kibble, but they'd eat me in a pinch. I darted to the side. One of the zombies turned to follow me, but she was slow, even slower than the fat Alpha-cub. I got behind her and snapped at the small fleshy tendon behind her ankle. She went down face first, a few of her two-legger fangs cracking as she hit the fake ground.

I wanted to finish her off, but Jess was looking like she had lost her will to fight. She had the metal stick pressed up against the third zombie's forehead and was merely trying to keep him at bay. I didn't think her tactic was going to work.

I barked at her. "Swing!" I yelled over and over. She looked at me pleadingly for help. I barked again, she needed to kill it on her own or she would begin to doubt her ability to survive; next she would be fear urinating like Ben-Ben. This wasn't a funny time, but it was a funny thought, and I planned on thinking about it later when we were safe.

"Riley!" Patches admonished me from behind the clear viewer. "She needs your help!"

"Then maybe you should get out here!" I yelled to the cat. She shut up after that.

I kept barking at Jess until something in her finally released; she let reason and higher thought go as she reached into the depths of her being and pulled out instinct. Survival took over. She realized this *thing* wanted to take what was most precious to us all: Life. She swung the stick much like I had seen on the picture viewer when Alpha watched a game he called baseball. The game made absolutely no sense, but the balls were delicious whenever I could get a hold of one.

When I was a puppy they had talked about sending me to puppy prison when I got a hold of one of the round, cow tasting things. He had kept screaming that a baby had signed it and that it was priceless. I still don't know what 'signing' is, or who Baby Ruth was, but I sure was glad She-alpha had told him in no uncertain terms that I was staying and that maybe he should put things out of reach of puppies. Although, in all fairness, I had jumped up on his chair and onto his desk and pushed the clear viewer material out of the way so that I could get to it. Seemed like such a waste to have the fun ball under clear viewer material.

Her first hit seemed to stun the monster but did not put him down. The second one split through his hairline. Vile smelling liquid began to ooze down its side. Jess gagged, but she struck again. I watched as the side of the head where she hit indented, the oozing became a gushing. The thing wasn't moving forward, but it still hadn't gone down. I thought Jess was done...until she brought the stick one more time against it. This time his head seemed to swallow the stick, a wet sucking sound ensued as the thing fell. The stick was pulled violently from Jess' hands. She let it go as she winced from the pain.

She was sobbing uncontrollably; much like she had been when she got off the plastic talking box at the house one time. She had told She-alpha that Bobby DiCarlo had broken up with her. I didn't know how the plastic talking box knew, but that wasn't important. I made sure that I was within petting distance for the next two days as she watered her eyes. There was a time and a place to be sad, this wasn't one of them. There were no zombies around us right now, but they were nearby, I could smell them. And if more than seven came, we would be in trouble.

"Do you need my help?" Ben-Ben was barking from the clear viewer on our side.

The dog was so dense, I bet he didn't even realize there was a way to get out and help. That was unfair, he had proved his reliability more than once; humans weren't the only ones that suffered from stress.

"Just look for more of them," I answered.

He seemed to like that answer.

I felt like I had to add this next part. "And let us know if you see any of them." There was more than a fair chance he would spot some and leave it at that.

Jess thought my barks were for her, didn't matter that they weren't, it seemed to get her moving. She had been looking down at the zombie by her feet. I couldn't tell if she was celebrating her victory, despairing in it, or just maybe trying to decide if she should pull her weapon free from its skull. She shuddered once and looked around at our surroundings. She immediately headed towards a wheeler that had its door open. It was the kind that the two-leggers that always wore the same fake skins drove. Always blue with a blue hat, some have a shiny hard piece over their breast, some don't—like the one that used to come to my Alpha's door almost every day.

I couldn't stand him. Most days he would come up to

the house. I could hear him moving around behind the door, and he would do something with the small paper holder that the Alphas called 'male?' (I never got any scent of male from it.) I would bark mercilessly until he would get scared and run away. Funny thing is, he would go to the next house and do it again, and they didn't have a guard dog like me at all. He was just a scared man that threatened to go into homes uninvited. I would bark at him through the clear viewer on the side of the house until he would leave there, too. Even pressing my paws and face up against the viewer to let him know I meant business.

This wheeler had the funny bright lights on top. The uniformed people it held, I didn't like them much either, but that wasn't stopping Jess from reaching in. She pulled out a short metal object and a firing stick that looked a lot like the one her sire had used. She leaned back in.

"The keys are in it, Riley," she said.

"Okay," I answered. I wasn't sure what she meant, and she had absolutely no clue what I had replied.

"Do you think there's gas?" she asked me.

"Do you think cats are the root of all evil?" I asked back, neither of us had an answer for the other.

I whipped my head around at the shouting from Ben-Ben. "Rileeeeeeeeyyyy!"

If this was about finding him bacon I was going to nip him in the behind for almost scaring the waste out of me. I could quickly tell this wasn't about food; that was more of a whine, this was a warning. I couldn't see anything from where I was, but I could hear the shuffling of feet. I ran to the other side of the wheeler, the blue fake-skinned man was approaching, and he was huge. I couldn't even imagine how he had fit in the two-wheeler to begin with.

He was holding a large, shiny stick in his hand. Although it didn't really seem that he knew he had it, he was holding it out in front of him as he came at me. I barked at him, hoping it would stop his advance, it didn't. I was longing for the days of the 'door hider' this blue fake skinner scared me like no other had. Flaps of skin dangled from the side of his face, I could see his teeth as they mashed together. Part of his top fake skin had been ripped off revealing a body that did not look like it had fared much better. Ribbons of meat hung from him almost to his knees.

Muscle and sinew glistened back at me, I tried to hold my ground, but every step he took, I found myself involuntarily backing up. Unlike the other zombies, this one seemed to have some spark of intelligence, like the cat. It watched me warily, almost willing me to attack. The ends of its ripped lips pulled up in what I had learned was the two-legger equivalent of a smile. On him, it looked like death. Its eyes followed me constantly until it caught sight of Jess, and the small smile pulled back even further to reveal blood-stained teeth with bits of meat stuck in between some of the larger gaps.

Jess was now in the wheeler and moving the seat when she caught sight of the aberration looking at her. The monster moved faster than I thought possible. Jess barely had time to shut her door, as it was; I think she caught the tips of its front paws. It didn't seem to care; it brought up its stick hand. The wheeler started up with a throaty roar.

The zombie paused for a moment, almost like it was searching its inner picture thoughts for what it was trying to remember. Jess got the wheeler moving as the zombie brought its stick down heavily on the back of the vehicle.

I barked in happiness as Jess got away. That was a mistake as the beast turned towards me. It moaned some deathly mournful war cry, and the pursuit began. I had not realized how much my torn paw hurt until I started to run for my life. Bits of rock and dirt were getting into the wound and made running extremely painful. I was thankful that two-leggers were wholly unequipped for pursuit. It would give up soon when it got tired and realized it couldn't catch me...ever. I ran around most of the entire fake grounds, further than I'd ever had to when Alpha or Alpha-cub were chasing me. But when one's life is on the line like now, it seemed wiser to run the extra distance.

I slowed up and was about to stop so that I could lick the debris clear from my wound when I heard him still coming. I had gained some distance on him from when we had initially started but that he was still this close was unsettling. I winced as I took a painful step and ran towards the grass hoping that the softer surface wouldn't hurt as much. I made sure to stay as far away from Jess and Zach as she moved the baby over to the new wheeler. I noted that Patches immediately got in the new machine, but Ben-Ben wouldn't as he watched me running for my life. He almost started running towards me until Jess picked him up and threw him into the wheeler.

I found myself running with only three legs, still faster than the dead two-legger…but not by much. And I was in pain and getting tired, the zombie seemed like he could do this for a full cycle of the burning disc. I was glad Jess had gotten away, and now it was time to fight or die. I stopped and turned to face my pursuer. The smile pulled so far back on his face that he literally split his lips. He raised the club as he advanced, this time he seemed to be reveling in the fact that he was coming slowly. I do not think it was hard for him to see that I was not faring well, my front paw was held up in front of me and I was panting heavily—partly from the pain and partly from the running. But he was truly insane if he thought I was just going to lie down and die for him.

I raised my hackles trying to look bigger; I got my front lower and bared my teeth. I rumbled a growl my ancestors would be proud of; then I heard the loud 'goose' sound the wheeler can make, this is usually followed by the Alpha shouting some colorful language and displaying one finger to other wheeler operators. I had, as of yet, been unable to figure out what that one finger meant, but it always seemed to make him mad or maybe it was the goose sound the wheeler made. I know I hated that sound. The zombie turned to the approaching wheeler. He seemed to be trying to figure out what to do.

Jess drove the car in between us. The window behind her was down. Ben-Ben was looking out at me, his tongue hanging out. "Hey, Riley!!!" he said loudly. "You coming in?"

"If you get out of the way," I told him, preparing to scrabble up the side and through the window.

"Oh yeah," he said, still not moving.

Time was running out, the zombie was coming around the car. Jess was fumbling with the small firing stick. Ben-Ben and I were about to get real close. I took a couple of steps and jumped up. I yelped as I grabbed the lip of the door with my front paws, my back legs were moving rapidly trying to seek purchase on anything in an effort to get me in the wheeler.

I yelped in surprise as I felt Ben-Ben's teeth sink into the fur and skin on the side of my neck, and then I silently thanked him as I figured out what he was trying to do. The small dog was helping to pull me into the car. I was afraid that if I lost my grip we'd both go tumbling out. My right rear paw finally caught on the handle, and I was able to launch inside just as Jess got the wheeler moving. I was pushed in to the seat from the movement as Ben-Ben fell to the floor.

"Thank you, Ben-Ben," I told the dog. I truly believe he tipped the scale in getting me in.

"You taste like chicken!" Ben-Ben said excitedly as he licked his maw.

"Don't get any ideas," I told him.

"Sorry," Ben-Ben said as he hopped back up.

"For what?" I questioned him.

He looked down to the seat where I was getting my breath back; I now realized it was soaked. "It's alright…this time," I told him.

"You're bleeding, dog." Patches said, looking back at me from her lofty position in the front.

"I didn't know you cared," I told her.

"Suit yourself," she said, looking back out the front clear viewer.

"That was close…too close," Jess said. I saw her shiver a bit. She reached her hand back to seek comfort from our contact. I moved my muzzle closer so she could touch me.

Jess drove further. My paw would not stop bleeding as I tried my best to not get it all over the place. From time to time I would catch Jess looking in the reflector back at me. I guessed she was trying to figure out what I was doing. She finally got so curious she pulled the wheeler over to the side of the hard ground.

She swung her head into the back. "You're bleeding, Riley. Are you hurt?"

I almost cracked up when Ben-Ben answered, and he hadn't even meant to be funny. "Riley, if you're bleeding aren't you already hurt?" he asked me.

"Two-leggers don't know everything," I told him.

"Are you sure?" he asked conspiratorially. "I mean, they know how to make bacon. That makes them pretty close to perfect for me."

I kind of had to agree with him on that one.

Jess had gotten out from her door and opened mine. "Oh, you poor girl," she said as she lifted my paw. I thought she was going to touch my torn pad. I would have had to let her know what I felt about that if she had. "I need to wrap that up." She looked up and down the road, when she was confident we were alone, she shut the wheeler down and grabbed the janglers. She opened the back of the machine. "There's a first aid kit in here!" Jess said excitedly. "And food!"

Ben-Ben nearly stepped on me in his haste to get out of the car. "Sorry, Riley," he said as he jumped down, "food is food!" He yipped more excitedly than Jess.

Even the cat seemed somewhat interested at the mention of food. Who would have thought evil had to eat?

"You did good," Patches said as she brushed past and out to see if she could get a hold of something.

The cat's words shouldn't have mattered because of the constant disdain we felt for each other, but still I felt proud that she had even noticed, and then I was mad at myself because I had let her words affect me. *Stupid cat.*

Jess came back to me a moment later. She had a small packet in her hand and some *bandages* she called them. She grabbed my leg and lifted it up. "Ooh that looks like it hurts, girl," she said as she brought the small packet closer to it.

Ben-Ben came up behind her. "Is that food, Riley? Why is she putting food on your paw?"

"It is medicine for Riley's injury," Patches explained.

I wanted to ask the cat if it hurt, but I just couldn't bring myself to do it. The sticky liquid she placed on my paw initially stung and then began to cool; I felt relief almost instantly from the pain.

"This will help, Riley, now I'm going to put a bandage on it. Don't chew this off." The bandage hurt some as she wrapped the wound and then she grabbed strips of sticky cloth and wrapped that around the bandage. "That ought to hold it in place," Jess said, seemingly admiring her handiwork. "Thank you," she said, grabbing the sides of my face and pulling herself close. She rested her forehead on mine. "You saved me again, girl. How will I ever be able to repay you?"

"You already have," I told her as I licked her face.

"Gross, Riley!" she shouted, smiling for one of the first times in a while.

"Does she taste like chicken?" Ben-Ben asked as he danced around her feet. "I'm starving."

"Okay, okay," Jess said, going back to the end of the wheeler. "Wow there's got to be over a dozen MREs back

here. I know what these are from Mr. Talbot!" She said as
she held one up.

I didn't know what a dozen, or what an MRE was, but
it was hard to not pick up on how excited Jess was about it.

A few moments later, when Jess had come back to the
front of the wheeler and had ripped some packets open, we
all got to find out what MREs were.

"What is this?" Ben-Ben asked in bliss. His face was
covered in the substance, and he was doing his best to lick it
all off of himself.

"Peanut butter," Patches told him.

"This might be better than bacon!" he said as he
brushed his face up against the seat back so that he could lick
the peanut butter from the cloth.

I ate something Jess called 'beef stroganoff' it wasn't
much better than the cat food I sometimes ate. Not because I
liked the stuff, but so that Patches wouldn't have anything to
eat. Although the last time I had done that, she had
eliminated water waste in my water bowl. Even after the
Alpha-female had washed it out twice it was a week longer
before I stopped smelling the cat in it. It was the last time I
had eaten her bad food. This was alright, though, because the
stuff made my stomach hurt anyway.

Jess was trying to give noodles to Zach, but he wasn't
touching them. His eyes were barely open and they seemed
to be staring at something that wasn't there. Even Ben-Ben
knew the importance of what was happening. He was
greedily eyeing the noodles that were dropping to the seat,
but he stayed away.

"Why isn't the cub eating?" he asked me.

"He's sick," I told him, looking at the baby.

"Very sick," Patches added.

I wanted to pull her face off for her words, but she
was right. Noodles were not going to fix whatever was wrong
with the cub, and even Jess with her two-legger nose could
smell trouble.

"I need to get him a doctor," she said.

Jess got back into the front and got the wheeler going, Ben-Ben quickly began to clean up the backseat.

"Is that good, Ben-Ben?" I asked, not trying to be nice.

"Oh, it's delicious," he answered, his tail wagging like crazy.

I could feel heat radiating off the cub as Jess drove down the hard ground, I had no real concept for how fast we were moving, but if how quickly the scenery changed was any indication, then we were moving quickly…maybe even faster than I could run.

Jess kept looking back to see how her litter mate was doing. His cheeks at first had been blazing the color of a setting burning disc, and now they appeared whitish. I could smell death. Patches had the unfortunate ability to go one step further.

"He's here," Patches said, her fur standing on end.

I shivered as I felt icy cold fingers brush up against my coat.

"Patches, stop him!" I barked.

Patches hissed and spat so violently that Jess pulled the car over. She looked quickly towards the cat and then to her sibling. "Zach? Zachary!" she screamed, scrambling to get into the back seat. "Oh my God, he's not breathing," she said as she pushed a slumbering Ben-Ben out of the way so she could lay her brother down.

It looked like she was doing that funny custom two-leggers do of pressing their muzzles together but there was more to it. She was blowing her breathe into her brother and pressing down on his chest.

"Patches!" I yelled.

"I'm trying!" she spat back.

Jess' eyes were leaking as she kept breathing for the cub. I wasn't sure if that was even possible, but she thought so.

"I think it's working!" Patches said triumphantly. "He's fading!"

"I think it's working!" Jess said breathlessly. "He's coming back!"

Zach coughed and spit up some brown bile, his breathing sounds came back in ragged gulps, but at least now he was doing it on his own. And then he started full-throat crying, a sound that was generally annoying, but right now sounded like timber wolves howling in the wild; I loved it. Jess grabbed a wet liquid container and put the small suckling device into her brother's mouth. He sucked the sweet liquid down contentedly, his eyes never straying far from his sister, as if in a silent thank you.

Jess looked exhausted as she got back into the front of the car.

"That was close."

"What?" I asked Patches.

"I didn't say anything," she replied, looking into the back seat.

I may have thought it was Ben-Ben, but after he realized the cub was okay, he went back to trying to get the peanut butter off his whiskers so that he could eat it. He looked like the damned cat the way he was brushing up against the seat.

"I saw my mommy and daddy. They said it wasn't my time yet."

"What?" I asked again. This time I knew who it was…I just couldn't believe it. "Zachary?"

"I love you, Riley," Zach said.

I almost fell off my seat. "You can talk?"

"My mommy just showed me how, she said it was the only way we would have a chance."

"Patches, are you hearing this?" I asked.

I wished I had looked to the front earlier, the cat was frozen in mid-movement, and her bottom jaw was hanging low, her eyes wide as she stared at the infant cub. I think the two-legger term was 'shocked'.

She jumped into the backseat and was straddling Zach's special seat. "This is impossible," she said as she got right up to Zach's face. "Say something."

"I love peanut butter!" Ben-Ben yipped as his head came up. "Hey, Patches, what are you doing back here? I mean grrrr, cat! I'm growling at you like Riley would want me to. Do I still have any peanut butter on my face?" And then he began to rub up against the seat again in a desperate bid to discover any as yet previously unfound treat.

"Human cubs cannot speak!" Patches shouted as if Zach was an insult to all she knew.

"Patches, what are you doing?" Jess asked. "Is Zach alright?" she asked as she nudged the cat to the side. Her smiling brother's face shone back, slightly red, but better than it had been only moments before. "I need to find a hospital," she said as she made the two-wheeler go faster.

"Speak, boy," Patches said indignantly.

For a moment I was beginning to think I had imagined the whole thing. Humans went crazy all the time; why not me?

"You're whiskers tickle," Zach said as he rubbed his face.

Patches sprang back and into me, normally I would have taken advantage of the proximity and given her a little bite, but I was too shocked myself to do much of anything beyond stare at the baby.

"Hi, Zach, do I have any peanut butter on my face?" Ben-Ben asked the baby as if it were the most natural thing. He moved his muzzle from side to side so the baby could see.

Zach smiled and said no. Patches pushed even further into me; she must have been scared if she was this close to me on purpose.

"This isn't possible," Patches said, finally removing herself from my side, but only by a few inches, I was fairly certain that if Zach said 'boo' she would be right back to her previous position.

"Sure it is," Ben-Ben said. He had a foil packet stuck to his forehead as he spoke. "We all just heard him so it must be, right?" he asked at the end as if right now he wasn't sure if he had made a valid point or not.

"Why have you never spoken before?" Patches asked, approaching, but from an angle as if she were stalking prey.

"I couldn't until Mommy showed me the way."

Patches' tail was wagging back and forth violently. I really wanted to bite it, but I showed unbelievable restraint and didn't.

"You sure are making a lot of noise, Zach," Jess said. "You feeling better?" she asked, looking through the small image reflector. The relief in her voice was easy to pick up on.

"Mom and Dad say hi, Jess, they are so proud of you," Zach gurgled.

"Oh, you sound so much better, Zach," she said as she reached her hand back and tickled the bottom of his foot. "And your warm, thank you, God," she added as she momentarily looked up.

I followed her line of sight to see if I could notice this God she spoke of and to.

"I don't think I like this," Patches said, her tail still swishing crazily about. "I don't like surprises. I like to know where my food is, where my water is, where my litter box is, and where my bed is. That is what I like. This I don't," she said as she hopped back into the front seat. She made sure to keep looking into the back at Zach.

I moved closer to Zach. He tightly gripped my cheek in his fist. "My mommy and daddy said we need to find Michael." And then he let go.

"Cat?" I asked.

"I don't know who Michael is," she answered, still peering intently at the baby.

"He's Justin's father," Ben-Ben said, trying to rub his

paw on top of his head to knock the packet off.

"Who?" I asked.

"Pheromone boy," Ben-Ben replied.

"How do you know this?" I asked.

"Jess took me for a ride when she took Justin home one night. It was the best ride of my life; I found a bag of potato sticks stuck between the seat cushions...even had some of the red sauce the two-leggers call ketchup on it. Oh it was so delicious, even the bag it came in was good, tasted like grease."

"Can you get back to the Michael part?" I asked.

"Oh, okay," Ben-Ben said. I could see him trying to rip himself from the memory of eating the old french fries. "Jess and Justin were smelling each other faces."

"Kissing," Patches interrupted.

"Smelling faces," Ben-Ben repeated, looking scornfully at the cat. "Now I know why Riley growls at you. Then this man comes to the wheeler and he had whiskers like us, and he knocked on the clear viewer, told Justin that he needed help moving something. Justin rolled the clear viewer down and told him he'd be right there. Jess said 'Hi, Mr. Talbot,' and the whiskered man said 'Call me Michael,' then he reached behind Justin and petted my head, said I wasn't an English bulldog, but that I was cute anyway," Ben-Ben said with his tail wagging.

"You believe that?" Patches asked me. "You can't be considering it can you, this from the dog who chases his own tail because he doesn't know what it is!"

"Hey!" Ben-Ben shouted. "Who knows where that thing has been!" The food packet finally fell from his head and he tore into it like he had found a box of hamburgers, completely forgetting that he had been a part of the conversation. "Whether he's right or wrong, we don't know where this Michael is or how to tell Jess what we know," I told Patches, trying to take in all that was happening here now. "Zach, you know about your sires, right?" I asked cautiously.

"They're on the other side," he said sadly. "I miss them."

I wasn't sure about the exact meaning of his words, but he was conveying the right tone. "And they told you how to talk to us?"

Zach nodded.

"We should kick him out of the car," Patches said.

"Don't listen to her," I told Zach.

"I didn't even say anything," Ben-Ben's words were muffled, his face stuck in the packet.

"Interesting," I said.

CHAPTER TWO

"Vegas! They should have doctors here, right?" Jess asked. The excitement in her voice faded quickly. The wheeler moved past some other wheelers that had been burnt like some of the food Alpha-male used to cook. And not all of them were empty; dead two-leggers were in more than one of the wheelers.

"Whoa what is this place?" Ben-Ben asked, shaking the packet off his muzzle. "I don't like it," he said needlessly. None of us did.

"We should leave," I barked.

Jess jumped in her seat. "You don't like it here either, girl? I need to get help for Zach, though."

"Not going to happen here," Patches said, putting her paws on the side clear viewer. Her tail was eerily still as if she didn't want the evil of the place to see her.

"I see lights up ahead," Jess said, bringing the wheeler to a stop. "Maybe the next city will have a doctor." She began to turn the wheeler around.

"You have some nerve coming here, pig!" someone shouted off to our side.

"Someone say bacon?" Ben-Ben asked.

"You know what we do to cops here?" another voice asked.

"I'm not a cop," Jess said softly.

I started barking, the voices were threatening.

"It's a K-9 unit, I HATE dogs!" another voice said.

"That's why you keep losing your bets," the second voice said just as our wheeler was lit up with a fake burning disc.

Patches dived under her seat.

"I can't see anything, Riley!" Ben-Ben said, still staring into the light.

I had turned my head. "Stop looking, Ben-Ben."

"Oh...better. Many spots!" he answered.

"It ain't no cop, Creighton. It looks like a kid and some dogs, maybe a baby," the one who had shined the light on us said.

I think it was the one called Creighton that spoke next. "Alright, kid, I want you to come out of that car nice and slow. No funny business, no guns. You got me? And I see you thinking about trying to get out of here. There are at least five rifles pointed at you, we'll fill that car with bullets before you can go fifteen feet. Are you willing to take the chance we'll miss everyone with you?"

Jess was frantically looking around as if one of us might possess an answer to this problem. We all heard the familiar sound of multiple fire sticks being primed and readied for use.

"I'm not a very patient person," Creighton said. "Never was and now that I don't have to be to fit in, it's gotten worse. Get the FUCK out of the car NOW!" he screamed.

Jess was fumbling with the handle to the door, she stepped out.

"Well shit, it's just a girl," the fake sun operator said.

"Keep your fucking eyes on the car, dumbass," Creighton yelled. "Icely is going to want to see her. Who else is in the car?"

"Please, I just need a doctor for my brother, he's sick," Jess said.

The figure that had been approaching stopped and backed up a step. "Is he a zombie?" Creighton asked.

"What?" Jess asked and then answered when she realized what he was asking. "No, not a zombie, flu maybe."

"Have any of you been bitten?" Creighton asked.

"No," Jess told him.

"Then welcome to Vegas, you are now property of the Republic of Icely." And then he laughed a cruel laugh as he waved some more men towards our wheeler. They all had fire sticks pointed at us.

The one named Creighton had a small light pointing inside the car. "A baby and two dogs, although one of them isn't going to fair too well at the games."

"I love games," Ben-Ben yipped. "You think they're talking about fetch, Riley?"

I doubted it, but I didn't say anything. And how had they not seen the cat?

"You a good boy?" Creighton asked me through the clear viewer.

I bared my teeth at him. I would have bit him just for calling me a 'he.'

"Ooh, we got a live one. I might actually put a few bucks on you. Steve? Gonna need you to come over here with the collaring stick," he said to someone on the side of him.

Steve came over holding a pole with a loose noose of what looked like a tether hanging from it. I bared my teeth again, this time in fear.

The other side of the wheeler opened up and Ben-Ben hopped into the arms of a male two-legger on his side. *Stupid dog*, I thought.

The man shut the door before I could get out that way. And where would I go anyway? Zach was still in his seat, I couldn't leave him.

"Bad men," Zach said.

"You know that?" Even in my fear I was able to wonder at what more knowledge he possessed.

"Not too hard to figure out good or bad, I'm a baby, not stupid."

"Sorry, your talking is new to me."

"Babies know more than anyone realizes, they're just

not developed enough physically to express themselves either through body language or speech."

"I'll keep that in mind," I told him as the one they called Steve placed his hand on the door handle.

"You be a nice, fella, okay?" Steve said, trying to soothe me with his voice. Much like Zach said, it was not difficult to see the malice behind his words.

I started a rumbling growl deep in my chest. I bared my fangs and made sure that I had long lines of drool hanging from my mouth.

"What the fuck kind of dog is this?" Steve asked, looking around.

The one called Creighton came around. "Looks like some kind of Bulldog."

"Pit bull?" Steve asked, sweat coming from his brow. "He looks like he could rip my arm off and feed it to me."

He was nervous. I could smell it all over him, good.

"Hey, little girl, you calm your dog down or I'm going to put a bullet in his head," Creighton said, turning to Jess.

"No!" Jess said, running back towards the car. "I'll calm her down."

"Oh, she's a bitch, fitting." Creighton said. "You got a minute to put this collar around her, Icely doesn't like to wait."

I was still growling and barking at the men outside when Jess came in the door she had got out from.

"Riley," she said softly.

I turned to her, my fear and adrenaline still rushing through me. I turned to her still barking savagely, I wanted to lunge, I wanted to attack. We were in danger!

"Riley girl," Jess said softer.

"Shoot the fucker," Creighton said to Steve.

"I might hit the baby," Steve said.

"Yeah…and I give a shit," Creighton said.

"Wait!" Jess screamed. "I just need a minute, she's

scared. Just back up a little, give me the damn collar. I'll get her to come."

"Give me the keys," Creighton said, being careful not to stick his hand anywhere in the car. Jess handed him the janglers, Creighton took the collar device from Steve and handed that into the car. "You've got two minutes." And then he stepped back a few paces.

"Girl," Jess said.

My eyes were blazing, my ears were pulled back. "Need to fight!" I barked at her. I watched out the front viewer as the idiot Ben-Ben was running around and through the legs of our captors.

"Riley, they'll kill you, please come out with me. We have no choice. I'm so sorry I got us into this."

Water was flowing from her eyes. We were in trouble, and I knew getting shot with a metal bee was not going to help fix anything. I was trying to get my anger under control; the fear was going to be another thing. I was scared for myself, but it was the safety of the pack which affected me the most.

I turned to the baby.

"Live to fight another day," he said.

I pondered for a moment the wisdom of his words. "How can you know that?"

"Thirty seconds!" Creighton yelled.

"Riley, please," Jess said.

I turned back to face her and placed my head down as she wrapped the tether around my neck. "Come around front," she said as she positioned the pole so that I could get into the front and out.

Creighton pushed Steve to grab the pole as Jess stepped out with me in tow. Steve ran up quickly and grabbed the pole. He jerked it around, twisting the rope around my neck, I yelped from the pain of it.

"You're hurting her," Jess pleaded.

"Lucky the bitch isn't dead," Creighton said, coming

up and grabbing Jess by the arm. "Steve, put the mutt in the kennels. I'm taking her to see the boss."

I turned just enough to see someone reaching in and grab Zach before Steve pulled me forward. I bit down on the pole; it was a lot harder than the sticks I used to fetch for Alpha.

"This is a strong one," Steve said.

"Yeah, but she'll never beat Thorn," another man said.

"I'll take some of that action," another spoke up. They were all laughing and having a good time, but it was an evil fun to those who weren't on their side.

I ripped on the pole, pulling Steve to the side.

"Fuck me," he yelled.

It was just enough that I was able to see Patches slink away from the car while none of the two-leggers were paying attention.

"What about this little fuck?" one of the men asked of Ben-Ben who was following happily behind. "Should we just feed him to the others? No one would bet on this little rat dog."

Steve was sweating from the exertion of trying to rein me in, his speech was labored. "No, those little terriers can be ferocious. Maybe we can have some sort of small dog fight. If nothing else, it'd be fun to watch."

"Your call, boss."

"I'll take him if he's not too big a pain in the ass." Creighton replied. "Just drop him at my house, I've got to take the girl to Icely."

I could see where we were heading. They were like the small animal shelters that the two-leggers used to put Patches in when she would go see the animal doctor. Maybe a little bigger, but the one we were heading for, it didn't look like I'd even be able to stand.

"Vick, Matt, go grab the kennel keep it in place while I wrestle this fucking demon into it," Steve said.

I could tell he was getting tired, but we were close to what the two-leggers called a kennel. One of the two-leggers was close to the front of the kennel, and I was going to let him know what I thought of that, teeth first. The other one grabbed him by the arm, though.

"What are you, a fucking retard? Get back here with me."

The rope pulled tighter around my neck. I was having difficulty getting any air, and I was starting to see black spots in front of my eyes. The spots got bigger as Steve pushed me into the kennel. I stopped fighting as my eyes began to close, my tongue hanging out.

"Not so fucking bad now, are you!" Steve screamed at me as he released the rope and slammed the door shut.

I had some small amount of satisfaction as I lunged up against the door and he stepped back.

"Stupid mutt," he said as he wiped his brow and walked away.

I was right. I could not stand in the small enclosure…or even turn around for that matter. Right now, that was alright, I was exhausted. I could not see Ben-Ben, Jess, or Zachary; the cat I did not figure I would ever see again. My neck had just stopped hurting, and my breathing was not as labored when a couple of different two-leggers stopped in a bigger wheeler. They came and grabbed my kennel and threw it in the open back of the machine. They didn't say anything, and I was too tired to bark at them. When we stopped, one of the men pulled my kennel out of the wheeler and let it slam to the ground. My whole body jolted as I hit the hard ground.

Once the pain subsided, I realized that I was next to way more than seven other dogs. They were all in different sized kennels like I was. I caught all sorts of snippets of conversation, ranging from 'I'm hungry,' to mostly 'I'm scared'; though some were threats about tearing another's throat out. I shivered from the savagery of the words. I slept.

It was long moments later, and the burning disc was coming back up. My throat hurt so badly; I just wanted some water and to be able to stretch my legs. They hurt so bad, not being able to stand was worse torture than the time Alpha-male had made me get in the indoor water holder. He had said I was dirty and that I needed a bath. I had let him know in no uncertain terms what I had thought of that! And right now that memory sounded like bliss.

I could hear dogs on the other side of whatever building I was in beginning to howl. After a while I saw the reason why. The two two-leggers that had brought me here were giving food and water to us. One was carrying a stick that had blue electric sparks shooting out from the end, the other had the bowls. I almost cried when they finally got to my kennel.

"You gonna be a good girl?" the one with the stick asked. "Otherwise I'm gonna shock your mangy hide."

The end of the stick pulsed in blue, didn't need to be as smart as a poodle to figure out that stick was dangerous. I pushed as far away from the end of it as I could.

The other man opened my door and hurriedly pushed my food and water in, spilling most of the liquid onto the bottom of my container. I rushed ahead before he got the door shut, I almost got to feel what that stick felt like, but I had been going for the water not the man.

"Fuck that was close," the man said as he fell on his backside.

"Dip wad, the dog wasn't going for you, look," the other said, pointing to me as I lapped at the water on the floor.

They fed and watered the next two dogs and then left. I was just finishing up the water, which was not enough, when I turned to the food. It was meat and I almost tore into it before I realized what it was.

"Hey, hey, new dog!" the brown dog next to me was shouting out. "You going to eat that? Because I will."

I wasn't EVER going to eat it, but how he thought I was going to get it to him eluded me.

"Hey, new dog, I'm talking to you!" the brown dog said, his earlier disposition changing to aggression.

"What do you want?" I asked, fear growing in my gut.

"Well I want your food and then I want to rip your insides out through the hole I tear into your soft underbelly," he replied.

"Why?" I asked, most likely whining.

"It's what we do…we're fighting dogs. The humans cheer at us while we do it. Winners like me get to eat more of the losers like you."

Now I knew where my bowl of food had come from.

The brown and black dog was laughing at me. "I'm going to be eating you later. I hope you taste better than you look."

My bowels seized up, my legs were cramping. I was hungry, thirsty, and scared. I buried my head under my paws trying to drown out the misery around me. I could hear the mean dog possibly yelling at me, or maybe somebody else, but I didn't care. I don't know how long I was like that. I had given up thinking I was ever going to get out of there.

The burning disc was almost out of sight when the big wheeler came back. They grabbed the brown and black dog and then grabbed me. We were next to each other, separated only by our kennels.

"Your humans aren't going to save you," the dog said to me. "Maybe I'll just eat you after I kill you, I like my meat warm."

"Why would you do this?" I asked him.

"Because the humans want me to, and they like it."

And he seemed happy with that answer. He never stopped looking at me the entire ride. Our kennels were dropped into a big pit made with hard, white ground; there was a small wall around the whole thing, I thought I could jump it, but everywhere I looked there were two-leggers…and most had fire sticks. The brown and black dog was put down on the far side of the pit. My crate was dropped hard, my head bounced first off the bottom of the kennel then the top.

He was being held at bay as one of the two-leggers who had given me water had his hand wrapped around the dog's collar.

"I'm going to kill you!" the dog was barking, his front legs lifting off the ground, the human struggling to hold onto him.

"Thorn! Calm down!" the man shouted.

The other two-legger quickly unlatched my door and ran towards the wall. When he realized I wasn't coming out of my kennel he came back and lifted the back of it so I fell out like biscuits from a box. Gruff laughter came from the humans all around me.

"Look at that dog!" someone shouted. "He ain't gonna fight! I want to put twenty bucks on Thorn!"

My face was dirty from scraping against the ground, my legs hurt as I tried to stand on them. I fell over when I realized I couldn't even feel them.

"Make that a hundred on Thorn!" the man shouted.

My legs felt like I was at the animal doctor and he was sticking many, many stingers into me. I used my face to push myself back up, wobbled on my legs, and took a couple of tentative steps. I almost fell over again but was able to stay up.

A loud voice came over the entire crowd, warning them that they only had two more minutes to place bets, whatever that meant. I circled around, looking for Jess, Zach, or Ben-Ben—maybe even Patches, I was *that* scared. When I didn't see them, I tried to see if there was maybe a way out.

"Don't even think about it!" Thorn was shouting. "I'll rip your hind legs off before you can leave this circle."

"You ready, boy?" the two-legger asked as he rubbed

Thorn's side. "Go make me some money." He let go of the collar.

Thorn charged at me, almost at full speed before he was halfway across the circle. I had never 'fought' another dog before. I had postured plenty, barked even more, but never anything like this. I was scared.

"Throat or belly? Throat or belly?" Thorn was asking himself as he pulled closer.

I was finally able to start feeling my legs. I was scared, but that didn't mean I wouldn't do what it took to survive. I lowered my whole body, the fur on my back bristling. I pulled back a snarl to let Thorn see exactly what he was charging into. I saw something in his eyes, but he was already committed. I sank lower.

"Look how scared that stupid dog is!" someone was shouting.

Thorn leaped when he was in range, so did I, but as he went high I surged low. I caught him in his mid-section like he had threatened to do to me. His forward momentum pulled him past me. My mouth was full of his fur, skin, and blood, I had ripped a piece of him clean off. He yelped loudly as he rolled into the dirt past me.

"Did you see that?" someone asked.

Another shouted. "Get up, you stupid fucking mutt, or I'm going to lose all my money! This shit is rigged!"

Thorn's breathing was labored, and he was in pain, but he wasn't out of the fight. I warily moved in closer, circling his form. He matched me movement for movement.

"It doesn't have to be like this," I told him.

"You bit me!" he barked.

"Oh, I didn't just bite you, I tore a piece of you off," I snarled threateningly.

"The humans told me you would be an easy kill!" he was shouting.

"They lied," I said as I still circled him.

"They're not even fighting, I should get my money

back!" someone was complaining.

I watched Thorn's back legs. He was compressing them, getting ready to spring. He launched, I moved to the side as his saliva-coated teeth and mouth slid past. I turned my head slightly and caught him mid-flight, my fangs sinking deeply into his soft throat.

"No!" he whispered as air from his shredded throat rippled around my maw.

His legs were scrabbling. He was a big dog, and I thought he might be able to pull free; so I began to shake my head back and forth, sinking my teeth even deeper almost to the point where they were touching. The tighter I squeezed the less he moved. His tongue rolled out of his mouth and he was still when I opened my jaws and let him fall to the ground.

I noticed for the first time that all of the humans around me were quiet. And then a small applause broke out, but that was overshadowed by the groans of those that had lost money.

"That bitch killed my Thorn!" the two-legger said as he approached, fire stick in hand.

The same extra-loud voice sounded again. It seemed to come from everywhere, "Stop, Isaac, the dog won fair and square."

"But!" Isaac started.

"Bring the dog back to the holding pen and give her some more water. If anything happens to her on the ride back, you'll be in this ring next."

Isaac looked as mad as She-alpha did when I had torn a very small piece out of her couch. I didn't know why she was so upset, you could barely even see it.

"Get in the fucking kennel!" Isaac shouted at me, threatening me with his metal bee sender.

I started walking away from my kennel, not exactly towards the man…but not away either. I could smell the fear pouring off of him. I wanted to hurt him and that scared me, too, I had never wanted to hurt a two-legger before—not a living one anyway.

"Not going to tell you again, mutt! Get in your kennel!" he shouted.

I kept walking until finally I was past him, not going too close. He might be afraid of me, but that didn't mean he couldn't hurt me, and I needed to stay strong so that I could get the others out of here.

"Brent, she isn't getting into her kennel. She needs to be put down," Isaac shouted to the voice.

Then the voice overhead laughed. "Oh, she's getting into her kennel alright, her new kennel!" The crowd roared as I walked into the much bigger crate. I could stand and turn; there was even a small fake fur I could use as a bed.

"That's Thorn's!" Isaac shouted.

"He's not going to need it anymore," the overhead voice said.

My heart was pounding, but I laid down trying to make the two-leggers believe that I was calm. I don't know why that seemed important at the time, but it did. Isaac rushed over and closed the door with the end of the fire stick then placed his foot against it before reaching down with his front paw and locking it.

He jerked the crate into the air with a grunt, rocking me back and forth.

"Treat her right," the voice said. "That comes from Icely himself.

"Wade, help me with this stupid mutt," Isaac said to the other man that was at the dog pen place.

I was back in the wheeler and then back in the small building with the rest of the dogs.

"The bitch beat Thorn," One of the dogs said, sounding surprised.

Isaac came back a few moments later carrying two bowls. "Here you go, fucker! I don't care what Icely says, you bite me, and I'll kill you. What do you think of that?" He was shouting and spittle was flying from his mouth.

I laid my head down in indifference.

"No meat for you! I will never give you a piece of Thorn!" he shouted as he pushed in the bowls. Thankfully not much water spilled as he slammed the door shut. He stared at me a few more moments through the opening on the side. I shut my eyes and pretended to go to sleep. When he finally left, I drank the water greedily and then sniffed at my food; thankfully, it was the dried cardboard ball bits that the two-leggers called dog food…and it was delicious.

CHAPTER THREE

It was late and dark, almost all of the other dogs had quieted down; some whimpered in their sleep, others that had been wounded in battle groaned. I listened to it all feeling strangely calm after killing one of my own kind. I did not ever want to have to do it again, but I was glad Thorn had died and not me. I was on the verge of seeing the 'in my mind pictures', hopefully it would be happy times with Jess on the swing and me chasing her feet back and forth and not the newer ones that I'd been having more and more of where the zombies were chasing us and none of us could outrun them—even me with my four legs—when I was startled awake.

"You okay?" Patches asked, coming up silently to the side of the kennel.

Had I drank more water I most certainly would have released some…and not on purpose.

"I thought you left?" I asked harshly, still trying to get the fear out of my heart.

"You know me not at all," Patches said as she looked at the door.

I wanted to yell at her that I knew her more than she thought, but I guess I really didn't. She could have easily left all of us behind, nobody saw her and nobody realized she was missing. They wouldn't even go looking for her. "Why did you come back?"

"I never left," she told me as she walked around the entire kennel.

"You could have," I told her.

"Yes I could have, but just because I like to be left

alone, Riley, doesn't mean I want to be alone. Does that make sense in that dog brain of yours?"

"It does, cat...I mean, Patches. And I'm sorry. I just fought another dog to the death and I am more stressed than I have ever been." As if to prove my point, my breathing became rapid just thinking about it. "Can you open the door?" I asked her, hoping.

"If I could I would have never gone to the animal doctor's."

"Do you know where everyone else is?" I asked.

"The stupid Ben-Ben is with the first human he met. The dumb dog is acting like the man is the king of the world. Jess and the cub that shouldn't be talking are at a house a little ways from here."

"How do you know all this?" I asked incredulously.

"It's easy to get around when the dog fights are going on, almost all of the humans go to them. I'm sorry I did not try to get you out of here earlier I did not know that you would fight so soon. But I have an idea now."

I thanked the cat for her concern and then listened as she explained what she wanted me to do. I wasn't sure if it would work, the humans seemed like a pretty smart species, but I was willing to try anything right now if it even possibly might get me out of this kennel and back with my pack.

Patches hid behind my kennel just as I started the most pitiful whining I had ever uttered. Even Ben-Ben would have been ashamed of me if he could hear me now. It wasn't long before other dogs around me began to bark at my 'suffering'. Within a small passage of time, what was once a nearly quiet building had erupted into noise.

A light much smaller than the burning disc came on overhead, the two-legger that was not Isaac—Wade I think was what he was called—came through the door. He was rubbing his eyes, much like what I had seen Alpha do when Ben-Ben would wake him up with his incessant fear barking.

"Shut up in here will you!" he shouted.

That did little more than get the dogs barking louder. I had to whine louder to be heard over them. The two-legger shouted something again about us being stupid animals, and all I could think was that I'd never seen dogs assemble and fight each other like the two-leggers seemed to always want to do.

I thought all my whining was not going to work, and that he was going to go back to bed, when maybe he heard me and started walking down the kennels to see what the matter was. The closer he got the more pathetic I tried to sound.

"Laying it on a little thick aren't you?" Patches asked from behind me.

I just kept whimpering, whining, and moaning.

"Oh crap," Wade said as he ran his hand through his small head coat. "What's the matter, girl?" he asked through the bars. "If something happens to you, Icely is going to think Isaac did it, and then we'll both be in big trouble. Shit, shit, shit. I'd better get Isaac."

I moaned louder, even making sure that some drool was coming out of my mouth.

"Did you eat something poisonous? You're foaming at the mouth," Wade said as he quickly opened up my kennel. He pulled me out by my collar. I stayed limp. He opened up my mouth looking for something I may have eaten.

"Now, dog!" Patches shouted.

"A cat?" Wade asked looking up as Patches jumped up onto my kennel. The dogs that saw her began to go crazy. "What's happening?"

"NOW, Riley! You have no choice!" Patches said as she kept eye contact with the man.

"I've never..." This time I truly whined.

Wade looked down at me, I lunged, and within the beat of a humming bird's heart, a spark of recognition dawned in his eyes as I flew into his face. My bottom teeth caught him under the chin and sank in, coppery tasting blood flooded into my mouth as I tore into him. He attempted to pull away from me and scream. My top teeth latched onto the top of his mouth and clamped it shut. I could feel his skin tearing away as he tried to stand. I bit down harder, about as hard as I could. Water was spilling from his eyes. His arms and hands came up and wrapped around my muzzle. He wanted to pull me away, but he couldn't, not with me attached like I was.

"His throat, Riley, his throat," Patches said.

I knew that, I just had to be able to let go of the man's face and get to his throat before he did something to hurt me or get away. The man's eyes were wide; the smell of fear was as dominant as was the urine he was spilling. I released my jaws, Wade fell backwards striking his head on the hard ground. He was holding his hands to the wounds on his face, rolling back and forth. His legs were scrabbling as he tried to run on the ground.

"Ucking mutt," he mumbled.

"Riley, he'll get help."

"I know, cat, I know!" I said with distress. Killing the dead two-leggers to protect my pack was one thing, but to kill a live two-legger did not feel right.

"I'll ucking kill you," Wade said with one hand holding onto his ripped lip. Blood was pouring through his fingers. He was sitting up now, his hand was reaching for a heavy looking tool; I think the humans called a monkey wrench. But I'd never seen one of those funny looking little animals ever use one.

I lowered myself down and approached slowly, my head almost level with my shoulders as I got close. A deep growl ripping through my mouth, my teeth pulled back coated in the slick blood of my victim, him.

Wade's eyes went from anger back to fear. "Wait, wait, good dog," he said, placing one of his hands up.

I had never understood the gesture from the humans.

It had never worked when Alpha-female put it up to stop myself and Ben-Ben from running on her wet floors, and it certainly wasn't going to work now. I ran past his outstretched hand, he turned his head trying to get his hand on the heavy tool. I bit deeply into his throat, more coppery blood shot into my mouth than the previous time. Blood was flying out from his body in great spurts.

His top lip fell to the side as the hand holding it let go. He reached for the wrench. I released his throat as he swung the heavy piece trying to crash it against my skull. He kept swinging his arm back and forth, maybe hoping I would run back into it. He pressed his free hand against the hole in his neck. When he stopped swinging the wrench, he used it to help him get up on his legs.

"Riley, you can't let him go," Patches said as she came up beside me, her tail swishing violently back and forth.

My jaw was pulled back in a snarl, but it was more from being sick of the entire encounter. Blood was cascading down the man's arm leaving a trail even Ben-Ben could have tracked. The man was starting to sway; he was losing too much vital fluid. The other dogs were absolutely howling now, anyone close was going to come and see what was happening.

"He killed a human."

"Is that possible?"

"I smell blood."

"What do you think they taste like?" another asked.

"Riley." Patches prodded gently. She knew I was having a hard time with this, but I had to think of Zach and Jess and even Ben-Ben now.

The man was stumbling towards the door, a strange strangled gurgling noise issuing forth from his mouth. He was trying to call for help, but the blood loss was too much and was clogging his airway. I was hoping that the vital fluid would leak out and he would just die, but it did not appear that was going to happen fast enough. He was possibly less than seven steps from the doorway when I ran after him. He turned once to look when he heard me coming, and it looked like he was going to try and move faster. I didn't give him the chance.

I bit down on the small rubbery feeling piece above the man's ankle. He fell face first; bits of his teeth broke free as his face smashed into the hard ground, and then thankfully he was still. Blood still pumped from his throat, but it was not coming out as fast as it had been. I was breathing heavy even as I watched the man take his final breaths.

"Wade! What the fuck is going on in there!" the other man yelled. He was approaching. I stopped watching the spread of red and turned around to Patches.

"Come on!" she said in alarm. "I know another way out."

"Am I going to fit?" I asked as I started to follow her. That cat could get into some pretty tight places. I should know...I'd gotten my head stuck in more than a few of them when I'd chased her. She jumped onto a cabinet in the corner and then through an open viewer that I thought I just might be able to get through or I would die trying.

"Holy shit! Wade? Fucking zombies!" Isaac screamed as he ran out of the large building.

Where are they? I thought as I jumped onto the small cabinet and then wrapped my front paws onto the front of the outside viewer. I pulled myself up as I put my head through. I was looking down to the ground which seemed pretty far away.

"Come on, dog, I'll catch you," Patches said, looking up at me.

I was so scared I nearly believed her as I jumped through the viewer, the ground thankfully was the soft kind and not the stuff the two-leggers put down and called ground.

"I thought you were going to catch me?" I asked Patches as I stood, making sure nothing had been hurt.

"I lied, get used to it," she told me. "Come on, when the humans realize that wasn't a zombie attack they're going to kill every dog they see."

"I don't like the sound of that."

We were hiding in the shadows of a house when a loud sound went off, it sounded like what the humans called a fire alarm, I knew the sound from when Alpha-male sometimes cooked. I couldn't get out of the house fast enough as great big billowing clouds of smoke would pour through the house. She-alpha would laugh and they would go out to eat, many times bringing back what they called 'doggie bags' although I very rarely got to eat them, so I never figured out why they called them that.

CHAPTER FOUR

Ten heavily armed men entered the kennels; they were a part of Icely's elite guard. Most of them were either prior military or had been actively serving when the zombie apocalypse started. A few were part of SWAT teams in Vegas, their leader was a vice cop from Miami. He had been on vacation when he found himself cut off completely from all he had known. It had not been that great a loss, his wife had left him three years previous and his mother—his only remaining relative—had been locked up in an old age home. Last time he'd seen her she hadn't known who he was and then proceeded to squat right in front of him as she loosed her bowels. For a moment he thought he caught a flash of recognition as she stood, then she had begun to cackle wildly. Detective Schools had decided to leave before she began the feces tossing portion of her routine.

The other nine men on his team fanned out as he carefully leaned down over the body.

"Clear," his second in command yelled. He spoke softly into a portable radio. "Zombies, boss?" Mannie asked.

"Not even close," Schools said. He looked at the wound on the man's leg, then he flipped the body over, not concerned with disturbing the crime scene. He studied the wounds on the man's face and neck.

"We got infiltration?" Mannie asked, preparing to talk into his radio again; this time about to get the whole settlement on high alert.

"Dog," Schools said as he began to cross the floor towards the open window.

"What?" Mannie asked, following his boss.

"A dog killed Wade," Schools answered.

"Are you fucking kidding me?" Mannie asked, looking back to the still form of Wade.

Schools walked over to the cabinet, he moved it out of the way and stuck his head through the window, but the dog was long gone.

"How?" Mannie asked.

"Well for some reason it looks like Wade opened that kennel and the dog that was in it decided he wanted out. Bit Wade's face first, damn near ripped his jaw off. Then he went in for the kill and tore through the poor bastard's carotid artery. And then Wade must have still been able to somehow stumble away when the dog figured out he hadn't finished the job. He hamstrung him by tearing his Achilles tendon in half. This is one efficient killing machine."

"Holy shit," Mannie said, rubbing his throat.

"Get Isaac in here." Schools sat down on the cabinet.

Isaac was escorted in a few moments later. He was looking around wildly, possibly for zombies to come flooding out from their hiding spots.

"Relax," Schools said as he watched the nervous man. "There aren't any zombies," he said as he stood and walked back over towards Wade's body.

"You...you're sure?" Isaac asked, temerity still lined his voice.

"What kind of dog was in that kennel?" Schools asked, pointing back to the only empty one in the warehouse.

Isaac's eyes opened wide at first, taking in the detail he had missed earlier, and then quickly narrowed as he perceptively put the pieces together.

"Damn dog, I knew I should have put her down," he said angrily, his teeth grinding as he spoke. "Bitch killed my Thorn."

Schools was not a fan of the dog fights and never watched. On occasion he would stay on the outskirts of the crowd, if only to keep the peace, but even that was too close for his liking. He knew why Icely allowed the sport; it kept the growing populace's blood lust at bay. The people that had survived the apocalypse thus far were usually the loners, the preppers, the über-mililtary types. These were not a broad sampling spectrum of the human population before the zombies came. For the most part, the survivors were the fringes, the outcasts of the previous society. They did not play well with others, and it was all Icely could do to keep them together as a cohesive unit. The people here were like over-dry kindling, and it would not take much more than a spark to set the illusion of community ablaze.

"Thorn? He was that huge Rottweiler right?" Schools asked.

Isaac nodded.

"What kind of dog are we talking about?" Schools was interested. He was trying to figure out what could have taken down the beast that seemed to have been part bear.

"Boxer, I guess," Isaac replied. "Short snouted little bitch!" he spat.

"You guess or you know?" Schools asked for clarification.

"How the fuck would I know? I'm not a damn vet."

"You do know who you're talking to, right?" Schools said, asserting his authority.

"I'm sorry, man, I loved that dog."

Yet you sent him to fight to the death almost every night, Schools thought. *Glad you don't love me*, he completed in his head.

"Boxer's are kind of spindly, fawn colored with a short black muzzle," Schools said.

"Naw, this mutt had the short muzzle but was brindle colored…thick chested."

"How tall?"

"About up to here," Isaac said, holding his hand about midway on his thigh.

"Sounds more like an American Bulldog."

"I don't give a fuck, I want in on the hunting party. I want to catch that thing, shoot it, hang it upside down, gut and skin it, and then I'm going to use its fur for a throw rug where I can wipe my dirty-ass boots every day until it falls apart."

"You done?" Schools asked of the other man's tirade. Isaac nodded.

"Alright then, you tell Icely what's going on here, and then you're in on the hunt."

"You want me to tell Icely what happened?" Isaac gulped.

"Yeah this building is under your supervision...right?"

"Yes," Isaac answered reluctantly, "but I didn't let that thing out of its kennel," he said, trying to deflect the blame. "That idiot Wade did, and it got him killed."

"I don't care if the dog somehow let herself out, go tell Icely we don't have zombies, and do let him know we have a man-killing dog loose. And before I forget, shut the damn alarm off."

Isaac looked liked a shady mob accountant heading into an IRS audit.

Schools told his team what they were looking for; the order was to shoot on sight if the opportunity presented itself. He figured it would never come to that, though. The dog was probably long gone. Any dog that valued survival enough to kill a man had reverted back to its wolf heritage and was even now attempting to make as much distance from the settlement as possible.

Mark Tufo

CHAPTER FIVE

The fire alarm had finally stopped. My ears still hurt from the noise of them. What I wouldn't do to curl up on She-alpha's lap and fall asleep. My throat hurt, and I wanted to stop for some water, but Patches kept pressing on.

"How much further?" I asked.

"Riley, I'm running to save your life. The humans are not going to shoot their metal bees at me. And what are you complaining about? Your legs are longer than mine."

I didn't see what the length of legs had to do with anything, but the cat said it, so it was probably right—or she was lying. But then I didn't understand the lie either, so what was the point?

Patches stopped by a row of hedges as a wheeler full of men rode past. "That was close," she said as she dashed across the street. "Come on that's the house."

I followed her; another wheeler drove past soon after.

"I think they're already looking for you," Patches said.

"Cat, I'm scared," I told her. I didn't want the two-leggers 'looking' for me. They meant me harm after I had killed one of their own. The most trouble I'd ever been in had been when I'd torn through the Alphas' garbage for a perfectly good turkey carcass, and even then, Alpha had merely laughed at me as he picked up the spilled contents of the bag. She-alpha had been madder because I got everything all over her fake fur flooring, but even she laughed as I chased and barked at the small loud pushing machine she used to 'pick' stuff up. I didn't trust that thing she called a 'vacuum'. I was protecting her from it as it followed her around the house, always one step away.

"We'll get out of here, Riley."

"I wish you were a dog, cat," I said to Patches.

She tilted her head in a questioning expression.

"It would be so much easier to say thank you if you were a dog," I told her.

"I think that's a compliment, and coming from you that's good enough. Let's get Ben-Ben," she answered.

"What about Jess and Zach?" I asked her.

"The humans will realize they're missing and come after them sooner. The person that has Ben-Ben is probably wishing he'd leave."

I snorted in laughter. Patches was a good ally to have, she was smart. It really was just too bad that she was a cat. We came up to a small two-legger home.

"He's in there," Patches said, looking at the house. She turned to keep an eye out on the wheeler path.

I stood up on my hind legs, my front paws were up against the viewer, I couldn't believe what I was seeing as I looked in.

"We need to leave Ben-Ben here," I said as I hopped down.

"Is he hurt?" Patches asked, turning her head just enough to look at me.

"Worse," I told her as I began to move away.

"I'm sorry for your loss," Patches said as she began to follow.

It was then we both stopped when we heard the fast staccato burst of Ben-Ben's yipping.

"Riley - Riley - Riley - Riley - Riley - Riley!"

"I thought you said he was dead," Patches asked, looking up at the window as Ben-Ben was jumping up and down.

"*You* said he was dead. He was doing tricks for the two-leggers for cookies," I answered her.

"You can't leave him, look at that face," Patches said

as her head went up and down watching Ben-Ben while he tried to get a view outside, by jumping up and down.

"He's an idiot. We're fighting for our lives...we have no idea how Jess and Zach are doing, and he's amusing the two-leggers for snacks," I said hotly.

"He's doing what he needs to do to survive. Do you think he could have won a dog fight?" Patches asked.

Before the night the zombies came I would have said 'no way' but I saw how ferociously he fought. And he had nothing but our pack's safety in his heart as he did so.

"Besides...he's your friend," Patches added before I could rethink my stance.

"Biscuits," I said. "You're right."

"Of course I am, dog, the sooner you realize that the better off you'll be."

I got closer to the window.

"Riley - Riley - Riley - Riley - Riley!" He was yipping crazily. "They have no bacon," he said softly and with a noticeable hint of sadness.

"Come out here," I told him as quietly as I could.

"I don't know how to open a door," he said, looking down at me.

"Scratch at it like you have to relieve yourself. The two-leggers know what that means and they'll open it for you."

"I already went," Ben-Ben whined.

"You went in the house again, didn't you," I accused him.

He looked down and whined.

"Two-legger - two-legger - two-legger!" he yipped.

At first I had no idea what he was barking about. "Hide, cat!" I said in alarm.

The light coming through the viewer was blocked as a male two-legger was looking out. "Whatcha see, boy?" the male asked as he kept peering out.

"There ain't nothing out there, Creighton!" another

male yelled. "Come on, man, it's your bid."

"You shut up now, dog, you hear?" the male said to Ben-Ben. "Come on."

The man and Ben-Ben left the viewer.

"What'd he say? Is he going to come out?" Patches asked, getting up from her hiding spot.

"Says he already relieved himself."

"Inside?" she asked. I nodded. "What is wrong with that dog? He's dumb even for a canine."

"Watch it," I told her.

She knew I was playing. "We can't wait forever. Once it's light out, we need to be out of this place. We may have to leave him."

I nodded in agreement, even though now I had decided I wanted the dumb dog with me. Our pack was already too small; we couldn't afford another loss. Although that wasn't all of it, I cared for the mangy little guy. Too many feelings, I didn't have the time to sort them out now; sometimes it was still difficult to realize I wasn't trying to eat the cat.

"Riley?" Patches asked as I was trying to figure things out.

"I know. Let's go get Jess and Zach."

"Again, I'm sorry for your loss," Patches said as we began to move away from the house.

"I noticed you said 'your' loss," I said, looking for Patches to elaborate.

"You're kidding, right?" she asked back. "Jess had a hamster once that I was closer to, and I had wanted to eat that rodent."

I snorted again. "Goodbye, Ben-Ben," I said. I would mourn his loss later.

We were four or five of the human dwellings away from Ben-Ben's new home when I heard his yipping.

Patches stopped and put her paw to her face; it was a very human like gesture.

"He's like sticky kitty litter you can't get off the bottom of your paws," Patches said sadly.

"The dummy is going to give us away." I was torn between running to get him and shut him up, or run and get away from him. But the dog would probably get lucky and follow us, yipping the whole way.

Patches must have been thinking the same thing when she asked her question. "Can he follow our scent?"

"Only if we were covered in bacon, and maybe not even then."

This time the cat snorted. "Go hide, Riley. I'll go get the pain in the behind."

And there it was, I still didn't completely trust the cat to do what she said even though she'd already saved my life a couple of times over. Old habits die hard. "Bite him once for me," I told her as I got underneath a large wheeler.

Some time passed before Ben-Ben's yipping finally ceased, and to Patches' credit I actually did hear him yelp. I could see pictures in my mind of Patches sneaking up behind the small dog and biting his tail, probably sent him running! The funny thought was a happy reprieve from the stress I was feeling. My legs were starting to cramp as I waited for the two to come back. It was taking so long that I was getting certain something had happened. It was possible that the male two-legger had taken Ben-Ben out with a tether, and if that was the case, there would be nothing Patches could do.

I could, though. The thought scared me, but there it was. I had killed a two-legger, and I would do it again for my pack. I started to ease out from under the truck. I banged my head on the bottom of the wheeler when the cat spoke.

"Where you going?" she asked.

"Riley - Riley - Riley!" Ben-Ben yipped.

"Dog!" Cat hissed loudly.

"Riley - Riley – Riley," Ben-Ben whispered.

I was mad at the dog, but it was impossible to stay that way, his enthusiasm was infectious.

"You alright?" I asked as I got out and stretched my legs.

"I only got twenty-seven cookies twelve bowls of food and no bacon," he said as he licked my muzzle.

"Does he really know numbers?" I asked Patches. She shook her head from side to side.

"How are you?" Ben-Ben asked me when he realized that's something he should have asked earlier.

"I'm fine, Ben-Ben, it's good to see you, too."

"So no bacon for you either then?" he asked sadly, his head dropping a little.

"How did you get out of the two-legger dwelling?" I asked him, trying to steer him away from talking about food. My stomach hurt from the pain of it, and I'm sure the large amount of blood I had swishing around down there wasn't all that good for me either.

"I went to the door and kept telling them that you and Patches were out there and that I needed to go outside so I could be with you guys. And that then we needed to go find Jess and Zach so that we could leave and go find Justin who was at the other side of the Great Move," he said excitedly.

Patches just kept shaking her head. "He's hopeless."

"Well it's the truth right?" Ben-Ben asked, his tongue lolling out.

"Did they have any other animals?" Patches asked.

"A bird, green and blue. It kept saying two-legger words."

"A parrot," Patches said, looking off into the distance, back the way she had come.

"You know about parrots?" I asked. I wasn't even sure what it was. I knew about birds, but for the most part they stayed out of my world and I out of theirs. I snorted again thinking about me up in the air.

"I ate one once." Patches answered my question. "It was mostly feathers, tasted bad, but it was going to tell the two-leggers I ate Jess' hamster.

"You ate Jess' hamster?" Ben-Ben asked. "I thought I killed it when I knocked its cage over and the water bottle cracked it on the head."

"You did. Jess' sires kept getting her new hamsters so she wouldn't know," Patches said. "Now that fat little hamster, *that* was a delicious morsel."

"Gross," I said. "Can we get out of here?"

"We'd better get going. Parrots are one of the few animals that can communicate with the two-leggers," Patches said.

"So the bird heard everything Ben-Ben was saying?" I asked.

Patches nodded.

"Come on, let's go," I said as I started to move.

"I only told the truth," Ben-Ben said, not understanding what he had done wrong.

Pretty much the way the dog always operated. With Ben-Ben it was a constant case of having to take the good with the bad. Sometimes the good far outweighed the bad, other times it got REALLY close. This might be one of those times where it got REALLY close. As if the two-leggers knew my thoughts, we could hear noise and a lot of it coming from where Ben-Ben had been enjoying his twenty-seven cookies.

"You heard that, too?" I asked Patches as she picked up the pace.

Ben-Ben turned to the sound. "Do you think they're going to the store to get some bacon?"

"Not likely. Move!" I told him as I nipped at his hind-quarters.

"Where is that fucking dog?" a two-legger shouted.

"Creighton, come on, man, don't tell me you really believe what the parrot had to say?" another male human spoke.

"I don't know. That was some weird shit. The bird said something about a great move. He's never said anything like that before," Creighton replied.

"It's a crazy bird—brain is the size of a peanut probably. Remember, man, the thing kept squawking that I was doing your old lady. And she hates me, who knows what's going through that pea brain."

"Yeah, my old lady really does hate you. I wonder why?"

Probably because I gave her a bad case of crabs, Lenny thought and then smacked his friend on the shoulder. "Come on, man, I'm down forty-two bucks. I want to see if I can get some of it back." *And then when you fall asleep I'm gonna kill that bird and then probably do your old lady again. It's the least I can do considering I've already lost enough money to you for future services.* He smiled the whole way back into the house. *Sometimes you win even when you lose.*

"They're not following," I told the group. I was hoping it would slow Patches up; she had a pretty good pace going. My fights had taken a lot out of me, I was sore and tired and hungry and Ben-Ben would not stop talking about bacon.

"Sunrise is in a few more hours. We need to get Jess and Zach before then," Patches said, not easing up on her loping run.

"Wheeler," I said, getting behind some garbage. Patches was a few feet ahead. She had gotten behind a big blue box that the two-leggers put pieces of folded paper into. I never knew why they spent so much time writing things on the paper only to throw them away. Just one of the many strange things the two-leggers did.

"What's Ben-Ben doing?" Patches asked.

I stuck my head up. He was just standing there, tongue hanging out, tail wagging expectantly as he waited for the wheeler to come into view.

"Get over here, dog!" I shouted over the approach of the big wheeler.

"Why?" Ben-Ben asked just as the truck came into view.

A large explosion issued from the fire stick one of the two-leggers had that was riding in the back; the metal bee sparked off the ground next to Ben-Ben's paw. Urine pooled around Ben-Ben's feet. He was frozen and couldn't move. The truck stopped right in front of him.

"You think that's the man-killer?" one of the humans asked.

"Yeah it rips out your ankle, dropping you to the ground, and then it eats each of your eyeballs, while you scream in agony for your momma," the man driving said.

"Really?" came the first man's voice.

"No, you stupid shit. That dog couldn't take a squirrel. And look, it pissed itself just looking at us."

"Should I kill it?" the first man asked.

"Icely's orders," the driver said.

"I wish it'd stop looking at me," the first said.

"Are you going to kill it or not? I'm getting sick of looking for a dog. You could kill this one and we could be done, tell everyone we thought this was it."

"Okay," the man in the back of the truck said.

"Biscuits," I growled.

"What are you doing?" Patches whispered to me. "You're going to get yourself killed," she said as she watched me getting into a lunging position. "Oh no way are you going to leave me with him," Patches said as she stepped out from behind the box. She meowed loudly.

"Hey, Hank, it's a cat," The man in the back of the truck said. "Should I kill it?"

"If you're going to do it, now's the time," Patches said as she brushed up against the leg of the box purring contentedly.

"It's just a fucking cat, kill the damn dog," Hank said.

I sprang up over the garbage and past Ben-Ben.

"What the fuck?" the driver said. The man in the back

of the truck still had his attention on Patches.

"What?" the man in the back asked the driver just as I sprang, my front paws catching the lip of the truck bed, my back paws gripping on to the wheel of the wheeler.

"Holy shit!" the man screamed as I dove into his body.

"Andy, you alright?" the driver asked through the viewer behind him. I was thankful he did not come out to help.

I had bit down savagely on Andy's arm and felt the bones shatter as I shook my head back and forth. He was begging for help. He had dropped his fire-stick and, with his good arm, he was trying to push me away. I let go of his arm and bit the hand that he had in my muzzle. I ripped three of his fingers off at the knuckle. His shrieks quickly became sobs.

"It's killing me!" he hitched. "Help me, Hank!"

"The driver has a gun, Riley! Get out of there!" Patches warned.

I had bit down on the side of the man's face when I turned to see the driver pointing a small fire-stick at me through the viewer, his hand was shaking. I let go of Andy and hopped down just as I heard the viewer shatter under the explosion from the metal bee. There were two more shots, but I was already running. Patches stuck a very large claw into Ben-Ben's behind to get him moving also.

"Oh fuck! I shot Andy," Hank said. "Andy, you alright?" Hank asked as I heard the door to the wheeler open up.

We were traveling fast. I did not hear Hank getting back into the truck, but it would have been impossible to not hear the fire alarm begin anew.

"Think that's for us?" Patches asked as we all were catching our breath behind a small human dwelling.

I had to look at her long and hard. "You're kidding, right?" She had asked it so seriously I wasn't sure.

"You'll catch on eventually." She smiled at me.

Ben-Ben kept stealing glances at me when he didn't think I could see him.

"What, Ben-Ben?" I asked when I caught him for maybe the seventh time, or it could have been the twelfth, but I didn't really know that number.

"Riley, you attacked a two-legger. You told me to NEVER bite a two-legger," Ben-Ben said.

"She saved your life, Ben-Ben," Patches said, interceding on my behalf.

"Saved my life from a two-legger? Why would they want to hurt me?" Ben-Ben asked, clearly confused.

"This is a bad place, Ben-Ben. They make dogs fight to the death here," I told him.

"You lie!" he shouted, standing up. "All two-leggers are like Santa and they give us food and sometimes bacon!"

"Ben-Ben, they took Jess and Zach, and we don't know if they're alright. I just fought another dog. I had to kill him because the humans wanted him to kill me. Not all humans are like our Alphas...or Santa for that matter."

Ben-Ben was still shaking his head. "I...I don't believe you, Riley."

"Stupid dog, what do you think that man in the back of that truck was doing?" Patches said angrily.

Ben-Ben was clearly confused. "I don't know," he said honestly.

"Well maybe if you weren't standing in your own urine you would have heard them talking about killing you," Patches shouted.

"I...I thought they were talking about something else," Ben-Ben said.

"They weren't, you dumb dog. We should have left you at that house," Patches said in huff, walking away.

I followed after Patches. I couldn't stand to be under the gaze of guilt from Ben-Ben any longer. I didn't hear him following for a few moments; I think he was considering going back to the house he was at.

"Do you think Jess and Zach are alright?" he asked, panting a little as he caught up.

"I hope so," I said tersely.

"This is it," Patches said as we stood on the outside of a fenced yard. The two-legger dwelling was the largest of any we had seen so far. "This is the home of the person that runs the town."

"Icely," I said off-handedly.

Patches looked at me, wondering I guess about how I knew. Patches fit easily through the fence. Ben-Ben would fit barely if he decided to go in at all. I'd be lucky if I could fit my head, and right now I really wasn't in the mood to try. The Alphas weren't there to laugh good-naturedly about it as they tenderly got me un-stuck.

"Patches," I said louder than I meant to. She was walking across the yard, and I guess just figured we were all behind her.

She stopped and turned, looking at me quizzically. "You're not going to fit," she said as if she had known all along. "We'll get her, you just be ready. Ben-Ben, you coming?"

"I won't bite a two-legger," he said—mostly to me.

"Fine, but I'm still going to need your help," Patches told him.

It was a little tighter for Ben-Ben to fit through than I thought, probably from all the bacon he'd been eating at Winke's and Fay's. I nudged him through harder than I probably had to. Patches outright laughed as Ben-Ben rolled backside over head. I turned so he couldn't see my expression.

CHAPTER SIX - The Previous Day

"What do you want?" the guard at the gate asked.

"Just tell Icely that Creighton has something for him," Creighton said as he looked out the window of his SUV.

The guard looked through the windshield and saw the wide eyes of the girl in the passenger seat. The guard waved them in as he opened the gate. "You wait in your car until I let him know. You got it?" he asked as he shut the gate behind them.

"It's me, Creighton, we're like best friends," Creighton replied to the man.

"Listen, I have my orders, you get out of that car, best friend or not and you're gonna get shot."

"Fine, fine, tell him I'm here," Creighton said in exasperation. "I'll wait like a good little boy in here."

The guard pointed to the man on the porch. "Hey, keep an eye on the smart ass here will you."

The man on the porch holding an assault rifle nodded.

"Why couldn't you just let us go?" Jess asked.

"First off, why would I? And secondly even if I had a conscience, which I don't, if I had let you go and Icely had found out, he would have hung me in the center of town by my neck," Creighton said as he wrapped his hands around his throat and stuck his tongue out, making strangled noises as he did so. He laughed at Jess' reaction. "Relax, I'm safe."

But I'm not, Jess thought.

"Icely says send her and the baby in," the original gate guard yelled from the porch.

Creighton began to get out.

"He said send them two, he didn't say anything about

you joining," the guard clarified.

"But I found her, I should be the one to present her," Creighton protested.

"Yeah, yeah, he thanks you for your gift. Now drop the girl off and screw!" the guard shouted.

Creighton hesitated for a moment, looking at the revolver on his hip.

"Don't do nothing stupid, man," the guard said. "Curly over there will cut your car in half before you can get that pea shooter out of its holster." As if to reiterate the point 'Curly' hefted his MP-4.

"Shit, this ain't right, man," Creighton said to the guard who merely shrugged. "Get out!" Creighton said to Jess, brimming with hostility. She started to cry. "I said get the fuck out!" he yelled as he leaned across her and opened the door. "Listen, you get out on your own, or I'm going to push your ass out and toss your brother after you."

"Why are you doing this?" she cried as she hefted a wide-eyed Zach onto her hip.

"Because I'm one of the bad ones."

Jess got out. Creighton laid a little rubber in Icely's driveway as he departed.

"Come on," the guard said almost tenderly as he motioned for Jess to come up the stairs. She moved as if she were a wooden marionette. When she finally stood before the man, he told her to put the baby down and raise her hands above her head. He frisked her, looking for weapons. When he was satisfied she had none, he told her to follow him. She scooped Zach up and clung tightly to him.

Jess noticed the two large opposite facing staircases. Her heart was thudding in her chest, but eased ever so slightly when she realized he wasn't bringing her up there.

"Come on, Icely wants to see you in his office," he told her as she hesitated.

"Am I going to be okay?" Jess asked.

The guard didn't respond as he knocked twice on a

large eight-paneled door. He waited a moment before entering. "Here she is, boss," the guard said as he lightly pushed her in the back and into the room. He shut the door and withdrew back to his previous post.

"Come in, come in," the man said as he rose from his seat, he was tall—NBA tall—not overly powerful looking, but he did possess a wiry strength. "The baby yours?" Icely asked.

Jess shook her head slightly looking around warily. "He's my brother."

"Parents dead?" Icely asked, although it sounded more like a statement than a question. "Of course they are. Why would you be out in this hot mess if they weren't? Did you have to kill them? Sorry, forget it. I've been around roughnecks so long I've forgotten how to act civilized. Please sit…have a glass of water."

Jess sat when she realized it wasn't so much a request as a demand. There was a set to his eyes that said he was very used to getting his own way.

"Can I see your brother?" Icely said as he stood, arms outstretched.

"Sis, please don't hand me over to him," Zach cried.

Jess gripped him a little harder.

"The baby, please," Icely said as his jaw clenched imperceptibly.

Jess reluctantly handed him over.

"I am SO going to remember this, Jess," Zach wailed.

Jess half rose to snatch him back, but Icely had already moved back on his side of the desk.

"Oh, he's a feisty one," Icely said as he held the crying baby high over his head.

"Please," Jess said as she stood.

"Relax. What kind of monster do you think I am?" Icely laughed.

Jess noted that Icely had not referred to himself as a man but rather a type of monster.

"I wouldn't hurt a baby...unless I had to," he said, looking at Jess. "You know they say these things are our future. I don't see it." He brought Zach face-to-face with him. "I think they're just smelly little wastes of time personally."

As if on cue Zach released everything he had been holding for the day. "How's that for smelly?" Zach gurgled.

"Oh, God," Icely gagged. "Take this thing from me." He held Zach out at arms' length.

Jess raced to grab him before Icely dropped him.

"Good boy," Jess whispered as she held him tight.

"I've prepared a room for you. There's adequate supplies for you and you brother, diapers, formula, all that crap. Now get that stink factory out of my office."

"Sir," Jess gulped, "when can we leave?"

"Leave? Why would you want to do that? Have I not been hospitable?"

"It's not that, it's just that we were trying to get somewhere," Jess stated.

"Well you're as far as you're going to get. You'll soon be one of my wives."

Jess' face blanched.

"Relax. If you're good to me, I'll be good to you...and your brother." He added the last part as an effective threat. "Go upstairs. Any of the women up there will help you. Get cleaned up and be ready for dinner in a few hours. Now go," Icely said as he sat back down.

If Jess had felt that she had walked woodenly going into the house, she was ill-prepared for her movement now; an I-beam had more flexibility than she did as she made her way up the staircase. When she made it the top, she was drawn to a room where she heard muffled conversations. She looked into a large sitting room where at least a dozen women were—some younger than her couldn't even be qualified to be called that just yet—most older than her. Some had vacant eyes as they stared off into the distance, others talked animatedly with the person next to them.

"A baby!" a smallish woman of Asian decent said as she ran over to Jess and Zach. "Oooh, a baby in need of a changing!" she laughed. "Come on, honey, let's get him cleaned up."

Jess allowed herself to be led by the arm. Most of the women present did not acknowledge her presence as she passed.

"Thank you..."

"Mia, my name is Mia." The woman led Jess to her new room.

"I'm Jess. What is this place?" Jess placed Zach down on a changing table.

"I'm sure you met Icely, right?" Mia asked as she cooed at Zach.

"I like her," Zach purled, small bubbles of spit forming through his lips.

Jess nodded to Mia's question.

"We are his wives." Mia pulled off Zach's diaper. "Oooh, you're a smelly little thing," she said as she tickled Zach's belly. She placed the offending diaper into a disposal canister set-up just for that purpose.

"All of you are his wives?" Jess asked incredulously.

"And so will you be," Mia said as she cleaned Zach up.

"But I'm not ready to be married…and certainly not to him." Jess panicked.

"Shhh, sweetheart, I know this isn't the ideal position to be in, but don't ever let Icely hear you talk like that or even some of these women. They'll throw you under the bus to curry favor with him. His 'favorites' get more privileges."

"I've got to get Zach and myself out of here, Mia. There's somewhere I need to be."

"You're here now, Jess. There is no leaving…not alive anyway. That man downstairs cares little for the lives of those around him in so much and only as far as he can control them. Marry him, let him feed you and take care of your baby."

"Brother."

"When your turn comes up, just moan at the appropriate times and think of happier times."

"What? My turn? As in sex?" Jess was now in full on panic mode. "Mia, I can't!"

"You'll get used to it."

"I saw some of the looks on those girls in there. Did they get used to it, too?"

"The world isn't what it used to be. A lot of them watched as their families were ripped apart. Icely is an asshole, but he's not cruel, at least unless you cross him," she said as she shuddered.

Mia made a blowing sound on Zach's stomach. He cooed as she did so. "He's adorable," she said as she put some powder on his butt and placed a new diaper on him.

"She's a keeper!" Zach bellowed.

"Thank you," Jess said as she picked him up. "You hungry, Zach?"

"Always!" Zach said reaching for her breasts.

"I'll feed him," Mia said. "You look exhausted. Get some sleep."

Jess looked at Mia.

"I'll stay in here with you while you sleep. Zach and I will get along fabulously! He reminds me of my kids."

"Kids?" Jess asked. "You don't look much older than me."

"Flattery will get you everywhere. I'm twenty-four, not *my* kids. I used to run a daycare center in Flagstaff. I was out here at a daycare convention of all things when the zombies came. Crock of shit that is, a daycare convention in Vegas, just a way for all of us to get away from the little rug rats for a few days. Thing is, I always wanted to be around them. Babies are always honest. They let you know when they're cranky, when they're hungry, happy, sleepy, or stinky," she said as she tickled Zach. "If only adults were as open as babies, the world would have been a better place."

"You don't mind?" Jess asked as she stifled a yawn. She sat down on the edge of the bed. She had barely heard Mia's response as her head hit the pillow and she drifted off to a better realm.

"Come on, Chubba Bubba, I'm going to heat you some food up."

Zach was staring at her breasts "What's wrong with those?" he asked, reaching for them.

"Typical boy, aren't you," Mia said as she grabbed some formula and a bottle. She quietly shut the door to Jess' room and headed downstairs. She was startled when she saw Icely waiting at the bottom for her.

"I see you've met my newest," he said coolly. "What do you think?"

"She's a sweet girl," Mia said guardedly.

"But?" Icely prodded.

"It's not my place to question you."

"If only all women understood it like you, Mia," Icely said as he began to stride away. "You're up tonight."

"Yay me." Mia said sarcastically—and very, very quietly.

"Hungry!" Zach told Mia in no uncertain terms.

She looked down at the cherub face. "Sorry, *mi amore*." She smiled.

CHAPTER SEVEN - The Following Day - Early Morning

I paced back and forth along the gate as I watched Patches and Ben-Ben get swallowed up in the dark. I was angry I could not be there to help. Lights were going on inside the house as the alarm blared. Two-wheelers were going into the yard and others were leaving, I followed to the point where they were going in and out. I watched as a man opened it up, and then he followed the car up towards the house. I ran in before he came back.

I was about as far from the fence as I was to the house, and now I was wondering if this was the smartest thing to do. I did not know where Patches and Ben-Ben were; and neither would they know where I was now. I crawled closer to the house and got next to the porch, which was lined with huge bushes that offered concealment.

I peeked my head out when I heard the door open.

"What the fuck is all this noise about?" a large man yelled as he stood at the entrance, a glass of foul smelling liquid in his hand. I could smell the pungency from where I laid.

"Another dog attack, Icely," the man who had been opening the gate said.

"All this noise for a fucking dog attack. I thought the Fourth Reich led by a zombie general was coming. Shut that shit down!" he barked.

The guard said something into a little thing he held in his hand, looked a lot like Daniel's toy. Ben-Ben had chewed up one of what Daniel had called a walkie-talkie, but I did not know why he was so upset, he still had one more. Two-leggers are funny like that. A few beats of my heart later the siren once again stilled, my ears rejoiced in the silence.

"How bad?" Icely asked once the siren whined down.

"Dead."

"Another dead? What kind of dog are we talking about? Cujo?"

"Cujo, sir?"

"If you had any education at all you'd know who Cujo was and then maybe you could do more in life than just open a stupid gate. Let's try to dumb this down for you, what kind of dog has killed two of my people?"

"Some sort of Bulldog according to Schools."

"Pit bull?" Icely asked.

The guard shrugged.

"You know you're fucking useless, right? Go guard something."

"Yes, sir," the guard said, as he came down the stairs his foot landed no more than a dog bone's length away from me.

Icely slammed the door shut. I stayed where I was until I was sure that the man that watched the gate was far enough away to not hear me before I crawled out from my hiding spot. The lights in the house began to go out. I stayed low as I went up the stairs. The front door was open a crack.

"What are you doing here?" Patches said from behind me.

I almost barked in fright. "Cat, you have got to stop doing that. I saw a way in, I wanted to help."

"How'd you get the front door open?" Patches asked as she pushed it open with her paw.

"I didn't, Icely slammed it shut. I'm not sure why it's still open."

"Must not have caught," she said as she strode in like she owned the place, which I was finding was a pretty normal reaction from her. If she was there, then it must be hers.

I pushed the door open wider to allow myself in. Ben-Ben was close behind me.

"I smell Zach," he said.

"Me too." My heart was happy with the scent of him.

"Which way?" Patches asked inside the entry way.

I could hear Icely off to my side, or more accurately, the cold water cubes in his liquid container as he stirred his drink around.

"Upstairs," I said as I sniffed around.

Patches and I stayed close to the shadows against the wall as we climbed the stairs. Ben-Ben was too busy looking around to realize we were trying to be undetected. His reluctance to believe humans could be evil might be his undoing.

The cat got to the top of the stairs first. "Next room," I told her.

The house was mostly quiet, but there were some conversations going on in the room we passed and in the room where Zach was.

"What do you think all the noise is about, Mia?" Jess asked someone that was in there with her. My tail involuntarily wagged at the thought of her being so close, she was safe!

"Wait, Riley, we don't know who's in there with her," Patches said.

"It's Jess!" Ben-Ben said excitedly.

"Did you hear that?" the other voice that must have belonged to Mia asked.

"It sounded like a dog," Jess said.

"Icely doesn't have dogs, can't stand them," Mia responded.

Patches and I moved as close to the wall as we could so we wouldn't be seen. I heard footfalls approach the door, and the door opened to illuminate the tail wagging features of a smiling Ben-Ben. His tongue was lolling out as he looked upon the woman who had opened the door.

"Oh, what cutey!" Mia squealed as she bent down.

"Ben-Ben?" Jess asked as she came alongside the

other woman. "What are you doing here?"

I came out of the shadows, my fur bristling, a heavy growl coming from my throat. All of my teeth were exposed, and I was low on my haunches as I approached the woman. She backed away, terror showed in her eyes. I could smell the fear shooting off of her.

"Riley?" Jess asked. I could smell a hint of fear on her as well.

"You...you know this dog?" Mia asked, looking for some hope that she was not about to be attacked.

"Wow you are truly scary looking," Patches said as she came up next to me.

"Shush, cat, I'm trying to intimidate the human."

"Well you're doing a fantastic job, but I think Jess and the woman are friends," Patches said.

"You think so?" I asked, still growling, but not taking my eyes off Mia in case she tried to do something.

"Zach is alright!" Ben-Ben said from inside the room. He was standing on the edge of the chair that Zach was propped up on sniffing at the baby's diaper.

"Took you long enough." Zach said, pulling at Ben-Ben's face.

"Riley, it's okay, she's my friend," Jess said, putting her hands up.

"Told you," Patches said as she strode in.

I stopped the growl, but I wasn't done glaring at the woman just yet. Partly because I had lost some trust of the humans and partly because I just hated that the cat was always right. I came completely into the room, Mia backed up even further.

I went over and took a quick sniff of Zachary. "My heart feels better that you are alright, Zachary."

"As does mine," he answered. "The man that owns this home is a bad person, Riley. We need to leave. Mia we can keep, though."

Ben-Ben looked up at Zach when he mentioned that

Icely was a bad man.

"Jess, tell your dog that I need to shut the door. If Icely sees these animals here, we'll all be in trouble," Mia said.

"Riley, can Mia get by?" Jess asked. She leaned down and rubbed my face. "Are you hurt, my sweet girl? You have blood on you."

'Not mine.' I wanted to tell her.

Ben-Ben looked over at me. "Will she still love you if she knows?" he asked.

"Stupid dog," Patches said as she jumped up on the chair with Zach. "You smell better," she said as she brushed her face up against his.

"You don't," he smiled.

Mia moved around me. For a moment I had a fear that she would cry out in alarm, but she stuck her head out and looked both ways down the narrow room and then closed the door quietly. "What are we going to do with them?" she asked.

"How did you find me, girl?" Jess asked as she rubbed my back. "How did you all find me?" she asked. She was nearly at tears as she stroked and rubbed each of us in turn.

"We need to leave," Jess said as she stood. "All of us."

"We can't," Mia said, "Icely has guards. Even if we somehow got out of this house—which I'm not sure if we can or not—no one in this town will help us."

"We just get a car and go," Jess said with conviction.

"You make it sound so easy," Mia said sadly.

"We can't stay here...I can't stay here. I will not marry him, and I will certainly not moan for him at the appropriate time, I would rather die trying to escape."

"He won't just let you die," Mia said, her feelings wounded. "He'll make an example out of you to everyone else that's thinking about crossing him."

"I'll take my chances," Jess said, heading for the bedroom door.

"Wait, wait, we have to wait until he goes to bed," Mia said.

"It's after three in the morning. When is that going to be?"

"Another hour at the most." Mia answered, "Unless..."

"Unless what?" Jess asked.

"Shh, I hear something. Oh shit, I think he's coming," Mia said as she went across the room and quickly extinguished the light.

I could hear the multiple thudding of scared hearts—mine included.

There was a creak outside Jess' door, followed quickly by a soft knock. The door began to open. "Listen, I know I said I like to be married to my women first, but I think I'll make an exception this one time," Icely said as he stepped completely in.

The twisted smile he wore froze as he reached over and hit the light switch. "Mia? What's going on in here—"

His words froze in his throat. I was to the side of him, my teeth bared. He looked towards the door he had just entered. I barked savagely.

"Move slowly, Icely," Mia said.

"This dog is the people killer," Icely said as he tried to avoid looking at me.

"What?" Jess asked. "She's not a killer."

"I have two dead men that will say otherwise."

I bristled as he turned to me. He began to reach for the small fire stick on his hip. He stopped and yelped when Ben-Ben bit down on his calf.

"Ben-Ben!" Jess said loudly.

As he wrenched his leg free from Ben-Ben's mouth, his hand went for the pistol. I launched, landing on his chest, I snapped at his face as we fell to the floor.

"Whoa, dog, whoa!" Icely said, moving his hands up and to the side.

My muzzle was so close to his face that we were almost touching; drool was dripping from my mouth and onto his face. My chest was heaving as I prepared to tear into him.

"Riley, no!" Jess said loudly. "Don't kill him! You can't kill him!"

"Kill him, Riley. I can feel his vileness," Patches said from the chair.

"Get this fucking dog off me now!" Icely said forcibly.

I growled, somehow getting even closer, until he stopped talking.

Jess reached down to touch my bristled fur. I barked three quick times. "Riley girl, pretty girl, this isn't you," Jess said calmly. I could hear a tremor of nervousness in her voice.

"Mia," Icely pleaded.

"Kill him, Riley," Mia said coolly.

"Bitch," Icely hissed.

"You bastard, you killed my best friend. Do you really think I love you? I loathe you, I hope that dog rips your diseased fucking face right off your body." Mia shook in rage as she uttered the words.

"I can't have my dog kill him," Jess pleaded.

"Listen to the girl," Icely said, maybe to me, maybe to Mia. "I might let you live if you get me out of this," Icely said, again I wasn't sure who his words were directed to.

All of my senses urged me to kill the evil that breathed in this man, but I couldn't bring myself to do it because of Jess. I couldn't stand being a bad dog in her eyes. I also knew I couldn't let him up either. He would grab his fire stick and kill us all. I think he could sense my hesitation, his hand began to lower.

"I'll take that," Mia said as she grabbed the pistol.

"You're dead," he told her flatly.

"I've been dead since the first time you laid your hands on me," she said as she checked the cylinder. "Tie him up, I'll cover him, and don't get any funny ideas, Icely, because if the dog doesn't tear you up, I will blow a hole in your chest. My first shot may go low, though," she said as she pointed the gun at his crotch.

"There's no rope." Jess panicked.

"Use the sheets," Mia told her.

Jess ripped the bedding off and approached Icely. "Think about what you're doing, girlie. I can make you a queen…especially since I'm going to need a new number one," he said, directing his attention at Mia.

Jess was shaking with fear. "I'd rather be a zombie than ever have to be with you," Jess answered, digging deep for her courage. "Roll over."

"You're both dead. I will hunt you down and make you pay for this over and over."

"Roll over," Mia said.

I placed my teeth on his neck. His body went rigid. "I think Riley is telling you to do what we want," Mia said.

Icely began to shift.

"He is not lying about hunting us down, Riley. Rip his throat out now while you can," Patches said as she got down beside me.

"I can't," I told her as I moved so that Icely could get on his stomach.

Then Patches did something that surprised me. She jumped up on his back and bit down hard on his neck, taking a small piece as he tried to reach around and get his hands on her.

"Don't!" Mia shouted as he moved back. "It appears all these animals are great judges of character or your lack thereof."

"What are you doing, cat?" I asked her.

"Killing him."

I scoffed at her words as I looked at the bite that was barely bleeding, I'd seen insects cause more damage.

Jess spent a few moments tying Icely's hands up. Mia bent down and checked her handiwork. "I wish it was tighter. Find something to put over his mouth."

"You are going to wish you killed me," he told the women as they rolled him back over and propped him up against the wall.

Jess shoved a black nylon sock in his mouth and then grabbed a silk scarf to tie around his mouth to hold it in place.

"Now what?" Jess asked as she stood up. Icely was glaring at her.

"Now I guess we find a car and get out of here."

We were heading down the small narrow room when one of the women must have heard something as she was half in and half out of her room looking to see what was happening.

"Get your ass in your room," Mia told her, pointing the pistol at her. The door slammed shut quickly. "We're not going to have much time. Are you sure you want to go through with this, Jess? He might let you live."

"And you?" Jess asked.

"Not a chance, not now."

"Well why are we wasting time talking about it then?"

We headed down the stairs quickly, when we got to the front door Mia told us to wait for a second. She handed the pistol to Jess, who had to shift Zach to her other side to get a good grip on the fire stick. "If anyone but me comes back through that door you'll have to shoot them, do you understand?" she asked a bewildered Jess. "Listen, girl, we're only going to have one chance and it's already slim, you may need to shoot your way out of this. Can you do it?"

Jess nodded slightly.

"Good, I should be right back." And then she went

out the door quickly and shut it behind her quietly.

I could hear thumping noises upstairs. Icely was either attempting to free himself or make his present situation known. He would be successful with either venture soon. I turned to go back upstairs and do what I should have already done.

"Come on, come on!" Mia said as she motioned with her hand quickly for us to come out the door.

I looked once up the stairs and followed everyone out.

"What's going on?" Jess asked.

"I got Icely's driver to get his car. Now if he shows up before the porch guard, we'll have a real chance," Mia said. She was looking around for danger.

"Patches, come here," Jess said as the cat walked to the corner of the house.

"Riley, the man with the gun is going to be here before the car makes it," Patches said.

"Give me the gun, Jess," Mia said calmly.

Jess handed it over, gladly I think. Mia softly padded to the corner of the house. She was right behind the cat who was watching the approaching man.

"Hello, kitty," the guard said. "Come here, sweetie."

Patches purred and rubbed up against the side of the house. Mia tensed as the man's footfalls got closer. The man's attention was rapt on Patches; one hand held the rifle to his chest, with the other he was reaching out and bending over towards the cat.

He barely had time to register he was not alone as Mia placed the pistol close to his head and fired. She turned as she did so, but the metal bee did its job as the man fell over. The side of his head had exploded outwards in a shower of blood, bone, and brain.

"Holy shit, Mia, what did you just do?" the man that brought the car up asked. He was standing by the car he had just exited. He had seen everything. I ran down the stairs. He had still not taken his eyes off the scene on the side of the porch. When he finally noticed me running towards him, he turned to get back into the car, but it was too late.

I hit the back of his knee and he fell face forward—the top of his head catching the body of the wheeler. He wasn't unconscious, but he also wasn't moving quickly either.

"Cat, let's go!" I yelled. She seemed to have frozen somewhat. She had played an integral part in the killing of the human. It had been necessary, but that didn't make it easier.

Patches ran towards me. Ben-Ben started barking, he was corralling everyone to head into the car; got to love herding dogs.

Jess ran to the passenger side with Zach, Patches went into the back, I followed her quickly, Mia hopped into the driver's seat, Ben-Ben ran over the prone form of the chauffeur onto Mia's lap and then into the back seat.

Mia had no sooner shut the driver's side door when the door to the house flew open. The imposing form of Icely dominated the entryway. He said nothing and he did nothing…and that was somehow worse as Mia got the wheeler moving.

Mia's hands were shaking on the wheel as she sped down the driveway. Jess reached over and grabbed the fire stick which she was threatening to drop.

"I've never killed anyone before," Mia said as she looked over at Jess.

"Well keep it to one," Jess told her as she secured the fire stick and then pointed out the front window, hoping Mia would follow suit and avoid the rock column that held the gate up.

The car swerved violently, Patches landed on top of me. For the briefest of moments I wanted to sink my fangs into her, and then it passed.

"Sorry," she said as she pulled her claws from my chest.

I winced as droplets of blood fell on the seat.

"I bit a two-legger, Riley. They're going to send me back to the pound now," Ben-Ben moaned, his head hanging low and his tail tucked neatly under his behind.

I nudged his face up with mine. "No one, Ben-Ben, and I mean no one, is ever sending you back to the pound. I will make sure of that."

"You did good, Ben-Ben," Patches said.

The car scraped the ground as we left Icely's yard. "Get Zach secured in the back, Jess, this is going to get worse before it gets better," Mia said as she concentrated on driving.

"We're not free?" Jess asked, but from her tone I knew even she knew the answer before she had asked the question.

Jess reached back and set a quiet Zach down and did her best to make the harness in the back of the car fit the baby as best as possible. As soon as she finished, the fire alarm sounded for the third time.

"Thank you, Riley," Zach said. "Thank you, all of you."

"I was missing the smell of your paper pants," I told him. "All of the credit goes to Patches, though, without her we'd all still be captive."

"I'm sorry, Riley, I didn't know," Ben-Ben added.

"How could you?" I asked, hoping to relieve his guilt.

"I should have, though. You were fighting to the death. Jess and Zach were being forced to stay with a man holding them captive. Patches is out there risking her life to get everyone free, and I'm trying to figure out how to get more bacon. What kind of pack protector am I?"

"The best kind," I told him. "You kept yourself in the best place to escape, you held on to your faith of me even when you doubted my actions, and when we were up against the wall you did something that went against everything you've ever learned. You are as much a part of this pack as any of us," I told him. He smiled at that.

"You know what would make this perfect?" Ben-Ben asked.

We all knew the answer, but we let him say it anyway.

"Bacon," he said proudly.

"We need to make it out of Vegas," Mia said as she looked in her rear view mirror, which had just lit up from the wheeler that was following.

"Will they keep following?" Jess asked as she turned to see. "There's two of them."

"At least for a while. Outside of Vegas is the unknown, and they won't be in such a rush to go exploring. It will take some threatening from Icely before a posse comes chasing us.

"How long until we're out of the city? Because they're gaining," Jess said as she sat back down.

"Five miles," Mia said as she maneuvered around a car that was coming from a side path.

"At least they're not shooting yet," Jess said.

"They won't, Icely wants us alive so he can kill us personally. If they stop us, Jess, we will need to take ourselves out. What he'll do to us will be so much worse."

I wasn't really sure what Mia meant by 'taking themselves out' but Jess' reaction let me know it was not a good thing.

"Good thing I have some Asian in me!" Mia yelled as she drove the wheeler up onto the path where the two-leggers like to walk. She was able to get past a large wheeler that had stopped in the middle of the wheeler pathway.

"Watch out!" Jess yelled as she placed her hands up by her face. The wheeler feet screeched as Mia turned sharply to avoid a light holder.

The wheeler started to slow down. "Mia, what are you doing?" Jess asked as she finally peeled her hands away from her face.

I looked out the front viewer. There was nowhere for the wheeler to go, large trucks were blocking the entire pathway including the footway.

"Now what?" Jess asked.

"How many bullets are in the gun?" Mia asked as she reached for it.

Jess pulled it away. "Not a chance, I haven't...*we* haven't come this far to just put a bullet in our heads."

"You don't understand, Jess, he's not just going to kill us, he's going to make us suffer. You will wish that you had put the barrel of the gun in your mouth and pulled the trigger."

"And what about Zach? Will you be able to kill him? Because I sure as shit won't be able to!" Jess screamed.

"Hey I'm right here!" Zach bellowed. "I don't want anyone shooting me!"

"You said they won't shoot us, tell them to move or you'll shoot them," Jess begged a defeated looking Mia, whose head was resting against the steering wheel.

"Might as well die trying," Mia said as she picked her head up. The wheeler lurched forward; the smell like Alpha's burnt dinner came from the rear feet as the wheeler gained speed.

Men scrambled from their blockade once they realized what Mia was doing.

"Put your seatbelt on, Jess, and give me the gun." Jess looked over at Mia. "I promise it's only for them."

Jess handed it over, took a quick look in the back to make sure Zach was still under the leash, and then she quickly buckled herself in.

"Riley, help me pull the baby behind Mia's seat," Patches said.

"You sure? But she's under the leash."

"It's too loose, he's not safe."

I tenderly grabbed Zach's foot. "Sorry," I told him around my mouthful of his leg.

Ben-Ben grabbed the front of his shirt as I pulled him over the edge and gently let him down onto the floor. "Oooh, a french fry," Ben-Ben said as he looked under the seat.

Mia shot metal bees from her gun. The big wheeler that had been directly in front of us was moving quickly to get out of the way. Between the bees and the car speeding down on him my guess was that he wanted to get out of the way.

"This is going to suck," Mia said just as our wheeler made contact with the front of the truck. Mia crashed up against her steering wheel as our wheeler spun to the side, she was able to get us going straight again within maybe seven feet. Her breathing was labored as she spoke. "That hurt," she mumbled.

"You alright?" Jess asked as she turned to the back. "Zach?" she cried in panic.

Ben-Ben barked around a mouthful of old french fries. "Right here!" he said, his tail wagging furiously.

"Oh, Zacky," Jess said as she tore her leash off and reached behind Mia's seat, grabbing for Zach, a half chewed french fry hanging out of his mouth.

"I really don't see why he thinks these are so good," Zach said as he spit the old spud to the ground, his face wrinkling up as he did so.

Ben-Ben dove down and snatched it off the floor before Patches or myself could, although why he thought we'd want it I really don't know.

"Sorry," Ben-Ben said when he finally brought his head up.

"It's okay," I told him.

"You okay, Zach?" Jess asked as she patted down his entire body.

"Except for my tongue…which now tastes like dirt," he chortled.

She hugged him tight.

"What now, kiddo?" Mia asked as she roared past the

Vegas sign.

"Colorado?" Jess asked, hoping her new traveling companion would want to go with her.

"Never been. Seems as good a time as any. Maybe get some skiing in," Mia told her.

EPILOGUE

"What now?" Gerald asked as they watched the car rocket past the blockade and out of the city.

"Well Icely said to not kill them. I would say that it was mission accomplished," Jerome said as he got back in his truck and headed home.

"Are you going to tell Icely they got away?" Gerald asked him.

"I'm going to pretend I never saw them coming, if I were you I'd do the same. If for some reason you feel the need for honesty, then please only throw yourself under the bus or I'll cut your throat. Understood?" Jerome asked.

"Loud and clear, never saw them." Gerald got back into his damaged truck and headed for home.

Jerome waited until his friend was out of sight before he doubled back and headed towards Gerald's home. The silver paint from the Mercedes Benz was all over the front end of Gerald's truck, and that was going to give him away. He knew his friend would not go down alone.

He parked his truck a few streets over and walked casually over to Gerald's house. He rang the doorbell.

"Hey, man, come on in," Gerald said with a beer in his hand. "Want one?"

"Sure," Jerome said as he shut the door taking a quick peek outside.

Gerald came over and handed the beer to Jerome.

"Sorry about this, man."

"About what?" Gerald asked as the blade slid into his stomach, the impact as hurtful as if a sledge hammer had struck him.

"Why? We grew up together," Gerald asked as he slid to the floor.

Jerome pulled the blade free. "You should have moved your truck quicker. The moment she hit your car you were a dead man...you just didn't know it yet." Jerome wiped his blade on Gerald's shirt. Gerald wrapped both his hands around the gushing wound. Jerome stepped back and popped the top on the beer. He took his time drinking it, waiting for his friend to take his final breath. "You always were slow," he added as he opened the door took a quick look around before exiting and going back to get his truck.

The Book of Riley: Part 3 My Name is Riley

Mark Tufo

Dedications:

To my wife, a thank you seems so simple but neatly sums up everything.

To my beta readers:

Joy Buchanan

Vix Kirkpatrick

I hope you both have an idea of how appreciative I am of your extraordinary talents and your willingness to use them to help me.

As always, to the men and women of the armed forces and first responders. Your sacrifices do not go unnoticed.

PROLOGUE

Icely was wiping blood off of his neck with his left hand; with his right he was pouring a stiff glass of scotch. Schools, his security chief, was standing in front of Icely's desk. His hands clasped behind his back. He'd been in the city since the beginning of the zombie apocalypse and he'd yet to see his boss so enraged. Schools turned slightly when the double doors opened up. Jerome Mueller, one of the gate guards, was escorted in. Icely did not turn.

"What's this about?" Jerome asked Schools nervously. Schools ignored him.

Icely held the cool glass to his neck. "Aren't you a guard of the eastern most route?" he asked.

Schools watched as Jerome licked his lips trying desperately to get some liquid into the rapidly drying hole in his face.

"I had the night off," Jerome replied.

"Is that what I fucking asked?" Icely said, turning, his eyes boring holes into Jerome. The guard took an involuntary step back.

"N-no, sir. Y-yes, sir. I'm a guard on the eastern most route out of town," Jerome stuttered.

"Notice anything unusual this morning?" Icely asked casually, sitting down as he did so.

"I-I had the night off, Icely. I...I don't know what you're talking about." Jerome said, his eyes darting about wildly from Icely to Schools.

"You missed all those fucking alarms?" Icely asked, holding the glass to his forehead, letting his head bow down a bit.

"I got drunk...um, yeah I went to the dog fights and got shit-faced," Jerome said, thinking he had hit upon a perfect alibi.

"I was there," Schools said, turning just a bit more. "I didn't see you, but then again, there were a lot of people. Did you see what happened to Thorn?" Schools asked, referring to the champion fighting dog that had lost his life to Riley.

Jerome's eyes widened at first in surprise and then narrowed when he realized Schools was attempting to trip him up. He once again licked lips that were beginning to stick to his teeth from lack of moisture.

"Fine. I didn't go to the fights...I still got drunk as a skunk."

"What am I to think, Jerome? If a man lies about one thing, he's likely to lie about another," Icely said. "You know as well as anybody that if the alarm rings, no matter if you have the night off or not, you have to go to your duty station."

"Fuck, Icely, for two alarms I went to that damn gate. Spent my damn entire night there waiting for nothing. Never saw so much as a pigeon shit on a statue. It was my night off!" Jerome said, hoping his loud vocals would profess his innocence.

"It's the third time I'm concerned about," Icely said softly and in direct contrast to Jerome's outburst. "Schools, tell him what you found." Icely rubbed the cool glass all over the top of his head.

"Found your gate partner Gerald dead in his home, stabbed to death," Schools said, studying the other man's face. He noted a hint of panic...and then the feign of surprise.

"Gerald's dead?" Jerome asked. "We've been best friends for years." Jerome tried his best to shed a tear. It wasn't working; it seemed that fear had dried up his tear ducts as well. "Knife to the belly, who would do such a thing?"

"Haven't you watched enough damn television to know better?" Schools asked. "Criminals really are stupid. It never ceases to amaze me."

"What...what are you talking about?" Jerome asked.

"I never said anything about him being stabbed in the

belly," Schools said.

Jerome reached to his side and pulled out a large knife. Schools thought the man might be an idiot, but he was quick as a snake.

"Gerald was a fucking asshole, Icely. He let them girls get away, I was just saving you the time of having to kill him yourself." Jerome held the knife out in front of him, dried spots of blood visible on the blade.

"How kind of you," Icely replied never looking up.

That is one cool customer, Schools thought.

"Dispensing the king's justice and all," Icely said, holding his glass up. "I guess I should thank you."

"You're welcome," Jerome said, relaxing a bit, not realizing Icely was being sarcastic.

Schools often wondered how there could be so many criminals running around when the vast majority of them were idiots.

"Bends, show him how grateful I am," Icely said.

Bends was the large man behind Jerome who had brought him to Icely. Bets had been taken on Bends' previous job – it ranged from bouncer to bodyguard, and a couple even had him as a mafia enforcer. He'd only smile when someone would ask, and the pot would grow larger as more and more guesses came in. It was Vegas and some of the old habits died hard; folks would bet on just about anything here.

Schools heard the whistle of the riot stick as it sliced through the air, and then the sickening crunch of bone as the baton splintered the side of Jerome's knee. It was hard to tell which came first – the scream, or the collision of Jerome's body with the floor. The knife, as if planned, flew through the air and landed flush on Icely's desk.

Jerome was rocking back and forth on the ground, knee up to his chest, both hands wrapped around it in a protective gesture. "My knee, my knee!" he kept sobbing.

"Shut the fuck up," Icely said in a conversational tone

as if he had asked the man if he would please pass the iced tea.

To his credit, Jerome mostly did. There was some slight sobbing but he bit back most of the cries.

"Bends, please sit him down," Icely said.

The big man grabbed Jerome under the armpits and neatly deposited him in one of the two leather chairs in front of Icely's desk. Jerome's posture never changed; he had been clutching his leg on the ground, in the air, and still was as he was seated. Tears were now freely running down his face.

"Know what I hate most of all?" Icely asked Jerome.

Jerome shook his head from side to side.

"Liars…I hate liars most of all," Icely said, taking a big pull from his drink.

Schools thought that was a slightly skewed view of the world considering Jerome had just killed someone. But then again, Jerome had lied *to* Icely while he had killed another.

"So what happened out there?" Icely asked. "And if you bring up that drinking bullshit again I'm going to have Bends shove that nightstick up your ass so far it'll tickle your tonsils."

Bends looked as his crowd-control wand wondering if it was long enough to do as Icely said. He deduced he would have to use part of his forearm to get the task complete, but that it could be done. *Gonna get messy*, he thought.

"The bitch got away. She slammed into the front end of Gerald's truck and took off. Gerald told me he got word we couldn't shoot them."

"See? How hard was that?" Icely asked, spreading his arms wide, a beaming smile across his face.

"I'm sorry," Jerome said.

"These things happen," Icely told him. "But you know what I hate almost as bad as liars?" Icely intoned. "Losers," he replied quickly before giving Jerome a chance to speak. "Bends."

With the one word, the stick was once again hurtling through space, this time making impact with the side of Jerome's head. An ejection of material sprayed from the strike, blood shooting up with bits of hair, scalp, and connective tissue. The second blow created a fissure; Schools could see the pink of brain as Jerome's skull separated by as much as two inches at its widest point. Jerome's legs were thrusting about violently as if in the throes of a mal-seizure.

Urine pooled in the chair and then trickled to the ground in a pattering. It was the smell of released bowels that nearly had Schools turn away. And through it all, Icely was staring intently at Jerome, his eyes nearly glistening with excitement as he watched the other man die.

"Want a drink?" Icely asked Schools when, after ten agonizing minutes, Jerome finally and thankfully stopped twitching.

"I don't like to start much before nine," Schools told him, trying to find some humor in this violent beginning to his day.

"Bends, get him out of here," Icely said as he got up to pour himself another drink.

"Icely, the girl and Mia have almost a two hour head start. When are you going to let me chase her down?" Schools asked. He thought the time away from the city and his boss might do him some good.

"Do you know where they're going?"

"How could I?" Schools asked. "And the longer we wait, the better chance they have of getting away."

"Relax, Schools, you're too uptight. Look at how at ease Jerome is," Icely said as Bends pulled the limp body out of the room. "I don't see you smiling…that not funny for you?" Icely asked.

"The punishment needed to be done. I'm just not a fan of the way it was carried out," Schools told him.

"Po-tay-to, po-tah-to, who gives a fuck?" Icely said nonchalantly.

"It's your call, Icely."

"I'll be ready to leave soon," Icely said. "Now go get a team together."

"You're coming?" Schools was shocked.

"I think the town will be just fine for the few hours I'm gone."

"That confident?" Schools asked.

"I am. I know where they're headed," he said as he tossed a picture onto the desk.

Schools reached over and grabbed it. The girl Jess was arm-in-arm with a thin boy only a little taller than herself; the Red Rocks amphitheater was their backdrop. He turned the picture over. On the back it read 'Justin & me 2010' with a few smiley faces and hearts drawn on it. Schools placed the picture back on the desk. "A little presumptuous, don't you think?" Schools asked.

"It was found in the car she came into town in. It's a zombie apocalypse…people only take what is absolutely necessary, and yet she has this on her." Icely grabbed the picture and rolled it into a ball, hurtling it at the wall. "She's going back to find him."

"It's possible, Icely, or maybe they were on vacation there. You have no proof other than—"

"I fucking said she's going there!" Icely screamed as he thrust himself up, his chair skittered to the wall.

"We'll be ready to leave when you are," Schools said as he turned and left.

CHAPTER ONE

"There's no one coming?" Mia asked for at least the seventh time, plus more. She kept looking through the rearview looker as if she thought it was broken. Every time she asked, Jess would turn around and look out the back.

"Nobody," she replied.

I sat there looking at my pack. Mia was our newest addition; she seemed like a nice enough two-legger and Jess liked her just fine. I was going to keep an eye on her for at least a little while, even if she had helped us escape. If the cat was right, there weren't very many trust-worthy two-leggers. Something that made my stomach hurt just to think about. I didn't necessarily believe the cat, but it seems to me she's been right at least as many times as she's been wrong and I am not going to have that little self-serving feline tell me 'I told you so' again.

"Mia smells nice, think she has any milk?" Zach asked.

Patches, who had been slumbering (seems that's all she ever does), jumped up when Zach spoke and had to work hard at not falling off the wheeler seat. Out of us all she'd been having the hardest time adjusting to the baby 'speaking'.

I knew what he was asking. I'd seen Zach suckle from his alpha's teat before. I did not smell that on her. If she had ever been with child it was a long time ago.

Ben-Ben was curled up and sleeping next to Zach, his

legs began to twitch and he would let out involuntary yips. I figured he was having a bad dream.

"Ben-Ben," Zach said, reaching a fat fist down to the dog's sensitive snout. He gripped a bunch of the dog's whiskers and yanked.

Ben-Ben pulled back awake, his eyes wide with fright. It took him a few moments to figure out where he was. "Riley, it was the worst dream ever!" he cried.

I figured he was dreaming about the lost defense of our home or any of the other bunches of things that had gone wrong since that night. Maybe he was even remembering his days at doggie jail. I shuddered thinking on any of them. I should have known beforehand when he spoke.

"There was this giant piece of bacon!" he started, drool falling from his maw. "It looked so soft, and fat was dripping from it. I just wanted to eat it so bad." He whined. "But every time I tried to move closer, the bacon would move, too. And then when it finally stopped moving, I was stuck in deep, wet ground. I couldn't move my paws, Riley. It was the worst thing ever!"

That's the worst thing ever? I thought. If only that was the case.

"Oh, you poor baby," Mia said, turning to look at Zach. "You must be starving."

"I'm starving!" Ben-Ben barked, licking her paw.

"Umm, Mia, you're drifting off the road," Jess said, bracing her hands in front of her.

We were all tossed around as the wheeler was jerked back onto the hard ground.

"Sorry," Mia said sheepishly. I could tell she was embarrassed.

Mia looked up again at the rear viewer. "I don't understand why he isn't following. He'd never give up so easily."

"It's a good thing, right? Maybe he just doesn't think we're important enough," Jess said with hope.

"It's not if we're important enough, it's that we defied him and he needs to make an example out of us. People will think if we could do it then so could they, and pretty soon his power will be undermined. He'll never allow that."

Two-leggers had horrible noses, and we had so much distance on him, I wasn't sure why they were so concerned. I had heard and shared in their happiness as they said we had entered into Arizona and then another strange place called Utah. How far could he track us?

I once heard alpha male say 'great minds think alike'. It was two summers ago and he had just come home from a place he called 'work'. (Sounded like walk to me, I never understood why I couldn't go with him). She-alpha had come out the front opener to greet him, kind of like a good butt-smelling. And before he could offer her his greeting, she said 'Ice cream'.

"Just what I was thinking – great minds think alike," he had replied with a smile.

I had not known what that velvety sweet treat was until we all piled into the wheeler and headed out to a small home that traded paper and metal for the stuff. Best trade ever! Can't eat paper or metal.

Jess' other brother Daniel, who died the night of the dead ones, had gotten a huge serving of the treat. When he went to lick it, part of it had fallen off and onto the ground. He had cried almost as much as when he had fallen off his two-wheeler and made life fluid come out his knees. I didn't see the problem; I had sniffed at the ice cream once and licked it clean off the hard ground, loving every tongue full, even at the end when my tongue got hot from licking the ground! Oh that was heavenly.

"We're two states over," Jess said. "How can he follow us?"

And just like that, the fond memory of the fallen treat was wiped from my mind.

"We're on the same road we left town on…Route 15.

How hard do you think it'd be?" Mia asked back.

"Can't we take another road?" Jess asked. I could smell the waves of panic coming off of her.

"Maybe, but I don't know the area and we don't have a GPS. Check the glove box for a map," Mia said.

Jessie unlatched the small container up front. "Whoa!" she exclaimed. I peeked my head around to get a look, hoping it was ice cream or maybe bacon-flavored ice cream so we could all be happy.

"Does it have bullets?" Mia asked.

"You tell me," Jess replied, handing it to Mia who took her hands off the steering device. The wheeler once again headed off the hard packed ground.

"Mia you're doing that drifting thing again," Jess said with no small measure of alarm.

"The two-legger might be a good one, but she's going to get us all killed nonetheless," Patches said. "I could drive better than her."

I snorted, thinking how her little legs would try to reach the go-faster and the go-slower pedals on the floor.

"It won't be so funny when we're upside down," Patches said haughtily.

I turned my head as far over as I could. It made my stomach feel funny, and I agreed with the cat AGAIN that 'no' it wouldn't be so funny if we were upside down. I barked to get Mia's attention. She looked at me in the rear viewer and she immediately gripped the steerer as the wheels bit into the soft dirt, sending the rear of the wheeler into what Jess called a fish-tail. That made no sense--it didn't smell like that gross stuff the cat liked to eat. Two-leggers are funny animals.

The burning disc was coming up as Mia stopped the wheeler. Jess got out and stretched and then opened the door so that the rest of us could get out. I hopped down, immediately followed by Patches. Ben-Ben looked like he was still sulking from his near-bacon experience. Jess had to coax him to join us.

"I'm hungry, Jess," Zach said, smiling as he reached for her nose.

"Are you hungry?" She nuzzled his face.

"He just told her, why can't she understand him?" I asked.

"I wish I couldn't understand him either," Patches said, going towards the sand.

"As much as I hate it Jess, we're going to have to pull off into one of these towns and look for supplies and gas." Mia shielded her eyes from the burning disc and looked around.

Neither of them were happy about it, and to be honest…neither was I. We had found Winke and Faye, but most two-leggers had been – at the best – distrustful; or worse, outright hostile. The last one taking us all, save Patches, hostage.

"There were signs for a place called Hurricane a few miles up," Jess said.

"Not sure I like the name, but it's as good a place as any," Mia said.

Ben-Ben walked over towards the side of the road; he lifted his leg, almost making water on Patches. She hissed and ran away.

"Next time you try that, I'm going to put a claw in a sensitive place," Patches told him as she groomed herself.

"Sorry," he mumbled.

He appeared as if he hadn't woken up too well. Still dreaming of his giant bacon slab I would imagine; but then again, which of us there right then wasn't. My stomach was twisting in knots thinking of anything to eat. I was tempted to ask the cat if she wanted to hunt the green lizard – chicken-tasting things – when Mia looked around and told Jess we should get going.

According to what Jess said, the place called Hurricane was twelve miles off of the main hard-packed road. It didn't sound all that far to walk, but with the wheeler blowing out cool air from the front I didn't see why we should go out into the heat…especially without any ice cream.

CHAPTER TWO

"Where are the bitches?" Icely said, staring through the front windshield. He kept getting closer and closer to the glass as if that would extend his viewing range. "Can't you make this thing go any faster? he asked Schools.

"I'm going faster than I want to be," Schools replied evenly. He had the Mercedes running at ninety miles per hour, well under what the high performance machine could handle but far faster should something come out into the road or already be there. Anything more than a subtle shift for avoidance at this speed would send the small tank hurtling through the air. "We'll catch them," Schools said. What he didn't add was 'if they went this way.' Icely's theory that the girl was heading back to Colorado was circumstantial at best. If they were, which he had doubts, they were on the right track. There were not many ways they get there from this part of the country. It was stark, open and an unyielding landscape.

Schools was doing the math. The women had a two hour lead on them, and at a modest sixty miles per hour they had a hundred and twenty mile lead. If they were heading to Colorado at this pace they'd catch up to them in four hours. The big 'if' was the destination. Icely had put together a team of four pursuit cars and a truck carrying a giant tank of gas. Mia would have to stop, and getting gas without power was not an easy feat for someone who did not have practice in it. Plus, they were traveling with a baby, supplies would become paramount – things in which they had an abundance of in the chase cars. Time was on their side, and then the giant 'if' came out.

"Icely, if they're going to Colorado—"

"Not if," he said coolly.

"Okay…fine. They will still need to pull over and get food for the baby."

"I'm going to tear that thing's head off," Icely said distractedly. "I was prepared to raise that smelly little thing, teach him everything I knew. Not now, though, not ever. I'm going to have that bitch watch, too. Maybe I'll even keep her around for a while."

Baby dodged a bullet there, Schools thought.

"We need to split up," Schools said. "Any one of these cars has enough to take out two women and a baby."

"And a people-killing dog. I saw the eyes of that dog, fucking thing wanted to tear my throat out."

Would that have been for the better? Schools thought.

"I'll take a fully automatic weapon over a dog any day," Schools replied.

"Fine…you tell the cars which way to go, but you make it abundantly clear I want Mia alive. And Jess," he added.

"Icely they have at least one gun. It's going to be much more difficult to do that. She's not going to just give herself up."

"And the baby, I want that fucking thing alive as well so that I can kill it personally with my own two hands," he said, completely ignoring what his security chief had just said. "Oh yeah keep the dog alive, too. Maybe I'll tear its throat out." Icely had a wild look to his eyes now. "Oh, and the stupid fucking cat, too. I want someone to toss the thing in the air like a pigeon so I can shoot it with a shotgun. Yeah…nothing would make me happier than to say 'pull'!" He laughed.

"What about the little dog?" Schools asked. It was meant to be sarcastic, but Icely didn't pick up on it.

"Oh, you can kill the little Toto fucking thing. All the others I want alive, Schools. You understand me? Your men kill any of my new toys and I'll play with their lives instead. You got me."

"Loud and clear, boss," Schools said as he told the driver to pull over.

The other cars followed suit. He spent a few minutes pouring over a map and telling everybody where he wanted them to turn off and Icely's specific instructions should they come across the runaways. There were groans of protestations.

"You have Tasers and pepper paint balls…use them," Schools said, shutting down their clamoring.

"Fat lot of good a Taser is going to do against a bullet," Lionel, Schools' second-in-command said.

"If you kill any of them, I suggest you find someplace else to live," Schools reiterated.

"That's as much a death sentence as coming back and telling Icely," Lionel replied.

"One way is less painful than the other." Schools folded the map back up.

CHAPTER THREE

According to Jess, this place was named after a great wind. I don't know what she was talking about, it was quiet; nothing was moving, not even the leaves in the trees. I saw some winged ones, 'birds' I think Jess called them. Patches seemed fascinated by the birds--kept licking her mouth every time she saw one fly by.

"Look at all the crows," Jess said, pointing to some tethers that were placed between a couple of the fake trees the two-leggers called poles. I followed Patches' line of sight. The tether seemed to be sagging from the weight of them.

"You believe in omens?" Mia asked Jess with trepidation.

"Should I?" Jess asked back.

"I don't like it here." Mia craned her neck to look up at the birds as she passed.

"Let's just do what we have to and go."

"Are those good to eat?" Ben-Ben asked Patches.

"Flying bacon," Patches replied looking out the back of the window. Ben-Ben immediately joined her; his back paws on the seat and his front resting up by the rear viewer. His tail was wagging so fast, I thought he might be capable of flight.

I was busy keeping an eye out for two-leggers of all varieties, living and somewhat dead. The only thing I'd seen moving since we got into Hurricane was the birds.

"Riley, I'm awfully hungry," Zach said, pulling my

attention away from the viewer.

I was about to respond when the car came to an abrupt halt. I had to admit it was funny when Ben-Ben was hurtling through space and fell into the back of Mia's seat. Patches had dug her claws in and hadn't moved an inch. I was just able to brace myself and keep from shifting too much.

"Damn fools, what the hell are you doing?!" someone shouted from outside the wheeler. I had to spin my head to see who it was. It was a large man in very short white fake furs that barely covered over his reproductive parts. He had more hair over his body than I'd ever seen on a two-legger. Could have been part animal as far as I was concerned, and that seemed to make him a better person in my eyes.

"He's got a gun!" Jess screamed.

"And no damn pants," Mia said as she tried to get around the man. He pointed the metal bee-slinger at the front of the wheeler.

"Shut off the damn engine," he told them, not quite as loudly. "Now!" He made the slinger do some sort of metallic sound.

"Not again," Patches said, standing next to me and watching.

"Is he a wolf?" Ben-Ben asked when he had finally righted himself.

I honestly had to think about it. He had thick, shaggy fur coming from his head and a heavy beard.

"Shut the fucking engine off," the man said again, this time placing the barrel of the weapon against the viewer. If he sent out a bee now Mia would be stung deeply.

She turned the wheeler off and placed her hands in the air.

The man looked over at Jess and then into the back seat.

"Put your damn fool hands down, grab the baby and the animals. Come on and be quick about it," the man said before turning away and walking off the hard ground and onto the grass.

"Mia? What do we do?" Jess asked.

"Start the car and leave," Patches answered.

Mia looked at the danglers, and then back over to the man; probably trying to figure out if she could get out of there before he could make the fire stick shoot.

"Grab Zach, I'll get the animals," Mia said, opening her door.

The wolf-man turned back around. "Hurry up, you damn fools, and do not slam the doors," the man said as he was looking about wildly and getting closer to a house.

Mia shrugged to Jess but opened the back door to the wheeler. "Come on, Ben-Ben," she said. I followed quickly behind.

Jess had opened the other side and grabbed Zach. Patches looked from open door to open door but did not move.

"Come on, Patches." Mia stuck her head back into the wheeler.

"Patches, come on, sweetie," Jess said, looking in from the other side.

We waited a few moments. The cat wasn't budging. She hissed at Mia when she reached in to grab her.

"Cat, what are you doing?" I asked, crowding in around Mia's legs.

"I'm not a dog," she said haughtily, "I don't come when I'm called like a common cur."

"Fine, you tell the dead ones that when they get here."

Her eyes opened wide and her head whipped over towards me.

"Shit, they heard. Let's go!" the man yelled.

"Zombies!" Jess and Mia said at nearly the same time. I could smell them coming.

"Patches, come on!" Jess said angrily.

"She does look somewhat like a cur," I said to Ben-

Ben as Patches leaped out of the wheeler and was catching up to Wolf-Man.

"What's a cur?" Ben-Ben asked as he struggled to keep up with my longer strides.

Wolf-Man held the door open as Patches, Jess carrying Zach, Mia, then me and Ben-Ben came in. He quickly shut the door and turned the knob. It made a large clicking sound.

He placed his fire stick next to the door and moved further into the room. He pulled a covering back on one of the outside viewers to look outside.

Mia quickly grabbed the rifle the man had put down.

"You know how to shoot that thing?" the man asked, never turning back towards her.

"I do," she said solemnly.

"Good…you may need to before all of this is over." The nearly naked man let the material fall back in place.

I was thankful for it. The room was a multitude of bright colors that hurt my eyes trying to take them all in.

"The name's Koala," he said with a wide, gap-toothed smile. "Like the bear, get it?" The man dragged his hand through the thick fur on his chest. "Is it the underwear? Sorry, I'll get a robe…don't get much company."

"I'm Mia, this is Jess and her brother Zach. The big dog is Riley, the little one is Ben-Ben and the aloof little one is Patches," she said quickly, getting the introductions out of the way.

"Circus in town?" Patches asked as she looked around the room much like I had. I did not know what she meant.

"It's nice to meet you all," he said genuinely enough. "Don't let Jumper bother you, he's not nearly as fierce as he looks," the man said before he departed the room.

"Should we leave?" Jess asked quietly.

Mia looked inside the gun and seemed content when she saw whatever she had been searching for. She strode quickly over to the other side of the room and looked outside the same viewer. "Can't," she replied, letting the dark take over quickly.

"Get off of me!" I heard, the voice sounding pretty muffled.

"Sorry!" Ben-Ben exclaimed, getting up quickly. He had jumped up onto the couch and sat down on the head of easily the oldest dog I had ever seen.

Patches approached warily, her tail dancing back and forth rapidly. The old dog did little more than follow her movement with his milky eyes. "How many seasons?" she asked the ancient one.

"Lost count after my fifteenth," the dog told her.

"You can count that high?" I asked, coming over.

"Higher if I had a mind to. Don't do much more than lie here anymore and watch dust settle. The name is Jumper."

Patches snorted.

"Always disliked cats," Jumper said.

I laughed with him. "Is your alpha a good person?" I asked, looking out for the safety of my pack.

"I've known a bunch of the humans in my time. He would be the best of them all."

"That doesn't necessarily answer the question," Patches replied.

Jumper's neck cracked and popped as he swiveled it to look directly at her. "You know, sometimes cats are too smart for their own good."

She sat and licked her front paw.

"He's never said a bad word to me or ever raised his hand in anger. His friends have told him over and over again that he should 'put me down' and he always tells them, 'when it's his time he'll go.' He carries my food over to me and he used to bring me outside to relieve myself. Now he has a place set up in the kitchen."

"I go in the house, too!" Ben-Ben yipped excitedly.

"Yeah, but he doesn't do it on purpose." Patches deflated the small dog's ego.

I knew what 'put down' meant. When George had got sick the alphas had talked about it. That was when he went to the animal doctor and never came home. I'd always thought the alphas knew everything; how I wished they'd let him live out the rest of his time, however fleeting it may have been. Just one more moon with him would have been worth it.

"I smell a lot of fear on your pack," Jumper said. "My nose is about the only thing that works…can't even chew my food anymore."

I heard Koala coming back from wherever he had been. Jess stood straight, and would have bristled if she were a dog. He came back into the room carrying an armful of fire sticks.

"Grab what you feel comfortable with," he told Jess and Mia as he placed them down on a large chair.

He sat down on the couch right next to Jumper. He had put on more fake furs and reached into a pouch and pulled out a crinkly container, I think the two-leggers called them baggies. Ben-Ben had come over to see if what was inside might be edible, he sneezed heavily when he caught a big whiff.

"Weed?" Mia asked.

"Not for me, never touched the stuff. More of a Red Bull kind of guy," he said as he pulled out a small jar of peanut butter from another pouch. "Jumper has glaucoma. I was able to get him a prescription."

"You got your dog a prescription for weed?" Mia asked.

"I'm not sure if it helps at all, but I do know he whines less about his pain after I give him some." Koala mixed a little of the potent smelling substance called 'weed' into the delicious peanut butter. I was salivating thinking about getting some of the sticky substance onto my tongue. "I've been with this dog through two wives and four moves. Used to drive a truck before all this madness started. This dog has seen more road miles than most men. Used to take him with me everywhere I went. Had to stop the last couple of years, it hurt him too much for me to move him in and out of the cab."

"Sorry," Ben-Ben said. Before I could ask him for what he jumped up and licked the entire mound off of Koala's palm.

Koala's mouth opened wide. "Oh-oh."

"What's 'oh-oh?'" Jess asked.

"You're little dog is going to be high as a kite soon."

"Will he be alright?" Jess asked, coming to his side.

"He'll be fine," Koala told her. "Hungry…but fine."

"I'm already hungry," Ben-Ben said, licking his chops while trying to force the peanut butter down. Koala reached down and stroked Ben-Ben's face.

"What is going on?" I asked. The question was immediately forgotten when Koala spoke.

"I am so sorry. I've really been alone for a while even before. Just been me and Jumper for the last five years. Sister lived up the street she'd care for him on my runs. I hit the lottery on my last trip. If you're hungry, the pantry is pulled up right to the back of the house."

Mia nodded at Jess who went out to the kitchen. "Holy crap" issued forth.

Patches followed Jess to see what she was looking at. I stayed put, just in case. I felt better about the two-legger, but I wanted to make sure he wasn't a deceiver like the cat said they could be. Ben-Ben was looking at Koala's hand, hoping more of the sticky food would reappear.

"This is incredible," Jess said, walking out the back of the house and into a huge wheeler container.

"I was heading to Louisiana," Koala said from the living room, "in preparation for the storm that was heading that way. When I started to run into zombies and the roads were getting choked with people just trying to get out, I turned around and headed home. I figured if I was going to die it was going to be with the one I love. I knew I couldn't haul that stuff in here, and leaving it on the street wasn't a great idea either. No way I could go out every time I needed something, either zombies or—"

"Others would get it." Mia finished. She had stepped over to the threshold and was looking at what Jess had walked in to.

"The bay window was old and I was going to need to replace it anyway, so I just backed my trailer right up and through the damned thing." Koala laughed.

Jess was looking at stacks of bottled water, pallets of granola bars, crates of dried food products, juice in boxes, even a few boxes of pet foods.

"This is incredible. How long will this food last?" Jess' question drifted out from the trailer.

"Longer than we have," Koala said softly, hugging Jumper's head.

"We?" Mia asked.

"Stage-3 colon cancer," he answered her. "And well, you've seen Jumper. I'm just trying to last longer than him so his last few weeks can be peaceful, not painful. You know what I mean?" Koala asked with a tortured expression on his face.

I could tell from the scents he was throwing off that he was saddened by the thought of losing his friend and also scared with the prospect of dying. Mia came over and placed her hand on his shoulder.

"I know how sick he is," Jumper told me. "I've been trying to hold on as long as I can so that he won't be alone when he finally releases."

"That's a good thing," I told him.

"Can I feed Zach and the animals?" Jess asked, coming back into the living room. She saw that Mia was sitting next to the man and his eyes were glossed over as if ready to tear. A questioning look passed over Jess' features.

"Yeah sure," he said, wiping his eyes; I guess before anything could spill down. "Please grab whatever you'd like.

There's more there than...there's plenty."

The same look of confusion was still on Jess' face as she turned back around. I was curious to learn about the man, but once I heard the familiar sound of a dog food bag being opened, my stomach took control. I went out into the kitchen and looked into the back of the food container room for the giant wheeler.

Jess put Zach on a chair with a small box of what looked like small crunchy donuts.

"Come here, Patches." Jess next put down a small bowl of food for the cat.

The cat, which usually sniffed around her food for long minutes and would then even sometimes walk away from it as if she didn't care, was a totally different animal this time.

"Sorry," she said as she looked up.

Bits of food were falling from her mouth as she said it. She was attacking it like I expected a wolf would attack a deer. And then I thought back. At least I'd been fed in Las Vegas; the cat hadn't eaten in days. I let her enjoy herself without me watching her make a mess. I've got to admit, though, the memory of that food flying around her head and water sloshing out of her bowl will bring me fond memories for a long while. She's always so dainty, dipping her head down and taking one piece chewing it long and carefully before going on to the next.

I thought that was perhaps the funniest thing I'd seen in a season when Ben-Ben went and did one better.

"Come here, puppies," Jess said as she got us a couple of bowls of food and water.

"I feel funny," Ben-Ben barked from the other room. He caught the corner of the wall with his shoulder as he walked into the room. He completely spun around so he was facing where he had just come from.

"Back already?" Mia asked from the living room.

"Riley, where are you?" Ben-Ben asked.

"Looks like the medicinal marijuana is starting to work," Koala said.

I followed Jess as she went to retrieve Ben-Ben. "Oh, you poor thing." She was smiling as she picked him up. "You spazz," she told him.

His eyes were half shut like he was going to sleep and his tongue was hanging out. She picked him up in her arms and walked back over to the food bowls.

"I'm flying!" he said excitedly, and then he licked Jess' face.

I thought the cat's wild eating was something to behold; she couldn't hold a cookie to what Ben-Ben was doing to his food. He had finished his bowl before I got more than a few mouthfuls down and then he had pushed my face out of the way so he could eat mine. "Sporry," he had mumbled as he did so.

Jess motioned with her finger for me to follow her. I came back out to the room where Mia, Koala, and Jumper were.

"Here you go, pretty girl," Jess said as she stroked my muzzle. She put down a bowl of food just for me. I had no sooner taken a bite, than I noticed Patches not more than a stride away, watching me intently, her tail swishing back and forth at a rapid pace.

"You eating in there, too?" Ben-Ben asked from the kitchen. "I'll be right out!" he said excitedly.

I usually liked to enjoy my food, but I wasn't going to get the chance today. I attacked that thing like it was cow meat and still I couldn't finish it before Ben-Ben tried to crowd me out, with Patches at his side.

"Isn't this food just the most wonderful thing you've ever eaten?" he asked the cat.

"I've had better," she replied, but that didn't stop her from eating.

At some point, Jess and Mia ate. Must have snuck it inside the great container, because I'm pretty sure Ben-Ben wouldn't have left them alone. When the small dog was done with his third bowl of food, his stomach was practically scraping on the fake fur flooring. He hopped up onto the couch, crawled over Koala's lap, and nestled in with Jumper.

"Don't let me get in your way," Koala said as he did so.

"He's warm...feels good," Jumper said as he shifted his head.

It was a little while later, the shadows in the house getting longer. Koala had lain down and was head-to-head with Jumper and Ben-Ben. Jess was sitting in one of the big chairs, Zach in her arms, and I was down by her feet. Patches had found some place else to sleep in the house. She liked her alone time and hadn't truly been afforded any lately, especially all crammed into the wheeler like we were. Probably trying to figure out a way for world domination knowing her.

The only one not relaxing was Mia. She would sit for a bit and then get up pacing nervously and then always go over to the outside viewer before she would start the routine all over again. I could sense her nervousness, so I went up to her as she was standing there, looking out. I figured if she petted my head she might feel better. I know it works for me.

"Stupid, stupid, stupid," she said over and over. She looked down at me when I nuzzled my head into her leg. "Hi, sweet girl. Got any ideas?"

"About what?" I groaned back as she rubbed my ears.

"I should have never left that stupid car out in the middle of the street," she said, standing back to look out the viewer.

I hopped up, my front paws resting on the small ledge so that I could also see what she was seeing. The wheeler was indeed out in the middle of the hard packed ground. Dead ones were all around it – well, I guess all around everything really.

"Icely comes looking for us...he's going to know

where we are," she said, biting at one of her fingers.

I thought if she was still hungry there was plenty of more food, no need to eat herself. Two-leggers are funny like that.

On our next trip to the window (Mia kept rubbing my head in a worried manner – I could do this all night) "Stupid, stupid, stupid" changed to "Fuck, fuck, fuck." She let the material fall back into place and moved quickly away from the window. I didn't see it, but it was impossible not to hear the paws of another wheeler moving across the hard ground or the loud beating of its heart as it stopped near to where we had.

"Jess," Mia said in a loud whisper, "Icely's here."

Jess nearly dropped a startled Zach she had gotten up so quickly. He cried from the sudden and maddened movement of his sister.

"Icely? John 'Icely' Huntington?" Koala asked.

"You know him?" Mia turned back from the window.

"Not personally...I've heard of him. Hard to be a truck driver in this region and not know about him. He ran most, if not all of the illegal trucking in the Nevada area. What's he want with you two?"

"He runs Vegas now," Mia replied. "We were held captive there."

"He runs Vegas? Pretty impressive for a thug. You guys important somehow that he would come this far looking for you."

"I was one of his wives," Mia said defiantly, looking for any sort of condescending look from Koala.

"I was to become one. Riley over there tried to kill him, Patches bit him," Jess said.

"And I think Ben-Ben urinated on his rug," Mia added.

Koala suppressed a snort at that. "Persian?" he asked.

"I think so," Mia said.

I looked over to the cat. "Rug," was her one word

reply. "Fake floor furs," she added when she didn't think I had understood her. I hadn't.

So Ben-Ben had finally made water inside when it was acceptable – good for him. Wish I had thought of it.

Koala walked over to the viewer and looked out. "Looks like there's four of them in the car. Nice to see the zombies are finally on our side."

"There's got to be too many zombies for them to get here right?" Jess asked.

"Doubtful," Mia said. "I don't think there could ever be enough zombies."

I wanted to see what was going on, I jumped back up and poked my head between the material and the viewer. There were indeed bunches of dead ones all around the car. A female two-legger got out one of the doors in the rear of the wheeler. She was carrying a deadly looking fire stick. An explosion of flame burst from the end of it as she sent more metal bees out faster than I'd ever heard before. Dead ones were torn in half. I think she was screaming as she swept the fire stick back and forth.

"Machinegun!" Koala pulled me away from the window. "Must have really been an expensive rug. Come on," he said to Mia.

I followed as Mia and Jess followed the man into the back of his house.

"We need to leave," Patches said to me as we walked. "Those people will kill us all."

"You have any ideas?" I asked her.

"Not me, I'm just the muscle," she replied coyly.

I turned to look at her. "You're funny, cat. I'm really starting to like you."

"Riley, what's going on?" Ben-Ben asked, slamming into the back of Patches he was running so fast. They slid halfway across the food room on the shiny ground.

"I could do without this one," Patches said as she extradited herself from the tangle of paws and fur.

I wanted to laugh, but I was so scared, and it was impossible not to pick up on the nerves the two-leggers were throwing off. They knew how much trouble we were in, maybe more so. I didn't exactly know what a machinegun was but it sounded wicked, almost like a pack of coyotes, or two cats. Any of them or all of them; pure evil.

"...only have the one shotgun and a couple of twenty-twos," Koala was telling the females when I caught up. "Not much use against a machinegun."

"Better than nothing," Mia said. "We've both got nine-millimeters, but not many rounds."

"Well I got plenty of rounds," he told them. He grabbed three of the small fire sticks, a couple of boxes of metal bees and headed back into the living room.

"Jumper?" Koala asked. The large dog had gotten off the couch and was standing next to it on shaky legs.

"If I die, it's going to be in defense of my human," Jumper barked softy.

I wanted to tell him that no one was going to die today, but I'd never been good at lying.

"Nobody is going to die today," Patches told him. She said it with such ease and conviction that I almost believed her.

More fire sticks had joined in the shooting.

"Damned fools, the more they shoot, the more zombies are going to come," Koala said as he quickly shoved bees into the sticks.

"That's a good thing, right?" Jess asked.

He stopped for a second, his head popping up from his task. "Yeah I guess that's true."

A few of the bees struck the house; it was so loud my ears hurt.

"You alright, Zach?" I asked, going over to his chair.

"I want my mom," Zach said tremulously, his bottom lip quivering.

Me too, I thought.

"I wonder if my time has come," Koala said, not really to anybody. I was not sure if I was the only one that heard him.

Jumper had creaked his way over to the front door and was waiting, expectant I guess the cat would say. I was impressed by his display but did not know how effectual he would be as a first line of defense. I would gladly add my teeth to his presence when the time came.

CHAPTER FOUR

"Well lookie what we got here," the driver of the car said. He was driving a non-descript blue sedan. It looked enough like a cop car, but that wasn't why Sedgwick liked it. Hated cops, loved the control.

"That's definitely Icely's car," Ned, the passenger, replied.

"Anybody in it?" the woman, Dianna, asked from the back seat. She seated a magazine into her Israeli built Uzi.

"Put the damn toy away," Sedgwick said. "You heard Schools, Icely wants the bitches alive."

"Yeah, well Icely and Schools aren't here," she said defiantly.

"Listen, Dianna, we got a good thing going on in Vegas. You ain't gonna fuck this up for us."

"Just stop the car so we can see if the little princesses are in there," she replied.

"The doors are open and there are zombies around…they're food by now," the fourth – and as of yet silent one in the group – said. His name was Nick Anthony but they called him "Grumper" because he was generally in a foul mood.

"I agree with Grumper," Ned said. "Just back the car up and let's get the fuck out of here. We'll tell him what we saw."

"We leave without a head and he'll take ours instead," Dianna said.

"Shit…she's right," Sedgwick agreed.

"I'm always right," she said as she opened her door.

"What are you doing?" Sedgwick asked.

If he said anything else it was drowned out by the blazing fire of her sub-machinegun. Zombies stutter-stepped as they received multiple rounds.

"The fucking head, Brain-child," Grumper yelled through the open door.

"This is so much more fun!" she screamed.

More than a few of the zombies folded in on themselves as their torsos were shredded, their heads dropping down by their knees. They would turn so they could keep looking towards the potential food source but could not reconcile the fact that they were no longer looking forward. Their legs would move in the only direction they knew, frustrating the zombies as they moved further away from their prey.

"That's hilarious," Grumper said as he got out of his side.

"Waste of fucking bullets is what it is," Ned replied, watching the action. "If they were in the area they sure as hell aren't now," he said to Sedgwick.

"Let them finish the zeds off and we'll check the car for any clues," the driver responded.

"Aren't you piss-wads getting in on this?" Dianna asked as she reached back in and got another magazine.

"Killed enough zombies for two lifetimes," Sedgwick told her. "Have a blast."

"Suit yourself."

"Psychotic bitch," Ned replied. "How the hell did she end up in our car?"

"She's my sister," Sedgwick said.

"Oh yeah." Ned laughed.

It didn't take long for Grumper and Dianna to decimate the local zombie population. Her gun was still smoking when Ned and Sedgwick got out.

"Keys are in it," Sedgwick said, getting in behind the

wheel of Icely's car.

"And apparently it works," Ned added as Sedgwick started the car.

"Quarter tank of gas." Sedgwick shut the engine down.

The street was quiet except for the steady thrum of the sedan engine and the occasional kicking of a piece of brass.

"Hijack?" Dianna asked.

"Possible," Ned told her, no gunshots to the car, though.

Sedgwick looked around, "Sure are plenty of houses they could be holed in right now. Probably even watching us."

"This sucks," Grumper said. "They can shoot at us, but we can't return fire?"

"Fuck that. I'm not taking a round for Icely, King of Vegas or not," Dianna said.

"Not often I agree with your crazy sister, Sedgwick, but on this one I do," Ned said.

"Is that anyway to talk about your blushing bride?" Dianna asked.

"Love you, honey." Ned blew her a kiss.

"Let's hope for all our sakes, theirs included, we can find enough of their tasty tidbits to bring back to the boss. That way his revenge is completed, we don't get shot at, and these poor bastards don't have to be tortured," Sedgwick said.

"Dear brother, are you going soft in your old age?" Dianna asked.

"I've done what I've had to in order to get through life, Dianna. Some of it – okay, most of it – unsavory, but I do not take enjoyment from the brutality of torture. That's Icely's thing, not mine."

"Yet you work for the man," she taunted.

"Like I said, I've done some unsavory things. I told

mom she should have gotten you checked out."

"Before or after she started smoking meth?" Dianna asked.

"Hilarious…and it was crack," Sedgwick answered her.

"Kids, kids," Grumper said, "let's just do this."

"See, Dianna, I told you he wasn't just another pretty face," Ned said about Grumper and his shock of red hair.

"I will shoot you." Grumper told him.

"Alright, let's check the houses, two to a house. Me and Grumpy will start on the right. Dianna, you and your boy toy to the left," Sedgwick said.

CHAPTER FIVE

"They're splitting up." Mia said, making sure to stay low and out of sight. "Shit! Two of them are coming this way!" She ducked down.

"You see movement?" she heard one of the men ask outside.

Within the span of a few seconds there was a heavy knock on the door. "Open the fuck up!" one of them yelled.

"What do you want?" Koala shouted through the door.

"Census survey."

"One, now piss off," Koala said.

"We're looking for somebody!" the voice shouted.

"I just said 'one.' And if you're looking for me, I'm not interested," Koala replied.

A loud shot rang out, I heard a metal bee crash into the door.

"Steel core door." Koala turned, smiling at the shocked face of Jess. She was entirely too scared to enjoy in his mirth. "Gonna need a bigger gun!" Koala shouted.

"Windows bullet proof too, asshole?" the man from outside asked.

"Shit. Gonna need some help, Jess," Koala said quietly. He pointed to a slot halfway down the door. "Need you to open that, okay?" She nodded.

Koala got down on one knee, he put the large fire stick up to his shoulder. "You ready?" he asked her. She looked sick, sort of the same color green I'd seen She-Alpha wipe away from Zach's rear end. Mia got behind Jess and placed her hands over the younger girl's ears.

"One...two...three." The slot opened with a noticeable squeal. Koala stuck the front part of the stick through the door and pulled the trigger. I whined; the explosion in the house was so loud. That was soft in comparison to the shrieks of agony that poured forth from the man that had been stung.

"My leg, my leg!" he was screaming.

I took a peek through the small slot before the fire stick came back in and Jess let it go. I didn't know which leg the man was crying about, the one he was using for support or the one two steps down on the small porch.

"Sedgwick!" the woman screamed.

Metal bees peppered the house, glass all around us shattered. Holes appeared on the opposite side of the room with loud 'thunks'. Furniture was being torn up way worse than Ben-Ben could ever hope to accomplish. Fake lights were shattering. The house was being destroyed. All of us, including Jumper who had expended so much energy to be standing, were as low to the ground as we could get.

Light streamed into the house from the many holes in the material that had covered the outside viewer and from the outside walls as well. If the woman kept shooting she would eventually be able to make her own entryway.

I could hear the woman approach, she was shrieking so loud. "Get a tourniquet on him!" she screamed. Their voices lost some volume as they pulled the injured two-legger away from the steps.

"Is there another way out?" Mia asked.

"The back door," Koala said sadly looking at Jumper. "My car's in the garage in back, but it's dead. Haven't bothered to get a new battery. Never figured on leaving, not on this plane anyway."

"Why are they shooting at us, Riley?" Ben-Ben asked, a puddle spreading underneath him.

I understood his fear, but couldn't he at least scoot

forward a few steps to get out of the wetness?

"We're going to have to stay and fight," Jess said, looking at Zach who she had shielded in her arms.

"Pistols against machineguns isn't a very fair fight," Koala said as he inched his way back towards the front of the house.

He carefully pulled himself up so that he could look out the bottom of the viewer. "He's going to die," Koala said to no one in particular. "Never killed anything."

"Not even a zombie?" Mia asked incredulously, coming up alongside.

The hairy man shook his head, which I knew meant 'no'. I came up alongside them; there was a heavy trail of blood leading from the steps to the wheeler the people had come in.

The lone female among them stood to the side watching the house as the two males tried to stop the vital fluids from leaking out of the injured one.

Patches about had me add my own puddle as she fought for room next to me. "See it?" she asked me.

"See what?" I asked back.

"Death," was her one word reply.

My fur bristled, I saw no such thing and I was happy for it.

Her tail switched back and forth in a jerky manner, I knew this meant she was agitated. Who wouldn't have been?

"It is gone and has brought the man with it. They will seek vengeance now," Patches said, dropping down and moving away from the viewer.

I saw one of the men stand and shake his head, the one that looked like his hair was on fire. The woman screamed 'NO!' I saw her put something into the bottom of her fire stick. Koala pulled Mia and me down as the metal bees once again flew.

"What had it taken, Patches?" I asked; the man was still lying there.

"I'm going to cut your fucking head off!" she screamed.

"Does she mean me?" Koala asked, rubbing his hand on his throat.

Jess had gone into the food room and then into the small room beyond. "There's zombies out here," she shouted over the bees.

"Zombies out front, too," Mia replied. "They're either going to have to try to get in here in the next minute or fight the zombies."

"Or leave," Zach gurgled.

"Wouldn't that be nice," Patches said. "Highly unlikely though."

"I don't really like it here," Ben-Ben moaned.

All was still for a moment as the crazy woman stopped shooting. Dust swirled heavily in the air making it difficult to breath.

"This isn't over!" she shouted, sending another spray of bees our way. Or at least we thought that until no new holes showed up.

We all heard the car drive off, and some more bee-fire, but they were using it to clear zombies from their path. I had crept back up to the viewer to watch their departure. The wheeler we had come in was destroyed. Holes were punched in it all over the front. Vital fluids leaked out from the bottom of the wheeler worse than the male that had lost his leg.

"They're going to get Icely," Mia said, resignation ringing in her voice.

"We need to leave...we all need to leave," Jess said.

"No car and close to a hundred zombies, we're going to have a hell of a time getting through them with .22s," Koala said, looking around what remained of the viewer covering.

He backed up quickly as a zombie arm shot through. I smelled excrement – that was Ben-Ben. Patches hissed and mewled loudly before jumping on to the couch. More hands and arms thrust through and became entangled in the shade maker. I backed away from the viewer and started barking when zombies approached my spot; once again arms and even torsos were thrust through the new opening. The viewer on this side of the house was lower due to the ground outside which sloped upwards; most of the zombies here we could see down to their waists.

If their brethren weren't pushing so hard from behind pinning their legs to the house, the ones in front would most likely just have fallen into the house. I barked when I heard glass in the back of the house break.

"The back door!" Koala said before heading that way.

Jess had Zach in her arms and was shielding him. Mia had come up to my side and started firing her short fire stick. Zombie necks whipped back as she sent metal bees into their heads.

"There's too many!" Mia cried out.

Glass was breaking all around us as the zombies fought for ways to get in. Then shots began to ring out from the kitchen. "Gonna need some help! Door is going to give!" Koala shouted.

I could see that Jess was torn. To shoot, she would need to put Zach down and she just did not want to do that. I went in to the kitchen to see if there was anything I could do. The door was indeed giving. I could see light coming from a crack as the zombies pushed on it. Koala had his back against the wall and his legs kicked out in front of him to brace the bottom of the door to keep it from opening. Zombies had broken through the top half, which was made of small outside viewers. When they saw him they struggled even harder to get in.

Every part of me wanted to bark at them, to show them how ferocious I was, and that they should leave before I attacked, but I'd seen enough of them to know that they didn't care. Even if I started tearing into them they would still advance.

"Help me!" Koala screamed again. His legs were shaking from exertion. I heard creaking as the door was taking more force than it could withstand.

Jess ran in--she had placed Zach down on the floor of the kitchen.

"Riley, I don't want to be here," he said to me.

"That makes two of us," Patches said, coming in.

"How many is that plus me?" Ben-Ben asked, tail tucked firmly between his legs. Another puddle sprouted from between his legs when Jess shot her fire stick.

Koala squalled, I thought he had been bit. "Hot brass, hot brass!" he was bemoaning as he brushed shiny things off the top of his head and face. I smelled burning flesh, it was not unlike—

"Bacon?" Ben-Ben asked, braving the fighting to see if his favorite food in the world was somehow being prepared in the heat of the action.

"Face," I told him.

"Sorry!" Jess yelled as she moved slightly to keep shooting. Her shots were effective, but as a whole ineffectual. The zombies in front were dead, but the ones behind kept pressing forward. The door was starting to splinter.

"Get out of here, Jess!" Koala said, beads of sweat forming on the top of his head and cascading down his face. "I can't hold this much longer."

"I can't just leave you. Come with me."

"What do you think is going to happen if I move?" he strained to ask.

Jess shook her head, but I think more in denial than in not knowing the answer to the question. Even Ben-Ben would be able to tell that as soon as he moved, the door would slam open and zombies would come streaming in.

Water was coming from Jess' eyes. "Where should we go?" she asked.

"The basement--the door is made from the same stuff as the front door. Should hold for a long time."

"Long enough for Icely and the others to get back," Patches said.

"One thing at a time," I said to her.

"Oh that's right, dogs can't multi-task. That means do more than one thing at a time if you needed an interpretation."

"Is now the time for that?" Zach asked.

"Babies that shouldn't be talking should not be telling me what not to do," Patches said exiting the room.

A dead zombie was bent over, half in the house, the tips of his fingers brushing up against Koala's pants. Thick blood flowed from it to him. He kept trying to shift to avoid the sticky stream. Didn't much matter, the zombie was being jostled from those behind him, the loose arms swinging back and forth pretty much covering the entire small room with their blood offering.

Zach was in the middle of the floor and Jess was putting more bees in her stick. Ben-Ben had turned away from me. I heard his low growl and, before now, never heard such a sinister noise from him.

"Holy biscuits, Ben-Ben, what's the matter with you?" I asked, turning. He was bristled, his small canines were flashing as his lips pulled back savagely.

A zombie stumbled in, its milky eyes fixed solely on the baby down by its feet. A fresh head wound by its ear oozed blood. It looked like the bee had scraped against the side of its head leaving an exposed skull that shone a sickly swirl of colors. Ranging from deep reds and purples to the gray of an exposed brain where the bee had dug in a little deeper. Ben-Ben launched himself as the zombie bent down to get at Zach who was attempting to crawl away. Ben-Ben latched on to the zombie's nose. The zombie's arms were still outstretched reaching for its food. Ben-Ben had pulled it close to the floor; his back feet were scrabbling on the shiny surface of the food room trying to gain purchase.

He was growling as he shook his head vigorously

back and forth. When the zombie couldn't see the baby anymore it started grabbing at Ben-Ben, I think it meant to make a meal of him if it could.

"Let go, Ben-Ben!" I shouted, just as the zombie's hands wrapped around his small midsection. The zombie was pulling him in closer as it began to stand. I caught as much speed as I could get in the close distance and crashed into his leg joint. I heard something break from the force, but it cared little as it fought to bring Ben-Ben into its blackened, diseased mouth.

Ben-Ben had let go of the zombie's nose and now had his front paws braced on the zombie's forehead and his back paws against the zombie's chest. He was struggling to keep himself out of its jaws. I got behind the zombie and tore at the tendon in the back of the man's ankle.

The tip of it smacked wetly against my nose as it snapped back. It stung for a moment, but I had bigger things to worry about as the zombie was falling backwards; there was not much room to maneuver and I didn't have enough time to get myself out from under it should I get pinned down. The thing had completely fallen on its back, but as of yet had not yielded its prize. Ben-Ben screeched as the zombie bit into him. I struggled to get towards the zombie's mouth as I saw fur and skin being pulled taut. Blood began to drop from Ben-Ben as he struggled to get away – his eyes nearly all white he was so afraid. I tore at the side of the man's face, skin sloughed off in my mouth. I spit out his chewed-up ear.

I had pulled off enough skin from his cheek that his teeth were exposed. Ben-Ben had a paw pressing up against its nose, the zombie's tongue kept flicking up trying like a snake to coil around it and bring it into those dangerous teeth. Every piece of the thing I grabbed came away in my mouth. Patches came up on the other side, I caught a glint of light off her razor-sharp claws as she plunged it into the zombie's eye. It popped like those funny things the two-leggers call balloons. White and red fluid leaked out from it and still the zombie pulled on the small dog. Ben-Ben's blood was now dripping on the zombie's face. I felt a hand sweep me away, I slid on the slippery surface as a fire stick went off. All was still for a moment.

"Ben-Ben, are you alright?" Jess screamed. She had put her small stick up against the thing's head and sent a bee deep into its brain.

Ben-Ben was howling and panting heavily. Jess scooped up Zach.

"Riley, Ben-Ben, come on!" Patches shouted to me as Jess headed for the door that led to the inside cave.

"Mia!" Jess shouted. There were zombies everywhere. I could not see our traveling companion through the lot of them.

Ben-Ben had rolled onto his side and was drawing his paws in.

"Not yet," I told him as I grabbed the scruff of his neck. I half dragged and half carried the small dog, following Jess.

Jess opened the door that led down. I could smell the coolness and the safety the cave afforded. I could hear her footfalls as she went down the stairs. I had kept the door open with my nose long enough for Patches to get through and to drag Ben-Ben onto a small landing. Just as quickly as she had gone down, Jess had come back up – this time without Zach.

"Thank God," I heard her mumble when she saw the three of us at the top. "You guys stay here. I've got to help them, watch out for Zach."

"I'll watch Ben-Ben and Zach," Patches told me as I looked from them to Jess who had just exited the door. I nodded to the cat and darted out before the heavy door could close. Almost immediately Jess was shooting, but she wasn't the only one. Mia had fought her way to the back door and was trying to help Koala. He was holding a zombie at bay with his arms locked out in front of him. The zombie had tried to descend on him while he was holding the door. I made my way in and around legs trying to get to him.

Jess shot a zombie that had stopped and was reaching down for me. I jumped over it as I headed for Koala. His arms were shaking from the strain of holding the thrusting zombie from getting to him. I watched as another one latched on to Koala's leg and tore a ribbon of meat from him. The man did not so much as cry out as the zombie dove down for more. I charged into the eating zombie; we both fell over and onto Koala who grunted from the added weight. I seized the zombie's throat in my jaw and ripped all the way down to its spine. I shook my head violently back and forth making sure as much meat would come loose as possible when I tore free. The zombie's head fell to the side when I let go, there was nothing left there to hold it in place. And still the mouth opened and closed endlessly. I grabbed the top of its skull and pulled it off of Koala. The damage had been done, though, as I looked at the festering wound on his leg. The stench of death was already about him.

Jess got as close to the other zombie he was holding away from him as possible. The thing turned to look at her, its tongue dancing around wildly in its mouth. Its nose was twitching quickly as it sensed the new source of prey. A look of shock and surprise creased its features as she placed a bullet through his upper lip. Cartilage, blood, and brain sprayed over Koala and me. Jess reached down and dragged Koala free from the door. As she moved him, the door moved as well. It got hung up when it pressed against the two dead zombies in the small room.

"Where's Jumper?" Koala winced.

I hadn't seen the old dog since the melee started. I didn't think that was good news; the idea that he could get to safety was not promising. The old dog could still learn new tricks as I was about to find out. Jess shot a few more times into the zombies that were trying to force their way through the back door, the bodies further blocking their path. She had granted us that elusive thing the two-leggers called time.

We went out from the kitchen with me in front and Jess supporting Koala. Mia had gone back to get the old dog and now she and Jumper were pinned against the far wall of the living room. His lips were pulled back in a fierce gesture I would not have thought he was capable of. One or both of them were bleeding from multiple wounds. Mia was putting more bees in her fire stick Jumper had latched onto one of the zombies' arms trying to pull it downwards. The zombie stumbled and fell at the old dog's paws. Jumper pulled at the back of its neck, his maw coming away with gristly pieces of the thing.

Jess' arm that was not supporting Koala was shooting as was the one Koala was not using to hold himself up. More zombies were struggling to get in but for right now, more were dying. A hole had finally broken through.

"Come on!" I barked. Jumper looked up, his eyes angry and tired...oh so tired.

Mia nearly fell over the fallen zombies before she got her legs under her. She and Jumper followed us quickly, as did the zombies. I waited until Jumper got past me and then leaped into the closest zombie. I wrapped my mouth around his knee and crushed the delicate bones. That wouldn't kill it, but would create a big enough jam up that we'd be able to escape.

"Hurry up!" Koala urged as if I needed the incentive.

He closed the door as soon as I came in. Mia, Jess, Patches and Ben-Ben had moved to the bottom of the stairs. Koala, myself and Jumper were on the top landing. Koala slid down the wall and into a sitting position as he tried to staunch the blood flowing from his leg.

CHAPTER SIX

"I'm in a little bit of trouble," he told Jumper. The dog had sat next to him licking his hand.

"Riley," Patches said from the bottom of the stairs.

I turned and barked savagely at her; she backed away as I shouted. "I don't want to hear about death anymore!" I told her, "Let him show himself instead of hiding in the shadows. What will come for him when I get rid of it?"

"Mia's been bitten as well," Patches said when I stopped.

I almost fell over from the shock. As it was, it was difficult getting air into myself. "How bad? Will she live?"

The cat shook her head 'no'. "And neither will Koala. The bite will make them like the others."

"I know what it does," I replied thinking back on Winke. "When will this stop?" I asked, hanging my head low.

I came down the stairs. Jess was crying, tears coming out of her eyes faster than the snake-like water pourer She-Alpha used in the back yard. I loved drinking water from that thing, though I hated when Daniel used to spray me with it. Okay that wasn't so bad either, he usually only did it when it was hot out and it felt good to get cool under the burning disc. Mia was working on Ben-Ben, putting what looked like an old shirt around his stomach to protect his bite. Jess was rocking back and forth with Zach in her arms.

When Mia was done putting the wound covering on Ben-Ben she got up and walked over to Jess. "Ben-Ben will be fine, a little bald, but the zombie only ate fur as far as I can tell."

"You alright?" I asked him with concern.

"He...he bit me Riley. It hurt so bad. Am I going to become one of them now?" he asked.

I honestly didn't know.

"What if I don't like bacon anymore?" he asked.

"He'll be fine," Patches said to me. "You fought bravely," she told him.

Now I knew he was going to die or the cat would have never said anything nice to him.

My attention was pulled away when I heard Jess speak. "I should be consoling you, not the other way around," Jess said sadly as Mia put her arm around Jess' shoulders. "If I hadn't forced you out of Icely's house you'd be fine," she wailed.

"You did not force me out, Jess. I jumped willingly at the chance to escape. I'd rather die here now than have had a long life under Icely's rule. I was his prisoner and you helped me escape. I will always be thankful for that." The two women clutched. "I'll gladly take these few hours of freedom with you over a lifetime of servitude for him."

"Oh, Mia," Jess cried again.

"Can I hold Zach?" she asked as they broke away.

Jess held the baby out.

"I'm going to miss your fat little cheeks," Mia said as she kissed his belly.

"Why?" Zach asked. "I'm not going anywhere."

"Are you talking back to me?" Mia asked with a smile.

"It's the polite thing to do," he responded.

"He really likes you." Jess sobbed.

"What's not to like?" Zach asked.

"I wish I knew how long I had left...maybe I don't. You know what you have to do, right?" Mia asked.

"What?" Jess asked, clearly appalled.

"I don't...I can't become one of them. Please don't let

me," Mia begged.

"What...what do you want me to do?" Jess asked. "You can't be serious, Mia, I can't do that!"

"You have to and you will, Jess. Who do you think I'm going to go after when I turn?"

"Why are they crying?" Zach asked me.

"Mia's sick," I told him, licking his chubby little hand.

"Kiss her forehead Riley, that will make her better. That's what my mom used to do to me," he told me.

"I wish it was that simple," Patches told him.

"Maybe if you gave her some bacon," Ben-Ben replied. He had gotten up and was standing next to Patches, leaning on her more like it.

"Bacon or kisses aren't going to fix this," I snapped. Ben-Ben looked more wounded from that than he did his injury. Zach just started crying.

"I've seen rats act more civilized," Patches said, throwing a little salt on my raw nerves.

I walked away and up the stairs. Koala was petting Jumper's head. He had tied the belt that held his robe together right below his knee. Blood still spilled, but at a much slower pace.

"I did not think I would see the day when my human passed," Jumper said, lifting his head when he heard me, his large ears still touching the floor. "I think it is an unnatural thing."

I was alarmed as I heard the zombies bumping up against the door although neither Jumper nor Koala were disturbed in the least.

"Jess, Mia!" Koala called out weakly.

Jess came to the bottom of the stairs. "Can I get you anything?" Jess asked, she looked and sounded so scared.

"I'm not feeling too well. Between the blood loss and the bite I don't think I'm too much longer for this world." As he was saying it, I watched as his hale color left him. Dark purplish black rings orbed his eyes; his lips began to pale and his breathing became labored.

"Please don't say that." Jess begged. "You'll be fine."

Koala coughed, a spot of blood striking the far wall as he did so, and more was dribbling down his chin. "I've asked God for a pass on this one," he told Jess as he picked up his fire stick.

"What?" Jess asked, her eyes growing large.

"My options were to have you do it or do myself. I didn't think it was fair to you so I asked the Big Man if just this one time would it be alright."

"If what would be alright?" she asked, but her actions and her tone let me know that she already knew what he was saying.

"I really just don't want you to watch. And if you should somehow make it out of here, which I truly hope you do, please take Jumper with you."

"Anything, Koala, I promise." Jess was crying.

"That's all, you might want to walk away now."

Jess nodded and was out of sight.

"Jumper I could not have asked for a truer friend," Koala said. He was interrupted by a racking set of coughs, bloody clots of phlegm hitting the far wall with audible plops. Blood was now freely flowing from his mouth. He struggled to get one of his fake feet off; he wiggled his toes a little then braced one end of the fire stick against the wall in front of him. I knew which end the metal bees came out of and he was doing it wrong. I started barking and approaching him to let him know he was making a huge mistake.

"Riley, he knows what he's doing," Jumper said calmly.

"Wrong end...wrong end!" I yelled in warning. "You can't let him, Jumper!"

"Hush, Riley," Jumper told me. "Let him go in peace."

I whined as Koala placed his mouth over the end of

the stick. He wiggled his toes again and placed them where the two-leggers front paws usually go.

"Wrong end," I whined softly through my nose.

"Let him do what he needs to do with the firearm," Patches said from below.

Fire-arm? Was all I got to think before the explosion brushed everything else aside.

Koala's head blew back, smashing against the wall he was sitting against. The stick clattered to the floor and what was left of his skull fell forward. Pieces of his head were imbedded in the wall behind him. Jagged pieces of red-striped, white bone dotted the wall, brain matter clinging to them as precariously as Jumper clung to life.

"It was the noble thing to do," Jumper said as he let out a long slow mournful howl.

I saw no nobility in it whatsoever; he had blown his head off with a fire-arm. I padded downstairs, my ears ringing from the explosion.

Jumper's cries continued for a little longer and then stilled. I figured what it meant; however, it did not make me feel any better about it.

"Is Jumper alright?" Ben-Ben asked from the bottom of the stairs. He had gotten up to look once the old dog had stopped.

"He is now," Patches told the small dog. "They're back together again."

Now that made absolutely no sense and I would have called the cat out on it if Mia didn't start to cough. Jess and Mia had been almost inseparable since we had come down into the man-cave.

"Koala was a lot braver then me," Mia said. "I'm so sorry."

"I can't, Mia, I just can't." Jess' face was twisted up in torturous agony.

"I'd do it for you."

"You're a liar."

That got Mia laughing. "Caught me there. I can feel it inside of me, Jess, like a predator it's stalking me…getting ready to pounce. To kill me." Jess clutched the woman's hand. "Only it's no great jungle cat, it's like…it's like a little fucking worm, millions, billions of them crawling inside of me getting ready to take over. You can't let that happen, Jess. I'm begging you."

I saw something change in Jess, right there and then. She got a set to her jaw. She wasn't happy in the least about what she had to do, but she'd do it. She got up and hugged Mia fiercely.

"I've only known you a couple of days but I just need you to know that I love you," she told the woman.

"Thank you," Mia told her as they separated.

Mia was sitting in a chair. Jess had placed Zach next to me off on the side. Jess got behind Mia and placed the end of her fire-arm against the back of Mia's head. Mia let out a shock of breath.

Her lips were moving and soft words were coming out. Jess picked up on the other woman's words and they said them together. "…forgive me my sins for what I'm about to do…" Mia fell to the floor at almost the same time the bee casing came to a stop by my paw. Jess and Zach alike were wailing.

"What did she just do!" Zach was screaming.

"What she had to," Patches told the baby.

Mia had fallen face forward onto the hard ground, her arms out by her side, her legs somewhat tangled in the chair. A growing pool of blood haloed out from her head. My ears were ringing from so much loud noise and my nose was stinging from the smell of smoke from the fire-arms. Jess had pulled her front paws up close to her mouth, one still clutching the bee sender. Tears came from her eyes, sadness washed out from her. I walked over and nuzzled my face to her leg. She didn't move she was so lost in her grief.

Our pack had been seven-plus-one strong we were

now back down to when we had left our home. Animals, two-leggers, and dead ones kept dying all around us. I had hope that we'd survive – but not much anymore. Jess looked inconsolable and Ben-Ben was wounded. That left me, Patches, and Zach to defend the pack. Last time I checked, sharp claws and a dirty fake skin weren't going to be enough, no matter how smelly it was.

"Do you think Jess will fit through the window?" Patches asked.

"Huh?" I asked. I was having a tough time thinking or more likely understanding. I guess I was somewhat lost in my own grief.

"Do you think she will fit through that window?" Patches asked, looking past my shoulder.

"I'm not sure if I'll fit," I told her when I turned to look. It was a small viewer set high up on the wall. It was smaller than the one I had climbed out of with Patches to escape the dog prison.

Ben-Ben looked up when we heard the dead ones walking on the floor above us. "Can't we stay here?" he asked pathetically.

"No food," Zach chimed in. His eyes had a faraway glaze to them. He was still looking at Mia's prone form on the floor.

"And the others said they'd come back," I added.

"No food," Ben-Ben said sadly.

I honestly couldn't blame him for fixating on that one problem; if it helped him forget all the death around us then more power to him. I motioned to Patches, pointing at Zach.

"I am not a babysitter, Riley," she told me.

"Just get him to look somewhere else. I have to get Jess moving--we can't stay here," I told her.

"Baby who should not be talking," Patches said going up to Zach. He didn't respond. "Can you not talk now?" she asked. "That would make more sense and make me happier."

"I don't feel so good," Zach told her. "My stomach

hurts."

Nerves and lack of food would do that. I just hoped he wasn't getting sick as well. I nudged Jess' leg again but she didn't move. I barked and she tried to shoo me away. I went over to Mia and as tenderly as I could I grabbed her front paw that was closest to me.

Jess didn't say anything until I started to pull on Mia's arm.

"Riley, NO! What are you doing?" She took a step towards me. I growled deeply, the fur on my back was bristled. "Riley?" she asked cocking her head to the side.

I got Mia's body moving as I pulled her along the length of the cave. The trail of blood could not be helped, but at least the shell of her was out of their sight. I came back when I had pulled her as far away as I could. Jess was looking at the thick swath of life fluid on the ground.

"Smart...for a dog," Patches said to me. "And you really can look ferocious when you put your mind to it. I mean, you don't scare me all that much, but the girl was petrified."

I was saddened I had scared Jess, but she was not giving me many options. It seemed to bring her out of her daze, though. She began to look around. She grabbed the fire-arm Mia had left behind and looked in it. She did not look overly pleased. She took in a deep breath and went to the bottom of the stairs where she let it all out in one great gust.

"Shit," she muttered before she went up the stairs. She came down a moment later with Koala's fire arms, her face visibly paler but resolute.

"No going out the basement door," she said aloud. "And it doesn't appear that this is a walk-out basement. That leaves two options...we stay or we go out a window."

Patches had already come to that conclusion. How was she so smart?

"Gonna be a tight fit," she said as she grabbed the

chair Mia had sat in and moved it over to right underneath the viewer.

If she heard or saw the blood fall from the chair, she paid it no heed. She stepped onto the chair and rubbed her arm against the viewer; the dingy light that had been coming in brightened.

"Shit," she said again, "there are zombies out there. Not many, but if I start shooting them, more will come."

"Patches, if we get out where will we go?" I asked her.

"We need another car, that is for certain. We cannot stay on the ground for very long," she said.

"Will the zombies follow me if I get out?" I asked.

"They will. Looks like they'll eat any old thing at this point." She smirked. "You mean to draw them away?"

"I do."

"How will you find us again once we get out?" she asked, looking like she actually had some concern. It could potentially be fake, but I didn't think so.

"I'll get them far enough away and then I'll circle around and pick up your trail."

"Oh, I almost forgot about that obnoxiously large thing you call a nose."

"Funny, cat. If you get away and get a wheeler and you don't find me soon enough, just go. You'll become the pack leader."

She looked at me but held her tongue. I'm under the impression she figured she was the pack leader the entire time. "You would sacrifice yourself?" she asked. I don't think she really held an understanding of the concept.

"For the safety of everyone else? Yes I would," I told her honestly.

"She's not going to let you out, you know," she said to me.

I hopped up onto the dead tree structure and placed my paws against the viewer.

"What are you doing, Riley?" Jess asked.

I pawed at the window silently; I didn't want the dead ones to take notice…at least not yet.

"I don't think this is such a good idea," Zach said.

"Why?" Ben-Ben asked. "What's going on?"

"Riley, you're just going to have to find a corner of the basement to do what you need to do," Jess said.

"I don't need to relieve myself," I grumbled at her.

"Stop, Riley, they'll notice." Jess came over to me.

"Open the doggone window," I growled at her.

She backed up.

"How to win friends and influence people," Patches said.

"Cat, how do I open this thing?" I asked.

"That lever needs to be pulled down."

"What's a lever, Patches?" I asked. I was getting angry now. I had a plan and I wanted to do it before I got too scared to even attempt it.

"That white small stick right above your paw is the window lever, you need to pull it down," she told me.

I draped my paw over it and yanked, it dug into my soft pads at first and then finally yielded.

"Riley!" Jess said, coming back towards me.

The viewer popped open a little, but not nearly enough to fit me through.

"Pull the window down, Riley," Patches told me.

Jess moved and grabbed me around the waist. Patches spat and hissed at Jess. I turned and leveled a fierce gaze on the girl.

"What is going on?" she asked, terror filling her eyes.

I truly was sorry that I had to do that, but she could have easily pulled me off my perch.

"I wish I knew what you guys were up to," Jess said. "Riley, why are you going out?"

The viewer was flat with the ground; it could not open any more. I lunged so that my front paws were gripping the outside of the house, my back paws were pumping in the air trying to get a paw hold on anything, I was coming up empty. I once again felt Jess's hands on my body, but this time they weren't trying to hold me back she was pushing me up.

"I don't know what you're doing, but I've trusted you since this started and I shouldn't doubt you now, my precious dog. Whatever you're doing...please don't get hurt." She kissed me on the neck before she got me all the way through the small viewer.

This is a bad idea, I thought as I moved away from the small shrubs that encircled the house. I checked out my surroundings, making sure I had a way to escape once the time arrived. I moved further from the house and Jess' frantic gaze...then I started to bark.

Jess' hand went to her mouth. *What are you doing?* she mouthed.

It didn't take zombies long to hone in on me. Within a few beats of my heart, the chase was on. I was pulling as many of them away from the house as I could.

CHAPTER SEVEN

"I swear to the Animal Gods, if that dog gets herself killed and I get stuck with you, Ben-Ben, there will be hell to pay."

"Hell?" Ben-Ben asked.

"Ultimate dog jail," Patches said.

"Oooh, that sounds bad." Ben-Ben cowered.

"You too?" Jess asked as Patches easily jumped up and grabbed the lip of the window pulling herself up and out.

Patches looked around quickly. She could hear Riley's barking trailing off as she moved further away. She turned and pawed the glass.

"What?" Jess asked.

"You cannot be this thick," Patches said to her.

"You want me to go out there?" Jess asked.

"See? I knew all humans weren't dumb," Patches said.

"How can they be?" Ben-Ben asked. "They know how to make bacon."

"Fair point," Patches replied. "Although I don't love it quite like you do."

Jess looked at Patches, confusion quickly becoming a dawning. "Riley is leading them away, so we can get out of here. How is this possible? I'm just not getting it."

"Doesn't matter what 'you get' get your ass out here!" Patches spat.

"Me next!" Ben-Ben yipped. "I really have to go."

Jess looked down at him and then to the window. "As good an idea as any." Jess picked up the small dog.

"Of course it is," Patches purred, "I thought of it."

Ben-Ben turned slightly just as Jess was pushing him through the window. "Goodbye, Mia. Goodbye, Jumper. Goodbye, Koala, may you always have a slice of bacon in your mouth." And then he was out.

"Fine prayer," Patches told him.

"Thank you," Ben-Ben told her. He moved a few feet over to the side of the house and hunched over, arching his back placing his backend close to the ground.

"What are you doing?" Patches nearly screamed at him.

"I have to go," Ben-Ben replied, clearly confused.

"Not here, you dumb dog! The zombies will smell it. You should have gone inside the house."

Ben-Ben cocked his head to the side. "You're kidding, right? Riley always yells at me for that…even when I tell her I couldn't hold it anymore. And now I'm trying to do the right thing and you're telling me I'm not. I don't get it?"

"Just hold it some more," Patches told the dog.

Ben-Ben grunted at her. "Where's Riley?" he asked, looking around like he just realized his friend wasn't around anymore.

"Where do you go?" Patches asked. "Did you miss the whole plan?"

"There was a plan?" he asked.

"Just keep an eye out for zombies."

"Which eye?" Ben-Ben asked.

"If I didn't think you'd start crying, I'd stick a claw in your nose."

Ben-Ben moved away.

"That's the smartest thing you've done today," Patches said, returning her gaze back into the basement.

Jess had picked up Zach and walked over towards Mia. Patches heard her murmur a small prayer and then she came back towards the window. She hesitated as she moved to put the baby outside. "I'm sorry," Jess told Zach as she pushed him through the window. He toppled a couple of inches to the ground. When he righted himself he had some leaves sticking to the side of his head.

"That was fun," he gurgled.

Jess made sure all of the safeties were engaged on the pistols and shotgun before she pushed them through the window.

"Anti-gun activists would have a field day with this if they saw it," Jess said as weapons surrounded her younger brother. Zach watched his sister put the guns down but made no move for them.

Jess grabbed the lip of the house and jumped up, the weight of her body coming down on the window. It shattered with a much louder crack than it should have. With no manmade sounds to speak of, the smashing of the glass pane traveled far. Jess paused for a moment and then began to hurriedly pull herself through the small enclosure as they heard footsteps coming their way.

RILEY

I've had better ideas, I thought as I ran from yard to yard.

I had a good number of zombies playing chase. Only some were the faster ones and they usually got stuck on fences, giving me enough time to catch my breath as I went through the openings in between. My throat was sore from all the panting I was doing, and I really wanted a huge bowl of water.

Only once so far had I had to fight my way out of a situation. I had run into a back yard and had been panting so heavily I had not heard the zombie exit the home from behind me. I'd been watching the zombies that had been following me. They were walking into the fence, which caught most of them high on their legs. Some would fall in or be pushed over and the pursuit would begin anew. Other times, the faster zombies would hit the fences so hard they would snap the dead trees, usually at the cost of their own broken bones that would snap louder than the wood.

It made no sense that they felt no pain and they seemingly never got tired. The closest thing I'd ever seen pursue food so relentlessly was Ben-Ben, and even he had his limitations. Maybe to the zombies I was one huge slab of bacon. That was the thought I had when I felt a foot stumble into me from behind. The zombie was bent over at the waist, her black mouth agape. Jagged teeth were gnawing ceaselessly as her outstretched hands tried to encircle my neck. I was glad the cat wasn't there to see me as I yelped. I tucked my tail between my legs and leaped.

In my panic to get away I did not watch where I was heading. I had kept my line of sight on her as I ran. The back of the yard had the smooth planked dead trees that rose much higher than I could jump and with no openings, it was not an avenue of escape. I slid to a halt as I turned my body. Fangs bared, lips pulled back, fur bristled, I barked savagely as she advanced. Her hands were still outstretched as I ripped three of her fingers off in one foul bite. Her blood-soaked fingers on her left hand tried to seek purchase. The best she could manage was a mild pinch on that side. Her other hand gripped a large swath of fur and pulled me towards her. I sank my teeth deep into the meat of her arm. She was unconcerned as she brought her mouth down towards the side of my face, looking to pull pieces of me away and into her mouth.

Ben-Ben had a history of eating some of the most disgusting things the world had to offer – on more than one occasion that even involved animal droppings, and still his breath had never smelled quite as horrid as this thing that leaned down for me. If the Death-being Patches said she saw had a smell, this would be it. I let go of her arm and wrenched myself free from her grasp, whining a bit as she took a fistful of fur with her. Her teeth clamped down on air. Her eyes went from satisfied, to confused, to enraged that I had not sat quietly while she ate me. At least that's what it looked like to me.

I latched on to the back of her thigh before she could spin and try to grab hold once again. I dug my front paws into the ground and violently whipped my head back and forth. The light fake furs yielded easily enough as did a substantial amount of her muscle. I ripped a wide red wet swath of it clean from her, leaving a gaping wound where she was once whole. The piece of meat was still rippling on the ground when she turned. I ran into the middle of the yard and she followed, dragging her damaged leg behind – her foot at a grotesque angle to the rest of her leg.

"How?" I barked.

The taste of her was sour in my mouth. This one zombie above all others bothered me to no end. Her pale, gray, moist eyes were locked on to me. She wore fake skins much like She-Alpha, and their size, build and looks were similar enough that they could be littermates. Maybe that was why I wished so hard that she'd stop chasing me. I needed this rest. Soon I was going to have to circle back around and try and find my pack and this zombie was not allowing it. I knew better than to posture an attack…I did it anyway. Tough to just ignore something that is instinctual. That was as much a part of me as looking out for my pack.

I ran at the zombie, coming close, and at the last moment I moved to the side and away from her outstretched hands. I quickly got in behind it. The zombie spun down as I'd hoped it would with its leg not working correctly. Dogs and even cats could get around pretty good with one damaged leg, two-leggers not so much. I had thought to crush her skull in my teeth, but the pain to my jaw would be immense and just the thought of tasting her mind did not sit well in my stomach. I went to the leg that was whole and ripped out a portion to match the other. She could come at me now, but it would be at a snail's pace.

I moved a few paces away. I was breathing heavily and needed to slake this thirst. First things first though as I took a few ragged breathes. My head whipped up with the loud cracking of the fence that separated me from the zombies. The chase was on again, I was not sure how much longer I could keep this up.

JESS

Patches was caught midway between wanting to flee to preserve her life and staying to protect the pack. "Damn you, Riley, if you get me killed I'm going to be pissed. Stupid guilt," she said softly, her tail the only thing moving.

Patches was peeking out from underneath the bushes. There were three zombies in the area; two seemed completely oblivious to anything going on and the third was sniffing the air. Patches could tell he had caught a scent of something, but as of yet had not located his prey.

Patches wished Jess would be quieter as she grunted her way through the window. The zombie would sniff, then stop and look around, take a step or two, then repeat the cycle.

He's hunting, she thought as she watched. He turned and she slunk back further under the brush. She thought he had a good idea where they were. She noted that the other two had turned as well even though they were further away and as of yet had not shown any curiosity whatsoever for her location.

There's some form of communication going on, Patches thought as she watched the feet of the other two begin to approach. "Hurry up, Jess," she hissed an urgent message to the girl.

Jess had just pulled her last leg out of the window. She checked on Zach and then stuffed the two pistols into the front pouch of the sweatshirt hoodie she was wearing. She grabbed Zach and then the rifle. The lead zombie was pushing up against the bushes, trying to force his way through. He made it about half way when he stopped.

"Wheeler," Ben-Ben said softly. Patches could tell there was a hint of excitement in his voice. "Two of them, we're safe."

Patches was not nearly as convinced. She knew there was no one out there looking for them or attempting to rescue them unless Riley had magically learned how to drive. "That'd be something," she said. "I'd like to see that."

Ben-Ben looked confused.

"Do not move, dog," Patches said, her tail brushing the ground behind her. "We don't know who is in those cars." At least the sound of the engines had the added benefit of drawing the two furthest zombies away.

Jess had propped the shotgun up against her shoulder as she sat hunched down by the side of the house. The business end of it was pointed up into the bushes where the zombie would meet his maker if he came one foot further.

She would have to shoot if he did, and if that happened, the people in the cars would know where they were. Patches hoped it didn't come to that. Zombies were dangerous to be sure but nothing in comparison to people. The zombie paused momentarily and then followed his brethren.

"Well, that's my car," a voice said. "Did you have to shoot it up?"

"Icely," Jess whispered under her breath.

"I didn't want them to use it to get away," Dianna said.

"Ever hear of pulling the spark plug wires?" Icely asked with some heat.

"There were zombies here and people were shooting at us. Sedgwick had been hit," Ned said.

"Yeah, yeah I get it, lot of shit going on," he told them. "Mia!" he shouted. "You going to come out on your own, or are you going to make me come in there and get you? It'll go worse for you if I have to do that! Well…scratch that, it's going to go bad for you either way, but you could at least be courteous enough to save me the trouble!"

"Zombies," Grumper said. "There's always fucking zombies."

Dianna lifted her machine gun, Icely pushed the barrel down. "You daft? You fire that thing and we're going to have a zombie party in under five minutes."

He reached into his car and pulled out a machete. He rubbed his thumbnail along the blade, satisfied with the sharpness. The tall man strode towards the nearest zombie. He pulled the arm wielding the large knife back, turning his hips like a professional baseball player as he swung. The blade met little resistance as it parted the zombie's Adam's apple, sliced through his esophagus, and then made short work of the delicate bones that supported the head. The zombie took two more steps before it realized it was now driving blind. The head fell with a sickening thud.

"That's how you do it," Icely said with a measure of satisfaction.

"I'll stick to my gun." Dianna turned away.

Grumper opened up the trunk to the car he had been in and pulled out a large tire iron. "Mind if I take one, boss?" he asked.

"Have at it." Icely pulled his blade free from the skull of the second zombie. He had struck it on the top of the cranium, determined to split the head in two. He had driven the blade entirely down to the base of the nose before the momentum and human material had slowed and finally stopped the blade. The zombie's head opened up like a butterfly.

"Well that's the stuff of nightmares." Icely laughed as he placed one foot against the zombie's stomach. As he pushed it away, he wrenched his blade free. The body jerked a few times on the pavement, and then lay still.

Grumper brought the curved end of the tire iron into the forehead of the third zombie. Blood erupted as if it had been under extreme pressure and seeking a way to escape its captivity.

"Weak," Icely said as the zombie kept coming forward.

"Thing's skull must be an inch thick," Grumper said.

"Or you're getting decrepit in your old age." Ned smirked at him.

Grumper reared back, his arms shivering as he planted another swing in the same spot, the bones cracking like an over boiled egg. Chunks of skull flew out from the impact; the zombie staggered but was still standing. Grumper walked a couple of steps away and picked up a piece of the skull. "Look at that fucking thing, it's a freak of nature," Grumper said turning the abnormally thick piece of bone around and around in his hand.

"Are you going to finish the damn thing off?" Icely asked, watching the swaying zombie.

"Sure, sure sorry." Grumper dropped the piece of bone and wiped his hand on the side of his shirt. His third blow went halfway into the brain tissue, it was all Grumper could do to pull his iron free before the zombie fell to the ground.

"Okay, Mia, get your ass out here. I want to be done with this and go home. And, oh yeah, bring your little friend out with you. I plan on sharing her with the whole city. The men will be thrilled to have her in the whore stables," Icely said.

Jess was shaking so violently she nearly dropped the rifle. Patches brushed up against her, hoping that some of her resolve would rub off on the girl.

"What about the man in there, Icely?" Dianna asked.

"What about him?"

"He killed my brother, I want to avenge his death."

"Then do it. I have no quarrel with him unless he

shoots at me."

There were a few moments where nothing happened and all that could be heard was the idle of the two engines.

"Really, Mia? You're going to make me come in there? Fine, Ned, get the grenades."

Jess' face blanched. Patches had only heard the word once before when Daniel played at war with his friends. He always made exaggerated explosion sounds and would say that everyone on the opposing side was dead, although that never happened. They would complain that they were sufficiently hidden so as to not be hit by the burst.

"I see movement in the house," Grumper said.

"Looks like zombies…and a shitload of them," Dianna said.

"Oh you don't even know how pissed off I'm going to be if they've already been offed," Icely said. "Well…clear some of the stupid bastards away so we can go in and see a half-eaten Mia."

"The explosion is going to bring zombies," Ned told him.

Icely grabbed his collar and jerked the man violently towards him. "Do I look stupid?" he spat into the other man's face. "Just get it done." Icely shoved him away.

Ned gave a quick look over to Dianna who clutched her weapon tight and then he quickly and cautiously moved towards the house.

"Zombies don't shoot, dipwad. Hurry up," Icely said.

"Fire in the hole!" Ned shouted as he pulled the pin on the grenade and lobbed it through one of the broken windows. He quickly ducked down underneath. Everyone took cover except for Icely.

Jess rocked as the house moved behind her. A blistering flame filled with detritus and furniture spewed forth from the window, raining debris down all over the front yard.

"Now that's what I call exciting! Let's go see if our

friends are okay," he said with mocking concern. "You first, Dianna, you seem to be all ready to start shooting that little toy of yours."

She hesitated for a moment and watched him reach for the large magnum strapped to his hip before she did as she was ordered. "Good girl," he said as she walked away.

She avoided her brother's blood as she climbed the steps. She checked the lock and kicked once at the door. Pain rocketed up her leg from the unyielding oak and iron door. Icely laughed, a grating noise issuing forth from him.

"Hilarious," she mumbled as she blistered the door lock with rounds.

The door swung open easily enough after the assault. She stumbled back from the smell of burnt decay. Zombie parts littered the entire room; it looked like a mad doctor's laboratory that had been stockpiling parts to create some disfigured, liquefied being. She had to swallow down hard to keep the gorge at bay.

"Looks like that bitch of yours is having a hard time," Icely said to Ned.

Ned came up behind his wife. His eyes began to water, his nose protesting against the odors that assailed it. Dianna walked in, her eyes rapidly scanning the room. She let loose a short staccato burst as zombies began to come out from different parts of the house.

"Shut the screen door," Ned said, pressing close behind her. He flashed a grenade in front of her.

"Another one?" she asked.

"Why not? How often am I going to have a chance to use them?" Dianna moved out of the way just as the zombies were about to cross the room. Ned pulled the pin and opened the screen door enough to toss it in. "That was stupid," he said as he grabbed his wife and jumped off the small porch.

The explosion ripped the screen door right from its hinges, sending it spiraling out to the roadway.

"Fire in the hole," Ned said belatedly.

Jess had cried out from the second explosion. Luckily she wasn't loud enough to overcome the blast.

Icely stopped the skidding door with his boot. "Maybe lay off the explosives, Ned. Remember me saying I wanted them alive?"

Jess pushed away from the house attempting to see around the corner. From this vantage point she could only see the flattened wheels of the vehicle they had come in. She stayed tight to the side of the house and inched herself closer to the front. She almost gasped when she saw Icely's white snakeskin boots in the roadway. She pulled back quickly.

Zach was fidgeting a bit, but even he knew better than to say anything right then. Patches had stayed close to Jess as she moved. Her attention was pulled away as she caught a foul odor; she mistakenly thought another zombie was on the prowl. Not more than a foot away Ben-Ben had resumed his defecating position.

He smiled wanly as Patches glared at him. "I really have to go," he told her sheepishly.

"Oh God," Jess mumbled. "What is that?" She turned to see Ben-Ben finishing up. She looked relieved that it wasn't a zombie, but somewhat terrified that Ben-Ben's masterpiece, such as it was, was blocking her only available path for escape.

"Not cool," Patches said, skirting a wide path around the scat. "Not cool at all."

"I really had to go." Ben-Ben pleaded his case. "Oooh…itchy butt," he said as he dropped his rear end to the mulch-strewn earth. He dragged himself with his front paws towards Patches. She hissed and ran further away.

"Who does that?" Patches asked.

Ben-Ben was all smiles and tongue when he finished.

They all stopped as they heard the approach of heavy footfalls on the hard ground. Jess breathed a sigh of relief when she realized Icely was heading in to the house.

"You coming?" he asked the driver of his car.

"Schools, post a man at the door. I want you to come in and tell me what happened.

"We've got to go," Jess said. Patches thought it was completely unnecessary to voice the obvious.

They clearly heard a lighter snap a flame as the sentry lit a cigarette. That seemed to be the spark Jess needed to get moving. Her eyes grew wide as she did some unnatural body contortions to get past Ben-Ben's offering. When they were back by the window they had escaped from, Jess forced herself through the bottom of the bush, looked around quickly, then pulled herself and Zach all the way through. She took off running across the backyard.

Dianna and Ned swept through the rooms, taking down four more resilient zombies before the top floor was clear.

"None of these are, Mia," Icely said as he picked up heads and looked at them whether they were attached to a body or not.

Dianna was in the master bedroom. She had checked out the en-suite bathroom and when she determined the room was safe, she went over to the window to take a look out. She thought she caught movement a few houses down, but it was so fleeting she couldn't be sure; and she wasn't going to tell Icely that she may have seen something. Odds were he'd tell her to go check it out herself.

Jess never looked back as she ran. She crossed through two yards and darted into the side yard just as she sensed a psychic tickle that someone was looking her way. She leaned up against the house, breathing heavy. She waited to hear the sounds of alarm or pursuit. When she was convinced she must have imagined it, she began to take in her surroundings.

She turned to her side. Ben-Ben and Patches were sitting staring up at her. "Okay, I know I'm not a world-class sprinter, but how did both of you beat me here? And more importantly, how did you know I was going to stop here?"

she asked, looking down at the two animals.

"Because at least one of us is as smart as you, if not more so," Patches purred. "And you really aren't very fast, especially carrying a baby and a rifle," she added, rubbing up against Jess's leg.

"I'm fast like the air!" Ben-Ben yipped.

"Do you mean like the wind?" Patches asked.

"That's what I said...I think."

"This is too close. Let me catch my breath and we'll move further away," Jess told them.

ICELY

Diana exited the bedroom just as Ned was opening the doorway to the basement. He stepped back quickly in alarm. Dianna rushed to his aid but he held his hand up. "It's alright, there's a stiff on the top landing. Brains blown out. Zombies must have got into the basement as well. Just wasn't expecting to see that."

"A little brain splatter making you lose your manhood?" Icely asked as he opened the door wider.

"That the dog killer?" Ned asked, looking at the slumped over form of Jumper.

"Are you fucking kidding?" Icely asked. "That damned thing is so old it couldn't chew a doughnut. I fucking pay you?"

Schools moved Ned out of the way. "That's not a zombie," Schools said as he got down on his haunches.

"Who shot him?" Icely asked. "A little domestic dispute gone bad?" He laughed.

"Offed himself," Schools said. "Took his shoe off so he could use his toe to pull the trigger. Must have stuck the barrel in his mouth because there's no entry wound, but he sure took care of business. Twelve gauge if I'm not mistaken. He was bit...the back of his leg is almost stripped clean of meat...must have hurt like hell."

"Same damn thing he killed my brother with," Dianna said angrily from behind them.

"Most likely," Schools said.

"Where's the gun then, genius?" Ned said.

"Good question." Schools said as he pulled his from his holster.

"Well, you're the most useless one here, Ned. Why don't you go down first?" Icely said. "Normally I'd send Dianna, but her tits are just too nice to have impaled with buckshot. Probably flood out the basement in silicon if that happened anyway. And no, you can't toss any more fucking grenades."

"Ned?" Dianna asked with concern.

"It's okay," he told her. "I'm coming down." Ned said, "I don't want to harm any of you."

"But I do!" Icely laughed.

Dianna looked at the gun in her hands. It would be so easy. Icely, though--it was like he was psychic. He turned to look at her, a wicked smile plastered across his lips. "What are you looking at?" he asked her before turning back to watch Ned slowly descend the stairs. "Hurry the fuck up, I'm double parked out there," Icely blared.

Ned moved quicker when his legs became exposed to anyone who was looking. He turned quickly from side to side, wishing that his eyes would adjust quicker to the murkiness in the room.

"Well?" Icely asked, nearly making Ned jump.

"No...nothing. I see blood, but no bodies."

"They're down there," Icely said as if he'd seen them with his own eyes. "Move some boxes out of the way or some shit. They'll come scurrying out like the rats that they are. And, oh yeah, look out for that fucking dog...it'll tear your damn throat out."

Ned swallowed hard, subconsciously hunching his shoulders and pulling his head down a bit to make less of a target for the nape-lusting mutt. As he shuffled further into the room, a spider web draped across his face, nearly making him loose a magazine of rounds. As his eyes finally adjusted, he followed the blood trail to the far corner of the cellar. A form was huddled there, still and unmoving.

"Got a body," he said as he approached.

"You're going to be next if you don't hurry up," Icely said.

He wanted to tell the man he was more than welcome to come down and look for himself if he was in such a fucking rush, but all that would get him would be a grenade for his efforts.

If there were more people down in the basement with him, they were masters in the art of camouflage because there just weren't that many places to hide. He prodded the body with the end of his muzzle. If the blood loss was any indicator, this one had expired long ago. He hooked the barrel of his rifle on the shoulder of the body and rolled it over; a sliver of light illuminated the once pretty, now distorted face.

Whoever had shot her had put the barrel of the gun to the back of her head. The bullet had ricocheted throughout her skull breaking her delicate facial bones. Her face had caved in on itself, giving her the sunken look of a woman three times Mia's age.

"It's Mia!" Ned shouted.

"Oh happy days," Icely said gleefully. "We're going to have so much fun."

"She's dead," Ned replied.

"What!?" Icely asked hotly. He came down the stairs fast, forgetting the potential for any imminent danger. "Where is the bitch?" he demanded as he came across the room. He nearly pushed Ned over in his haste to get to her. "Oh, Mia, what have you done?" he asked tenderly. "I loved you in my own way." He sat down hard on the concrete. He placed his gun to the side and cradled her head, stroking her hair. "We had good times, me and you. Then you had to go and fuck it all up." He pushed her head off his lap. "This is what I get for trusting I suppose. It's a good lesson to learn A hard one…but a necessary one."

He bent and picked his gun back up. Just when it looked like he was going to turn and leave, he pulled his leg back and kicked her lifeless body. It was impossible to not hear the sound of snapping ribs as he repeatedly drove his boot into her. Schools and Dianna had come down and were watching the entire scene.

Icely turned and wiped his glistening forehead. "Well…not nearly as satisfying as I would have hoped, but it will have to do. So, mister detective man, what happened here and where are my other little treats?"

"You done?" Schools asked as he approached the broken and battered body.

"For now," Icely told him.

Schools turned her back over so she was face up. She had been such a beautiful woman, reminded him of his own ex-wife a little. He despaired at seeing her so broken.

"Mercy killing," Schools said as he stood up.

"So that I wouldn't get to her?" Icely asked.

As good of an answer as any, Schools thought. "She was killed before she turned into a zombie. She was bit on the arm."

"I wish she had turned. I would have kept her as a pet. I could have fed my enemies to her. Where's the other girl? She's not in here, and somebody had to do Mia in."

"Maybe it was the guy upstairs?" Dianna asked.

"Did I ask you to say something?" Icely wheeled on her. "Why don't you make yourself useful and go make us some sandwiches or some shit."

"She could be right," Schools said. "Not sure why he'd go back up the stairs to kill himself as well, especially since traversing those steps would have been near impossible with the wound he had."

"No, this was the girl. That sweet little bitch and her

baby brother, they did this, they took my Mia from me and now I have to exact my revenge," Icely said icily.

Schools couldn't help himself and it almost cost him his life. "Icely, it's just two kids, let them go. If you're away from town too long, anything's bound to happen."

Icely's gun was pressed to School's head before he could even come to the realization. Schools put his hands up. "Figured you'd see it my way," he said, putting his pistol back. "This is about respect. What do you think those peasants in Vegas are going to think if I come home empty handed?"

Schools shook his head.

"I'll tell you what they'll think. They'll think Icely is weak and that they can get away with whatever they want. No, that will never do. I've got to show a clear message to those who are thinking of crossing me. Ned, get your useless tit-carrier of a wife and grab a body bag from my trunk. Bag the bitch and then we're leaving." Icely headed back upstairs.

Ned looked over at Schools. "Don't, Ned, don't say it, don't think it." Schools followed his boss out of the house.

Icely was leaning against his car, smoking a cigarette when Dianna and Ned finally came out of the house wrestling Mia's black vinyl-clad body. They were by the bumper of Icely's car when Icely spoke.

"What the fuck are you doing?" he asked in between puffs.

"What you told me to do," Ned said with an edge.

"Never once did I say put her dead ass in *my* car, that's just fucking creepy. Put it in yours."

"Now what?" Schools asked as Ned and Dianna duck-walked the body over towards their car.

"Grumper, pop the fucking trunk will you?" Ned asked. The back of the car rocked momentarily as they unceremoniously deposited Mia's body into the trunk.

Ned quickly shut the lid.

"You tell me, detective man," Icely said staring up at

the sky.

"Well…she's either real close, or she got a car and she's miles from here," Schools said.

"They used to pay you money to come up with this shit?" Icely asked, flicking the butt of his smoke away.

Schools shrugged his shoulders. "My guess is she's still around. She probably can't start a car without keys and that means going into homes to look for them. That's dangerous all by itself. Any car she finds in the road with keys in it is most likely drained of gas which involves another stop for her."

"Door-to-door it is then," Icely said.

"You can't be serious? That's how Sedgwick got killed."

"Oh, I'm serious. I'll send Dianna up first, and then when she gets killed, I'll send Ned."

"And then?" Schools asked.

Icely merely smiled.

"I've got a better idea."

Icely nodded his chin in an 'I'm listening' gesture.

"You are under the impression that the girl is set to go to Colorado."

"I'm positive," Icely reiterated.

"Then let her."

"What are you talking about?" Icely asked.

"Odds that we find her in this town are slim. Odds that more of us get shot are probably pretty high. Let her get whatever she needs. She will still be heading to Colorado so all we'll need to do is wait."

Icely stared long and coolly at Schools. "That's not fear speaking is it, Schools? I'd hate for my head of security to be afraid of something, especially a little girl and that big bad wolf of hers."

I'm more afraid of you and what you'll do, Schools thought. "The dog merits some fear," Schools said. "And the girl has proved resourceful. This is the best course of action.

There's the chance she's already escaped here and we'll lose valuable time looking for her ghost."

"Maybe you're alright after all," Icely said, wiping his hand along the side of Schools' face.

"I saw a dog!" Grumper shouted. He was standing next to his car. "Brindle colored. And zombies," he added.

"Already left? I doubt it. Get in the damn car," Icely said.

Grumper and Icely's driver, a dour-faced man named Rick, pulled around Mia and Jess' disabled ride and sped down the road to where Grumper had seen the dog cross the roadway.

"Went that way," Grumper said, sticking his hand out the window. He was pointing towards a small front yard that led into a back yard by way of a gated fence. The gate hung askew from the fence, the damage looked fairly recent.

"Well go get him!" Icely yelled.

"By myself?" Grumper asked.

"Bring the titted wonder and brow-beaten husband, you dipshit."

All three doors opened almost as if on cue. Dianna checked her safety, Ned put on a heavy jacket. Grumper glared back at Icely as he got out of the car.

"Watch this," Icely said to Schools, smacking him on the shoulder. "Gonna have a little fun," he said privately, then he stuck his head out the window. "I want the dog alive, the zombies you can kill, unless one is the girl. Her I'll keep." He laughed.

Schools shook his head minutely. "Icely, I brought these people because they're some of the best I have. I don't consider them expendable."

"Then that's where we differ, isn't it?" Icely was looking intently at Schools. "Relax, It's one mangy dog against three adults. I think they'll be fine."

"This is bullshit," Dianna said to Ned as she followed him through the broken gate. Grumper was bringing up the rear. "A couple of rounds into his car and we could be rid of him."

"You forgetting about Maggie?" Ned asked. Maggie was their daughter; she was staying at Icely's home while her parents were away on the hunt.

"If Icely were dead..." Dianna started.

"If we came back without him, there's no telling what his guards would do," Ned replied.

"They love him as much as everybody else." Dianna stated.

"Meaning not at all." Grumper chimed in.

"You willing to risk your...*our* daughter's life on that?" Ned asked.

"Just find the damn dog," Dianna said dejectedly.

"Not going to be that difficult." Ned pointed with his rifle to the far side of the yard. The dog was moving back and forth in the corner of the yard not allowing the zombies to get a hold of her. She would occasionally glance up the entire length of the security fence that had her penned in.

"That dog is the man killer?" Grumper asked.

Riley froze for a moment when she heard the human speak. She turned and looked directly at him, the look of confusion on her face quickly dissolved as she bared all of her teeth.

"Oh fuck she's scary looking, put a round in her, Ned," Grumper said, changing his earlier stance on the dog.

"I put a round in that dog, Icely will put a round in me," Ned said. "Come on let's surround the thing."

"And then what? Tell her to sit? I don't think she's going to listen," Dianna said. "Maybe just say we got here too late and the zombies got her.

RILEY

I heard the loud explosion noises back by the house where I had left Jess. I desperately wanted to get back to them and make sure that they were alright. The noise was much louder than the time Ben-Ben had nosed open one of She-Alpha's storing places in the food room. He had knocked over one of what she called 'pans' but which I thought of as 'incredible heated aroma producer'. A stack of them had poured on to the hard ground in the food room.

Ben-Ben had stood frozen in fright as the pans clattered all around him. He had received a decent scolding for that. He had awakened the entire household, including Zach and myself. I had not known it at the time, and I'm sure the two-leggers would not have appreciated it, but he would get into the pan container every night and lick them, trying to eat traces of the food they had held earlier. The two-leggers had placed locks on the containers after that; even the cat would not have been able to get them open. I wondered for a moment if the sound had frozen the poor dog like it had the last time.

I had to keep running further away. I had two of the fast zombies chasing me and they would not stop. It would do no good to bring them back towards Jess. I could hear the wheelers moving, but I had to get across the hard ground, otherwise the zombies were going to catch me. I realized my mistake the moment I entered into the back yard, but by then it was too late to turn around. The zombies were not more than a couple of steps behind me. My hope right now was that the fence had a weak spot that I'd be able to get through. If not…it was time to fight.

The zombies were fast in foot speed but not reflexes. It took them time to 'catch up' when I moved from side to side. I was gauging just how long when I heard a two-legger speak from the other side of the yard. I stopped long enough to snarl at them. The closest zombie nearly caught my tail as I pranced to the side and then in an instant I got an idea the cat would be proud of; I mean, not that I cared or anything. I ran past the unfurled hands of the zombies and through their legs, heading directly for the two-leggers and the deadly fire-arms they were carrying.

The male in front was aiming his fire-arm at me. I slowed long enough that the zombie behind me almost stepped on my rear paw. Timing was going to be everything. His expression changed as he saw the zombie barreling down on him. The weapon in his hands moved up and fire poured from the end as the zombie behind me hit the ground.

I was close when I heard him yell 'JAM!' Sounded like something the young two-leggers used to make sandwiches with. The female was moving past the male with the sticky food, her gun up. She fired as well and I heard the second zombie fall. By that time I was weaving between their legs. There were too many of them and they had too many weapons for me to stand and fight.

All I heard was a bunch of talk as I tried to make distance.

"That was close."

"Casing is stuck."

"Get the fucking dog."

And then I felt blistering pain as something struck across the side of my head. Day faded to night as I tumbled to a fall.

ICELY

"That, my friends, is how you catch a dog," Icely said, wielding a bloodied gun stock. "Ugly little bitch, isn't she?" The dog's tongue was lolling out and its eyes were rolling up into its head. A trickle of blood leaked from its left ear. "Put it in your trunk," he told the stunned trio.

"I don't want to touch that thing," Grumper said.

"Get her ass, I'll get the business end," Ned said.

"Poor thing," Dianna said.

"This is a smart fucking dog," Ned said as they deposited her in the trunk.

"What are you talking about? It's just a stupid mutt."

Grumper closed the hatch.

"I don't think so, man." Ned stated. "Did you see her? It was like she knew to bring the zombies towards us, that we'd have to deal with them first. She would have gotten away if it wasn't for Icely."

"Bullshit," Grumper said. "Just a stupid mutt."

"Just a stupid mutt that killed at least three people," Dianna said.

"Then if she is a furry Einsteinian mass-murderer, I'm not too glad she's in this vehicle," Grumper groused.

"In this we are in agreement," Ned said.

"Yo, little bitch, we have your mutt!" Icely yelled a few times, making sure to stay quiet for a few moments each time that he did in order to listen for any sort of reaction. He had almost struck pay dirt on the first go-around.

CHAPTER EIGHT

Jess began to stand up when she had to place one hand over her mouth to stifle her scream and with the other push Patches away. "What the hell, Patches?" she asked, noticing the droplets of blood that welled up through her jeans.

"Fool girl, what do you think he'll do to you or your brother if you go out there!" Patches spat back.

Jess recoiled. She had never seen the cat act so aggressively towards her or any person for that matter.

"They have Riley?" Ben-Ben asked, struggling to keep up with the conversation. "We've got to get her back!"

"You too?" Patches asked. "Got any good ideas that DON'T get us killed?"

Ben-Ben's head bowed a lot like Jess' did. "It's Riley, Patches," Ben-Ben said sadly.

"I know, little dog, I know, but there's nothing we can do right now. There are six of them, and they all have guns," Patches said in as soothing a voice as possible.

"Oh, Riley," Jess sobbed.

Jess jumped when she heard Icely yell again. "Listen, little bitch," he bellowed. "I know you're heading to Colorado. Just so happens I'm heading that way, too. If I don't see you soon, I'm putting a bullet in that dog's skull. It doesn't have to be like this," he added almost sweetly.

Jess let loose a sob as she heard the cars pull away. "How...how could he know where we're going? How am I going to get Riley back?" Jess asked as she slumped back down the side of the house.

Patches wheeled on Ben-Ben. "This is your doing!"

"What?" Ben-Ben cried.

"You told that bird!" Patches said, referring to the parrot in the home in Vegas Ben-Ben had been staying at.

"Stupid bird," Ben-Ben sulked.

Jess and Zach were going at it tear for tear, each seemingly trying to outdo the other.

"Why are you crying, Zach?" Patches asked, trying to calm herself down.

"Because I'm a baby," he replied. "This is what I'm supposed to be doing. I miss my mommy and my daddy, my brother…Mia, and now Riley. I'm hungry and my diaper is dirty."

"That's a lot of good reasons," Ben-Ben said solemnly.

"That's a lot of good reasons," Patches echoed.

It was the smell that finally got Jess moving. "Zombies," she said softly, looking about wildly. She scooped Zach up, wishing he had some sort of hearing protection in case she needed to shoot. "I'd just better make sure that doesn't have to happen," she told him. "We have to find a car," she said aloud.

"There's my Jess," Patches said supportively.

"That way we can chase those bastards down and kill them," she said with vehemence.

Patches did NOT like the sound of that. In her own way she was saddened by the loss of Riley. But risking the lives of the rest of them in a fruitless bid to get her back was not a wise decision and she would do what she could to make sure that didn't happen.

Jess looked from house to house as she walked down the street, being mindful to stay in the shadows as much as possible. She dared not attempt to enter one; too many dangers could be hidden within those walls. She had gone more than a mile before she had found a car that wasn't completely out of gas or did not have its keys.

She approached the vehicle cautiously. It appeared as if the person who had vacated it had just done so. The door stood open and the keys dangled from the ignition, a Power Rangers keychain glaring a shocking pink back at her. The dome light was on, possibly not as bright as it could be but it shone a dull yellow.

She looked from the car to the convenience store ahead of her and back again. Patches hopped onto the driver's seat and then over to the passenger's.

"Hurry up!" she meowed.

Jess was not quite as convinced the ride was theirs. She thought to ask the person in the store if it would be alright if she could borrow it or perhaps get a ride. "Yeah stupid." Jess berated herself, "I'm sure they'd be more than willing to drive to Colorado so they could get in a gun battle. Take the stupid car."

She knew it was a dog eat dog world now, more so than it ever had been. But taking this car was paramount to killing the person inside that store; perhaps they had a family they were trying to provide for.

"Ben-Ben, get in the car! And then she'll have no choice," Patches said.

Ben-Ben hopped in, he placed his front paws on top of the steering wheel and was looking outside the windshield. "I sure could go for a biscuit," he said, looking at the storefront.

Jess took two steps towards the store when she saw the door begin to swing outwards.

"I...I'm sorry. I wasn't going to take..." she started, and then the words caught in her throat.

What came out the door had been human once but that was a long, long time ago. Whoever had vacated this car most likely now resided in the intestinal walls of the creature that stared back at her. Pure malevolence radiated off of the zombie that stared back at her. Not only did it want to eat her, but it appeared as if it wanted to make her suffer as it did so. The zombie had ragged strips of flesh hanging from its sallow cheeks; milky white eyes ringed by dark black circles stared intently at her. It wore a grey t-shirt, the logo on the front stained in blood and gore. Jess was just able to make out 'What would T—' the rest was ripped away or obscured by viscera. A savage bite had torn part of its thigh away, but that did not seem to impede its movement as it started towards her.

"Stop," Jess said weakly, attempting to reason with it.

"We have not saddled ourselves with the smartest human," Patches screeched. She hopped over onto the driver's side. "Help me, Ben-Ben," Patches said as she pressed down on the center of the steering wheel.

"I would, but I don't know what you're doing," he replied.

"Use that fat head of yours for more than chewing! Press your paws here!" Patches said in a panic.

She reared back and used her entire body weight to press upon the horn. On the third attempt, Ben-Ben finally picked up what she was doing. Sort of. It wasn't necessarily what she was thinking but it worked when he face-planted himself into the center of the wheel. He fell away reeling but had accomplished what he'd set out to do as the car bleated out a response. Both Jess and the zombie paused their prey-and-game contest to look.

The zombie started running, Jess turned to get back in the car. She nearly sat on Ben-Ben who didn't have the wits to get out of her way as she sat. Patches was staring out the front windshield as the zombie caught the front edge of the car. He spun slightly as he lost a little of his momentum. Jess shut the door just as he came around. He leaned down so he could look through the window at her. She pulled back as he was no more than inches from her.

"Start the car, start the car, start the car!" Patches begged.

"I agree with the cat!" Ben-Ben barked as he pulled himself free.

Zach's eyes were the size of saucers. "They're right!" he intoned.

Jess was transfixed, almost as if the zombie were a snake charmer and she the snake. A long gray-black tongue streaked with blood fished through the fissure in the zombie's face. He licked the window leaving a trail of innards most likely from the previous owner of the car. The zombie's hand came up, black cracked fingernails scraping at the smooth surface attempting to gain purchase and get at its newest meal. The hand lowered, its head cocked to the side as it came in contact with the door handle. It was working at thinking so hard it was almost audible. Jess just watched in terrified horror.

Her breathing stopped when she heard the mechanical sound of the handle being moved. In the silence, the occupants of the car heard the hitch catch slightly and then fall back into place as if the zombie hadn't quite figured out the puzzle. Patches hoped it didn't have the dexterity to open the door, but she wasn't leaving anything to chance. She was terrified and had forgotten to retract her claws as she ran across Jess' thighs. She plummeted on the door lock, pushing it down. She turned to Jess, getting between her and the visage of the zombie. She hissed and spat so loudly she was finally able to release the invisible grasp the zombie had upon Jess.

"Start the car!!" Patches yelled. "Or so help me, when I'm done with you you'll wish the zombie had gotten a hold of you!"

Ben-Ben was cowering in the back seat, his tail firmly entrenched under his belly. "You scare me, Patches."

"You're hurting me!" Jess cried.

Patches hopped back over to her side. It was then she noticed the welts of blood seeping through Jess' pants where her claws had been. "I'm sorry but if it gets us out of here..."

She left the rest unsaid, it really didn't need clarifying.

The zombie was once again working at the handle. Something was working in his festering brain as the attempts became more frequent. His expression began to change when he realized he was having no success. The crust on his face cracked as his eyebrows furrowed in first confusion and then tilted downwards in anger. Jess jumped as one fist slammed into the window and then another. Her hand shot to the ignition, the dome light dimming as she tried to turn the car over. The engine whirred slowly as a spider web crack appeared under the assault of the zombie.

"Oh poop, oh poop, oh poop," Zach exclaimed.

The car finally started with a catching sputter just as a crack bisected the entire length of the window. Jess was once again staring at the zombie. Patches dug a claw into her hand that was still clutching the key.

"Fuck, Patches!" Jess said, pulling her hand towards her mouth so she could lick her wound.

One quick wince and her hand went to the transmission column. She almost compounded their problems as she slammed the car into drive and tried to create a new drive-in opening for the store. The zombie careened off the rear of the car as he came back for them. The car revved in high gear as Jess inadvertently placed it in neutral. The zombie had come up the trunk and slammed his fist on the rear windshield.

"Is he behind us?" Ben-Ben screamed not daring to look. "He is, isn't he?!"

Jess finally got the car in the right gear. Her wheels screeched as she reversed out of the parking lot, the zombie going for a short ride with the group.

When Jess had enough room, she once again placed the car in drive, the transmission changing gears with a sickening thud as she didn't slow down and stop to make the change.

"Is it gone?" Ben-Ben asked, his paws overlapping

his eyes.

"Sure," Patches said.

"Thank the biscuits," Ben-Ben exhaled. He hazarded a look behind him; the zombie stared back at him. A puddle of urine formed on the seat as the zombie slid down and away.

"Sorry," Patches said sarcastically.

Ben-Ben didn't say anything, but he didn't think he would forget the cruel joke anytime soon.

"We've got to find Riley." Jess said.

Do we? Patches wondered.

The Book of Riley: Part 4
My Name is Riley

Mark Tufo

This book is a work of fiction. Names, Characters, places and events are a product of the author's imagination. Any resemblance to actual names, characters and places are entirely coincidental. The reproduction of this work in full or part is forbidden without written consent from the author.

Dedications: To my wife because without her, I'd be screwed!

Thank you to my beta-readers, Vix Kirkpatrick, Joy Buchanan and Kimberly Sansone. I lucked out when you guys hopped on board to help out!

As always to the first responders and men and women of the armed forces, you have mine and my family's admiration and respect for all the sacrifices you endure to keep us all safe.

A shout out to my friend across the pond Steven Simpson, he promised me the best fish and chips should I ever visit his fair country, I'll be over at 5!

Chapter 1 - RILEY

It was the smell that finally got me awake. My dreams were troubled, and I was happy to be away from them, but the reality of my situation was worse. I was in the company of death. There was the scent of the two-legger that was Mia and the odor of decay—faint for now, but it would be overpowering soon. My head hurt so badly. I could feel sticky, dried life-fluid on my ear, but that was nothing compared to the crushing pain in my head. I whined softly through my nose, wishing I could go back to sleep. It hurt every time the wheeler hit any kind of bump on the hard-packed path. I closed my eyes tightly and gritted my teeth wishing the pain would go away.

And even that, as bad as it was, was still nothing compared to the sense of loss I felt for Jess, Zach, Ben-Ben and maybe even the cat as well. I could only hope that my plan to lure the zombies away had given them the opportunity to get away. Patches seemed more than capable of leading them to safety. As long as she didn't revert back to her normal state of Cat First and everything else third, they should have made it away from Icely and the zombies.

I let loose a small growl just thinking about him—the vibrations rattled up my skull and caused no small amount of discomfort. All I remember was running away from the zombies and through the legs of one of the two-leggers; I'd turned slightly to see if they were in pursuit. When I turned back, it was too late. Icely was in front of me…and then I'd felt him strike me.

Now I was trapped in a wheeler with Mia's body. I could hear voices in the front of the wheeler—it was two males and a female—I believed them to be the same ones from the yard, but it was impossible to concentrate. The wheeler mercifully stopped and the two-leggers began to talk.

"Check on the dog," I heard Icely say off to my side. I wanted to growl but I had enough wits about me to realize the pain it would induce.

"You're kidding, right?" I heard one of the males ask from the front of the wheeler I was in.

"Yeah, I'm fucking kidding. Now check on the dog or you'll be back there riding with her," Icely said. I could hear the anger in his voice.

The wheeler moved up and down as all of the two-leggers got out.

"Cover me," one of the males said as I heard something metallic scrape the trunk next to me. The light that poured in forced my eyes shut; it was like I was being struck all over again. I whined, angry I had shown weakness in front of them even if it was involuntary.

"Is it alive?" one of the men asked.

"She just whined, idiot," the female said.

"Give it some water," Icely ordered.

Someone poured water over my muzzle; it felt so good, the cool liquid wetting my fur. I moved my tongue, trying to lap up as much as I could before it spilled to the floor of the trunk.

I felt a hand stroke my side. "She's a beautiful dog," the woman said.

"This ain't fucking PETA, Diana," Icely said. "That dog has killed more people than you. You'd better keep that in mind. Alright, I want to go a little further and then we'll stop for the night."

The trunk shut, thankfully blocking out the blinding light. The movement of the car lulled me back to sleep.

Chapter 2 - JESS

Ben-Ben awoke from his nap with a start. "Rileyyyy!" he cried. "The zombies are coming and they took the bacon!"

"There's no zombies, no Riley, and certainly no bacon," Patches said, looking down at the small dog that had rolled off the seat.

"What?" Ben-Ben asked, trying desperately to come up from the depths of his dream state and also from the car floor. "Riley hasn't come back yet? She wouldn't leave us."

"It's alright," Zach soothed, his small, fat fist reaching out to touch the dog's head reassuringly. Ben-Ben moved in closer when he realized the baby couldn't reach.

"It's far from alright," Patches said.

"Ben-Ben doesn't need to know that," Zach admonished the cat as he ruffled the fur on Ben-Ben's muzzle.

"Yeah, Ben-Ben doesn't need to know," Ben-Ben said, his eyes half closed as he enjoyed the ministrations from the baby.

"You guys all awake?" Jess asked; her voice had a lilted anxiety to it. Even Patches, who was not all that in-tune with other beings' feelings, could feel the stress radiating off the girl.

The cat, much to her chagrin, found herself asking 'What would Riley do?' She moved off her seat and onto the center console so she could rub up against Jess, hopefully alleviating some of the anxiety they both felt.

"What am I going to do, Patches?" Jess asked absently, rubbing the top of the cat's head.

"Well, you can keep doing that for now," Patches replied, stretching so her head brushed up against Jess' shoulder.

"What am I doing?" Jess asked as tears fell from her face. "I lost Riley and Mia, and I'm trying to find a boy I broke up with a year ago. Even if he wanted to be with me, I'm sure he's dead just like everybody else!" By the time she got to the end of her sentence she was near to hysterics, so much so that Zach began to cry in response.

"Everyone's not dead!" Zach wailed.

"I miss Santa!" Ben-Ben began to whine.

Patches moved back to her seat next to Jess. *Riley would never let this happen.* At one time, she thought getting rid of the dog was the best thing possible for the group…well, at least for her. But now she wasn't sure…not so sure at all. That angered her. She was going to stick her claws straight into Riley's snout the next time she saw her.

Chapter 3 - RILEY

When I awoke next, my head did not hurt as much. Other than that, I did not know how long I'd been in here. It was cooler, so I thought the burning-disc might be down and the light of my ancestral wolves must be shining. I felt stronger for that. The small amount of water I'd received had helped, but was not nearly enough to slake my thirst. I had to get out of here somehow.

I rolled slightly so I was on my paws. I could stand most of the way, more so than in the first kennel I had been housed in. The material above me was the hard stuff the two-leggers called metal. Even with my strong jaws, I knew it was impossible to bite through it. I'd once chipped a tooth as a puppy when I'd bit down on the chain that Alpha-male had me on in the backyard. He'd said it was so I wouldn't run away. Why he thought that, I didn't know. This was my pack. Where would I have gone?

"Sorry, Mia," I whined as I stepped over her and towards the front of my compartment.

I could hear the two-leggers talking. Something about how they should shoot Icely and be done with it. Sounded like just about the best idea I'd ever heard. The wall of the compartment was covered with fake fur. I nipped at a piece and clenched it tight in my front teeth. The material pulled away easily enough; behind it was a flat piece of tree. THAT I knew I could chew through—I'd once destroyed a door made out of the same stuff. Alpha-female had been so angry. Alpha-male had merely laughed and told her that "maybe

Riley doesn't like the laundry room any more than you do." He'd stopped smiling when she'd told him that now they had to get another one. I was glad she'd meant a door and not a dog.

"You owe me one, Riley," Alpha had said as he'd rubbed my head and went to the store. I could only hope he felt that I'd paid him back.

"Did you feel that?" the man named Grumper asked.

"What?" the female asked; her name was Diana.

"Something in the trunk," Grumper replied.

"Yeah, Mia's come back to life." Ned laughed.

"Hey, man, that shit's not funny," Grumper said.

"I guess it really isn't," Ned agreed.

"Do you think so?" Diana asked.

"Mia? No. She had her brains scrambled. She's dead," Ned told her. "Probably just the mutt rolling around."

"Do you think she can get through the trunk?" Grumper asked.

I was also wondering that same question.

"Naw," Ned said. "An older car maybe, but there's framework behind your seat and there's only three or four inch holes, not to mention the woven metal *in* your seat."

"Three or four inches? That's big enough for her to get her muzzle through," Grumper said.

"Did you hear the part about the metal slats behind you? You're fine, you big baby," Diana said.

"Then you sit back here," Grumper challenged.

"Not a chance," Diana told him.

"You fucking mutt, you come through here, I blow that ugly head of yours clean off!" Grumper yelled.

I slowly retracted from position and back over Mia to my original location. Sadness struck deep as I sat there. The further we moved, the further I got from my pack that desperately needed me. Ben-Ben was loyal and could be fierce, but he was not a leader. Jess was mired in indecision, her caution sometimes creating an inability in her to make choices. The one who could best lead them was an infant; he had greatness in him but did not yet possess the means to use it. Patches was the leader by default and that made me scared. She was smart, resourceful and predatory…it was that last thing that cut both ways. She would stand and fight as long as it was safe for her to do so. If she felt the tide was turning, she would abandon the battle at any cost to those around her. It wasn't truly her fault; it's just the way cats are. They are solitary animals that survived by stealth and maybe deception. I couldn't prove that last part, but it made sense.

The wheeler was still moving and Grumper had stopped smacking his seat to make sure I wasn't trying to get through. I heard Ned speak, "We need gas."

"Shoot your high beams at Icely," Diana said.

"I'd rather shoot the asshole with something else," Grumper muttered.

The wheeler slowed down and finally stopped. A door opened.

My fur bristled at the next voice I heard. "What do you want? Your pussy hurt?" Icely asked.

"We need gas," Ned replied evenly. I could tell he was trying his best not to let anger creep into his voice. It was easy enough for me to detect and I wondered why the two-leggers couldn't pick up on the stresses in their communication. They always thought they were so smart, and yet they missed the simplest things.

"Do I look like a fucking gas station?" Icely asked, his voice trailing away.

The door slammed shut and we were once again moving.

"His asshole gets bigger and bigger," Ned said. "I wish it would just hurry up and swallow him whole."

Diana laughed.

"I'd pay to see that," Grumper said.

The speed of the wheeler began to decline and we stopped again.

"Hold on," another voice said, "let me just do a quick check around before you guys get out."

"Alright. Thanks, Schools," Ned said.

A few moments later, Schools came back up to the car. "It's all clear, but let's hurry this up. I don't like being in the open like this, especially at night.

"I'm with you on this one." Ned agreed. What he didn't say but his tone said clearly was that he'd be with him on whatever he wanted to do, even if that meant shooting Icely. At least that's what I hoped.

"Is he planning on stopping for the night at any point?" Diana asked Schools softly.

"He's blazing through an eight ball of cocaine right now. I don't think he's going to come down for another day or two," Schools replied.

"That's just fucking great," Grumper said grumpily.

"I'll keep an eye out, let's just get rolling quickly," Schools said as he moved away.

"Where the fuck is the gas lever?" I heard Ned ask.

"Down by your left-hand side," Grumper said. "But be careful, it's right next to the trunk…"

I heard something above me click.

"…release." Grumper finished.

"Fuck," I heard Ned whisper.

"What's the matter?" Diana asked.

I stood up and the ceiling moved as I did so. The hard packed ground was lit up by the Wolf-Disc. It took me a moment to realize I was staring at freedom. I turned back to Mia. "I wish I could take you with me," I said to her as I slipped out from the back of the wheeler and onto the black ground.

"I popped the trunk," Ned said.

"You did what?" Diana asked in alarm.

"The fucking two levers are right next to each other!" Ned said in the same tone as his wife. "Grumper, go shut it."

"Go fuck yourself," Grumper told him.

"The dog was nearly dead," Diana said. "She's not going to do anything."

"Then you go out there," Grumper told her.

"Fine, you fucking baby," she said.

I could hear the metallic sound as she readied her bee shooter. Her door opened and I realized I didn't have anywhere to run. It was completely open ground to the back of the wheeler. On the driver's side and a little further up sat Icely in the other wheeler. On the other side, Diana was coming. I could see her fake feet come out.

"Great, now I'm going to look like a damn sissy," Grumper said as his door opened.

I was crouched down closest to him. He moved quickly and I ducked underneath the compartment I had been in. There was a loud slamming as he pressed the lid of the trunk down.

"Easy as pie," he said, his voice relaxing.

"I told you the damn dog was dying," Diana said as she got back into the wheeler.

"Hurry the fuck up!" Icely shouted.

"Dipshit, the zombies won't hear that, will they?" Grumper whispered sarcastically.

"Hand pump is in our trunk," Schools called from across the lot.

Grumper walked away and was back a few beats of my heart later. His fake feet stopped not more than two cat spans away; he was standing by seven metal discs stuck in the ground. He bent down and stuck his finger in a catch I had not seen. The disc was moving when his head whipped my way. He was looking straight at me. I had no choice but to do what I did as I charged out from under the wheeler. My mouth opened wide as I launched; the front of my mouth caught him on the meat of his cheeks even as he was falling backwards.

A strangled cry came from him as his hands wrapped around my waist, trying desperately to push me away. The harder he fought, the further I sank my fangs in. He stopped trying to push me away when he realized that to continue to do so would mean he'd lose half his face.

I furiously shook my head from side to side. I could feel the membranes of his muscles tearing. Bones in his face started to snap as I bit down harder. An explosion sounded as the ground next to us flew up. I had pulled Grumper down to the ground with me. He had stopped fighting and was now merely whimpering. I turned to the side, subsequently taking his face with me. The woman was out of the car, pointing her bee shooter at me. I pulled Grumper so that he was in between her deadly tool and me.

"Grumper!" she shouted.

"What is it?" Ned asked.

He was getting out of the car. I saw movement off to my right. The other man, Schools, was looking as well. I don't think he could see anything from that distance, but it would only be a matter of time before he came to check out what was causing the woman so much distress.

"Well lookie here!" Icely leaned out his window. "Fucking dog is killing Grumper. That's fucking hilarious!" he shouted. The wicked looking bee slinger however was not.

Bees riddled the ground all around us, a couple even biting into Grumper as I turned slightly to make the man the only target available to Icely.

"You're hitting him! You fucking idiot!" Diana shouted.

"What did you say?" Icely asked, stepping out from his car, his hatred burning brightly.

I saw a chance to escape, as he was fixated on the woman. I let Grumper's face go. He smacked wetly to the ground as I bounded off into the night. A bee came dangerously close just as I ran down a small slope. It had to be Schools—he was the only one that was not in the escalating argument I heard raging behind me.

"I should just shoot your stupid asses!" Icely was

shouting.

"He's still alive." Schools bent down over Grumper. I had slunk back up the small embankment to check for pursuit, none of which was coming.

"He's too stupid to die." Icely walked over, his heavy gun hanging down by his side. "Well I can fix that," he said as he fired a bee at pointblank range into Grumper's chest.

Diana sobbed.

"Let's go." Icely rubbed his nose and walked back towards his car.

"When is enough, enough?!" Ned shouted.

"When I say so!" Icely yelled back.

"How many of us have to die because of your wounded pride?" Ned asked.

"At least one more," Icely answered, menace lacing his voice.

"Ned, get back in your car," Schools said, trying to keep the scene from unfolding into anything worse than it already was.

"Fuck you, Schools. Grumper was my friend," Ned yelled at Schools, but he was looking at Icely.

"Bitch, you'd better control your man or you're going to have a pair of orphans," Icely warned Diana, not taking his eyes off of Ned.

"Come on, Ned," Diana said.

The two-leggers wanted to kill each other; I wished they'd just get it done. At least then Jess and the rest would be safe. That was another funny thing about the human animal, what they said and what they actually wanted to do where sometimes very different. Dogs had it right; there was no deception among us. We eat if we are hungry, we drink if we are thirsty, we fight if we are angry and we cuddle if we want comfort. Straightforward and honest…two-leggers could learn a lot from us.

"Ned, you think you can get your gun up before I can blow a hole in your chest?" Icely asked.

Ned stared at him a few seconds longer and got back into his car.

"That's a good bitch." Icely turned to get into his own ride.

"That was close," Icely's driver Dent said. He'd gotten the nickname because of his inability to keep a car free of damage.

"Shut the fuck up and drive." Icely grabbed his mirror, and did a couple of quick rails. He leaned back after sucking them up, making sure none of the white lightning shot down his throat.

Schools got in and looked over to the driver who simply shrugged his shoulders.

"Where to?" Dent asked.

"You too? You stupid motherfucker. Same as it ever was!" Icely was yelling.

Schools noticed Icely's pallor did not have a healthy hue. He thought that could be attributed to the coke, but maybe not.

"Colorado it is." Dent put the car in drive, pulled out of the gas station and into the night.

Ned was sitting in the driver's seat staring straight ahead, his body taut as a guitar string. He started to laugh.

"What's so funny?" Diana asked nervously.

"We didn't even get gas," Ned said through his tears. He hitched a couple of more times—sometimes it was more of a cry, other times more of a laugh—and then he spoke, "You need to cover me."

"You think that mutt is still out there?" she asked with trepidation.

"I'm positive that fucking mutt is watching us...waiting for an opportunity to rip our throats out. It's a demon, Diana...no, no I take that back she's a vengeful angel making us pay for our sins."

"Don't go getting all philosophical on me, let's get the gas and get out of here." She checked her gun.

"I'm filling this car, Diana, then I'm driving back to Vegas."

"We can't, Ned. He'll kill us. He'll probably kill the girls...or worse," Diana pleaded.

"We're getting the girls and we're leaving. I'm thinking Montana...maybe we can get on with a militia group. Gotta be dozens of them survival groups up there."

"How can we be sure they'll be any better?"

"Really, Diana? Worse than a drugged out psychopath? We've already made him mad. Do you think once this is over he's going to let bygones be bygones? If he doesn't kill us outright he'll find a way to do it. We mean nothing to him—we've never meant anything."

"Schools won't let that happen," Diana pleaded.

"Huh!" Ned snorted. "He's just as concerned at saving his own skin as we are. He's not going to go too far out of his way for us. You'd better believe that."

"I'm scared, Ned."

"Yeah, welcome to the club. I'm getting gas and heading back home as fast as I can. We grab the girls and we're gone."

"Okay," Diana replied meekly.

Ned stepped out into the night to my deep bass growl. I was less than three feet away. My teeth were bared, saliva hanging in thick strings. My muzzle was pulled back and my body was tensed like a spring.

"Wha-what's the matter?" Diana asked the rigid form of her mate.

"I'm a dead man," was all he said back.

Diana quickly tried to get out of the car. I looked over her way.

"No, no, no!" Ned said to her and then turned to me. "I know what you are. I swear to you on my life and those of my family, I'm through. I've done a lot of things I'm not proud of, and it's something I will have to live with for the rest of my life...which may or may not be that long by the looks of you. If you let me live, I promise I will try to do good, to raise my daughters, to do right by them." Ned had his front paws raised above his head.

"Ned?" Diana asked tremulously.

"Hush, hon, I'm making a deal with God," Ned said.

I barked savagely. "Two-leggers are stupid," I told him. "I don't know *that* two-legger…you, though…you I know, and if I ever see you again, I'll tear your throat out." I took a step closer so I could get a good clean scent off of him. He went rigid, closing his eyes and raising his face towards the sky. "I'll remember you," I barked and turned, melting back into the shadows and heading off in the direction Icely had gone.

Chapter 4 - NED

"What the fuck was that?" Diana asked, finally getting out when she saw her husband move.

"A second chance," was what he told her as he furiously pumped gas into the car.

Chapter 5 - ICELY

"Where the fuck are dipshit and dipshittier?" Icely yelled, smacking the back of Dent's seat.

"They still had to get gas, Icely," Schools replied.

"They should have caught up by now." Icely bent back down over his mirror. "Pull over. We'll wait for them here." Icely snorted again.

Schools got out of the car and started doing the math in his head. They'd driven about twelve miles and it would take somewhere in the neighborhood of ten minutes to refuel the car. "They should already be back on the road," he said aloud. "Ten, fifteen minutes at the most."

"What the fuck are you going on about out there?" Icely asked. "Is anyone else cold? Shit."

Schools walked further away. He heard a door open and was relieved to find out it was Dent.

"The boss is asleep, I don't know how though 'cause he did enough coke to keep a sorority up for a week. What should we do?" Dent asked.

"I guess we wait."

When the ten-minute mark came and went with no sign of Ned and Diana, Schools wasn't overly concerned. At twenty minutes he was. He was fairly certain the devil dog had gone back to finish the job it had started.

"The odds that she was able to get both are slim, especially Diana."

"You say something?" Dent ambled over. "Say...where are those two?" he asked as if he were just remembering what they had stopped for in the first place.

Schools thought it highly unlikely the two were dead. His cop instincts began to kick into overdrive. *No, they left,* he thought. *They're heading home for their kids and getting the hell gone.* He was angry; not that they left, but rather that he was not afforded the same chance as them.

"Should we get the boss up?" Dent asked.

"Be my guest," Schools said. "Nothing quite like waking up a pissed off coke hung-over man."

"Yeah...maybe I should just let him sleep a little longer," Dent said wisely.

And just maybe that will give Ned and Diana the time they need. They'd better be flying, though. If Icely wakes up and decides to pursue, it will be close. Dent was notorious for hitting shit with his cars, but only at slow speeds and generally when attempting to park. On the open roadway he was damn near a magician. Schools wasn't sure exactly what Dent did in his previous life but that he wasn't a racecar driver meant that he'd missed his true calling in life.

Three hours is what they need. Enough time to sustain their lead, grab their kids and get the fuck out. Schools looked over to Icely. His head was thrown back against the seat, white powder coating the base of his nose and upper lip. *One errant lick,* Schools thought, *and Icely will put enough coke back into his system to wake up.*

"They're not coming," Dent said after a few hours. Both men were sitting on the guardrail. The sun was just beginning to make its presence known

"Who's not coming?" Icely asked, sitting up groggily.

"Ned and Diana haven't shown." Schools got up.

"It's only been a couple of minutes," Icely said, wiping his nose. "When did you get so anxious? Sometimes you're just like a tittering little hen."

"Boss, it's been more than two hours, probably closer to three," Dent said, standing next to Schools.

Icely's eyes went wide as he extracted himself from

the car. "Two fucking hours and nobody thought waking me up was a good idea?"

"What difference does it make?" Schools asked. "We can only pursue one objective, them or the girl."

"Listen, you little twat," Icely said, standing directly in front of Schools, "I decide who is worth pursuing, not your little piss ant self. You hear me?"

"I hear you loud and clear," Schools told him.

"I'm going to skin them alive when we get back, always wanted to try that," Icely said as he drifted off.

"You still think they'll be there?" Dent asked Icely.

"Oh, they'll be there." Icely snarled. "They're too stupid to make it on their own…they're all too stupid, present company included. *Especially* present company. You smell that?"

Schools wondered how the man could smell anything with the constant flow of drugs up his nasal canal.

"Stupid smells?" Dent asked.

Chapter 6 - RILEY

I'd been moving at a trot—faster than a walk, slower than a run—a pace I felt I could keep up for as long as I needed. Following the wheeler was easy; the wheels left a burnt smell on the hard packed ground that was simple to follow. The small sliver of Wolf Light was falling behind a distant hill when I got the first hint I was not alone. I began to hear twigs snap in the underbrush on the side of the road. At first it was distant and singular and then it grew in volume and numbers. By the time I chanced a look behind me, more than seven zombies were on the roadway coming after me. It was too much to hope that they were tracking the same two-leggers that I was.

I started running faster. I could do this for a while, but I got the impression they could do it forever. I was looking off to my side, deciding which avenue of escape would be best. To my right was heavy underbrush. I'd be able to move fairly quickly through it while they would get stuck. On my left was a small metal barricade and on the other side of that a somewhat steep drop-off. It looked like I could easily traverse it; the clumsy two-leggers, though, well…they'd be falling all over themselves and that sounded like some decent entertainment. I decided to go the way of the hill. I'd drawn up alongside the metal barricade and was just about to jump over when I spotted a wheeler not too far up. The burning-disc was just beginning to glint off the viewers. Three men were around it, and one of them was Icely.

Then I had a better idea, a much better one. The

stupid cat would be so proud of me. Not that it mattered. I was going to lead the zombies right to them. I was getting tired, but hatred burns its own fuel, and I had enough of that to go around. It was Icely that finally turned in my direction. I was close enough to hear them.

"What the fuck?" he asked.

Schools turned when Icely spoke. "It's the fucking Pied Piper."

I didn't know what piper meant, but I sure did like pie.

"Kill that fucking mutt!" Icely screamed.

"I think the zombies following it might be more of a concern," Schools said, bringing up his bee shooter.

"Fuck them, kill the dog!" Icely demanded, his bee shooter waving around wildly.

I'd done my job. The zombies had seen the two-leggers and they were like Ben-Ben's bacon to them. I was the cardboard-like dog food in comparison. I could probably stop running and be safe now—at least from the zombies, not the metal bees, though. I hopped over the barricade. I thought about hanging around but thought better of it. No matter who won, the victors would come looking for me afterwards and I needed to get some water, food and rest. In that order.

***

"Son of a bitch," Schools said.

"Where'd the fucking dog go?" Icely asked. Shots were now ringing out.

"We need to get back in the car."

"Screw that, I want the dog!" Icely shouted. "Did the zombies get her?"

"She jumped the guardrail," Schools said as he started pushing Icely back towards the car. "Dent, let's go."

Dent was unloading his magazine into the oncoming horde. "Got to be dozens of them," he said in alarm as he fumbled quickly with a jam.

"Come on, man, we have to go!" Schools said to the both of them. He was still trying to wrestle an unbelieving Icely into the car. "We don't have the weapons or the position to fight that many!"

Schools finally got Icely into the back and Dent wasn't too far behind. The zombies were within ten to fifteen feet when Dent's door slammed shut.

"The fucking mutt led them right to us!" Icely yelled.

"It would appear that way," Schools said with no small amount of admiration.

"My bitch of a grandmother had a dog, thing used to shit on its own damn bed it was so stupid. Not this dog though...no, we come across a fucking dog that's read the Art of fucking War. What is this shit?" Icely asked, his question laced with doubt. For the first time since he left Vegas he began doubting his reasons for being there. "Just the crash from the drugs, that's all." He tried to prop himself back up.

"You say something, boss?" Dent asked. Schools noticed the man was fumbling around with his pockets. The car began to rock as zombies smacked into it from all sides.

"Yeah, I said get us the fuck out of here." Icely did his best to keep the rising fear and dread from his voice.

"What's the matter?" Schools asked Dent. The man's face had paled considerably in the last few seconds. In truth he was starting to resemble the countenances of those that had completely enshrouded the car.

"I lost the keys," Dent whispered.

"Fucking find them!" Icely screamed. Dent flinched.

"They're on the other side of the street," Dent said, pointing weakly to a guardrail they could no longer see. "I put them on top of my pack of smokes. That way I knew I wouldn't forget them."

"Hey, dipshit, maybe you could have just left them in the car. Ever think about that? Fucking moron. Well...go get them," Icely said as if he was telling the man to get a loaf of bread at the corner store.

"Icely—" Dent started and stopped as the barrel of Icely's gun pressed up against the side of his head.

"You'll go get the keys or I'll kill you. It's amazing how simple things can be."

"Icely, he can't get over there now," Schools said, trying to alleviate the mounting scene.

"You want to take his place?" Icely asked, waving the gun towards Schools.

Schools shook his head.

"Icely, please, man, I don't want to get eaten," Dent pleaded.

"I always told you cigarettes were going to kill your ass," Icely laughed.

"If he opens that door, the zombies are going to get in." Schools tried another tactic.

"You sure are sticking your nose deep into my business," Icely said icily.

"Fuck you, Icely." Schools squeezed the trigger of the gun he had pushed up to the back of his seat. Acrid smoke rose up from the burning material. A stain of spreading blood formed on the left side of Icely.

Icely was staring at Schools, seemingly in shock that his second-in-command had sworn at him or, for that matter, shot him, Schools was uncertain which. Schools angled his pistol to get another shot, but Icely was too fast bringing his own gun around. He fired, hitting Schools in the side of the head. Skull fragments struck the windshield as the deflected bullet broke through the heavy safety glass. Spider-web cracks radiated out from the strike.

"I'm-I'm…d-d-dying," Schools stuttered involuntarily.

"Was it your brains leaking out that gave it away?" Icely asked. "Stupid fuck."

Schools' mind began to race through images of earlier

and better times; anything it could grasp on to keep the reality of the unfolding event from panicking him. "The water is so warm," he said with a faraway gaze.

"Stupid fuck," Icely repeated as he drilled Schools in the forehead with another shot. Dent was staring in shock. "You haven't got the keys yet?" Icely said, swinging his gun back around.

Dent fumbled with his lock. It took some serious force against his door to get it open against the press of zombies.

"Make sure you shut the door!" Icely laughed even as he heard the first of the zombies tear into his driver. "Bet that hurts." Icely reached over the seat and pulled the door closed quickly while the zombies fixated on Dent.

"Help me!" Dent begged.

"Man, you're already dead. Oh shit, look at this!" Icely brought his hand out of his pocket. "Shit, I had a spare key on me the whole time." He pressed the key up against the window. An anguished Dent looked back. A zombie tore his left ear off as another bit through his side. He was dragged down to the ground. "The lesson of the day, kiddies," Icely grunted as he climbed over the seat, "is to not trust anyone with your life. Once a cop, always a cop, huh, Schools?"

Icely started the car and barreled through the throng of zombies with enough force that some came up the hood and smacked down onto the windshield, further damaging the glass.

"I would have gotten us out of here…sure, after Dent got out, he was too stupid to live. I was doing evolution a favor. But you, man? What the hell?" Icely asked, propping up Schools' head with the barrel of his weapon. "Nothing to say for yourself?"

Chapter 7 - RILEY

I heard muted gunfire and then the starting up of a two-wheeler. I was far enough away that I didn't have to worry about either adversary. I'd found a small stream at the bottom of the hill, which I was now drinking from greedily. I was busy enjoying the feel of the cool liquid coating my throat when I heard a branch break to my side. I raised my head slowly, not wanting to give too much movement for a predator to take notice of. An animal near to my size came out from behind some bushes. It was brown and had some white spots on it. It triggered something deep within me. This was food.

A much bigger version of what I now figured was the baby came out. This one did not have white on it but other than that the coloring was the same. The young animal dipped its muzzle into the water. It was then I noticed that the infant and the adult were both panting heavily, their sides going in and out rapidly as they tried to get as much air as possible. The mother was too terrified to drink; she was looking around frantically. Her eyes were wide as she did so. It certainly wasn't because of me. I don't think that either one of them had noticed me yet. I got down low and took a step towards the small one.

The deer…yes, that was what it was, a deer. I got that name from somewhere deep inside of me. The young deer looked up quickly, its gaze pinned me to my spot and then, as if it didn't recognize what I was, it moved on. I took another step towards it. I was three or four more away from grabbing it and pulling it down. I froze when the infant's eyes grew as wide as its mother's. I turned to see what it was looking at. My heart nearly stopped; three wolves were looking back.

"Is that ugly thing a dog?" one of the wolves said. "We should kill it."

"Mist, I want the deer. The pups cannot survive on dog meat," the wolf in the middle said.

"It's another predator, Tundra," Mist said.

"That thing's a predator?" The third wolf said with derision.

"Fine, Mist, if the ugly dog disturbs you so much, kill it. Flanks, you and I are going to get that deer," Tundra said.

The two larger wolves lunged for the deer that had once again taken up flight. "We'll come help when we take them down," Flanks said.

"Don't worry about it. I'll join you on the hunt when I'm done." Mist began to circle. "What is your captive name?" she spat.

"R-Riley." My heart was hammering in my chest. The wolf across from me was nearly double my size and ferocity.

"Well, RaRiley, I hope you enjoyed your last little bowl of food the humans gave you, because you won't need to worry about accepting handouts anymore."

I wanted to ask her why she wanted to kill me. She hated me just for what I was and that was enough of a reason for her. Run or fight? I spun and ran. If I'd had a bigger tail her teeth would have clamped down on it.

"You cannot run from me," Mist snarled with anger.

Watch me, I thought.

I could hear her jaws snapping behind me. If she was close enough to be trying to bite me, I needed to do something quickly. I darted to the left and spun to the bushes on that side. Mist was slower to react and had more weight to deal with in order to change momentum. I gained some precious time as I got to the bushes that hugged the water. After that it was just expansive openness. Would she get tired of chasing me? I guess I was going to find out.

"I figured dogs to be less smart. Why are you delaying the inevitable?" Mist said as she changed her direction and followed.

I was left to wonder if this wolf somehow knew Patches—they sounded similar. At least with the cat it was disdain and not outright contempt. The wolf crashed through the bushes. I heard small twigs snap as she pursued.

I ran along the base of the hill. If I dared to look, I think I was actually putting some distance between the wolf and myself…and then I realized what she was doing. I was running flat out in fear and she was pacing herself for the long haul. She'd tricked me from the outset. She was bigger, faster, and more powerful. I was now trying to weigh my choices: turn to stand and fight, or be dragged down from behind. Both of those were about as savory as the cat's disgusting fish food.

"Why are you stalling what we both know is going to happen?" Mist asked from much closer than I would have liked.

"Why?" was all I was able to push out of my heaving chest.

"You ask why? You mean less than nothing to me. You are not food, nor are you kin. You are a manmade abomination. Humans have twisted our lineage to suit their own needs and produced whatever you are…an enslaved being that lies around all day and is fed in a bowl."

I didn't see the problem with the food in a bowl thing. I mean, who wouldn't want food delivered to them? The two-leggers had stuff brought to them all the time, most of which they were always willing to share.

"I respect the deer we hunt more than you. They suffer the icy coldness of the nights, and the brutal drenching of the summer rains. They endure the biting insects that draw our life fluids from us and they, like us, are hunted by the humans and their long weapons. While you do what? Fetch a ball? You are less than useless and for that I will tear your throat out and leave you for the birds. At least they will get some sustenance from you."

Maybe her arguments were valid. I'd never thought of it that way. The fact remained though that I didn't want to die. "I loved your kind, I was honored to be a descendant," I managed to say.

"Descendant?" she scoffed. "Because we both have four legs does not make us relatives."

My legs were getting heavier the further we went. My previous run, the injury from Icely, add to that my lack of food and water and they were all beginning to take their toll. I was slowing down and Mist was laughing.

"You run decent for a dog, but you are already beginning to falter. I have not even hit my stride yet. Turn and die...at least have that much honor," she howled.

It sure would have been easier. I pressed on.

Chapter 8 - JESS AND THE GANG

"Is that a body?" Jess asked, looking off to her right into the gas station parking lot.

"She acts like that's the first one she's seen," Patches said, glancing quickly.

"This is hard on her," Zach replied.

"He looks familiar." Ben-Ben had his paws on the window as his head turned. "He was one of the men from Jumper's house. I miss Jumper, he promised me some bacon snacks."

"Are you sure?" Patches asked. She turned to look at the now rapidly fading scene.

"I saw him," Ben-Ben said, thinking about his long lost snack.

"When?" Patches asked.

"When I was scratching my bum," Ben-Ben said.

Zach let out a small laugh.

"Disgusting dogs, what do humans see in you?" Patches asked, turning back around.

"That's good news, right?" Zach asked. "One less of the bad people."

"There are still four of them, Baby-that-should-not-talk. And how I wish you wouldn't," she added softly.

"I heard that," Zach said.

"No kidding," Patches dripped sarcasm. "There are still four of them, though."

"I wish Riley were here, she'd know what to do," Ben-Ben said sadly.

The next fifteen minutes were ridden in silence, as each occupant in the car was lost in thought.

"Zombies!" Jess said as the car screeched to a halt.

Ben-Ben once again fell to the floor. "You should really brace yourself better," Patches said.

She had her front paws on the dashboard, her tail twitching back and forth as she looked out upon the zombies ahead of them. They had not yet seen the stopped car. She noticed they were busy with something. The runnels of blood flowing down the street were the only clue she needed to figure out exactly what it was.

"Too much of it to be a dog."

"Of what?" Zach asked.

"If I was talking to you, I would have started with Baby—"

"That should not talk. I get it," Zach murmured.

A couple of the zombies on the fringe of the feeding frenzy turned around to look straight at Jess. There was no hesitation as they started to run at her.

"Shit," Jess said.

"Shit," Zach mimicked.

"I will agree with you this time," Patches said.

"Oh, I don't like them." Ben-Ben said as he stared between the two seats at the onrushing zombies.

"You don't say?" Patches asked, her tail gaining in momentum as the zombies neared.

"What?" Ben-Ben asked. "I did say."

"Stupid dog." Patches meowed loudly at Jess, "Move, girl! It's clear behind us!"

Patches was flung back into her seat as Jess pressed down hard on the gas.

"You should brace yourself better," Ben-Ben said happily, his tongue hanging out.

"Shut up, dog." Patches was trying her best to make it look like that was what she had meant to happen.

"Good one, Ben-Ben," Zach said.

The car rocked as a zombie struck the quarter panel. "Oh, God." Jess tried to swerve to avoid more of them.

"She's really close to the guardrail!" Zach looked over to his side.

Patches' eyes grew wide as she looked down the steep embankment. The headlight on her side shattered as Jess hit two more zombies, her left front beginning to crumple from the assault. Sparks flew up on the right side as she was forced into the metal. Patches dove into the backseat and to the far side of the car away from the drop-off. The scraping of metal on metal was deafening within the confines of the vehicle.

"I just pooped," Ben-Ben said. He hopped into the vacated front seat, partly to get away from his 'mistake' and partly because he got to sit up front for once.

Patches was terrified as zombies were pressing up along her side. Jess was single-minded in her determinedness to pull away from them.

"Faster!" Patches howled.

"Yeah, what the cat said!" Zach wailed.

"That looks like fireworks!" Ben-Ben sounded fascinated as he peered at the shower of sparks.

"You're terrified of fireworks," Patches reminded him.

"Yeah, you hid under the table and peed," Zach agreed.

"You guys know about that?" Ben-Ben sounded ashamed. "Whoa, that's a big dog," he said as the sparks stopped.

Jess had finally pulled the car away from its fiery embrace with the safety-rail. "We're past!" she shouted triumphantly.

Patches let out a sigh as she looked at the zombies giving chase behind them.

"The big dog is chasing a smaller dog, I think they're playing," Ben-Ben said, his tail wagging furiously. "I want to play!"

Patches came up next to Ben-Ben. "That's a wolf."

"I just got here. Do you want me to move?" Ben-Ben asked.

"It can't be," Patches said.

"What?" Zach asked.

Patches thought for a moment about not clarifying her words. She didn't know if she thought better about it because Ben-Ben would eventually figure out what was going on or if it was just the right thing to do…at least by dog and human standards. The right thing for her would be to let the wolf finish off Riley once and for all so that the meddling mutt would not guilt her into helping 'the pack' at the most inopportune times—times when she could save herself and avoid personal injury at every cost.

"It's Riley," she finally said.

"That big dog is Riley? It doesn't look like Riley." Ben-Ben was looking hard.

"The other one, dumb-dumb," Patches said.

"Oh yeah, that's Riley!" Ben-Ben started barking excitedly. "She sure does look like she's having fun."

"You're a dolt, she's running for her life," Patches hissed.

"Patches, you have to get Jess' attention!" Zach exclaimed.

She knew if she did nothing in the next ten seconds it would be too late. Even from this distance, Patches could tell Riley was flagging. She thought very highly of herself as she pierced the relative quiet in the car with her wail.

"What, Patches?" Jess asked, looking over.

Ben-Ben was staring out the window, his tail going a mile a minute and Patches was caterwauling at her. She leaned over to try and get the same view as the small dog. "Oh, my God!" The car surged ahead on an intercept course; she began to frantically beep the horn.

"This is fun!" Ben-Ben yipped loudly over the noise.

Chapter 9 - RILEY

My heart hurt, the exertion was too much. My steps were faltering; the wolf was relentless in its pursuit. It was nearing fight time. I would not be dragged down like a rabbit or a deer.

"Close now, dog. Can you feel my breath upon your hindquarters yet?" Mist asked.

I picked a point up ahead where the small upslope would give me a height advantage; that was where I was going to make my last stand. That's what I truly thought it was going to be. She would not be fooled like Thorne. I was going to die today, but she would suffer some wounds as well. Maybe next time she would think twice before killing another dog. Probably not though, she didn't look like a wolf that had many regrets.

I was approaching the do or die—mostly die—spot when I heard a wheeler horn off to my left. I barely had the energy to look towards it. The horn wouldn't stop though—it was a lot like the wolf. 'It can't be.' I thought after finally glancing over. It was entirely too far away and I did not recognize the wheeler but that there was some small animal or animals in the viewer looking back at me was almost beyond doubt, although possibly, it was just a figment of hope. At this point, what did I have to lose? I'd already resigned myself to my fate.

I found something deep inside of me, maybe it was ancestral, and just maybe and more importantly, it was the canine part of me. I surged ahead with a newfound purpose.

"Enough is enough, dog!" Mist spat out. She sounded like she was winded a little bit. Good. She had also heard the horn; that I was heading back up the slope and towards it, I had to believe, was causing her a moment of concern.

The wind was flying by my face as I ran for my life. It was difficult to make out who was in the car as I galloped, my vision going up and down to the rhythm of my paws. The hard packed ground curved slightly towards me and that was where the wheeler stopped. It was a straight line from where I was, to where I was pretty sure I needed to be. I could now feel Mist's heavy labored breathing right behind me. She was closing in before I could make it. I had nothing more to give.

A heavy paw swipe caught me in my flanks, and I tumbled down. A cloud of dirt erupted as I flipped over two times. My paws sought purchase as I sprang back up. Mist had gone by me as I was falling. She now stood between me and the excited, yipping Ben-Ben.

My heart was elated and heavy, I was so close, and now the end was near. I was happy that at least they were safe. Mist was snarling and snapping at me as we faced each other.

"No, Ben-Ben!" I heard Jess scream. The small dog was running towards us.

"I want to play!" he was saying.

Mist spun to what she figured was a new threat. "What is that?" she howled at him.

It would have been impossible for Ben-Ben to not see the malice etched on her maw, and yet he still came forward.

"Oooh, you get bigger as I get closer," he said, ears pulled back and tongue lolling as he ran.

"Stupid dog," I heard Patches yell as she followed in pursuit.

"These your friends?" Mist asked, spinning back to me. "A cat and a rat?"

"Friends and pack-mates," I answered, lowering myself in expectation of an attack.

"Wow she's pretty!" Ben-Ben said as he got closer. Mist again turned.

"She's deadly!" I warned him.

"He doesn't get it," Patches said.

Even the three of us together were no match for the timber wolf. I just hoped that she didn't see it that way and would leave.

"First you, and then I'll take care of them," she said as she launched.

"So much for wishful thinking," I said.

The sharp sound of a fire-arm report made Mist yelp in distress. She cut short her flight and sharply veered away back down the hill.

"Oh yeah, the one with the fire-arm is also my friend and pack-mate...plus, she feeds me! Stupid wolf!" I barked.

Mist howled and was gone.

"Riley, Riley, Riley!" Ben-Ben said, jumping around like the crazy dog that he was. "Who's your wolf-friend?" he asked, looking the way Mist had gone.

"She's no friend of mine," I told him. "Wolves are jerks."

Patches and Ben-Ben stayed next to me as we walked slowly back towards Jess. I couldn't muster much more than that. Patches repeatedly scanned the area in case Mist decided to come back.

"Oh, Riley," Jess said, putting her fire-arm down.

She hugged me tight around my neck. I was thirsty and dog tired, and I was still shaking from the exertion of getting away from Mist—and I guess even the closeness of my demise—but it was still one of the sweetest things I'd ever felt. Water leaked from her eyes.

"Good to have you back!" Zach shouted from inside the car.

"Oh, I'm sorry, Zach." Jess let my neck go to check on the baby.

"It's good to have you back," Patches said.

"You mean that?" I asked her.

"Not really. And we should get going…the zombies are coming." She hopped back up into the car and took the front seat. I didn't have the energy to argue about it with her.

"We have to go." Jess was looking to the rear of the car.

"The girl is always a day late," Patches said.

I wanted to ask her what that even meant, but even that seemed like an effort. Jess helped me up into the backseat; I couldn't make the small leap. Ben-Ben slammed his snout into my backside in his haste to get in the car. Not to get away from the zombies, but rather to be next to me.

"I missed you." He snuggled close. Normally I would have pushed him away, but right now, his company was very welcome. "The cat's been mean to me," he whispered as I drifted off to sleep.

My dreams started off good enough; Jess and Winke were making bacon cookies in our old home. Ben-Ben kept looking from them to the back door. "Riley?" he asked in a strange nasal whine. It was not his normal bacon happiness.

My attention was pulled to the door. Alpha-male was outside, staring at us through the viewer. He looked all right at first and then his skin began to change from its healthy color to that of a late-day blue. I could see this clearly, even though it was dark out. His pale face glowed like the Wolf-Disc. He opened his mouth and his teeth elongated, as did his nose. I was trying to back out of the food room, but my paws kept losing traction on the slippery surface. Jess had her back to the door and was paying no attention at all to the horror behind her.

Winke had stopped moving completely; he was frozen in place, a lump of bloody something in his fist. The only thing not still was the blood that fell from his hand and onto the top of Ben-Ben's head. At first it was merely drops, and then it began to come down hard. Ben-Ben was bathed in it. Icely was behind me, laughing in his cruel way. A zombie-

Mist was staring at me through the viewer now. The handle to the door began to twist as she was letting herself into the house. I yelped loud enough to wake myself up. At first I didn't know what I was looking at as my eyes adjusted and then I realized it was Ben-Ben's nose; it was closer to my eyes than my own.

"Hi," he said.

He was too close to focus so I pushed back and stood up. It was dark out, and at some point Jess had stopped the car. She was outside, sitting on the front of the car with Zach in her arms. He was getting some food, something that didn't sound so good at the moment as I struggled to let the sleep images go. I heard soft footfalls above me.

"Patches on patrol," Ben-Ben said when he saw me look up.

"Why aren't you getting food?" I asked him.

"I don't want to ever leave your side again, Riley."

"Ever?"

"Ever," he reiterated.

"Oh boy, this is going to be fun," I told him. "Well...let's go get you some food then."

"That would be great, Riley because, I really do think I'm starving to death. I've only had two cans of food, thirty six cookies, twelve pieces of beef jerky and eighty-nine floor fries."

"Only eighty-nine?" I asked.

He nodded sadly. "Only eighty-nine."

Had to give the dog credit, all his talk about food actually worked my appetite back up. "Let's go see if we can get you another can of food or two."

Jess slid off the wheeler with her brother. "You guys hungry?" she asked.

Ben-Ben was dancing around crazily, sometimes spinning around all the way.

"There are no zombies nearby," Patches said from the top of the wheeler. "This is what I've been doing while you've been gone."

She was making it sound like I had voluntarily left to stay by the great salty water.

"It's been me that kept them all safe," Patches said.

"Thank you," I told her.

I didn't know what else to say. I think she expected me to fight her. She was more than welcome to pack leader, the position had nearly gotten me killed three or four times. She'd be better at it; supposedly cats had nine lives. She could stand to lose a few; maybe it would make her more humble.

I could feel her gaze upon me as I ate. I let her stew. She was too exhausting to deal with, especially now that I was still weakened. Jess tilted a bottle of water into my mouth and I tried as best as I could to not let any spill. The cool liquid felt so good as it slogged down my throat and into my nearly full belly. When she pulled the bottle away I began to walk a few paces away from the car, Ben-Ben tripping me as he stayed close.

"Ben-Ben, I need to relieve myself," I told him.

"Okay." He looked up at me, his tongue dancing around.

"Alone, Ben-Ben."

"Okay," he repeated, still keeping pace with me.

"I thought you were kidding about the never leaving my side thing."

"Nope," he said honestly.

"I'm going over to that bush alone, Ben-Ben, you follow me under it and I'm going to hold you up by your tail."

"That would hurt, Riley."

"I know."

I crawled under a bush and to a small clearing. Ben-Ben was whining softly from the distance between us. I'd never been pulled up from my tail, but it must hurt if the little dog wouldn't follow with just the threat of that hanging over him. Then I felt bad that at some point in his life he had experienced such a painful sensation.

"You done yet, Riley?" he asked. I didn't even get a chance to respond before he spoke again. "What about now? You've been gone an awfully long time."

"I love you, Ben-Ben," I said, amused.

"I love you, too," Ben-Ben answered sincerely.

"Get a room!" Patches mewled.

"What's that mean?" Ben-Ben asked while I was thinking it.

"She's just angry because of who she is." I finished up.

Ben-Ben's head was cocked to the side as I came out. He didn't know what that meant either. "I really have to go too," Ben-Ben said.

"Then go." I looked back to where I had gone.

"You want to come with me?"

"No, but I'll wait out here for you."

"I'd like that."

I could hear him turning and turning as he looked for the perfect spot and then the grunting began as he was trying to force through it quickly.

"It's okay, Ben-Ben, I'll still be here when you're through."

He grunted louder in response. "Almost done."

"You're going to hurt yourself," I laughed.

He came under the brush, his butt dragging on the ground.

"Riley, you need to talk to him about that," Patches said from her lofty perch.

Ben-Ben and I walked back to the car.

"How you doing, girl?" Jess asked as she petted down my back.

"Much better now," I told her truthfully.

"I know you can't really understand me, Riley," Jess began "But I'd swear sometimes that you do. I'm tucking

Zach back into his chair and then I need to get some sleep. Can you watch out for us?" She put her face next to mine and hugged me tight.

"Yes," I woofed softly in her ear.

"What does the stupid girl think I've been doing all along?" Patches asked bitterly.

Jess let me go, scratched briefly behind Ben-Ben's ear, and attempted to reach up and pet the cat, but Patches moved away. Then she got in the car.

I turned to Patches. "She doesn't understand, but I am thankful for everything you've done," I told her. I hoped that would calm her down a bit. If the flicking of her tail was any indication, it had not worked as well as I'd hoped.

"Stupid human and stupid dogs they own," I heard her mumble.

"Do you want to get some sleep?" I asked her.

"Yeah, I'm so tired," Ben-Ben answered instead.

"Might as well. She won't know it was me that protected her anyway. You'll just take all the credit." Patches jumped down.

"I'm not looking for praise, cat, I'm just doing my best to keep us alive," I told her. She was starting to get me riled up.

"Says you," she replied before she hopped up into the car.

"Are you staying out there?" Jess asked, looking at me. I sat down next to her door. She leaned over and shut the back one when Ben-Ben and the cat were inside.

"I'll be next to you in my thoughts." Ben-Ben stuck his head out the viewer.

"That'll be close enough," I told him.

"Okay." He ducked back down.

I'd done only one trip around the wheeler when I heard him snoring. I noticed Patches glaring at me. She stayed like that for three or four more times around. I made sure to never look up at her—I was afraid she'd attack.

Eventually, at some point, she got sick of the game and had gone to sleep herself.

I'd seen a deer and a strange prickly looking thing lumber across the road during my watch. The deer had bounded off quickly; the strange looking animal had looked my way once and kept shuffling along. For that I was thankful. It looked slow enough, but those spiky things all around it looked dangerous.

The burning-disc was just coming up as the cat jumped out of the window and next to me. I was startled; I think she may have laughed. One of Jess' arms stuck out the window as she stretched.

"I slept longer than I meant to," she said, getting out of the car. "We could be to Justin's by tonight, Riley."

I wagged my tail in response. Anything that made her happier, made me happier.

"We should get going." She opened the door so I could get in. "Where's Patches?" she asked in alarm.

"I didn't know you cared?" Patches said sardonically from across the road.

"Oh...there you are," Jess said with visible relief.

"Give her a break, cat, she's doing the best she can." I hopped in.

"What did you two eat last night?" Patches asked. "It smells like one of Zach's dirty diapers over here."

"That would be Ben-Ben," I said.

"Probably," Ben-Ben said happily as he watched me get in with him.

Patches sauntered over to us.

"Any day, Princess," Jess said to Patches. She was getting excited about her potential reunion; it was easy to smell the pheromones coming off of her.

"I would have gone with 'Queen' but Princess is a good start," Patches said as she hopped into the wheeler.

She looked quickly and noted that I was in the backseat. Her eyes got big for a split second before she took the passenger seat triumphantly. I was amused at that. She was welcome to it; there was more room in the back to sleep, something which I planned on doing in the next few moments.

Ben-Ben got down on the floor of the car and was resting his head mere whiskers from me.

"We doing this again?" I asked.

"Yup." was his happy reply.

"Fine, but no licking this time," I told him before I closed my eyelids.

Chapter 10 - ICELY

"Fuck I'm cold."

Icely sat shivering in his car. He had pulled off the highway and onto a turnoff reserved solely for emergency vehicles. He was hidden from only the most prying of eyes where he had parked.

"You cold, too?" he asked the still and lifeless form of Schools. At some point he had stopped to strap the man in position after he had slouched down again.

"You're not cold? You look like you're freezing, man." Icely said.

Fat beads of sweat were running off of Icely's brow as he shook throughout the night. His rest had been fitful, and more than once he had cried out while he slept. Schools though had kept a constant vigil and Icely thanked him for it when the sun crept up.

"You're a good friend." Icely clapped the man on the shoulder before he stepped out. "Fucking birds are chirping, crickets are making cricket noises, I think I saw a rabbit. It's like a Disney movie out here. Want a smoke?" Icely asked Schools. "Sun feels good…a little too hot though." His body went from shivering a few moments previous to sweating profusely.

Icely's head was hanging low; drops of mucous coming from his nose. He would occasionally wipe those away. It was the sticky sensation on the back of his neck that he found the most disturbing; more than once he had reached back there and rubbed, the hand coming back covered in an oozing, viscous, gel-like fluid.

"Got an infection. The fucking cat." He looked at the goop in his hand. "Doesn't that beat all, Schools?" Icely asked. "Man-killing dog, and it's the cat that's doing me in. Ain't that a fucking peach? Guess I'm going to need some white-lined antibiotics." He laughed, as he got back into the car. "Come on, Schools, move a little so I can get in the glove box. I'm not shitting you, man, move!" he shouted when he realized the dead man wasn't moving fast enough. Icely pulled his gun out and pressed the barrel against Schools' head, he did so with enough force that Schools fell over.

"Why didn't you just do that in the first place?" Icely asked as he reached over and grabbed the cocaine. Icely had just done his second rail and was feeling better when he heard a familiar far off sound. "Pigs? No offense," he said to Schools. "You still pissed about the whole gun to the head thing, man? That was nothing. Here let me help you up." Icely propped Schools back into a sitting position. "Man, you want one of these lines? You look worse than I feel."

Icely's attention was once again pulled to the noise of the approaching car. "Well ain't that the shit." Icely looked at the passing car. A multi-colored cat was staring straight at him through the passenger side window.

"Fuck, Schools, you were right, man. All we had to do was wait for her! Hot fucking damn! Put your seatbelt on, we're going for a ride!"

He started the car and pulled out quickly, sending gravel shooting out from behind him, his wound slowly draining blood. Icely was too far gone to care.

Chapter 11 - JESS and the GANG

"Icely," Patches said softly. She may as well have said 'bath time' it had cut so quickly through my sleep.

"What about him?" I asked, lifting my head up.

"He was on the side of the road." Patches turned to look out the rear viewer.

I stood up quickly to share the same view.

"That wasn't a long nap, Riley," Jess said as she looked at me through the small reflective viewer. "What are you two so interested in?" she asked. "Oh, God, no." We all watched Icely's car pull onto the hard packed ground. "It can't be." Her earlier happiness had been completely obliterated. Fear swirled around the wheeler like a tangible force.

I got back down to make sure Zach was strapped into his funny seat. Ben-Ben had got back down to the floor. He was shivering and fear relieving. I did not yell at him. I wanted to do the same.

"He means to kill us," Zach said to me.

"Figure that out all on your own, Baby-that-should-not-talk?" Patches mewled.

I would have berated her, but Zach hadn't even seemed to take note of her words. Plus, I could tell she said it just because she was as scared as the rest of us.

"What's he doing?" Jess asked, looking into the reflective rear viewer. We all figured it out as soon as the wheeler swung violently to the side from Icely's impact. I fell to the floor and Zach 'umphed' loudly as the wind was knocked from him. Patches hadn't moved an inch though. I figured she had those razor claws buried halfway into the seat she was on. Jess cried out in alarm as Zach began to wail.

"Are you alright?" I asked him as I got up off of Ben-Ben who didn't seem to mind the company all that much.

"I'm fine," he mumbled as my back paw pushed down on his muzzle.

"I meant the baby, but I'm glad to see you are alright as well."

Zach sniffed, his bottom lip quivering as tears stained his face. "I'm okay," he said.

"He's coming back," Patches said.

I braced for the next hit. Wheeler feet screeched on the hard pack ground. The sound of breaking things was louder this time. Our wheeler went side to side as it appeared Jess was fighting with the wheel.

"She's going to drive us right off the road!" Patches yelled.

"Like to see you do better," I said through gritted teeth as I strained to keep myself from once again falling over.

"I can't lose him," Jess said frantically. She kept looking in the rear viewer.

There was an explosion as the glass to the rear viewer sprayed into the backseat.

"Oh, my God! He's shooting at us!" Jess cried. "Zach are you alright?" she asked as she turned around. There were some small pieces of the viewer in his lap and a small cut on his cheek, but other than that, he was fine. "You're bleeding!"

"It's just a scratch," he told her, trying to calm his sister down.

Jess reached back and touched Zach. When she was confident he was fine, she steadied the wheeler and pressed down harder on the go-faster pedal. For the moment at least, she was able to pull away from Icely.

I shook my body and a bunch of the viewer pieces fell away. Ben-Ben was sparkling, he was coated in so much of it, but since he had his head buried under his paws, I figured he was alright as well.

"Cat down! Cat down!" Patches squealed.

I turned quickly around. She had fallen to her seat and was screaming bloody murder—had that same sound I'd heard before at home when the local Toms came to visit her. How she found that irritating sound flattering was beyond me. The noises Zach's brother made out of his behind were much more entertaining than those wails. Yet she would strut around like Prince Charming himself had come to date her. (I used to really enjoy when Jess read Zach his bedtime stories.)

Patches was clawing at something in her side. I was convinced the metal bee had struck her. I could not imagine her small body being able to absorb such a shock. I'm ashamed to say this, but I was trying to figure out if I would miss her or not.

"Did the metal bee get you?" I asked her, panting from distress. Maybe that was my body's way of telling me I would miss the fleabag.

"What gave it away?" she asked.

"Where?" I moved in closer. I didn't see any blood.

"Right here." She was pointing with her claw. She couldn't turn her head enough to see it. "Oh, Riley, I'll be with my ancestors soon."

"I have no idea what you're talking about, cat."

"When you die you see all of your family members again, stupid dog."

I turned to Zach. "Is that true?"

He nodded.

"I'll see Santa again?" Ben-Ben whined from below.

He wasn't technically family, but I saw no reason to make the little dog any sadder. "Sure, and he'll have bacon."

"That would be wonderful," Ben-Ben said from under his paws.

I turned back to the cat. "Move your paw, let me see."

"You touch me and I'll stick this in your eye."

"Move, Riley." Jess pushed my head away. "Oh, you poor thing," she said as she pulled a small piece of blood-coated viewer from Patches side. "All better?"

"Who's the baby now?" Zach asked.

"That…that could have been deadly." Patches stood back up.

Another bee struck the car as Icely had decided to hit us with something other than his own wheeler.

"There's smoke coming up from his car," Patches said, looking out the rear. She was careful to stay mostly hidden behind her seat.

"I-I think he screwed his radiator up," Jess said triumphantly.

"He's coming again." Patches got down onto the seat.

Jess ducked down as Icely shot multiple bees. Near as I could tell, none of them were close. Then my side of the car dipped down and there was a loud flapping sound.

"Flat!" Jess yelled out. "Shit."

"Flat?" I asked Patches.

"It's like the car lost a shoe."

"Is that important?" I asked back. I was really hoping it wasn't. I'd seen all of the kids play around the yard without them on, even after they would occasionally step in Ben-Ben's droppings. Alpha-female had a special secluded spot for us to go in the back of the yard. Ben-Ben didn't care or couldn't remember; he would go wherever and whenever the mood struck.

Patches nodded back to me in response. "He's got worse problems, though. There's heavy black smoke coming from his car."

"That's good right?" I asked.

"Yes, except we'll all be walking soon."

Icely could move faster than Jess, especially since she was going to have to carry Zach. Plus, he had a fire-arm. This

Mark Tufo

was bad.

"He's slowing down!" Jess said with excitement. "What was that?" she added as we all heard a loud sound come from the rear of the wheeler.

"Big piece of tire just came off," Patches said.

A couple of more bees buzzed by the car and then…nothing. I stuck my head to look up, by the time I did, Icely was standing beside his car, melting away into the distance.

"We're going to lose him," Jess said happily. "Now I just need to change this flat."

She was quiet for a moment before she spoke again. "I'll just go a little further before I do though."

As the smell of burning wheeler shoe got real strong within the car, Zach began to cough. I was concerned that he was not getting enough clean air. And then, luckily, the smell stopped. It was quickly replaced by a grating sound and a shower of fire behind the car.

"She's driving on her rim," Patches said.

How does she know all this stuff? I thought. As long as the wheeler was still moving I was okay with the loud sound and the small fires.

"That's as far as I can go." Jess pulled the wheeler over to the side of the hard path. "I hope they have a spare."

"Spare what?" Ben-Ben asked. "Food packet? Because that would be nice. I get hungry when I'm nervous."

"Who knew you were always nervous?" Patches asked. "And she means tire. Spare tire."

"How far back is Icely?" I asked.

"Not far enough," Patches replied.

Jess got out and opened the side door to get a better look at her brother. "Oh you poor thing." She kissed his cheek. "I'm so sorry."

"It wasn't your fault, sis," he gurgled.

Jess went to the rear of the car and opened it up, I followed. "I don't even know what I'm looking for," she said as she pulled stuff out. "Why didn't I pay more attention when Dad tried to show me how to do this? Seemed like something I'd never have to worry about. Oh, Dad. I miss you and Mom…and even Daniel."

Patches had come up beside me; she kept looking from Jess to back down the path we had just come.

"Uh-huh! The jack! Now what do I do with it?" Jess asked.

She placed the 'jack' under the car and did something to it that made the wheeler start to rise up into the air. I backed away as did Patches. Ben-Ben was staring at us from the rising doorway.

"This is fun!" he yipped.

"Okay, the car is in the air. Now what?" Jess asked.

No idea who she was asking, even the cat had a blank expression on her face.

"I've got to take the wheel off, that's right." Jess grabbed a heavy stick made from metal and went over to the flat. "Rightie-tightie, leftie-loosie."

I shrugged my shoulders; it was funny because Patches did the same. Jess was grunting and groaning. The wheel began to turn, although from her tone I could tell that was not what she wanted it to do.

"He always made this look so easy," she cried out.

I noticed that the wheeler was moving slightly forward every time she tried to do whatever 'leftie-loosie' meant.

"The jack is moving!" she cried in alarm.

"The jack isn't moving, the car is," Patches clarified.

The wheeler rode forward a little bit as the jack fell over; there was a crinkling of metal underneath the wheeler as it came down.

"Are you guys alright?" Jess asked, sticking her head into the back of the wheeler.

"That wasn't as much fun as I thought it would be," Ben-Ben said, jumping out.

"Maybe that's a good idea." Jess pulled Zach's seat with him in it out of the wheeler. She put him down a few feet away from the back end. I went over and gave him a kiss. He looked like he could use one.

"Oh...that makes sense. I should loosen the lug nuts before I jack the car up."

Ben-Ben was in the middle of the road taking care of some business.

"What?" he asked when he saw Patches and me looking at him. "I have to go when I'm nervous."

"What don't you have to do when you're nervous?" Patches asked.

Ben-Ben grunted out, "Sleep."

"Too bad. I'd almost never have to deal with you if that were the case." Patches started to walk away from us. "I'm going to keep a look out for Icely."

"I got one loose!"

It was some time later when she announced that she had finally got the last one loose. She started to tug on what she called 'the rim'.

"Sometimes, Jess, you really do let your blonde shine through." She laughed. "NOW, I need to jack the car up."

The wheeler went back up into the air. Jess once again started pulling on the rim. Nothing happened. She even feebly kicked it a couple of times.

"It won't come off!" she screamed.

She smacked it a couple of times with the metal stick and still nothing. She went back into the back of the wheeler and came back with a heavy ended stick.

"This ought to do the trick," she said to herself.

The loud gonging sound had me concerned that Icely might be able to hear it and would come running. I could see Patches sitting far up the pathway and she had yet to turn our way. I figured she'd come running if he was.

The wheeler was swaying back and forth as Jess tugged, pushed, banged and kicked the rim. On her last kick she slipped and landed hard on her backside where she began to cry uncontrollably. I went over to her and licked one of the hands that were covering her face.

"Oh, Riley, I can't even change a flat. How am I going to protect us?" she wailed.

"I thought *you* were protecting us?" Ben-Ben asked of me.

I shushed the small dog.

"We should go," Patches said as she trotted up.

Chapter 12 - ICELY

"Piece of fucking shit!" Icely was screaming as he slammed his hands down on the dashboard and steering wheel. Black smoke billowed up from the hood and into the interior, a heavy knocking sound coming from the engine block.

"Can you fix a thrown rod?" Icely asked Schools. "Fine just sit there, you fucking lump, I'll take care of it myself. What the fuck do I pay you for?" He stepped out of the non-functioning car. He popped the hood and was immediately surrounded by a cloud of acrid engine smoke. Oil was dripping down from the ceiling of the hood. He could hear what little water remained boiling in the bottom of the radiator.

"Well that can't be good. Schools, man, come on out here and help me will you?" Icely reached out to touch the top of the manifold with a shaking hand. "Withdrawals? Well no reason for that." He went back inside the vehicle and pulled out a small mirror. "Want a bump?" He offered a rail to Schools. "Maybe it will liven your dead ass up. You're a horrible co-pilot." After completing a gram, Icely grabbed his gun and headed onto the open road. "Fuck it, if I can't drive, I'll just fly." He spread his arms out as he walked.

Icely stayed as close to the centerline as possible. He realized he would drift off the road if he didn't pay enough attention. His lips were cracked and dry. His mouth felt like he had swallowed a tablespoon of sand. His eyes burned and his chest sometimes felt like someone was hitting it with a hammer. Throughout it all, a slow steady pulse of puss oozed from his neck wound.

"Screwed the pooch on this one," he croaked. "Nope, nope, that's wrong...the pooch screwed me." He laughed, an arid sound coming from his throat. Heat shimmered off the roadway giving it a surreal, watery appearance. "Ain't that the shit? Schools you seeing this? Looks like the Sahara, man."

At one point, Icely found himself walking through some scrub brush. "How the fuck did that happen?" he asked, coming out of his fugue state. He quickly righted himself. "How long have we been walking?" Icely stopped and placed his hand up by his forehead to shield the sun. Off in the distance he saw something. "It can't be."

He was running forward even as he finished saying it.

Chapter 13 - RILEY

"The wheeler isn't working yet," I told the cat.

"And it never will. The rim is frozen on." Patches started walking down the road.

"I don't see any ice?" Ben-Ben said as he sniffed around the jack.

"What are you doing, cat?" I barked after her.

"He's coming," she responded without ever looking back.

The mysterious 'he' was not in doubt. However, how I was going to get Jess to abandon the wheeler was a different story. I lightly nipped at her shoulder and tried to pull her towards me.

"What are you doing, Riley?" She looked at me, water still flowing from her eyes.

I pulled harder.

"Stop, Riley!"

"Are we playing?" Ben-Ben asked as he grabbed her side and started tugging with me.

"The both of you just stop it!" She attempted to push us away.

I growled loudly and ferociously as she did so.

"That doesn't sound like playing." Ben-Ben let Jess' side go.

"Get up!" I barked savagely at her.

"Riley, you're scaring her and me," Zach said as he began to cry.

"Icely's coming, Zach, your sister needs to get

moving now! Cry louder," I told the baby.

Jess stood up, partly to get away from me, but mostly to get to her brother.

"I've got an idea," Zach said as he kept crying.

"Icely's coming?" Ben-Ben asked as he ran over to the side of the roadway.

"Didn't you just go?" I asked.

"I'm nervous!"

"Zach, are you okay?" Jess asked as she picked him up.

The baby kept crying as she took him out of his seat. She placed him on her hip and hopped him up and down a little, something which generally made him giggle uncontrollably. This time, however, he just kept crying. She placed him up higher so his face was next to hers. Deep-throated cries came from him. I was impressed something so small had so much volume.

Jess began to walk towards the back of the car and somehow Zach found another level. His face reddened with the exertion of getting that volume level. The funny thing was, when Jess started to walk towards the front of the car, he stopped completely. At first I had no idea what he was doing, but whenever Jess did anything but walk straight down the roadway following the cat, he bellowed. She took longer than me to figure it out, but then again, I knew why. As soon as I did know, I joined him. When he cried I would bark and then get in her way if she was not following the desired course. Ben-Ben almost messed it up when he once again thought we were playing and would get in her way no matter which direction she was going.

"What's going on?" she asked, pulling Zach away to look into his face and then down at me. Maybe it was the cat that finally got her. "Where's she going?"

"Thanks for waiting," I said sarcastically to the cat as we finally caught up.

"Took you long enough."

Chapter 14 - ICELY

"You think this is a trap, Schools?" Icely asked as he came over a rise to see Jess' car in the middle of the roadway. Then his concern quickly became glee. "Naw, no reason for a trap, the bitch could have just easily left me behind. Looks like her car is out of commission!" His steps, which had been faltering, picked up again.

Chapter 15 - JESS

Hesitation still reigned supreme within Jess. We were headed in the right direction, but she kept looking back. "We have no supplies...no food or water or anything for Zach."

"We have our lives," I told her, but I knew without the food and water the time span on even that was limited.

"My feet hurt, Riley," Ben-Ben moaned.

I was not sure how far we had walked, but I was hurting as well. Patches was stoic even though she would stop from time to time to lick her paws. Jess was getting tired and her footfalls began getting shorter in distance.

"We need to rest, find some shelter," I said.

Jess went to the side and sat on the heavy metal barrier.

"I'm going to look for water," I told the group. I crawled under the barrier and away.

Jess said nothing as I left. I could smell flowing water but it was far off and getting Jess to follow me would be difficult. My ears perked when I heard shouting in the distance.

"I see you, bitch!"

Icely, I thought. All thoughts of water were forgotten. I was heading back up to the group when I got a better idea.

"Riley, we have to leave!" Jess cried. Ben-Ben was barking incessantly in warning. I could hear them as they started heading away.

"He'll catch up or he won't," Patches said, as she led them.

There's the cat I know and loathe, I thought as I stayed off the road and went back towards Icely.

"Don't run! I want to get this over with!" Icely was laughing. "How far do you really think you're going to get? How far did you really think I was going to let you get? Stupid bitch, I would have treated you like a queen! A queen of whores!" And then he started coughing.

I got low, almost crawling as our paths came closer and closer.

"I saw your car! You shouldn't have driven on your rim, that's real bad for the suspension!"

"Stop following us!" Jess shouted back.

Icely started laughing anew. "Like that's going to happen. That baby must be getting heavy. Don't worry, I'll lighten your load soon enough. I'm not even going to bury you guys when I'm through...I'll let the birds feast on your eyes!"

"I hate birds," I said to him as I crawled back out from behind the metal and onto the roadway. Icely's back was to me.

He turned; he looked horrible—not as bad as the zombies, but not a whole lot better either. His color was ashen and I could almost feel the fever heat radiating off him from my present location. His red-lined eyes flew open momentarily in fear as he turned to see me.

"You're still alive? That's not possible. Now I'm seeing ghosts, first Schools and now you."

"Oh, I'm alive." I bared my teeth and got low.

He pointed his fire-arm at me with a wavering arm. He closed an eye as he tried to take aim at me. In my anger I had forgotten to take into account the bee slinger. I heard metal on metal as he pulled the trigger. No loud explosion and certainly no bee. He pulled the trigger again and again.

"Seems I'm out of bullets, mutt. So now what?" he asked.

"Now you die," I told him as I advanced slowly.

"This is the way it should be don't you think? Mano-to-dog-o," he said as he laughed again. "I will not lose my fucking empire to a damned dog. I worked too damn hard to let it go now." He turned his fire-arm and swung his arm out, I guess to test the weight of it to be used as a club.

I circled around.

"Come on, mutt! I've got a date with your little bitch! And I don't want to keep her waiting."

He staggered as I slowly went around him. I feigned a charge and he swung viciously, the fire-arm making a whistling noise as it cut through the air. He may have been sick, but he wasn't dead, and he still had more than enough power to inflict some serious damage if I let him. If I did die, I was going to make absolutely certain that he would be in no condition to follow Jess and the rest.

"You're really starting to piss me off!"

I darted to my right, Icely struggled to keep up. As I dodged back to the left, I went in and bit hard on the back of his calf. I hated that I was using Ben-Ben's tactics, but this wasn't about herding sheep; this was a life or death struggle, and I would do whatever it took to make sure I was the victor and he was the loser.

"Motherfucker, that hurt!" he shouted as he simultaneously kicked out with his leg.

I winced and jumped back. He caught me on my sensitive snout. I took satisfaction in the fact that I saw his blood leak onto his fake furs.

"Well I guess you drew first blood." He had touched his wound with his front paw and was looking at the redness there. "It's not who draws first, though, it's who draws last...and I plan on pissing on your dead body." He lunged at me as he spoke.

I had not been expecting his attack and nearly had my skull crushed when the fire-arm club came dangerously close to my head.

"Ooh so close. You won't be that lucky the next time.

I should have just shot you when you were lying in that trunk. Well, lesson learned. Let's dance," Icely said menacingly as he kept a watchful eye on me.

I noticed he would raise a hand up to his head when I barked as if the noise somehow was hurting him. I made sure to do it as fast and as loud as I could.

"Shut up, mutt! My head is splitting!"

"Not yet," I told him. "But soon."

Icely kept moving closer to the side of the road. It was when he bent down cautiously that I saw the reason why. He was looking for objects to throw at me. He picked up a chunk of the path. I yelped loudly when it struck me in my hindquarters.

"Next one is going to be in that thick dog skull of yours," he said, bending down to retrieve another piece.

I launched. He stepped back and stood up as I came in. I fell short of my target—which was his face—but I was still able to strike. I bit down on the inside of his thigh and could feel his blood begin to coat my teeth. His cries of agony were punctuated with a swinging of his fire-arm laden paw. It had enough force that I was jarred loose. He'd caught me in my ribs and hit hard enough to knock the air from me. I rolled away, coughing in an attempt to breathe.

"FUCK!" he bellowed. "You must be a bitch, damn near made me a eunuch!"

I backed up. My entire right side hurt and I still had not caught my breath.

"Riiiiley, are you alright?" Ben-Ben asked, running up.

"Stay away from him!" I told the small dog.

Ben-Ben pulled up short.

"Aw, isn't that cute. You got fucking back-up. How about I kill that little dog so you can watch?"

"Try," I told him. Something in my growl gave Icely a reason to pause.

"You're right, I should kill you first. It would be the

smart thing to do. But then again, I didn't get to where I was with my smarts." He turned and ran towards Ben-Ben, arm upraised and ready to strike.

Ben-Ben's eyes got huge as the big man barreled down on him. Fear urine spread out below him. He looked like Jess did sometimes when she watched what she called a 'scary movie'. She was always careful to make sure that I snuggled next to her on the couch when she did so. I honestly didn't know what she was afraid of; the images on the box never once came out and harmed anyone. I started to run at Icely, but his lead was too great. If Ben-Ben didn't move, he was going to get hit and hard.

A blur blazed by Ben-Ben and struck Icely's paw. He yelled out as I watched Patches jump easily to the side, avoiding his swipe.

"Move dog!" she hissed, making sure to stay away from Icely.

"Fucking cat, you scratched me!" he yelled as he held up his paw. Blood oozed from an angry wound on the back of it. "You're the one that got me sick."

"You're welcome," Patches said, moving away from what appeared to be clumsy attempts to get her. I'd seen Patches elude the entire family easily in an enclosed space when they told her it was time for a flea bath. How Icely thought he was going to catch her out in the open was a mystery.

Patches had delayed him long enough that I was able to catch up. He let out a loud 'oomph' as I hit the back of his legs. He fell hard onto his knees. I heard a loud cracking as he did so.

He struck and rolled, dropping the fire-arm to cup one of his legs. "You broke my fucking knee-cap!" he was shrieking. "This can't be happening to me! I'm getting my ass handed to me by the animal farm." He started laughing; it was raspy and during parts of it he coughed, but it was a laugh nonetheless.

Jess and Zach had come up and were now watching.

"Bitch…" Icely started. "I mean, Jess, help me. You get me out of this I'll let you run Vegas. I was…I was just kidding, I was never going to hurt you." He paused. "Okay, we both know that's a lie, I was going to fuck you up good and then let everyone else do the same. I'm a businessman, though, and things change. Let's make a deal."

Jess stayed where she was. "Kill him, Riley," she said evenly.

"Wait…wait! You come to my city, unannounced and uninvited I accept you into my home to make you a queen and now you want to kill me? You ungrateful little cunt."

"He smells bad," Ben-Ben said to me as he circled around and came up beside me.

Icely kept turning his head from side to side to keep an eye on all of us.

"Sick," I answered.

"Dead soon," Patches added.

"Riley, you can't kill a man in cold blood," Zach said.

Cold-blood? I'd never heard of such a thing. All blood was hot.

Jess put Zach down and approached the downed man. She brought her paw up. In it was a fire-arm.

"What now, bitch, you going to shoot me?" Icely spat.

We all flinched from the explosion as Icely's head slammed hard against the ground.

"He's dead," Patches said as she watched something leave the ground. Her head moved upwards to track it then whipped down as if whatever was going up had fallen. Then she walked over to Zach.

Jess stood over Icely's body for a few moments longer, not moving away until Zach began to cry. Ben-Ben raced to catch up or more likely get away, either way, I didn't fault him. I waited until they had begun to move away before I went over to Icely's body and sniffed. I wanted to make completely sure he was dead; when I was convinced of this I moved on. For the briefest of moments I thought about urinating on him much like he had threatened me, but then thought better of it. If that sick bully of a man had wanted to do it, then that just meant it was wrong. Even us 'lowly' animals don't debase those we kill for nourishment or even in defense.

The rest of the day was traveled in near silence except for the grunts of Jess as she readjusted Zach or the licking of paws when we paused—not much was said. Jess was having a difficult time with the killing of Icely. I wished I could tell her how necessary it had been and she'd even done him a favor. The fever that racked his body would have killed him eventually anyway, and it would have been a long, drawn out, painful way to go.

The day had darkened up as thick brown-black clouds covered the sky. Rain threatened to fall, and it gave the light a murky quality. The burning-disc was once again starting to hide. It would be difficult for the Wolf-Disc to shine through the cover. I felt nervousness and fear from Jess. This wasn't the excitement-fear she felt when she watched the image box, though. This was closer to terror. We were stuck out in the approaching dark, in the open, without shelter or a wheeler. The lack of light meant little to Patches; Ben-Ben and I, we'd be okay, but Jess and Zach would be nearly blind. Two-leggers feared the dark like no other animal. Many creatures thrived when the burning- disc went down…they weren't one of them. Of all the things the two-leggers can do, it still amazes me how much they can't.

They can't see in the dark, they can't run very fast, they have small teeth, small noses, and no claws. It makes sense that they make the world as tame as possible, because they are ill suited for the wild. The higher power they believe in has a strange sense of humor. He (or she) creates a world full of animals that are completely adapted to their surroundings and then he (or she) drops man in the mix. No wonder they sought out wolves as companions early on—without them they would have never stood a chance. It was a funny thought to help get through the mundane and the pain of the long walk but it would do little to get us out of our present situation.

"A dealership!" Jess exclaimed.

Patches looked over at me with a questioning expression. Holy dog biscuits there was something the smug little feline didn't know. It mattered little to me that I didn't either.

"They have wheelers there!" Ben-Ben yapped.

How he knew was beyond me, all I knew was that Jess walked off the hard ground and onto the much softer grass and towards this 'dealership'. Zach was beginning to get irritable, he was uncomfortable, hungry, and I believe his skins were dirty—at least that was what the smell indicated. The baby was being brave, but even he had his limits. Jess stepped on every noise-producing object she could. Fallen twigs, old liquid holders…didn't matter to her, she was completely unaware of how dangerous her surroundings were.

"You and Ben-Ben are almost ghosts compared to how noisy Jess is," Patches said as she moved away just a bit. "She's going to garner some unwanted attention."

The cat was right, it was just the *way* she said it. Not as if we should try to make Jess and Zach quieter, but rather, we should leave them before 'we' all got attacked. Luckily, Jess did get quiet and down on her haunches as we came across what I could only describe as a wheeler farm. They were all stopped in neat rows, any and all of them looked fine to me. The light was nearly completely gone, but I thought there was enough left that Jess would also be able to see all the wheelers. However, her hesitation led me to believe otherwise soon enough.

"Do they put gas in new cars?" she spoke barely above a whisper.

"Tell her to hurry up," Patches said. "I can smell the foul ones."

I also caught a faint whisper. They were either very far away or inside the building all the wheelers were parked around.

"Riley, you ready? I want to pick out a car; hopefully the keys will be in it. If not, we'll spend the night in it and find them in the morning." Jess rose into a half crouch.

We got into what Jess called a 'cross-over'. She fumbled around quickly, looking for the janglers, but the small light in the car seemed to unnerve her and she kept looking up at it. She was right to be concerned; anything out there would be attracted to it.

"Sleep it is." She doused the light.

"The baby needs water," Patches said as Zach slept restlessly.

I did not sleep well that night. I was concerned for Zach and sniffed at him repeatedly to make sure he was all right. I kept a vigilant watch as well. I did not want to get surrounded by the zombies in a wheeler that would not move.

Ben-Ben was in his traditional spot on the floor. He spoke just as I began to hear the morning birds. "There are no floor-fries, Riley. I sure would like some."

"It's a new car, stupid dog," Patches said.

"They still should come with floor-fries." Ben-Ben scraped at the fake fur flooring, hoping some were hidden deep within.

Jess' arms stretched out. "Well that was an uncomfortable night. Time to find some keys. Riley, you keep an eye on everything," she said as she opened her door.

I almost folded her leg over as I rushed out to be by her side. "Not a chance."

"Okay, I guess you're coming." She stuck her head back in. "Patches, keep an eye out."

"Whatever," Patches replied.

I glared at her, but she was busy pretending not to

notice me as she licked her side.

The closer we got to where Jess thought the janglers were, the more nervous I became. There were definitely zombies in there. Jess walked up to the large viewer and cupped her paws around her face to look in.

"Zombies," she said so softly that someone without my ears would not have heard. She backed away quickly. "I saw two of them, Riley. Now what? I need those keys. I have got to get Zach some formula and new diapers. This sucks." She looked down and opened her fire-arm up, making sure she had enough bees. "Two zombies that I can see and four bullets. I can do this, I can do this."

"We can do this," I told her. At least I hoped.

"You ready, Riley?"

She began to walk to the door. She let out a startled scream when a zombie banged up against the glass. It had been a small adult female before it became a zombie. She looked like she really enjoyed floor-fries before she started eating people. Her brown dress was in tatters, her teats hung low on her belly, round scabs covered most of her gray skin. A blue-black tongue licked over her bloodstained teeth. Hair hung from her head in clumps. Her calf muscle flopped down onto the ground with each halting step she took to keep up with us.

"That makes at least three zombies," Jess said as she did her best to avoid the zombie's gaze much like Patches had only moments earlier to me. I would not have been overly shocked if she began to lick her side or paws. "I need another weapon." She moved away from the building and to the nearest wheeler. She opened up the rear and after a few moments pulled out a metal stick.

I didn't like the metal stick—that meant she had to get close. It was always better to send the bees; they traveled far.

"Here we go again, Riley."

We went back to the front doors. Jess didn't

immediately enter as I thought she would. She waited until the first zombie came to us before opening the door and quickly stepping back. The zombie did not hesitate as it came at a direct line for her.

"Bees," I whined as the zombie came closer.

Jess stood her ground, the fire-arm in one paw the stick in the other. When I realized she wasn't going to shoot I advanced on the zombie.

"No, Riley."

The damaged leg made the zombie slow; she was still coming at us, though. When she came into range, Jess swung the stick, the sickening sound of shattering teeth breaking through the still of the morning. Bits of blood-red bone fell to the ground. The zombie kept moving forward. Jess swung again, hitting it on the side of the head. She had ruptured the skull, but not deeply enough to make the zombie stop its forward progress. Jess was backing up as the zombie kept moving in.

I wanted to bark to scare the zombie off, but I'd learned that didn't do anything good and would only notify other zombies or people that we were around. Jess stumbled a little as the back of her legs hit the front of a wheeler. She recovered in plenty of time as she had put some distance between herself and the shuffling zombie. She swung again, hitting nearly the same spot on the side of the head. This time the zombie did go down. It landed knees first, much like Icely had, and then rolled to the side, head whipping down onto the hard packed earth. It shook for a few moments and was still. Jess poked it with the stick, making sure it wasn't playing dead, I suppose. I knew better. Jess had put much of her body weight into both of those killing blows.

"One down," she said grimly.

"Bees next time," I pleaded.

We went back to the front door. I made sure to go in first. The smell was overpowering. I could smell little else except for the death and decay. Jess was gagging. Dead bodies had been dragged around the entire floor. Entrails and bones were everywhere.

"Oh, God, this is horrible," Jess said, bringing her forearm up to her nose.

A zombie had noticed the light coming in from the opening, and when its eyes settled on us, it came running. This one was not hampered with an injury. I barked because Jess was not looking in the right direction; her gaze was on the floor. Harm was not coming from there.

She turned and fired. Her bee smashed into a flower holder. Her next shot hit the zombie in the chest, his steps slowing for a moment as he received the bee. By the time Jess took her third shot, her fire-arm was nearly touching the zombie's head. Gray brain matter littered the floor, adding its own to the putrid mix.

"One shot," Jess said more to herself. The third zombie was having a difficult time getting towards us as it repeatedly slipped, not able to get traction on the slippery organs. Jess' paw was shaking as she held the fire-arm up. "Wait," she was saying over and over.

"Wait for what? Shoot it," I begged.

"Another one?"

We both saw as a zombie came out from a back room. Jess was alternating her looks from one to the other. The zombie that had come from the back was further away but was moving quicker towards us. The floor must have been cleaner where it was. I couldn't be sure, but it looked like they were going to get to us at about the same time.

Jess was looking from the door to the slipping zombie to the running zombie and back again. We could not walk any further; Zach wouldn't make it. The janglers were the most important thing. I moved into the pathway of the running zombie.

He was running too fast for me to feel confident that I would be able to get a bite in that would debilitate him. I could not take the chance that he got by me. His eyes were fixated on Jess, so much so that he did not run around things so much as into them until they yielded, sending desks and chairs flying. That would be my chance. I turned so my side was facing him and his right leg struck it. I howled in pain as my back end began to spin. His left leg came up and hit me under my jaw, sending me up off the ground for a moment. The pain I felt was momentary though as I celebrated. I had achieved what I had desired. The zombie was falling to the floor, fast and hard.

This one had the smarts enough to brace for his fall to keep his face from smashing into the hard ground. When I stopped moving from the impact, I lunged for the zombie. For one horrifying second, I did not think I was going to get the traction I needed. He was already starting to push himself up when I landed all four paws on his back, pushing him back to the earth. I heard Jess' shot just as I bit deeply into the back of the zombie's neck. I shook back and forth until I started to hear the muscles and tendons tear. I ripped back when I was confident I would take a significant part of him with me.

I let the rotten meat fall from my mouth. The zombie had moved enough that I fell to the side. He pushed up quickly and gained his feet. He tried desperately to hold his head upright. It kept falling forward so that his chin was hitting his chest. Then he did something I wasn't expecting—he braced his head with his hands to keep it straight. He swiveled his head with his front paws until he was once again locked on Jess who was staring down at the body of the zombie she had just killed.

Jess' gaze came up to see the living scary-night pictures coming toward her. I ran and hit the back of his legs, causing him to once again go to the floor. This time he couldn't move his paws and his head hit hard. I heard bones break; I did not know if they were facial or skull.

"Move, Riley!" Jess was coming. She had her stick raised high and hit the exposed glistening bone, shattering it into fragments. The zombie's front paws splayed out by his side and it was dead. "Wow that sucked," she said through heaving breaths. "Well, if there were any more zombies, they definitely would have come out by now unless they're scared."

"Well that would make two of us."

"Alright, let's do a quick check around to make sure there's no cowering zombies. Then the keys, and if God is really looking out for us, a vending machine or two."

The building was plenty big. We checked a place Jess called the service center, parts department, and employee lounge where Jess let out a small squeal of delight as we looked at a row of big boxes made of viewers.

"We'll come back here for sure. Let's find the damn keys first, though."

We had entered into another room she called an office. She walked over to a metal box. "Please don't be locked."

The door to the box swung open, seven times seven (and maybe more) janglers were hanging on small hooks.

"Jackpot!"

Then she was quiet, her merriment quickly melted away to consternation. "How am I going to tell which keys go to which car? I just figured they'd be marked with the name of the car, not all these damn numbers. What the hell do all these numbers mean?" She sat down hard in one of the chairs. "It'll take me hours to try all these damn keys."

"Then we'd better get started." I nudged her paw with my nose.

"You're right, Riley. Stop feeling sorry for yourself, Jess. Okay let me get the others. We'll at least eat and drink while I figure this out."

"Sounds good to me." I couldn't wait to get the taste of that zombie out of my mouth and the grumbling of my stomach let me know that even floor-fries would be welcome right now.

"Nice décor," Patches said as we walked back in.

Jess had left every door and window open that she could. It had helped some, but nothing short of Alpha-female's 'spring cleaning' was going to help this. I actually enjoyed those times. Alpha-male would take us to the park for the entire day. He said it was much more fun being away with us and not having to do any of the cleaning. I agreed, not that I was going to do any cleaning, but being with him and George had been among the most pleasurable days of my life.

The group had moved deep into the building while I was looking at the 'ago' pictures in my head. I caught up just as Jess was throwing a chair at one of the viewer boxes. It bounced off and clattered loudly on the floor.

"Well I wasn't expecting that." She grabbed Zach from where she had placed him and moved him to the furthest corner of the room. "Okay…everyone back." Patches was next to Zach, and of course Ben-Ben was right underneath Jess' feet.

"Ben-Ben, move," Jess and I said at the same time. He moved closer to the box.

"Dog is as thick as a hamster," Patches said.

"Come over here, Ben-Ben," I told him. I was standing in the doorway to the employee lounge.

We ate until our bellies were full once Jess broke through the viewers. There was a lot of sweet and salty stuff and something that the cat called beef jerky—Ben-Ben's personal favorite. It took the gnawing away from my stomach, but it wasn't satisfying. I wanted real meat, but this was still a nice respite from the hunger pains. We drank water from one of the viewer machines—even one that had vitamins, that one was a little strange, but it was wet and cool and both of those were things I very much wanted at the time. There wasn't much that Zach could have. However, Jess did get some fluids in him and he perked up a bit. Jess found a box and filled it with everything she could get. Once the wheeler was full she went back and put all the janglers in the box as well.

"I guess I'd better get started," she said as she placed the box of janglers in the seat next to her.

She smacked the steering wheel after she tried way more than seven sets of janglers. Patches had perched herself up on the hood right next to the front outside viewer. She was peering intently at something and then to Jess, she did this constantly until she spoke to me.

"Riley, can you make the girl come out here?"

"She is busy and mad, I'm not so sure I want to bother her," I said honestly. "She looks like that one time when she was going out and was having a difficult time deciding on which fake furs to put on. I told her she should just go out without them, but she didn't listen. Two-leggers are funny like that, they don't like to have their genitalia exposed, although how are other two-leggers going to smell them properly if they don't?"

"Have her come out to me." Patches was ignoring me.

"How do you expect me to do that?"

"Think of something," was her terse reply.

So I did. "You want her to come out by you?"

"I said that. Didn't I?"

I was tempted to press down on the wheeler noisemaker and see if I could scare the obnoxious tone from the cat.

"Smack your paw on the viewer."

She looked at me like she wanted to say something rude again and then maybe she figured out it was actually a good idea.

Patches touched the viewer like it was water, so basically hardly at all.

"Smack it," I chided her.

"I'll smack you," she mumbled, but at least this time she hit the viewer harder. Jess ignored her. Patches kept doing it, harder and harder until there was actually blood on the viewer.

"What are you doing, Patches?" Jess and I said simultaneously.

Jess got out of the car. "Are you alright?" Jess lifted up Patches leg. "You poor thing." Patches hissed until Jess let go, she then once again smacked the viewer.

I think the events were just too much for the furry feline. She'd finally gone bonkers; not that cats were all that far away from that line to begin with, but still, it was painful to watch in someone I sort of had respect for.

"What, Patches? I don't know what you're trying to say or do?" Jess asked.

"I'm not trying to say or do anything, you silly human, I'm trying to show you something." Patches smacked the glass again.

Jess watched as the cat's paw came down again, small patters of blood sprayed out from the impact.

"Stop…" Jess started and then paused. She looked a little longer at the blood.

What is she looking at? I thought.

She moved her face closer and then wiped some of the life fluid away. Suddenly, her head whipped up and looked directly at Patches. "How…how could you possibly know? You beautiful, wonderful cat." She picked Patches up and hugged her tight, twirling her around.

"Do you think if I make myself bleed she'll do that to me?" Ben-Ben asked.

Jess kissed Patches face repeatedly. I don't know which of us was more disgusted, the cat or me.

"Put me down and start the car, human."

Jess twirled around a couple of more times before gently putting Patches down. She got into the car and quickly started looking at the janglers' tags. She didn't even try to put them in the wheeler before she discarded them outside.

"What did you do?" I asked the cat.

"Cars have identification numbers much like your dog tags. It's in case either one of you gets lost, you can get returned to your owners."

"That's what that was for?"

"They have to put those numbers on you both, because you and cars are about equally as smart."

"Did she just say dogs were stupid?" Ben-Ben asked. He stuck his head up from the floor; I would imagine he was still looking for the elusive floor-fries.

I nodded.

"Yeah, well if we're so stupid why do we get to wear leashes?" Ben-Ben said triumphantly.

"I'm not even going to answer that." Patches began to lick her wounded paw.

"I won," Ben-Ben said as he dove back down.

I just shook my head. "He's not representative of all dogs."

"Whatever."

Jess let out a triumphant scream as she held a set of janglers high. "Let's go, Patches," she said happily. Once she got the wheeler started, she strapped Zach in as well as she could without his special seat.

"Three quarters of a tank, that'll work." She locked the doors and started to drive. "We find some stuff for Zach and then my next stop is to see Justin. Please be there."

It seemed whoever this God person Jess was praying to often was finally delivering on her pleas. Jess found a place she called a 'Wholefoods Market'. The front viewers had been smashed in, but it looked more like from a battle with zombies than from people taking things. At least half of the shelves still contained stuff and more importantly, formula for Zach. Jess said the diapers weren't the right size but they were close.

No zombies, and the wheeler was stuffed with enough food and water to last for many burning-disc cycles. It was time for me to catch up on some much needed sleep. I have no idea how long I slept, but I felt very refreshed when I was awoken to Jess crying.

"What's the matter?" I asked, looking around wildly for any signs of danger. Zach was looking at me, but he appeared fine. Ben-Ben was on the floor snoring and Patches was looking out the viewer at something. I didn't see any approaching zombies or two-leggers so I did not understand why Jess was so upset.

"We're here." Patches pointed with her paw.

"Where?"

"Read the sign."

"You can read?" I asked.

"It's actually very simple," she said with disdain. "Oh, that's right, I should have known a dog would not be able to."

"Not the time, cat. Why is Jess crying?" I growled.

"This is Little Turtle."

"Where Justin lives?" I asked excitedly. And then I looked around, taking my time. Many of the buildings around us were burned to the ground; some even had smoldering smoke rising up from the ashes. "It can't be." Dead zombies and torn apart two-leggers littered the ground; a great battle unlike anything we had seen so far had been waged here. And it did not look like the two-leggers had won.

Jess opened her door and left it open. I don't think on purpose, though. She was just lost in her distraught feelings.

"Where's she going?" Ben-Ben asked through a yawn.

"Don't know, but I guess I'll find out." I hopped out after her.

Jess was walking back and forth as she avoided the dead. "One-oh-three, this is his home," Jess said as she walked through the shattered front door. The inside looked much like the outside...destroyed. The dead were strewn about. The smell had a physical presence it was so overwhelming. Jess seemed not to notice.

"Justin?" she asked tremulously. She called his name out again and again. Jess looked to the right of the opening. Some of the go-uppers had been removed.

"No stairs? That's genius," Jess said. "Could they still be up there?"

If they were, they were dead, I thought. I smelt none of the living.

"We need to get up there." She pointed excitedly.

"I don't think that's a good idea," I gave her a nasal whine response.

Jess looked around the floor we were on. She grabbed a small table and wrestled it over the obstacles to get back to the go-uppers. She let it drop over the hole; it barely covered the opening.

"You're going up that?" I asked her.

She answered my question when she went up. She leaned most of her weight on the handrail. She was most of the way over when the table slid down and came hurtling for me. I jumped off the small landing and away as the table hit the wall.

"You alright?" she asked.

I poked my head back around to make sure nothing else was coming my way. She had gotten her back paws onto the step above her. She was pushing up with her arms on the rail until she was standing the funny way two-leggers do.

"That was close…getting down ought to be a lot of fun." She went up the rest of the stairs.

"Not without me."

I ran up and leaped. I had not figured out just how big the hole was. My front paws landed all right. My backs paws, however, were dangling in open space. I barked in panic as I kicked out, trying to gain traction on something, anything. My front paws were sliding; I was about to find out how far the drop was when Jess came back down and grabbed my paws.

"Riley, you're crazy."

She pulled me towards her. When enough of me was on the step she wrapped an arm around my waist. I licked her face and went up the rest of the way, happy to be away from the hole. The upstairs looked much like downstairs—dead zombies were everywhere.

"How did they get up here?" Jess asked as she stood next to me.

She moved back quickly and shrieked when her foot struck something. We looked down to see a wet skull. It was not that of a two-legger, though. The teeth were much too large.

"That's a dog," Jess said. "Oh poor Henry." She began to cry again.

I did not know Henry, but from the torn up zombies, it was easy enough to see he had died in defense of his family. He was a brave dog and I would mourn for him.

Jess reached down and grabbed a piece of material. There was a tag much like mine hanging from it. She turned it over. "Bear? Did they get another dog? Where's Henry?"

We walked straight ahead and into a room where the two-leggers slept. A large hole was in the wall with dead zombies stuck in part of it. That explained how the zombies had gotten up here. We checked out the entire upstairs. There was no sign of any other people, living or otherwise.

Jess had picked up a small go-upper. "Well, this will help us get back down…maybe." She was looking at it and then up.

"Why would they have a ladder in the middle of a hallway?" She stood it up and climbed quickly. With her front paws, she pushed open a small door in the ceiling. She jumped up and pulled herself into it. I barked in anger. There was no way I could follow her, and if she got into trouble, she would be all alone.

"They got out!" She poked her head back out. "There's a hole in the roof, they got out! Now I just need to find them!"

She turned around so that her back paws were coming out of the hole. She hopped down and was again by my side. We got back down the missing go-uppers—thankfully easier than I had got up. When we got outside, Jess looked around. A strange mixture of excitement, fear, and sadness all radiated off her body. We had arrived where the boy Justin lived and he was not here.

"Now what, girl?" Jess asked, gently rubbing my head. She looked back to the wheeler. And that's where we ended up going.

"He not there?" Patches asked.

"No."

"So then why is she driving into the complex?"

The wheeler was rocking back and forth. Jess tried her best to not hit any of the fallen but it was impossible. The stench was nearly unbearable every time she ran over the bloated body of a zombie. More than once she had to stop so she could evacuate the contents of her stomach.

Thankfully we didn't go too far, even the trash-eating Ben-Ben wasn't looking so good.

"Well, the clubhouse is still in pretty good shape. Riley, you want to come check this out with me?" she asked pleadingly.

She didn't even need to pose the question; she merely had to open the door. The large tree-built structure in front of us was quiet, nothing moved. The front doors had been completely smashed in, which I was finding out was a good thing. It usually meant any zombies that would have been trapped inside were now out and hopefully gone. We went up the stairs and inside. There were more scattered remains of humans and destroyed zombies. It was hard to not step on the discarded casings of the metal bees, there were so many of them.

"What happened here?" Jess asked as we moved slowly throughout.

To the left was a large room where once many chairs

had been set up. The two-leggers liked to get together and talk; I think most of them just enjoyed listening to their own voices without ever really having anything to say. Two-leggers were the only species I knew that talked the most without actually saying anything.

We went further in, almost all the way back when we found what looked like an entire two-legger store.

"Oh, my God." Jess said as she looked at the boxes and containers of food and drinks. "There's enough here for us for months." She got closer and started rooting through the different packages. "Formula and…and diapers!" She turned and grabbed my face. "Riley, look at all this stuff! It's incredible!"

"Any dog food?" I asked.

I welcomed the cardboard meat bits after our last meal of saltiness and sweet. I don't know if she actually understood me, but her next words were of great comfort.

"Dog food and even cat food, too!"

That was reason to celebrate—the first part at least. Cat food was horrible; my stomach gurgled just thinking about what the feline feasted on.

"Let's get everyone and eat and then I'll figure out what we're going to do. Dad always used to say it was easier to make a hard decision after a good meal."

I ate more than I can ever remember, even Ben-Ben, who ate like he had a tapeworm, seemed sated. He laid a few paces away from me, on his back with all four paws up in the air, his eyes half-closed.

"I can't move, Riley," was all he managed to get out.

Zach seemed much better after a thorough cleaning and his fake milk. Even surly Patches had stopped taking verbal swipes at every one.

"We can't just leave all this here," Jess said after we'd all rested for a bit. "I can't fit this in the car though, no way. Riley?"

She was asking if I wanted to go exploring again. I

didn't want to do much more than let my full belly scrape the ground, but I got up with her.

"Patches, you keep an eye on things?" she asked hesitantly.

"Sure, sure," Patches barely managed. Her mouth was nearly as closed as her eyes.

Jess shut the door to the food room and we went back out, past the meeting room and outside.

"I wish I knew where they went."

She shielded her eyes from the sun. We went around to the back of the building. "Locked," she said as she pulled on a heavy wooden gate. We walked around the whole fence looking for a way in. "That might be a good place to stay for a while." She peered through to the other side.

All I saw was hard packed ground and another door into the building on the other side.

"Riley, we could be safe in there. This fence is still intact and so are those doors. I could bring the food down here, and who knows, maybe Justin is still around and they're using that food as well."

I wanted to tell her that I smelled no signs of the living. Even over all the dead I would have detected something.

"What do you think?"

Anything that was going to get us out of the wheeler for a while was good with me.

She went back to the gate and used her back paw on the handle to help her climb up and over. Once inside she opened the doorway and let me in. She placed a rock so the gate would not close again.

"Shit, these are locked too," she said as she pulled on the doors. "Think, think, Jess. Okay…I know there is not a way in from upstairs, the windows on the side are barred. It's this way or no way." She tapped on a small viewer next to the door. "This leads into a small office and then the basement."

She grabbed a rock, stepped back and threw it. She missed. Her next throw hit, the smash of the glass sending a crow squawking away. Jess cleaned out the sharp bits and then started climbing through.

"I don't know if I'm going to fit." She grabbed a chair and brought it over. She was about midway through when her legs kicked. "I'm stuck!" There was panic in her voice. If there were any zombies on her side she wouldn't have a chance. "I can't reach anything!"

She struggled for a while longer, her legs kicking back and forth until there was a thud and a loud 'oomph' as she fell through the window and to the floor. She was unhurt, though, as a few seconds later she opened the back door. She twisted something on the handle and also found something to make sure that this door would not shut.

"When did they put a jail down here?" Jess asked as we walked around the entire floor.

There were two of the two-leggers' bathrooms—one male and one female, which I also found funny. Why did they care so much about not doing elimination in front of the other sex? Besides eating and breathing, it was one of the most basic of living-being functions and they sure didn't care about doing those two things in each other's company. I'll say it again, and not for the last time, what a funny species. According to Jess there was also a pool table—although I didn't see any water in it—and a racquetball court on this floor.

"This will be perfect. We have plenty of room to sleep down here and this is pretty safe. The only weak spot I can see is in the racquetball court."

"And the viewer you crawled through," I added.

"If it wasn't for those stupid windows in the racquetball court, we'd be all set."

I'd also noticed how dangerous they were; the cat had been looking down at the both of us. The vision still scared me.

"That's really the only way in," Jess said, looking up. "Hi, Patches. Okay let me think about this. I can only lock the door while I'm inside the court and then I wouldn't be able to get out except by going through that window up there. I'd need a rope or a ladder. I could do that. Lock the door, climb up a ladder, and come back around. That'll work."

And that was exactly what she did. First though, she grabbed Zach, brought him down and placed him in the waterless pool table room. Ben-Ben and Patches had followed. The small dog began to look around and sniff everything. I was determined to stay by Jess' side.

"Do NOT mark anything inside here, Ben-Ben," I said sternly. He gave me that downtrodden look that let me know that was exactly what he had been preparing to do. "We're going to be staying for a while, and I don't want to have to smell you constantly. You can go outside, but stay inside the fenced-in area."

"We're staying here?" Patches asked.

"Seems that way."

I bounded off to catch up to Jess. I don't know how many trips she made to get the food and supplies, but we were both exhausted by the time she called it a day.

"That's not even half of it," she said, looking at the small mountain of materials.

Ben-Ben was guarding it with glazed over eyes, his tongue hanging out, and a strange cocked expression on his face. "Is that all bacon?"

"Found some candles."

Jess lit them. The room, which had been losing light quickly, was once again illuminated.

"I don't like that." Jess was staring at the windows, which were beginning to blacken. They were level with the ground, but had heavy metal bars over them, making entry impossible.

"Let's cover those up. Just because I feel safer doesn't mean I want anyone to know that we're here. The light from the candles could attract all sorts of unwanted visitors."

"Yeah, and they might want to take our bacon," Ben-Ben said, wrapping his paws around a chew toy Jess had given him.

It was a somber night; on one end, we were all safe, and we had eaten to our hearts content...except for maybe Ben-Ben. On the other, we had lost friends and family along the way, and our original reason for coming here was nowhere to be found. We could stay here for a good long while...and then what? At some point, Jess would want to once again seek out other two-leggers and we would be back on the ever-dangerous path.

Chapter 16 - JESS PLUS FOUR

"Can you believe we've been here almost four months?" Jess asked me as she made another mark on the wall.

All I knew was that we'd been here long enough to gain some meat back on our bones. Jess had to actually limit Ben-Ben's food intake as his belly was coming dangerously close to the floor. He was not happy about it and would continually pester me about sharing with him. He'd attempted to eat Patches food only once; it'd had taken more than three burning-disc cycles for the wound she had put in his nose to stop hurting. Zach was mobile and had started crawling around. He moved pretty well on four legs for a two-legger. I personally thought he should stay that way, two-leggers were not fast runners.

After a few days of being there, Jess and I had gone on a couple of explorations of what remained of the buildings. She'd found all sorts of fire-arms which she always took back with us. There was no sign of Justin, though. And with each passing day, she got a little more morose, although she put on a brave face for Zach and the rest of us. Her body, however, could not hide the scents of sadness that fell from her. I'd even heard her crying on more than one occasion late at night in the bathroom. We knew nowhere else to go. This place had all we needed except the companionship she craved.

I didn't know where the zombies had gone, but that they weren't here was good enough for me. Every once in a while we'd hear shots or engines, but always off in the distance. Jess struggled with going out and seeing who it was and huddling together and staying safe. The weather was getting warmer when we heard an engine that was getting closer. Ben-Ben and I had been out in the fenced-in area chasing a rabbit around. On more than one occasion he'd smacked into the fence as the rabbit had gone back under to the other side. He never quite figured out when to stop, or maybe it was all the added weight he had on him kept pushing him forward.

We were having fun with the rabbit, and I think the small animal knew it as well, because it would come back in from a different part and we'd start the chase anew. Although, when the rabbit saw Patches, it would duck back under and not come back until the next day.

"Want me to kill that thing?" Patches asked.

"You hear that?" I perked up.

"Truck," Patches said after me. She turned and went back into the clubhouse.

"Almost had him that time," Ben-Ben said excitedly. I didn't have the heart to tell him he wasn't even close.

"Shh."

He looked over to me and then he caught the sound. "It's a bacon truck," he said softly.

"What's a bacon truck?" I asked, looking at him. "Forget it. We've got to hide, it's getting closer."

Jess came out the door holding a giggling Zach.

"Bacon truck!" Ben-Ben barked to Zach.

Zach looked to me.

"No clue," I told him.

"Ben-Ben, Riley, in now," Jess said sternly.

Once we were in, she immediately shut and locked the door. She put Zach down and grabbed a fire-arm making sure it had bees in it. The truck approached and then stopped. It was on the opposite side of us by the front entrance. The next thing we heard froze us all; footsteps above us. Whoever it was, was now on the top floor of the clubhouse.

"Is anyone here?" the man screamed. Jess jumped as furniture was being over-turned. "I know you're here!"

Fear coursed through all of us.

"Icely's dead, right?" Patches asked.

He was…I knew he was! Could this be some of the people that were with him seeking vengeance?

"Mike, I should have stayed with you," the man said. The screaming was much more subdued and devolved into racking sobs.

The pain in the man's cries was evident from where we were. Jess stood up.

"What are you doing?" I asked softly.

"Riley, come with me, he needs help." Jess stood up.

"Are you going to let her do this? This is a bad idea," Patches, ever the altruistic one, said.

"The two-legger needs help," I huffed.

"That doesn't mean he isn't dangerous," she replied.

And she was right, but Jess was going with or without me. Jess had one hand on the door as she kept looking back at Zach. She was also questioning her decision. It was his next words that made her move.

"*O, mí Dios, ayuda me.*"

"Come on, girl." With that, she stepped through the door.

We stayed close to the side of the building as we came around. A large wheeler was still running. The two-legger had driven it halfway up the steps. We cautiously made our way around it and into the front of the building. A two-legger was sitting in a chair; his paws gripped his bowed head, a fire-arm in one of them. Water from his eyes fell to the floor in heavy drops.

Jess and I were no more than a few steps away when he looked up at us with red-rimmed eyes.

"Who…who are you?" he asked as he let his hands drop.

"Put the gun down," Jess said, leveling her weapon on his chest.

"Shoot me, I have nothing left to give."

"I don't want to shoot you, I just don't want to get shot." Jess sounded so sure of herself. She'd grown a lot in the last few months.

"You...you live here?" he asked as he put his weapon down. The words were tough for him to get out of his choked throat. I thought I caught a hint of hope or desperation, I guess those can kind of be the same thing.

"What are you doing here?" Jess asked, wisely not answering his question.

"I used to live here, for a little while anyway. It's the last place I remember feeling happy. I...I don't know why I came back. Maybe I figured I'd be able to find it again, the happiness that is. I didn't, though. It's gone and I can never get it back."

"Get what back?"

"My wife and my kids." He started sobbing again. "I went to get some supplies and the fucking zombies found a way in! Tore them to shreds, and by the time I got back, there was nothing but bones. I buried them, put a gun against my head and pulled the trigger. For a full minute I thought I was dead, gun wasn't loaded...go figure." He laughed just a bit, but there was no merriment in it. "I knew it was the easy way out, but after they were gone, what was the purpose of living?" he asked, looking up at Jess. "Everything I did was for them, everything. I came back here. I wanted to die in the last place I had truly felt safe and loved. Now the beauty of it is that I don't feel any better here than at any point in the fifteen hundred miles I drove to get here."

"Who are you?" Jess asked, clearly nervous, I think more for the broken man than for herself.

"My name is Alex, Alex Carbonara."

"I'm Jess, this is Riley," she said as she touched my shoulder.

I went over to the man. I sniffed at him and his fire-arm on the ground. I gripped the handle in my teeth and pulled it away.

The man's eyes got large as he watched.

"Smart dog," was his reply.

"You have no idea," Jess told him.

"I mean you no harm, I thought I'd be alone when I…" He choked up. "I just thought I'd be alone."

"What happened here?"

"Isn't it evident? How long have you been here? Have you been here the whole time?"

Jess shook her head. "I came looking for someone."

"I'm sure they're dead." Alex said morosely.

"Don't say that!" Jess was on the verge of tears.

"I'm sorry, that was cruel. I've been tumbling down a slippery slope since I lost my family. Who are you looking for? Some people had to have escaped this devastation."

"His name is Justin."

"Talbot?" Alex asked.

"You know him?" There was hitch in Jess' voice.

"Mike Talbot's son? Sure I do. I came back and saved them on Christmas Day no less. Then I did the singular most stupid thing in my life; I parted ways with them."

"They're…they're alright?" Jess asked. I could tell she could hardly believe the words coming out of her mouth. Worry and pain scents were intermingled in everything she said.

"They were the last time I saw them. That was a long time ago, though, especially in this world we live in now. Only takes a second to lose everything."

"But he…they were alive?"

"Yes."

"Where are they?" She was nearly hopping as she asked.

"Maine I would imagine. Mike's father and brother have places up there."

"I have to go." She almost walked out. I didn't think it was too particularly wise to turn her back on this man; she still didn't know much about him.

"Alone? You're going to go alone? It's too dangerous."

"I came from California to find him, I can't stop now."

"But not without losses right? I can see them clearly etched on your face."

"There's nothing for me here."

"There's life, isn't that enough?"

Jess thought about it. "No," was her solemn reply.

"Maine is a big state. Are you just gonna go door to door?"

"I-I don't know, I'll figure it out when I get there. There has to be a phone book or something."

"There's badness out there."

"I know."

Jess got closer. She lowered her fire-arm and touched the man's cheek, wiping salty water away. I growled as he grabbed her hand. He let go quickly, although I do not believe he had meant it in a threatening manner.

"I'm sorry, I didn't mean to frighten you. It's been a while since I've felt human contact. Thank you for that."

"I wasn't frightened, Riley is just a little over-protective."

"Friends?" Alex asked me, showing me his front paws opened up.

"Not yet," I told him, not getting close enough for a pet.

"I understand," he said to me. He looked up to Jess. "Can I come with you? Maybe you're the reason I'm here. I'm just not ready to die yet."

"I...I don't know..." Jess hesitated.

"Mike is one of the most admirable men I have ever had the privilege of knowing. He fought to allow my family to seek sanctuary within these walls when they still stood. Marta mistakenly thought the devil inside of him would be our doom, when in fact, it was that very demon that saved us all. My children loved him…especially when he brought Henry around.

"Henry's okay?"

"Who is this Henry?" I asked curiously.

"Almost the same breed as your Riley. She an American Bulldog?"

Jess nodded.

"I know he's an English Bulldog, Riley, but I think you two would get along fabulously," Alex said to me.

"Like George?" I whined.

George had been at my alpha's home when I was brought there. I loved him like no other. When he died I was unsure if I would ever get over it.

"If he can help us find this Henry, then I say we take him," I said as I looked up at Jess.

"You trust him?" she asked.

I walked over and let the man rub his paw over my fur.

Jess paused. "If Riley trusts you, then so do I."

Alex rose, I stepped away quickly.

"We'll work on this." He stooped down to place his face next to mine. If he trusted me enough to not rip through his face, then I would take that as a good sign. There was goodness in him; it however was covered in a deep sadness.

"There's more of us," Jess told him.

Alex began to sob anew when he saw Zach. "He's not much younger than my boy. Can I hold him?" he asked through a curtain of tears.

"Most certainly not!" Patches said, getting in between the two.

"You have any bacon?" Ben-Ben asked, jumping on the man's leg.

"Ben-Ben down," Jess told the dog.

"Riley, why did you let this strange man down here?" Patches asked, her tail swishing back and forth.

"Jess trusts him…and so do I for that matter. He's lost his family and there is a deep sadness around him."

"I don't care," she replied, "humans are bad."

"Not all of them. Now let him hold Zach, it will give him some comfort. He is going to help us find Justin."

"What?!" Patches shrieked. "We are not leaving this place. We have everything we need and more."

"It's what Jess wants."

"What about me…us, what about what we want?"

"Patches, Jess is suffering. She wants to be around her own kind. I know as a cat that is not something high up on your list of priorities, but two-leggers crave being around others. They are like herd animals in that regard."

"I like it here, dog," she said haughtily. "The road is no place for us."

"For once, cat, you and I are in agreement. Where Jess goes I will follow, though. Do you like it enough here to stay by yourself?"

"I will think on this."

And she was serious. She moved out of Alex' path and allowed him to pick up Zach.

"His face has fur, too." Zach pulled on the man's scraggly-bearded cheeks.

"He likes you," Jess said with a smile. "When should we leave?"

Alex and Zach were staring intently at each other. "Are you sure?" he asked. "It's just not safe."

"Nowhere is safe, Mr. Carbonara. I'd rather die trying to get to Justin, than spend the rest of my life here."

"I understand that…I do. Tomorrow then? We'll leave in the morning. Now that I'm not…umm…planning on doing what I had originally intended on, I find myself to be extremely hungry. Do you have any food you could spare?"

Jess laughed and led him to the food room.

He just stared and gazed upon it.

"Eat what you want. Pretty sure we're not going to be able to take it all with us."

"I helped get all this," he said as he walked into the room.

***

The burning-disc had no sooner broken over the sky than Alex shook Jess awake. "We should get going, kiddo," he said gently.

"Dad? Sorry," she said as she sat up. "He used to say that to me when it was time for soccer practice. I guess for a second I was hoping this was all a bad dream."

"It is," he said, walking away. "I packed my truck with as many supplies as I could fit in it. Got plenty of diapers and formula and food for the animals."

"How long have you been up?" she asked while stretching.

"I didn't sleep."

Patches was nowhere to be seen as we gathered up a few more things. I was going to miss this second home. While maybe not happy here, we had been safe, and that was a lot to give up for the unknown.

"Patches, I can smell you. Are you coming or not?" I asked.

"You and that damned elephant nose of yours," she said haughtily as she came out from under a bush.

"Have you made up your mind?"

"I have." She didn't tell me what it was, but when she hopped into the open door I was able to figure it out.

Once we were all in the car, I spoke to Patches. "Now I'm not saying I would have missed you, but I'm glad you came."

"I know," Patches said, and then curled up her tail around her body and went to sleep.

"Are we going to get some bacon?" Ben-Ben asked softly.

The day was going by quickly. I was saddened about leaving Little Turtle, but had happy thoughts at the idea of meeting this Henry. If he was half the dog George was, we would get along great. I loved Ben-Ben, but I'd eaten biscuits that were smarter than he was.

"What was that?" Alex asked as the car sputtered. "That was weird." He smacked his front paw on what he called the dashboard. "Never done that before."

"Let's hope it doesn't do it again," Jess added.

"So what's your story, Jess?"

"Do you mind if I give you the short edition? The long one is too painful."

Alex nodded as he grabbed her hand for support. She seemed to appreciate that.

"That first night...I was dead asleep. Wow, that was a bad pun."

Alex laughed.

"I hear my dad screaming to my mom about getting his gun. Took me a lot longer to wake up and realize what was going on back then than it does now, that's for sure."

"Constant vigilance will do that to you."

"Daniel, my brother, was saying something about zombies. I thought for a minute he was having a bad dream and then I heard my dad's gun go off. I'd never been as scared as I was then, at least up until that point in my life. I've been plenty more scared since then."

"Me too."

"My mother is screaming about calling the cops. Then my dad is telling us all to get in the bathroom. I still had no idea what was going on. Riley was covered in blood and I couldn't see Ben-Ben, but I could hear him barking savagely."

"She said I was savagely," Ben-Ben said proudly.

"And then, when I was finally fully awake, I was in

the bathroom with mom and my two brothers."

"I was there as well," Patches said indignantly.

"Dad came in a few minutes later. He was covered in blood just like Riley. He was crying…said something about having to kill our neighbor's daughter. It made no sense. I asked him why Emily was here in the first place and what could she have possibly done that would have necessitated him killing her. Now I was afraid because I thought he was going to have to go to jail. Then they started to hammer on the door. My dad's eyes became wild until he opened the bathroom window. He told me I had to go out there first so I could catch Zach…we were on the second floor. I told him I wasn't doing it. My brother told me it was zombies outside our door and that I had to go down. I thought they were all nuts, but something was smashing at the door and it was easy enough to tell it wasn't going to hold out for long.

"It was a tight fit I got through, though. My dad held on to my arms as long as he could. By the time I dropped down, it wasn't more than five or six feet…maybe less. Then my mother is at the window hanging Zach down. I was like…you have got to be kidding me? I play soccer, I use my feet a lot, but I never really catch stuff, no real hand-eye coordination and now my mother wants me to catch my baby brother. I mean, this is life or death stuff, I can't miss. I was freaking out. My mom is telling me to focus, and all I can think to do is throw up. She didn't even tell me when she was going to let him go, she just did. He seemed to hang in the air for ten seconds. He didn't cry, though."

"I was too scared to," Zach said.

"I could hear the wood of the door starting to give way in the bathroom. My other brother's face peeks through the window above me. He's coming out headfirst and I remember thinking I wanted to smack him. There was no way I was going to be able to catch him—he outweighed me by twenty pounds. Didn't really matter." Jess hesitated. "His…his screams still wake me up at night." She looked over to Alex. "We've been on the run since."

"I'm sorry for your losses," Alex said to her sincerely.

"I'm so sorry for yours," Jess told him.

"Thank you."

The somber silence was welcome after Jess' retelling of that first day. It had brought back the pain of missing our home and the he and she alphas. Life was much simpler when all I had to worry about was whether or not I would get caught sleeping on the off-limits couch. I was thinking about dozing again when the wheeler shuddered.

"You feel that?" Alex asked.

"I did, did you run over something?" Jess asked.

"No, there's nothing in the road. The car's been acting funny since we passed Bennett. Okay…well, it stopped now. Could you please get me a pen out of the glove box…and a piece of paper, too?"

Jess handed him the items he'd requested.

"This might work better if you do it." Alex pulled a folded up piece of cowhide from his pocket.

"What's this?" Jess asked as Alex handed her a piece of paper from within the cowhide.

"It's Mike's address and directions. I want you to copy it and stick it someplace safe."

"You already have it, what do I need it for?" Jess asked. I could sense the tension in her voice.

"No, no, it's not what you're thinking. I'm good for now. I've got you guys to think about and it would be good to see Mike and his family again. This is just in case. The world is so dangerous, and if something should happen or we somehow get separated, I would feel a lot better knowing you still knew how to get there."

"Okay, but this is just a precaution?"

The wheeler shuddered again and this time it shut off.

"What the hell?" Alex asked. He turned the janglers and a bunch of the small false burning-discs came on, along with some bells and alarms. Then the wheeler started again.

"That's not good," Jess said with concern.

"Not good at all," Alex echoed. "I wonder." He peered intently at a sign on the hard pathway.

"What?" Jess questioned.

"We're coming up on a town called Vona."

"Okay?" she asked, clearly confused.

"I think we're going to need to switch out cars before this one dies for good and I have just the one in mind. Won't he be surprised? Thought the man was going to cry the day we left it behind."

"What are you talking about?" Jess asked. She was smiling, though, because so was Alex.

"How well do you know the Talbots?" Alex had a broad grin on his face.

"I dated Justin for two years before we moved. Spent a lot of time with them. Why?"

"Do you know what Mike drove?"

"He had an old Jeep right? A red one. Treated it like one of his kids. I remember Justin wanted to take it one time when his parents were out of town. Nicole talked him out of it; she said their dad would disown him if he got caught."

"He had to leave it in Vona. We were attacked and there was just no way to get it back. I wonder if it's still there."

The wheeler had pulled off the large pathway and was now on a much smaller one. We passed a few small two-legger dwellings and places that they exchanged paper and metal discs that the two-leggers called money.

"Holy shit," Alex said as he stopped his wheeler.

"Is that it?" Jess asked.

"I can't believe it's still here. You stay put, I'm going to see if it still runs."

I kept a watch out for him. There were a fair number of zombies on the ground. They were enshrouded with a heavy covering of dirt and sand. Whatever had happened here had been a while ago. I saw no signs of life or un-life.

"Sounds great!" Alex said excitedly as he started the wheeler. "We're not going to be able to fit as much stuff in here, but at least it runs…and that's much more important. Let's take what we can, although I'm really hoping to be there in three days at the most. Can you drive a stick?"

Jess shook her head.

"Okay, maybe four days then."

The Jeep was much smaller than the truck. Even with Ben-Ben on the floor rooting around for food, the backseat was tight. There was hardly enough room for Zach, the cat, and myself. Patches seemed to be the most disturbed by our proximity. I loved the new smell of Henry; the Jeep was heavy with it.

"Floor-fries!" Ben-Ben yelled triumphantly. There was some snorting and chewing. "And floor-jerky! And floor-something!" He ate it all.

We had gotten back onto the large pathway, but had not been there long when Alex stopped the wheeler.

"Everything alright?" Jess asked, looking around.

"Fine, fine. Sorry, but I just thought of this. You really need to learn how to drive a stick."

Jess was about to ask him why. I could see her lips forming the words and then she figured out why that would be a good idea.

"Okay, show me what to do," she said as she got into the driver's seat.

"First, you want to press the clutch in, put the Jeep in first gear and then let—.."

I was nearly flung from my seat as Jess had the new wheeler bucking around. The wheeler stopped after a few feet.

"That wasn't too too bad," Alex said with a laugh.

Jess tried it many more times than seven before she got it out of what Alex called 'first gear' and then into higher numbers. A few times it sounded like hard metal was breaking apart underneath us.

"Glad Mike isn't around to hear this."

"Am I hurting the Jeep?" Jess asked with concern.

"It'll be alright, you're starting to get the hang of it. First gear is always the toughest."

She had the Jeep up to a fast speed. I figured at this point it would be safe for me to once again try to get some sleep.

"Kansas is huge." Jess was stifling a yawn.

"We're almost through it. Want me to take over now?"

"Let me just get to the end of the state."

The next time I awoke, we were in a place called Missouri. Jess was outside, first cleaning Zach and then feeding him. Alex was walking around. Patches and Ben-Ben were already outside.

"With both of us driving we should make good time. I'd like to get gas soon and also top off these tanks." Alex tapped a red can on the back of the wheeler.

"I hate getting gas," Jess admitted.

"Yeah, I've noticed that for some reason zombies like to congregate at gas stations. I wonder if they like the smell."

"Or it masks theirs," I said, stretching and getting out.

"Hi, Riley, I put food out for you and Ben-Ben." She pointed to the side of the car. Ben-Ben was muzzle-deep in the rapidly emptying bowl.

He looked up as I approached, food bits flying all around him. "Starving," he offered as an apology. He didn't stop eating though.

"He's your friend," Patches said as she dipped her head delicately into her bowl, grabbing one or two morsels and chewing slowly.

Alex started driving. He pulled into a gas station not too long after. The burning-disc was just beginning to hide for the night as we pulled out. "I hope all of our refueling stops are that easy," he said, finally relaxing. He was as tense as I'd ever seen him while we were there, and constantly made sure his weapon was ready.

The night was a blur. As far as I could tell, Alex had not stopped again. When Jess awoke, he let her know that they were in Indiana.

"Already? Wow. You must be exhausted. Want me to drive now?"

"I do, I'm going to pull over refuel the tank with the gas from the cans. Then we're going to have to look for a good place to fill up again."

"Where is everyone?" Jess asked as she stood guard. "I'm having a hard time believing there are no more people left."

"There are some people left, maybe as many as six million or as little as three. But in a country this big, we could drive for days and not see any of them, especially when the majority of those survivors are hiding."

"Wait, you're saying that out of a country of three hundred or so million people, there's only three to six million left?"

Alex nodded.

"How…how many are zombies then?"

"That's a harder number to figure out. At first I think their goal was infection, turn as many people into zombies as they could. It was victory by mob, a sort of survival instinct. What defense civilians and the military could muster was largely ineffectual—the odds were too great. But millions were destroyed. When the zombies somehow realized the tide had turned and they were winning, their goal became not recruitment but—"

"Sustenance," Jess finished for him. "And now?"

"They pulled a truly human trait, they over-harvested. At some point they realized this, and many of the zombies that are still around have gone into a stasis-like hibernation. On the low end, I think there's fifty or so million up to a maximum of a hundred million zombies still out there. And

I'm just talking the US. I have no idea how the rest of the world faired...probably worse because they didn't have as many guns."

"Worse? Is that possible? What are we going to do?"

"Right now our goal is tomorrow. Okay, we've got gas, let's get rolling again."

I braced myself as Jess once again got the wheeler going. I only banged my head once against her seat.

"This car reeks of this Henry dog," Patches said.

"Isn't it wonderful?" I replied.

"There's no more food down here," Ben-Ben whined.

"You're getting fat," Patches told him. "You keep that up and the zombies will catch you and eat you."

"I am not fat. Riley, tell her."

I said nothing.

"Riley?" the small dog beseeched.

"You have been eating a bit more," I said.

"A bit? The dog is starting to look like a furry foot stool."

"I eat when I'm nervous," Ben-Ben said in defense.

"You eat when you're nervous, happy, sad or afraid. You even eat in your sleep. I see your mouth chewing while your eyes are closed."

"Riley, make her stop. She's hurting my feelings."

"She's just playing," I said as I looked over sternly at Patches.

She glared back at me. "Fine I'm playing. Fat dog." That last part she mumbled softly. I was glad Ben-Ben hadn't heard it.

He dove back down, looking for more food remnants.

Patches pointed. "See?" she mouthed.

I shrugged.

"Footstool, that's a funny one, Patches," Zach said.

The cat turned quickly. "You're another thing I don't want to have to deal with, Baby-that-should-not-talk." Patches lay down and curled her tail around herself.

I could feel the tension ease and hope rise as we passed through more imaginary boundaries the two-leggers had created. At least the scenery outside the wheeler was getting more interesting, from flat expanses to tree-lined, hilly roadways. We stopped two more times for the smelly liquid the wheeler liked to eat. I noticed the wheeler was almost as much of a mooch as Ben-Ben. Alex had driven after the last stop.

"Is everything okay?" Jess asked as she awoke.

Alex had stopped the wheeler and, with a small smile on his face, he pointed.

Jess rubbed her eyes and then did it again. "Is…is it really Maine?"

"Well, the sign says so. If it's not, we're screwed."

"How far?" Jess asked, shrugging off the sleep in the span of a heartbeat.

"I think he said it's about three hours from here."

"I can't…I can't believe this. Thank you so much, Alex." Jess' eyes were leaking water.

"Stupid girl is going to dehydrate before we even get there," Patches said. "And if this Henry tries to eat me, I'm blaming you."

"Me? I don't even know him."

"You dogs are all the same," she told me.

"Is three hours long?" I asked her. I forgot how much I didn't want the cat to know what I don't know.

"This day will still be light by the time we get there," she answered. I think she was partly excited as well or she would have given me some sort of snarky response.

Alex had not driven far when he spoke again. "I…umm…need to pull over."

"We out of gas?" Jess leaned over to look at the panel.

"Personal matter, I don't think that beef stew from last night is sitting all that well."

"I told you I thought it smelled funny." Jess was

smiling.

"He's been releasing gas all morning," Ben-Ben said softly from under his seat.

"Why haven't you moved then?" Patches asked.

Ben-Ben looked at the cat like she'd grown two tails. "It smells like food is why," was his response.

"He's so gross," Patches said to me.

The wheeler stopped.

"I guess this is as good of a place as any." Jess opened the door to get Zach. Patches, Ben-Ben, and I got out.

Ben-Ben started following Alex who was heading to a small building.

"How about a little privacy?" Alex asked him.

"Okay," Ben-Ben replied, still following.

"He means you," I told him.

"What? I just want to watch. I won't bother him."

"You being there will bother him. Two-leggers don't like to be watched."

Zach was still fast asleep. Jess was able to change his diaper and get him back in his seat without him even stirring.

"I'll be right back," Jess said, patting my head.

Besides Zach, I found myself alone at the wheeler. That was when I got my first sniff of trouble. My immediate thought was Alex and his bad beef stew. How could he not have smelled the taint that came from the hard container it was in?

This wasn't odor from offal though, this was…zombie! I started barking loudly. "Zombies, zombies, zombies!!!"

Patches was first back. "Where?" she asked as she jumped onto the front of the wheeler.

"I don't know yet." I was running around the wheeler trying to pick up from what direction it was coming.

Ben-Ben also started barking.

Alex and Ben-Ben came back around from the small building. "What's going on?" Alex asked as he was struggling to get his fake leg furs back on.

My fur was bristled and my lips were pulled back.

"Oh, God," Alex said, grabbing his nose. "Where's Jess?"

She was where the zombie smell was coming from. Alex tossed the janglers onto the seat of the wheeler and we both ran across the hard path and down a small ravine.

"Help!" Jess screamed.

She was scrambling up a tree. Zombies were all around. Alex grabbed me around the waist and pulled me down so we couldn't be seen. I was struggling to get away from him so I could go and help Jess.

"Riley, shh," he said softly. "She's okay up there for now. We need to figure out how to get her down safely. You running in there and getting yourself killed is not going to help."

I understood his words and the sense behind them, but my first instinct was to do all I could to help her NOW!

"When are we going in?" Ben-Ben asked, coming up next to me.

"Shit," Alex said looking over. "Riley, Ben-Ben. Come with me, I've got an idea." He once again grabbed me to make sure I came with him.

"We can't leave her!" I was whining.

"We're going right back, Riley, I promise. I need to get more bullets."

"What's going on?" Patches asked once she saw us.

"Jess is treed with zombies all around and Alex is getting more bullets so we can rescue her." I explained. My heart was breaking that we were taking so long.

"Okay, everyone in the car. Let's be safe while I get ready."

Patches and Ben-Ben got in quick enough. Alex had to physically force me in. He followed me into the wheeler. He placed the janglers in the wheeler and started it up.

"What...what's going on?" I asked in confusion.

"He's leaving without her, humans always only think about themselves," Patches said. I could hear the alarm in her voice.

Before I could begin barking at him, he spoke. He said a small prayer to the Great Two-legger they worship, and then…

"I'm coming, Marta, I'll be with you and the kids soon."

He opened the door. I tried to follow, but he shut it quickly. "I'll get her back here, Riley, you get her to Mike's safely. This is where I get off."

"What? What's he saying?" I slammed my paws against the viewer.

"Sometimes humans surprise me. He is going to sacrifice himself for Jess."

"NO, NO, NO! He needs our help. Open the window, cat!" Spittle was flying from my mouth.

"It's a manual window, I cannot."

I jumped all around looking for a place to get out. I was trapped. I was imprisoned as Jess and Alex fought for their lives—one to hold onto it and the other to give it away.

Chapter 17 - ALEX

Alex snuck back to where he had originally been. He arose and spoke, "When you see an opening, you run. Do not hesitate, do not stop, the Jeep is running. Get in it and get out of here. Do you understand?"

He started firing, not waiting for her nearly imperceptible nodded response. The zombies turned to look at Alex who was shooting as he moved to the left, pulling the zombies away from the front of the tree. His shots were ineffectual in that they weren't finding kill zones, but they were wildly successful in garnering the zombies' attention away from Jess.

"RUN!" He yelled, his hand shaking wildly as he tried to put more bullets in his pistol while he ran.

Jess wanted to cry out after him, to help him, to get him to follow her, but that had never been his plan from the onset. "Thank you," she sobbed even as she was mid-flight.

Two zombies turned when they heard her loud thud as she hit the ground; the pursuit was on. She was grasping at weeds and small saplings to help pull her up the ravine quicker. The two zombies chasing her were less than ten feet away. Alex' screams of pain urged her forward.

A zombie stepped on her left foot as it slipped on a loose rock; pain rocketed up her leg. It felt a lot like the sprain she had suffered in last year's championship soccer game. She'd gritted the rest of that contest out and she sure wasn't going to quit now, not with the ultimate prize on the line.

An aching roar traveled up the length of her leg and lodged in the bottom of her skull with each step. She hardly noticed.

"Marta the kids look good." Alex gurgled out with his last breath.

***

"It's Jess!" Ben-Ben yipped excitedly.

"And she's got company," Patches added.

"She's not going to make it! I need to be out there!" I thought I was going to go crazy. Jess was in trouble and I could do little more than watch.

"We can do nothing, Riley," Patches told me.

"Patches, if she dies, we all die."

Making sure she realized the dire straits that she was in personally was the only way I could sometimes get the cat involved. She got it; with no way out of the car, we'd die of thirst. I don't think she'd die of starvation, though. I'm pretty sure she'd feast on all of us before she'd let that happen.

Jess' head whipped back as a zombie grabbed a fistful of hair. She screamed out in pain and terror. She lurched forward, nearly losing her footing as she was losing her balance.

"Come on, Jess," I said, watching.

The zombie kept a handful of her hair as she wrenched herself free.

"That's it...RUN!" Patches was getting into it now. Whatever her reasons, it was welcome.

The wheeler rocked as Jess slammed into it. She had been running so fast that she hadn't the time to slow down. The zombies were upon her as she opened the door and was sliding into the seat. Jess screamed. She was being pulled from the wheeler as a zombie gripped her shoulder and was trying to get her back out.

As soon as I saw daylight, I jumped out. I crashed

into the chest of the zombie that had Jess, sending him to the ground, fingernails popping free from his hand as it was torn from Jess. I ripped through what remained of his fake furs on his chest before moving up to wrap my muzzle around his throat. His hands encircled my neck and simultaneously began to squeeze and try to push me away. His grip was so tight I was beginning to lose air. I felt something punch through the side of my muzzle; it felt like I was on fire. The second zombie had taken a bite of me! I heard the door to the wheeler close. All that mattered now was that I had given Jess enough time. That was my last thought as the world lost its color.

"George, is that really you? I've missed you so much," I told my old friend. "Where are we?" He turned silently and led the way.

***

"Riley! OH, GOD, NO!" Jess was in hysterics.

"Let me out!!!" Ben-Ben was screaming. "I've got to help her! I promise I'll never ask for bacon again, please, please just let me out!"

Patches watched silently, her twitching tail belying her calm demeanor.

"Oh, Riley, I will miss you." Zach was crying.

The zombie that had ripped into Riley stood up, a large swath of fur-covered skin in his mouth. He turned his gaze on Jess. He lowered his head and ran into the Jeep window; the glass spider webbed.

Jess slid the Jeep into gear. It bucked for twenty or so feet before stalling. The zombie was running next to her window, when she stopped, he head-butted the glass again. The cracks widened and lengthened.

Ben-Ben had hopped onto the seat to look out the back window. "She's still there!! Get her!"

"Ben-Ben, she's gone," Patches said in an attempt to

calm the dog down.

"You'd like that wouldn't you?!"

"Nothing could be further from the truth," Patches said as she stood next to him.

Jess got the car moving. The zombie ran after them for a quarter mile before they could no longer see him.

Jess' sobs dominated the remainder of the ride. "She gave her life for mine."

"That is what friends do," Patches said. "Goodbye and dog's speed, Riley."

***

"Nicole, tell Dad we have company," Mark Talbot, Mike's nephew, said from his lofty guard post.

Nicole had been bringing him lunch when they heard the crunch of tires on gravel. She shielded her eyes from the setting sun to see a red Jeep swing onto the long driveway.

"Dad?" she asked as she looked upon the truck. "It can't be. We lost that in Colorado." Nicole, even though she knew the impossibility that her father had gotten his Jeep back and had come home, was still inexplicably drawn to it.

"Nicole, what are you doing?" her over-protective Uncle Ron shouted out from the deck.

"Someone's here!" she shouted, moving closer.

"I can see that, but we don't know who it is!"

The door opened and a young female got out, tears streaked her face.

Nicole paused and hesitated. "Jess? Jessica, is that you?" And then she ran to the girl.

PULSE
Mark Tufo

Copyright 2013 Mark Tufo
Discover other titles by Mark Tufo
Visit us at marktufo.com
http://www.facebook.com/pages/Mark-Tufo/133954330009843
http://zombiefallout.blogspot.com/
http://twitter.com/#!/ZombieFallout

This is how the end began

"Hey honey, you're home early. How was work?" Julie asked as she placed her gardening gloves by the sink. She had a large satchel full of tomatoes and cucumbers which she hefted onto the counter.

"It was good, normal stuff. You know, trying to create universes and God particles and such," Sam said, he was the leading scientist at the Super Collider facility at the University of Colorado in Boulder.

"Any luck with that?" Julie asked, brushing the dirt off her knees.

"Well…no black holes, so I consider that a victory. How's the garden?"

"We may get a melon or two out of it if I can get the bugs to stay off of them. Speaking of which, I think I gave a good pint or two of blood to the local mosquito population. Look." She pulled her shirt up slightly so he could see the angry red welts.

"Whereas I am happy that you are showing me all that skin, I wish it were for other reasons." Sam leaned down and kissed her stomach.

"Yeah, well maybe if you figured out a way to keep the bugs away from me, I wouldn't have to go soak in an oatmeal bath to get the itch to go away. I'll get dinner ready when I get out."

"No rush," Sam said as he headed to the garage.

"Hey! No weapons of mass destruction, okay?"

"It was one time." He smiled at her. Sam opened up the door that led to the garage; Radio Shack would have been envious of all the circuitry and electronic tools he had warehoused there. Building and testing new types of gear was a hobby Sam had enjoyed since he was old enough to learn how to wield a soldering gun.

"Bugs," he said aloud. "The problem is bugs. Do I build another giant bug zapper?" Julie had made him dismantle the last one when a sparrow had flown into it, the poor thing had vibrated and fried for half a minute before finally dying. "Yeah, that didn't work so good, plus I think it only attracted more bugs into the area. So I don't want an attractant…I want a repellant. How about something that shoots out a citronella-based fog? No, I hate that smell," he said to his muse.

"What about a pitch or a vibration?" He wondered if there would be a universal pitch or vibration that would cause bugs to move away. Some bugs, like ticks and spiders, were attracted to vibrations; that was their primary hunting technique. "Chemicals? No, Julie is allergic to DEET. Shit, this may be a little harder than I thought."

Sam began to doodle on his iPad. What he absently drew looked a lot like an old RCA tower complete with the lightning bolts emanating from it—which in actuality signified radio waves.

"That's interesting," he said, looking at his picture. "What kind of current am I talking about to get that kind of signal? A few capacitors in series…hmmm I wonder."

***

"Are you coming to bed?" Julie asked from the doorway.

"Bed? What happened to dinner?" Sam asked, looking up, his eyes red-laced.

"Honey, that was five hours ago. You said you'd come and get some in a minute. I've seen that look in your eyes before so I brought you some instead. It's that full plate of lasagna next to you."

Sam looked over at the cold dish like he was seeing it for the first time.

"Do you want me to re-heat it for you?"

"The what now?"

"I'll see you in the morning. Try to get some sleep."

Julie closed the door.

***

"Sam, please tell me that at some point you came to bed last night," Julie said with a yawn. The sun was streaming in from a window on the far side of the workroom.

"I did it, Julie!" Sam said excitedly.

"What did you do, honey, besides pull an all-nighter? You can't go to work after staying up all night, you're bound to create a vacuum in space or something that will suck the entire universe into it."

"That's always a possibility," he said to her honestly.

Julie shuddered." Sometimes I wish you had just kept that professorial position instead of going into applied sciences."

"When's the last time a professor won the Noble prize?"

"When's the last time a professor threatened to rip the fabric of the time-space continuum?"

"Well, there's that. But that's not what I wanted to show you. I think I may have fixed your bug problem."

"You're still on that? I thought for sure you would have moved on to time travel or something."

"That's tomorrow. Come on." He grabbed a small two-foot tower.

"What's that?" Julie asked.

"It's a solution. Now, when I can have more time to work with it, I'll be able to produce a version that works off a portable power pack," Sam said as he plugged in a long extension cord.

"Batteries? Are you saying a model that runs on batteries?"

"Yes a portable power supply."

"Okay."

"You may want to step back a little," Sam urged his

wife as he placed the mechanism next to Julie's garden and plugged it in.

"Sam?" Julie asked nervously.

"Further," he told her.

"I'm not going anywhere unless you are as well."

"Fine, fine…let me hit the power switch. It takes up to a minute until the capacitors hit full wattage anyway."

Same clicked the on/off toggle and quickly moved away; grabbing his wife as he did so. A large swarm of black flies hovered near the device, they were illuminated by the early morning sun. A minute clicked by, then two.

"Does it kill them through sheer amount of elapsed time?" Julie asked with a smile.

"You're funny. I wonder what's happening." Sam took two steps towards the machine. "Wow did you feel that?" he asked.

"No, but I saw a faint blue pulse of something come from the top of it. Sam, look!" Julie said excitedly.

"At what? I don't see anything."

"Look above your machine."

It took him a moment. "The black flies are gone."

"Not gone, Sam, they're dead. I saw them fall to the ground in one massive heap."

Sam approached the device cautiously. He reached around; fumbling with the toggle switch until turning it off. "It's okay now." He motioned to his wife. "You're right." He was getting down onto his hands and knees. "They're all dead." He picked some up and was holding them out for his wife to see, but she had already moved past and into her garden.

"Look!" she said. She was holding a Japanese beetle. "It's dead too. I've been trying to get rid of them for a month!"

They were both in awe as they found all manner of dead insects: spiders, ants, flies, and mosquitoes.

"What about grubs?" Julie asked.

"I…I honestly don't know. Let's find out." He went over to his wife's shed and grabbed a small handheld garden hoe. He turned over the soft earth until he found what he was looking for. He ran his finger over the thick white worm looking for any signs of life, there were none.

"This…this is amazing!" Julie shrieked.

Something niggled deeper in the back of Sam's mind, but the excitement from his wife drowned it out. He barely noticed that the beneficial earthworm had perished alongside his more troublesome cousin.

"You made this last night?"

Sam nodded, smiling like an idiot.

"You need to patent this. We'll be fabulously rich! I'll finally be able to afford the brand-name macaroni and cheese!"

"You're always living beyond your means, Julie, and now you're just talking gibberish. Do you really think I should seek a patent?"

"Are you kidding me? Home gardeners around the world will be groveling at your feet to get a hold of one of these," she said as she lightly tapped the top. "Is it dangerous?" She pulled her hand away quickly.

"I don't think so," he responded haltingly.

"You don't think so? Pretty sure the EPA is going to want something more than 'I don't think so.' When I saw the flash, you asked me if I had felt something. What did you feel?"

Sam thought about it for a second. "Well…the hair on my arms started to stand, and then I felt something like a mild electric shock travel over the surface of my skin. Which makes sense, every living being has a current of low voltage electricity running through it. I created a transmitter that will disrupt that signal. And you didn't feel anything from where you where and I did, so that makes the effective range about twenty-five feet…give or take a foot."

"A twenty-five foot diameter bubble?"

"To the sides and up yes, the signal is severely hampered by the ground. I'd have to run tests, but at this voltage and amperage I can't imagine it going more than a foot or so down."

"And it won't harm the plants?"

"Can't see why."

"What about using it in a home?"

"I'm not sure, Julie. Why?"

"Sam, if people didn't have to use pesticides anymore, just think of the benefits in that alone."

Sam could see all the good that Julie spoke of, and coming from her, it made perfect sense; but then again, she didn't have a mean bone in her body.

"Alright, alright. I'll draw up a schematic and a description of what it can do. We'll get a lawyer and file a patent. Happy now?" he asked, but the way his wife was twirling around in her bug-free zone was proof enough.

***

"Hi, Sam, Julie," Arnie Bassenger Attorney-at-Law and family friend greeted his clients. He waited until he got them in his office before he gave them both hugs. "I don't want everyone out there thinking I do this with all my clients," he said with a smile. "Sit, sit, you guys want a soda or something? I'll have my secretary grab you one."

Sam shook his head in the negative. "I'd love a water," Julie said.

"Jen, can you get a bottle of water please?" he asked into his intercom.

Julie was halfway through with drink when Arnie looked up from the papers in front of him.

"Um, I want to be as candid as possible." He looked at the couple.

"Go ahead," Sam urged.

"Does this do what you say it can?"

"Without a doubt Arnie. I've built three working models and have tried them in a variety of locales on all manner of bugs, and to a one, it has killed them all."

"Sam, does anyone else know about this?" he asked in a hushed tone.

"Just us three."

"Wow." Arnie sat back. "This thing…this thing is gold, Sam. Maybe more so. What's it cost to make?"

"I've tinkered with a few of the designs, but each of the three has been under a hundred bucks."

"Under a hundred?" Arnie ran his hand through his hair. "What's your target price?"

"I haven't really thought about it, Arnie."

"I have," Julie said, "I figured we could sell them for around three hundred and fifty bucks a piece."

"What?" Arnie and Sam asked simultaneously and for differing reasons. Arnie thought the price too low, Sam too high.

"Listen, both of you," she explained. "I got the parts list from Sam's diagrams and did some virtual bulk shopping for the parts. And I also got quotes for fabrication of some of the base and support structures."

"You've been busy," Sam said to his wife in amazement.

"Well now that I'm not fighting a Japanese beetle infestation I've found that I have way more time on my hands…and stop distracting me. So, with buying parts in bulk and outsourcing some of the fabrication, right now I figure the Pulsinator…" She got some quizzical looks with her name. "We can work on that. Anyway, I've got it to fifty-five seventy-two to build each one."

"And if we get a factory set-up, there will obviously be an additional start up fee, but eventually the cost per unit will go down significantly," Arnie chimed in. "I want in on this, ground floor, Sam, I'll invest everything I've got. You've discovered something revolutionary and I want to be a part of it. I've got a few questions."

"Go ahead." Sam was fidgeting. It was not that he was adverse to making money, it had just never been his main priority in life, and the way Arnie was talking, people were going to start lining up to throw it at him.

"How big can you make this thing? Sorry, sorry...let me clarify. Would a farmer in Kansas be able to use say a giant tower version of these?" Arnie was also excited, large end models could be the Cadillac of the line, earning huge bucks and even getting subsidized by the government so that Joe Farmer would be able to have larger yields of crops.

"I don't think so, Arnie, not without having a series of them. All of the tests I've done on this smaller model yield a sphere twenty-five feet across. It has to do with the pulse as it travels through the air and is met with resistance and gravity. I've done the math, no matter how large the tower gets or how much power is run through it, in theory the maximum it would be able to send a signal is a hundred yards, although I have not built one to those specifications. I didn't figure there would be too many home gardeners with an area that large."

"Okay, we'll revisit that one."

"Arnie, I'm not sure what you want to revisit. Physics isn't going to change because you want to sell to farmers."

Arnie's expression downturned for a moment until he realized the opportunity for hundreds of millions was staring him in the face. *Damn shame it wasn't going to be billions though,* he thought. "Okay, what about the power supply."

"What about it?"

"It says here your first two prototypes used hundred and twenty volt home power and the third used a car battery. Will there be a possibility for a model that does not need an extension cord or a forty pound battery? Having a hard time seeing seventy-two-year-old Gloria-the-gardener lugging a cord or a battery around."

"It's possible, Arnie, but we're not talking about an LED light here. This thing needs a fair amount of juice to operate properly. I mean, it will send out a pulse with a nine volt battery…although only about a foot or so."

"Portable models for hiking! Oh, my God, I'm a genius!"

"I'm not sure that's feasible," Sam started.

"I actually think it's genius," Julie stated. "A smaller model, maybe mounted to a backpack, running off a couple of cell phone or tablet batteries…I would think that'd be enough. Even if it only went out ten feet or so, time it so it goes off every couple of seconds so that the way is always clear for the hiker."

"I…I guess that's possible, but I'd have to do studies on if it's harmful to people in the long term."

"That was my last question. Is Chester Chipmunk or Billy Blue Jay going to be affected by this? PETA will be down our throats in less time than it takes to cash our first check if so much as a sparrow falls from the sky."

"With the current circuitry, I can't imagine one burst, or even two hurting anything bigger than a field mouse." A lone sentence reverberated in his subconscious and was quickly buried over. 'With the current circuitry'.

"This is incredible!" Arnie stated. "I'll get on this right away. I'll even have a real estate friend of mine look into some warehouse space.

Sam was beginning to blanch as Arnie talked.

"That would be fabulous. This is so exciting!" Julie exclaimed. "Sam, are you alright?"

"He's fine," Arnie interjected. "Anybody faced with this type of success can be overwhelmed…I know I am. Now go celebrate, I'll take care of everything."

Julie was slightly concerned as she led her husband out of the posh office.

Department of Homeland Security - Washington D.C.

"Corporal Kables, the Department of Defense just pulled this off of the new patent list and sent it over. Do you want me to do anything with it, or should I file it away?" PFC Coffers asked his non-commissioned officer in charge.

"Let me at least take a look at it. They thought enough of it to send it our way," she replied.

"Not sure if that signifies anything important, Corporal. Just last week they sent us an electronic pooper scooper." The PFC dropped the file on her desk.

The sun was getting ready to set when the corporal finally looked back up. She grabbed the file and her notes and headed to her superior officer's office. She knocked on the doorframe and waited for him to wave her in.

"You're still here, Corporal? I thought I was the only one that stayed late. You do know that the Air Force doesn't pay overtime?"

"Sir, I need to show you something that came in this morning," she said with all seriousness.

"What the hell is this?" Colonel George Elders asked as he put his glasses on. "The Pulsinator—zaps bugs dead? The DoD sent over a pending patent for a bug zapper? Why?"

"It's something with the way it works, sir. They thought it could be important, but they just didn't have the time to look into it."

"Oh? And we do? For Christ Sakes, just last week we intercepted a dirty bomb off the coast of the Florida Keys and they want me to look into a damned bug killer? What are they afraid of? That Raid will sue for copyright infringement?"

"Sir, it's not technically a bug zapper."

"Continue, Corporal, you've apparently already looked into it."

"I have, sir. I've spent the entire day looking at. Sir, it

sends out a signal that apparently is able to interfere with an insect's own electric current...thus rendering it inert."

"Do you mean dead?"

The colonel looked at his subordinate with a crinkling in his eyes. She was a great soldier and he was going to have her promoted to sergeant next week, he just hoped at some point she would use less obtuse wording; he needed a thesaurus every time he read her reports.

"Still sounds like a damned bug zapper to me. What of it? We both know ninety-nine percent of what is submitted to the patent office is pure crap."

"Sir, you know that I am an electronics enthusiast,"

"Yes, you like to build things as a hobby. How many times do I have to tell you how jealous I am of your working, full-scale R2-D2 astromech. I do believe my grandchildren love you more than me every time you bring it over."

"Sir," she smiled back, "I've studied this schematic. This is the one percent. I believe it will work."

"Great for him, sounds like he'll be the next Bill Gates."

"Sir, the invention as it stands would be a great boon for his target clientele, local co-op growers and home gardeners."

"Corporal, I'm still not understanding your concern. I'm sure there's more."

"There is, sir. This device can be made more powerful."

A light began to brighten in the colonel's head. "How powerful, Corporal?"

"It's impossible to say without actually building a model, but with some minor changes and additions...this zapper could kill a human."

"What's the range?" the colonel asked, standing up. His heart was racing a little faster than his doctor would want it to.

"The current model says it has a twenty-five foot

sphere as its 'kill' zone. But with modifications, it could be brought up to as much as a football field."

"From a grenade blast zone to a Sidewinder missile."

"Sir, there's more."

"Of course there is."

"Anyone with a little know-how and availability to three hundred bucks will be able to make one."

"You're telling me that any sick-o with a soldering gun will be able to make a device that could wipe out a city block in the beat of a heart?"

"I am, sir."

"Get the DoD back on the line. Actually…screw them, we'll take care of this. I want you to give me a list of everyone that is involved on this project. Addresses as well."

"Then what, sir?"

The colonel stared at his subordinate; the decision he was about to make was not to be taken lightly. "Corporal Kables, are you absolutely sure about your hypothesis?"

"I am, sir," she told him confidently.

"I don't see what my choices are, Corporal, but to implement executive order 241.5. I will give this list to Tonney Emery."

Corporal Kables swallowed hard. She had just handed down a death sentence to everyone involved in the Pulsinator project all in the name of national security. She'd never met a person in her life with eyes as flat as Emery's. It seemed to her that death was always within a hand-span of the mercenary.

"Go home, Corporal, have a drink. Hell, have a couple. This will all be over by tomorrow at this time. You've done your country a great service here tonight."

"It doesn't feel that way, sir."

Tonney

Tonney Emery was a hard man; he'd been forged in the deserts of Iraq, the mountains of Afghanistan and the jungles of Mozambique. There was very little he had not seen or done during his tours of duty. Every time his country had called, he'd done above and beyond what was required of him. Not because he was a patriot, but rather because he despised the enemy, and an enemy in his mind was anyone that stood in the way of him and the completion of his mission. It mattered little if they were women, children, or American citizens; an obstacle was meant to be overcome, plain and simple.

He sat outside Arnie Bassenger's office dressed in a three-piece suit, posing as a Mr. Pauling who was patiently awaiting his appointment. Arnie's secretary Jen Carroll did all in her power to not look in his direction; something about the man stirred a deep-seated fear within her. He'd been amicable enough when she'd greeted him, but she'd felt like a gazelle looking into the mouth of a crocodile. His eyes had shown no warmth and his smile could freeze water.

"Jen, I'll see Mr. Pauling now," Arnie said over the phone.

"Thank God," Jen breathed quietly. She turned to tell the man, but he had already arisen and was heading for the door.

"Hello, Mr. Pauling." Arnie extended his hand across his desk. Tonney sat down without shaking the proffered appendage. "Straight to business. I like that," Arnie said as he sat.

He was feeling much of what Jen and even Corporal Kables felt. It was like the man before him was wearing a disguise—as if a wolf were able to put on a human coat and blend in perfectly with society. He may look normal enough, but his mannerisms and demeanor would belie his true persona. He now wished that he had not pushed back his lunch to take on this man's urgent request to see him in regards to something of the utmost importance.

"Who else knows about the Pulsinator?" Emery asked, opening up his briefcase and tossing the file onto Arnie's desk.

"What? What is this about? Has Sam sought outside council?" Arnie grabbed the file. "Wait…this is the patent request. What are you doing with this? Is this corporate espionage? The courts don't look favorably on this type of thing. I mean, I knew you vultures would be all over this idea once it was made public but beforehand? How could you possibly get your hands on a pending patent? That is a government regulated…wait you're from the government."

"Sit down," Emery said with malice as Arnie began to rise. "Now, I asked you a question. And just so you will be more willing to comply, here is my court order." Emery pulled out another set of papers these ones folded up in his suit pocket.

Arnie took a moment to go through the legalese. "Jesus, it's just a bug zapper. You make it sound like it's a terrorist threat."

"Mr. Bassenger, do you think I'm here because Homeland Security believes this to be just a bug zapper? So I'm going to ask you again…who else besides you, and Sam and Julie Randolph know about this?"

"There are some investors, over at—"

"Okay, more specifically, who has seen these plans?"

"Just the three of us."

"I'm going to need your files."

"Now just hold on! I don't see anywhere in this warrant about the confiscation of materials."

Emery had been looking intently in Arnie's eyes, when the lawyer spoke and Emery received the answer he was expecting, he pulled his silenced pistol from his briefcase.

"The files, Mr. Bassenger."

"You...you can't do this. Of all the people that know what their rights are, I think I'm at the top of that list. I'll have your ass in jail by tonight."

Emery pressed the elongated barrel above Arnie's eye. "The files."

Arnie put his hands up and stood slowly. He walked over to the corner of his office and moved a chair out of the way so he could get to a small floor safe. Within a minute he was back at as desk.

"Sit." Emery motioned with his gun. He took a moment to look through the paperwork.

"Anything on your hard drive?"

"Too easily compromised."

"Smart man. Dead...but smart."

Arnie began to rise in alarm; the round caught him just under his left eye. The impact sent his wheeled chair rolling back on the hardwood floor.

"Thank you for your time," Emery said as he grabbed all the paperwork and headed out.

Jen was happy to see him go. It was twenty-five minutes later when she discovered her boss. Her description to the police would have a man with a much larger nose and midsection, and whereas Emery was bald, the suspect the police would be looking for would be blonde.

***

"Hello, Mrs. Randolph, my name is Dan Modzik, Arnie Bassenger and I were just talking about a potential investment opportunity. With the kind of numbers he was throwing around, I thought it would be wise if we could arrange a meeting."

"I'm sorry what was your name?" Julie asked over the phone line. "My husband is drilling something, I can barely hear."

"Oh, that's excellent, your husband is at home. I'm

not too far away and would love to discuss this matter in more detail."

"Arnie never said anything about—" And then the line was dead. "Well that was strange. Sam...hey, Sam!" she yelled louder.

"Yeah!" he shouted back even though he'd stopped with the power tool. "Oops...sorry."

"Just got a call from a man who says he's an investor and has been talking to Arnie. He wants to come over and meet us."

"Yeah? Arnie never said anything. Guy sure moves fast though. Alright, let me go get cleaned up."

"Naw, I'm sure he'll have complete confidence in a guy covered in wood shavings."

Sam headed into the bathroom to get the bigger pieces of debris off of him. When he was done he walked into the kitchen and grabbed the phone off the wall. It was a few moments later when he turned to his wife, his face had blanched of all color.

"Sam, what's the matter?" she asked, putting down the tomato she had been washing.

"Ar-Arnie's dead." He let the phone slip from his hand after missing the cradle.

"What? Are you sure? How can this be?"

"I just got off the phone with his receptionist."

"Is Jen alright."

"Shaken up. She says a guy came in, shot him, and left. She said she'd call later but the cops were all over the place."

"Oh, my God." Julie placed her hands up by her mouth.

Sam and Julie both turned as they heard a car coming up their long gravel driveway. Sam paled even more if that were possible.

"Julie, what did the man on the phone say again?" He went into the living room to look out the sheer curtains.

"He said something about investing in the Pulsinator."

"Is that it?" he asked as the car was rapidly approaching.

"Wait…he said something about just talking to Arnie."

"Julie, get my gun."

"What? You don't have a gun."

"The shotgun over the mantle…and hurry!" he added as the car stopped.

She reached up and grabbed the antique. "Sam, we weren't alive the last time this was fired and we don't have shells."

"Yeah, but he doesn't know that," Sam replied as he grabbed the gun from her hands.

"You can't just brandish a weapon, Sam."

"Arnie…our friend…was just gunned down, and now some guy we've never heard from before is coming to our house. Is this a chance you want to take? Besides, I won't point it at him unless I have to." Sam opened up the front door. The man was halfway up the walkway. "That's far enough." Sam was holding the shotgun down by his side. The man hesitated his hand drifting close to the inside of his jacket.

He thought better of it as he plastered on a face only a crocodile would be fond of. Chills fingered up Sam's spine as he witnessed the veneered smile forced on the stranger's face.

"My name is Dan Modzik, Mr. Randolph. I just got off the phone with your wife, she said it would be alright to come and talk to you both."

"Arnie give you my address?"

"That's right."

"And when did you talk to Arnie last?" Sam asked.

Emery realized his mistake the moment the words came out of his mouth. "I just left his office."

"Thought so." Sam brought the gun up to his shoulder. "Arnie's dead, but I'm fairly certain you already knew that. Now I suggest you get in your car and get the hell out of here."

"Let me get this straight so we're clear," Emery stated as he walked closer. "A family friend of yours was just murdered in his own office and you think it was me, but yet you're just going to let me go? That doesn't make too much sense unless that Remington Model 1889 double-barrel shotgun you are pointing at my chest is empty. I can see by the heavy sheen of dust that it's most likely been hanging above your fireplace for a decade. Maybe you should hire a maid. Now get in the house." He pulled out his pistol.

Sam let the shotgun fall down by his side.

"Good boy," Emery said as he roughly spun Sam around and forced him over his own threshold.

"Maid my ass!" Julie said hotly as she placed the leads of her Taser against Emery's neck and squeezed the trigger. He went completely rigid, his head smacking into Sam's back as he fell face forward.

"Holy shit, Julie! When did you start carrying a Taser?" Sam asked incredulously.

"It's for bears."

"You just stunned him with a bear Taser?"

"Would you rather I let him shoot you? Did you see that smile? I thought death was grinning at me."

"That's as apt a description as any. Now what?"

"Take his gun, check his pockets. I've got zip ties in my shed. I'll go get them."

"We really need to talk about what goes on down in your garden," Sam said when Julie came back with a fistful of ties.

"It's to hold the plants up to the stakes. And last month, Betty down the street said she had a bear in her yard. I decided I didn't want to be mistaken for berries or something and have him eat me."

"Fair enough."

Julie turned the man back over and pulled his hands behind his back. She used two ties and fastened it tight. She then rolled him over and did the same to his ankles. "*CSI*," she told her husband when he looked at her with a questioning stare.

"When did you become a bad-ass?" Sam looked upon his wife with a newfound respect.

"What?"

"Nothing, nothing." He had his hands up. "I don't want you Tasing me or doing judo or anything else I might not know about. Can you use Chinese throwing stars?"

"Now you're just being silly. And they're shuriken throwing blades for your information."

"Okay, Wonder Woman, now what?"

"Well, it seems to me we caught Arnie's killer. I say we call the cops."

"I wouldn't do that," Emery croaked out.

"Well we know *you* wouldn't do that," Sam told the man who was straining against his bonds. Sam dialed the numbers.

"Nine-one-one, what is your emergency?"

"Yes my name is—" There was an audible clicking through the line.

"Let me guess." Emery struggled to sit up. "Your nine-one-one call was interrupted and then a female came on the line saying that help is on the way and to remain where you are...then the handset died. Is that the gist of it?"

"That's exactly what happened," Sam said, placing the phone down.

"So?" Julie replied, "Isn't that exactly what the operator would say?"

"Would they also kill the line? Go ahead, check it. It's as dead as you two should be."

"He's right." Sam placed the phone to his ear.

"What's going on?" Julie asked Emery.

Mark Tufo

"Well, I've just become expendable and we're all burned. A clean-up crew is coming, most likely in a bug extermination van…which would be ironic. Don't you think? Although it could be in an appliance repair van as well. There will be three shooters all dressed up in blue jumper uniforms that will conceal a silenced sub-machine quite well. The hacks will put about twenty rounds in each of us. It's actually quite messy."

"Why? What did we do?" Sam begged.

"Listen, I'm just a government hit man. Correction, *was* a government hit man. Now I'm a mark just like you two. Can't believe I let a waif with a Taser end my career." He was shaking his head from side to side. "As to the reasons why Homeland Security wants you dead, I'm not entirely sure, it has something to do with your recent patent application though."

"What? Homeland Security wants me dead over a bug zapper? That makes no sense." Sam was running his hand through his hair.

"Listen, we can figure this out later but right now A-1 Exterminators is on their way. They'll most likely be here in less than five minutes, and if we're here, we're dead. They may be hacks, but they're professional hacks with enough firepower to drop this house. You need to untie me and we need to go, now."

"You said it yourself, you were going to kill us. Now you think we should just let you go? Even if we somehow believed your story, why wouldn't we just get in our car and take off? Seems the exterminators will get rid of you and we can go to the police station," Julie told him.

"You could do exactly that. What are you going to do though when Homeland Security comes and obtains custody of you from the police?"

"This still makes no sense, I made a bug killer."

"Listen, Sam, you need to think really hard about this at another time," Emery told him.

"What's to say we let you go and then you finish the job and wave off the men?" Julie asked.

"You can't seriously be thinking about letting him go?" Sam asked.

"Covering all my bases honey. I've heard about things like this."

"On *CSI*?" Sam asked.

"I'm burned. I'm less than useless to them, and just because I'm a killer does not mean I want to be killed."

"Sam, remember when we met?" Julie asked as she walked over towards Emery, producing a knife seemingly from thin air.

"How could I forget? Two of the best things happened within a week or so of each other. I met you and then got the job with the university collider program."

Emery turned to look at Julie with more scrutiny. "You're a clearing agent?"

Julie grabbed Emery's bound hands and placed the blade of the knife up against the plastic. She leaned in towards Emery as she pulled upwards, severing the cords. "I was. You attempt to harm him in any way and I'll stick my knife through your Adam's apple and then I will twist it around so the flat of the blade restricts your airway even as blood is filling your lungs. It is a death unlike any other. Do you believe me?"

Emery nodded. "We just may have a chance." He rubbed his wrists, trying to get feeling back into them.

"Our meeting was no chance," Julie told Sam as she stood. "It was my job to access what kind of security liability you might have been."

"What?"

"Honey, just know that with every fiber of my being I'm in love with you. When we first met it was just my job, two weeks later, when the risk assessment was done, I put in my notice. I'd fallen completely for you."

"Aw...that's so sweet. Can we get the fuck out of

here now?" Emery asked. "Someone's coming."

"It's an ice cream truck for Christ's sake," Sam said, "What the hell is going on here?"

"Must be new." Emery stepped away from the window.

"So you're trying to tell me three assassins are going to come out of an ice cream truck, that's absurd!"

"Listen, Sam. We live twenty miles from the suburbs, this is as close to the wilderness as you can be without living in a tent. Our driveway is clearly marked as a private entrance not a roadway, what business at all would an ice cream truck have here?"

"Oh, I don't know, selling a snow-fucking-cone maybe?"

"I get your concern and your questions. But for now we're going to play it safe."

"Weapons?" Emery asked.

"Nothing that would make this a fair firefight. We're leaving."

"We just going to drive on by?" Emery asked.

"Nope, let's go." Julie ushered her husband towards the back door.

"Let me just get my laptop." He ran down the hallway; within a moment he exited his home office with the portable device.

"Where are we going to go on ATVs?" Sam asked as the stood in the shed.

"Where they can't follow. Can you drive one of these?"

Emery nodded.

"Sam, get on," Julie said as she started the machine.

They took an old logging trail that led away from the back of their home, within minutes they were a mile away.

"What now?" Sam asked his wife.

"We'll go to my sister's, borrow her car, hole up in a hotel, and figure out our next move."

"No," Emery objected. "The second they realized you weren't in that house, everyone the both of you know will be under surveillance. You've got to get us close to town on these trails. I'll boost a car and take us to a safe house."

"You have a safe house?"

"I've seen enough agents get...umm...forcibly retired to make sure I have an alternate means of survival."

"Who talks like this? What's going on? Don't you think perhaps that, if the possibility presented itself, your employer may one day wish you dead and that maybe you should seek other employment?" Sam asked sarcastically.

"Well, the dental plan is for shit, but once I finished you two off, I would have received a cool half mil, not bad for three hours of work."

"Three lives for five hundred thousand dollars? This is who you have allied us with, Julie?"

"Right now, Sam, he's our best chance. And for the time being at least, we share a common goal."

"And when he cuts another deal?"

"Oh, I would imagine he'll try and kill us."

Emery nodded.

"This is insane. I made a fucking bug zapper. If it's because the feds want it for themselves, they can have it. I don't give a shit about the money."

"It's something else," Emery said. "I don't know what, but it's not the money."

They had just stopped on the outskirts of Boulder when Emery spoke.

"You hear that?"

It was difficult to hear anything after the heavy engine noise of the ATVs.

"Helicopter," Julie said looking up.

"It's the game warden's. It's alright." Sam pointed at the large green and white logo.

"We're the game." Emery was quickly snapping off branches and placing them over the ATV. "I suggest you two do the same."

Sam grabbed Julie and pulled her a few feet away from the cooling machines. "I think this is all going a little too far. There is not some huge government conspiracy to stop the extinction of bugs by killing me and you."

"Are you already forgetting that Arnie is dead, Sam? And what about reptile-eye over there, less than ten minutes ago he was going to scramble our brains inside our heads. And I for one like exactly how my brains work…without alterations."

"Did…did you have sex with me to see if I would spy or do espionage?" That seemed to be the thing that Sam was getting hung up on the most in their new reality. "You know my alarm bells went off when you came up to me at that bar. I should have known, you were just too damned gorgeous. Want to know what I thought at first? I thought my friends had paid you to do it."

"No one paid me…well, that's not quite true." She smiled. "Listen, I told you how we met was planned, the rest was not. And no," she punched him in the arm, "I did not sleep with you because I'm a spy. I'd already left the agency. I loved you then like I love you now."

"Have you ever slept with anyone while you were what? *Clearing* them?'"

"I'm going to pretend you didn't just ask that. Come on, let's hide the ATV."

Sam and Julie watched as Emery emerged from the woods. He'd told them to wait there while he 'boosted' a car and that he'd pick them up soon.

"What's to say he doesn't turn us in or just get a car and leave?" Sam asked.

"Ever heard of the phrase, keep your friends close and your enemies closer?" Julie replied without looking over towards him.

"That is one of the least comforting things I've heard in quite some time."

Sam spun around when he heard the explosion. Julie merely bowed her head.

"What was that?"

"Our home," Julie said sadly.

"Julie honey, what the hell is happening?"

"I don't know, Sam, but here comes our ride."

"Are you kidding me? He couldn't pick anything a little less conspicuous like maybe a snow plow?"

"What would we need a snow plow for? There are no zombies," Julie said seriously. She was walking towards the roadway less than a hundred yards away across a field.

"A Gulf Wing Recreational Vehicle…and top of the line no less. What's the matter, were they out of fire trucks?" Sam asked as he boarded the large vehicle.

"We've got to move," Emery said with a pinched expression. "They're getting ready to cast a net."

"What?" Sam asked as he was nearly flung into a seat.

"They're going to shut the roads down and do vehicle searches," Julie filled in.

"I still don't see how that's not a good thing. We've done nothing wrong, at least you and I haven't, Julie. I hope he fries for killing Arnie. No offense," Sam added that last bit when he looked up and realized Emery was peering at him through the rear view mirror. "You know, screw that, I do mean offense. I've been friends with Arnie since he negotiated a deal with the neighborhood bully so we could use the slide at the city park when we were both seven. So basically, Emery, you can go fuck yourself. My life was damn near perfect right up until the second I met you."

"I didn't put the hit out on you, Mr. Pocket Protector. You've apparently pissed someone off so severely that they felt the need to eliminate your ass. And now, thanks to Mrs. Super-Spy, I'm forced to play for the away team."

"At least until such time as your former team desires your return," Julie said.

"Or that," Emery replied.

"Fuck this." Sam moved away from the two and to the middle of the RV where he sat down at a small dining table.

Julie was looking over a map and telling Emery which the least likely observed routes may be. Sam opened up his lap top. "Fine, they fucking want my invention they can have it along with everyone else," he murmured as he waited for his computer to find a satellite signal for an uplink. "Here goes nothing." He pressed send.

"Sam, what are you doing?" Julie asked, looking back at her husband.

"I'm giving them what they want."

"What exactly does that mean?" Emery asked.

"I uploaded the schematics for my invention to the net."

"I don't think that was such a good idea." Emery was peering intently at the road. "What you do now affects us all, you maybe should have discussed it with us."

"Like you would have discussed putting a nine millimeter round in our foreheads?"

"Good point, but I use 40s…much more reliable kill round."

"Sam?" Julie asked, coming to sit by her husband.

"It's gone. I sent it to everyone on my contact list which includes hundreds of tech bloggers around the globe. It's out now and nothing less than an extinction event is going to bring it back. The feds can go fuck themselves."

"Whereas I can sympathize with your sentiment, I don't think that was the appropriate play here. And by the way, Julie, it looks like your skills have been lapsing."

"What?" she asked, going back up to the front. "Roadblock, son of a bitch." She was staring at the red and blue lights as were they all.

The RV didn't have a chance to pull up to the front, a team of seven SWAT members descended on the large vehicle, weapons drawn.

"We pulling a Bonnie and Clyde or a Butch Cassidy and Sundance Kid?" Emery asked in all seriousness.

"They all died," Sam replied.

"Yeah, but in one of them they went out with guns blazing." Emery was reaching down and checking the status of his pistol which was now firmly in Julie's hand.

The side window of the RV was broken in and a flash grenade was tossed in. The effects of the released tear gas were compounded by the sonic boom. Within seconds, Sam and the rest of the traveling party had rifles pointed at the backs of their necks. Handcuffs were put on all of them and they were wrenched from the ground and ushered out the door.

"I don't know what you guys did, but you are officially number one on Homeland Security's most wanted list," the captain of the SWAT team, Dillon Brewster, said. The trio were led into the back of a prisoner transport vehicle.

"My wife and I haven't done anything wrong, Captain Brewster, this is all some sort of a misunderstanding. I work on a super-collider."

"Maybe you figured out how to make a black hole. What do I know?" the captain said.

"You too?" Sam asked.

"Captain, sir, there's someone on the radio says its urgent they talk to you," one of the policemen said as he ran up.

"This is it, boys and girls, the order is in to just shoot us and be done with it." Emery watched the captain talk animatedly into the cop's car radio handset.

"They can't just shoot us on the side of the road," Sam said hopefully.

"Is he swearing?" Julie asked. "He sure looks pissed."

The captain was storming back to them, an expression of pure anger flooding his features. "Listen, I don't know

Mark Tufo

what kind of bullshit you pulled or what is going on." He turned Julie around and undid her handcuffs, followed immediately by Sam. "But you two are free to go. Seems there was some sort of misunderstanding like you said."

"I told you!" Sam said happily. "These bastards blew up my house, though. Now what?"

"Well, this one is being handed over to Homeland Security for murder and grand theft. My suggestion to you two would be to get on the horn to your insurance company and get a claim going. I'm sorry about the flash grenade," the captain said as he shoved Emery into the back of the van.

"What's a little blindness and deafness among friends," Sam said sarcastically.

What Comes Next

"What a horrible day!" Sheila, Julie's sister said as she got up to get Sam and her husband John another beer. "What now, honey?" She had come back in and was rubbing her sister's shoulder.

"Well...we rebuild our home I suppose and try to move past this entire thing."

"You know you two can stay here as long as you want," John said as he took a long pull from his beer.

"We appreciate that," Sam said. "The insurance adjuster told us that we get a hotel allotment as part of the claim. I think a little time away is exactly what we need."

"They have Arnie's killer, though?" Sheila asked.

Julie nodded. "We would like to stay here a couple of days until the claim goes through if that's alright."

"Of course, sis, our home is your home." Sheila gave a hug to her little sister.

***

"I can't believe they just backed off after you uploaded the file," Julie said as they lay in bed that night.

"What would be the reason to keep hunting us down?"

"I guess...but there's still something missing."

***

They and the rest of the world would get the answer less than a week later just as Sam and Julie were heading out the door and off to the Marriott for some much needed rest and relaxation.

John was seeing them off when a news bulletin broke through the baseball game.

"We are just now receiving reports that a bomb of

some sort was detonated in Paris. It is confirmed that at least a thousand people have been killed."

An aerial image next to the anchor woman's head showed hundreds of bodies on the ground as if they'd just stopped whatever activity they were doing. The anchor had her left hand up to her ear.

"Francois, we understand you are live on the ground? Is the feed ready?" she asked. "I'm sorry, folks, this is a fluid situation, but a bomb has killed thousands in Paris. We are about to get a live feed from the ground, the images you are about to see are graphic and disturbing, they are not intended for all audiences. If you have any children in the room we strongly suggest you move them away."

The warning had no sooner come from her lips when the ground feed came on. People that had been walking their dogs, jogging, sitting on a park bench drinking coffee, playing Frisbee or laughing, had all fallen to the ground. There was some blood, but not in amounts that would be expected from a severe bomb blast.

"Oh, God," Sam said as he moved away from the front door and closer to the sixty-inch flat screen television.

"What is it?" Julie asked as she got to his side. Her hands flew up to her mouth as she gasped.

"Charlene, what you're seeing here is the devastation wrought by this cowardly terrorist attack."

"Forgive me, Francois, I sympathize with the devastation to your countrymen, but this does not look like a bomb scene."

"You're right, Charlene. The police have completely barricaded the area off from everyone…including reporters, but the cameraman has zoomed into the device that we believe was detonated. It seems that it has emitted some sort of pulse, killing humans, and animals alike."

"And bugs!" Sam cried.

Check out these other titles by Mark Tufo

Zombie Fallout Boxed Set

All the books you love in one easy to go e-box! Perfect for when you have to leave your house in a hurry! TAKE YOUR EREADER!

Zombie Fallout

It was a flu season like no other. With the H1N1 virus running rampant through the country, people lined up in droves to try and attain one of the coveted vaccines. What was not known, was the effect this largely untested inoculation was to have on the unsuspecting throngs. Within days, feverish folk throughout the country, convulsed, collapsed and died, only to be re-born. With a taste for brains, blood and bodies, hordes of modern-day zombies began scouring the lands for their next meal.

This is the story of Michael Talbot, his family and his friends: a band of ordinary people trying to get by in extraordinary times. When disaster strikes, Mike a self-proclaimed survivalist, does his best to ensure the safety and security of those he cares for. What he encounters along the way leads him down a long dark road, always skirting on the edge of insanity. Ensconced in a seemingly safe haven called Little Turtle, Mike and his family, together with the remnants of a tattered community, must fight against a relentless, ruthless, unstoppable force. This last bastion of civilization has made its final stand. God help them all.

Zombie Fallout 2: A Plague Upon Your Family

The Talbots are evacuating their home amidst a zombie apocalypse. Mankind is on the edge of extinction as a new dominant, mindless opponent scours the landscape in search of food, which just so happens to be non-infected humans. This book follows the journey of Michael Talbot, his wife, Tracy, and their three kids - Nicole, Justin and Travis. Accompanying them are Brendon, Nicole's fiancée and Tommy, a former Wal-Mart door greeter who may be more than he seems. Together they struggle against a ruthless, relentless enemy that has singled them out above all others.

As they travel across the war-torn country side the Talbots soon learn that there are more than just zombies to be fearful of: with law and order a long-distant memory some humans have decided to take any and all matters into their own hands. It's not just brains versus brain-eaters anymore. And the stakes may be higher than merely life and death, with eternal souls on the line.

Zombie Fallout 3: The End...

As the world spirals even further down into the abyss of apocalypse, one man struggles to keep those around him safe. Michael stands side by side with his wife, their children, his friends and Henry the wonder Bulldog along with the Wal-Mart greeter Tommy who is infinitely more than he appears. Whether Tommy is leading Mike and his family to salvation or death remains to be seen...

Zombie Fallout 3.5 - Dr. Hugh Mann – Prequel

Before there were zombies there was the virus...
In this Zombie Fallout prequel, Mark Tufo tells the story of the virus that started it all.

Zombie Fallout IV: The End...Has Come and

Gone

"The End…has come and gone. This is the new beginning, the new world order and it sucks. The end for humanity came the moment the U.S. government sent out the infected flu shots. My name is Michael Talbot and this is my journal. I'm writing this because no one's tomorrow is guaranteed, and I have to leave something behind to those who may follow." - From Mike Talbot's Journal

So continues Mike's journey, will he give up all that he is in a desperate bid to save his family and friends? Eliza is coming, can anyone be prepared?

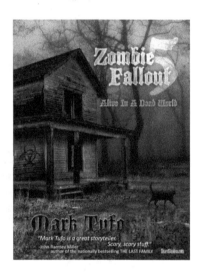

Zombie Fallout V: Alive In A Dead World

Eliza turned to Tomas: "This is the end…he is no longer alive in a dead world."

In this installment of Mark Tufo's action-packed Zombie Fallout series, Mike Talbot and his family continue their fight for survival as Eliza plots their demise.

Zombie Fallout VI: 'Til Death Do Us Part

Mark Tufo's Zombie Fallout novels have their share of memorable characters. Throughout the series, we have become acquainted with Michael Talbot. We've gotten to know Mike's wife, Tracy, their children, and several other characters, including Mrs. Deneaux, BT, and Tommy.

One character here, however, deserves special mention - that of Eliza. In Zombie Fallout 2, we discovered the queen's origins. In particular, we learned of her transformation from human to vampire. Subsequent novels in the series, indeed, affirm this villain's bloodthirsty nature. Eliza will not rest until she sees to the destruction of the entire Talbot clan.

Now, in the latest novel in the Zombie Fallout series, the moment has come for the final showdown. But as BT, Gary, and Mrs. Deneaux prepare to face Eliza, they have other worries. With Mike still missing, they cannot help but fear the worst.

Is Mike alive? Will the Talbot's defeat their nemesis once and for all? Readers will learn the answers to these questions and more in the much-anticipated sixth installment of the Zombie Fallout series.

Zombie Fallout VII: For the Fallen

Mike is back

The battle with Eliza is past. Now Mike must strike out once again in a desperate race against time as his son and best friend are succumbing to the zombie virus within them. What he does not know is that an old foe has risen up and a more insidious threat has emerged to not just the Talbots but all of humanity.

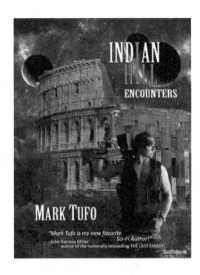

Indian Hill

This first story is about an ordinary boy growing up in relatively normal times who finds himself thrust into an extraordinary position. Growing up in suburban Boston, Mike Talbot undergoes the trials and tribulations of all teenagers, from the seemingly tyrannical mother, to girl problems to run-ins with the law. From there, he escapes to college in Colorado with his best friend, Paul, where they begin to forge new relationships. It is one girl in particular that has caught Mike's eye, and he alternately pines for her and laments ever meeting her.

It is on their true "first" date that things go strangely askew. Mike finds himself captive aboard an alien vessel, fighting for his very survival. The aliens have devised gladiator-type games - games of twofold importance that they use both for entertainment value and to learn about human strengths and weaknesses. The aliens want to better learn how to attack and defeat humans, and the battles are to the death on varying computer-generated terrains.

Follow Mike and Paul as they battles for their lives and try to keep the United States safe.

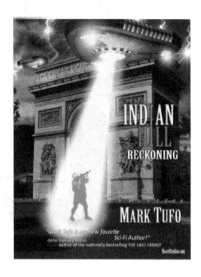

Indian Hill II: Reckoning

Reckoning starts where the first book in the series left off. After escaping from the Progerian alien vessel, Michael Talbot is given the opportunity to hide in obscurity with the rest of the human race or rise to the occasion and once again find himself immersed in a battle that he wants nothing to do with.

Mike goes home and decides to join whatever resistance force can be mustered to repel the oncoming invasion. As humanity gets thrust towards the abyss of extinction, two women in love with the same man make a desperate bid to travel across the country to reunite with him.

Mike will suffer the ultimate betrayal from those he loves the most. Will mankind fall and be ground to dust like so many other civilizations, or will the tiny humans thwart a takeover? Only time and shed blood will tell.

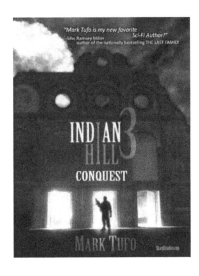

Indian Hill III: Conquest

And so the end begins...Indian Hill introduced us to Michael Talbot, an ordinary boy thrust into extraordinary circumstances when he finds himself captive aboard an alien vessel and forced to battle for his very survival in gladiator-type games. As Michael learns, the aliens were using him to learn about human weaknesses in preparation for an impending invasion.

In Indian Hill 2, Michael escaped from the alien ship and joined whatever resistance forces could be mustered to repel the oncoming alien invasion.

Now in the final chapter of the Indian Hill trilogy, Michael joins forces with an unlikely alliance in a desperate attempt to head off humanity's mass extinction. This is the long awaited conclusion to man's very struggle to survive against overwhelming odds and an aggressive alien species hell-bent on enslaving the entire world.

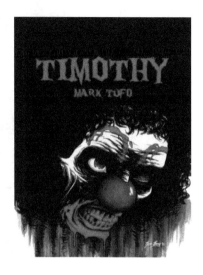

Timothy

Timothy was not a good man in life, and being undead did little to improve his disposition. What will a man trapped in his own mind do to survive when he wakes up to find himself a zombie controlled by a self-aware virus?

Tim 2

Timothy lived a life only a psychopathic sociopath could enjoy and understand. When he was bitten on the first day of the zombie-apocalypse he turned the tides on a single-minded virus he affectionately called Hugh. Together they terrorized a city before seemingly meeting their untimely demise. Nobody could have foreseen his resurrection, Tim's close call with death has done nothing to temper his missions in life, to live, to eat and to rule the world.

Tim is back and he's an asshole.

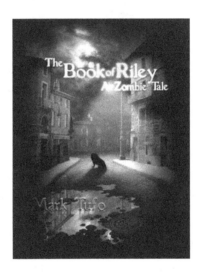

The Book of Riley: Part 1 - My Name is Riley

When the zombie apocalypse strikes without warning, one dog will hold the fate of her pack in her paws. This is the story of Riley, an American Bulldog who takes charge when the dead begin to walk. Follow along as she struggles to protect her pack from danger. Traveling with Riley are Ben-Ben, the high-strung Yorkie; Riley's favorite two-legger, Jessie; Jessie's younger brother, Zachary; and Riley's archenemy, Patches the cat. They are a rag-tag group of survivors who, when pushed to the limit, realize they are all that each other has.

The Book of Riley: Part 2 - My Name is Riley

In the second part of this unique horror tale from acclaimed author Mark Tufo, Riley, an American bulldog, continues to defend her pack in the midst of a zombie apocalypse. When the zombie apocalypse struck, intrepid American bulldog Riley quickly discovered it was up to her to keep the pack safe. Together with Yorkshire Terrier Ben-Ben and former archenemy Patches the cat, Riley helped to keep the zombies at bay while favorite human Jessie traveled cross-country to find safety for herself and her baby brother, Zachary.

But after a long journey, Riley and the gang arrive in Las Vegas - one of the few remaining inhabited cities - only to find that it has been taken over by a group of thugs who rule through fear and brutality. Making matters worse, ruler Icely and his gang have taken to staging dog fights as popular entertainment, and Riley catches their eye. With Riley forced to fight for her life and Jessie locked up in the home of Icely himself, the future is uncertain. Will Riley save the day once more and help her pack escape?

The Book of Riley: Part 3 - My Name is Riley

In this third installment, Jess aided by her four legged friends escapes the self-proclaimed King of Vegas and flees across state lines in a desperate bid to stay one step ahead of the vengeance seeking mad man.

Riley and company come a cross a unique ally that helps them on their quest to avoid recapture from Icely and his gang. Jess is one step closer to finding her way to Justin but is dogged each step of the way, by zombies and thugs. Can Riley and the ever petulant Patches along with the bacon loving Ben-Ben be able to keep her safe?

The Book of Riley: Part 4 - My Name is Riley

In this fourth and final explosive installment in the Riley saga, Jess finds herself once again alone in her quest to get back to her boyfriend. More determined than ever she vows to not let anything get in her way and Riley does her best to help Jess keep that promise, but will it be one in which she pays the ultimate price to keep? Ride along as Jess. Zach, Riley, Patches and the bacon-devouring machine known as Ben-Ben continue their journey.

The Ravin

This is book one of the Indian Hill series in a more youth friendly version.

Coming Soon - The Prey! Book Two in the Youth Adventures of Michael Talbot.

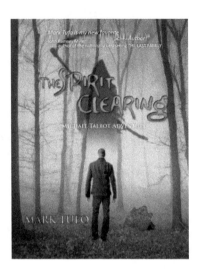

The Spirit Clearing

Mark Tufo's novels often center upon a single figure - that of Michael Talbot. Fans have joined this unforgettable character in numerous adventures. They've accompanied Mike in his struggle to navigate the apocalyptic world of the Zombie Fallout series. They've cheered him on his quest to save mankind from an alien threat in the Indian Hill books.

Now, in The Spirit Clearing, Tufo presents a Michael Talbot adventure like no other. Our hero wakes one morning to find himself in the hospital. Blind in one eye, he is the sole survivor in a horrific car accident. Soon Mike discovers that his injured eye allows him to see what others cannot. When he tells others of his visions, no one believes him.

Overcome by confusion, Mike feels as if he's caught between one world and another. Then, hope arrives in the form of the beautiful Jandilyn Hollow. Will she be able to pull him out of the depths of his despair? Can love transcend even death?

Join Mike as he embarks on his latest adventure, in this eerie, well-paced tale. Full of twists and turns, The Spirit

Clearing will keep readers guessing until the very end.

Callis Rose

Callis Rose is a girl blessed with a gift from above or cursed with a ruthless power she barely understands, it's really just a matter of degrees. As her family life is turned asunder she is thrown into an indifferent Social Services program where she defends herself the only way she knows how. Callis is moved from home to home until she finally settles at the Lowries. As she starts her first day of high school she meets both her favorite and least favorite person, both happen to reside at the same household.

Mindy Denton makes it her single mission in life to destroy Callis, even as her brother Kevin falls deeper into love with the mysterious and beautiful girl who is hiding something from them all. Follow along in Mark Tufo's newest adventure.

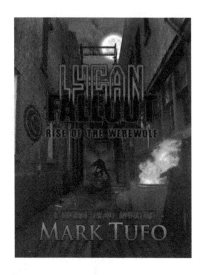

Lycan Fallout

The world of man was brought to its knees with the zombie apocalypse. A hundred and fifty years have passed since man has clawed and climbed his way from the brink of extinction. Civilization has rebooted, man has begun to rebuild, to create communities and society. It is on this fragile new shaky ground that a threat worse than the scourge of the dead has sprung. One man finds himself once again thrust into the forefront of a war he wants nothing to do with and seemingly cannot win. Follow along as Michael Talbot attempts to thwart the rise of the werewolf.

Zombie Fallout available in Spanish and Hindi

CUSTOMERS ALSO PURCHASED:

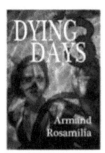

**ARMAND
ROSAMILLIA**
DYING DAYS
SERIES

SHAWN CHESSER
SURVIVING THE
ZOMBIE APOCALYPSE
SERIES

Travis Tufo
Red Sky

JOHN O'BRIEN
NEW WORLD
SERIES

JAMES N. COOK
SURVIVING THE DEAD
SERIES

HEATH STALLCUP
THE MONSTER
SQUAD

CPSIA information can be obtained
at www.ICGtesting.com
Printed in the USA
LVHW080240160720
660832LV00017B/1038

9 781494 733667